STANDING OUR GROUND

BILL PERCY

Black Rose Writing | Texas

ISBN: 978-1-68433-423-0
PUBLISHED BY BLACK ROSE WRITING
www.blackrosewriting.com

Printed in the United States of America
Suggested Retail Price (SRP) $21.95

Standing Our Ground is printed in Palatino Linotype

*As a planet-friendly publisher, Black Rose Writing does its best to eliminate
unnecessary waste to reduce paper usage and energy costs, while never compromising
the reading experience. As a result, the final word count vs. page count may not meet
common expectations.

DEDICATION

I'd like to dedicate *Standing Our* Ground to two women, Karla McGray and Judie Mattison, who have done exactly that through long careers, first as ministers (among other things) and in later life, like me, as writers. These two dear friends have finished profoundly important memoirs this year, and I hope that *Standing Our Ground* will measure up—despite being fiction—to the quality and significance of their work.

ACKNOWLEDGEMENTS

Writers will tell you that a book is the product of many people's hard work—from family members who put up with long spells of writerly sulking and silence as he or she works through tough problems; to the developmental, copy, and proofreading editors who take the author's messy product and skillfully, patiently, and without bruising the fragile authorial ego, shape it into something worth reading; to the publisher and the publisher's teams—editorial, design, marketing, sales—who midwife the final product and launch it into the world.

In my case, my thanks go first to my wife, Michele Brooks, always my first, best, and most patient reader. Next, my gratitude goes to my sister, Sue Haasis, who takes Michele's red-penciled notes and adds her own comments and insightful help. Thanks also to my two editors— Lorna Lynch for the developmental and copy edits, and Kim Cheeley for the proofreading. Nothing about *Standing Our Ground* and my earlier books would work as well without their care. Thank you, too, to Reagan Rothe and his team at Black Rose Writing. Lastly, my Monastery Valley books are immeasurably improved by David Levine's wonderful cover designs, and *Standing Our Ground* is no exception. All these folks are skillful and accomplished, and at the same time, a delight to work with. Thanks to you all.

And last and certainly not least, thanks to you, my readers. Your feedback and interest in my work have been invaluable. I am always eager to get back to the desk and the computer when someone asks, "When's the next one coming out?" It's a great motivator to know people are waiting. Thank you for your support.

STANDING OUR GROUND

PART ONE

A person is justified in the use of force or threat to use force against another when and to the extent that the person reasonably believes that the conduct is necessary for self-defense or the defense of another against the other person's imminent use of unlawful force. However, the person is justified in the use of force likely to cause death or serious bodily harm only if the person reasonably believes that the force is necessary to prevent imminent death or serious bodily harm to the person or another or to prevent the commission of a forcible felony.

Montana Code 2017, 45-3-102. The *stand your ground* law.

SATURDAY, AUGUST 25

1

9:37 p.m. The hands on the big Howard Miller wall clock above her cubicle seemed like they hadn't moved in an hour. Deputy Andi Pelton yawned and then called home. Ed would still be up. Just as he answered, she yawned again. Stifled it.

"Hey, kid," Ed answered. "How's the shift?"

"Shoot me. I've never been so bored. If this was Chicago, we'd have four, five drive-bys by now, a couple rapes, runaway kids. Here, everybody must be in bed." She glanced up at the clock: still 9:37.

"I miss you on these evening shifts."

That touched her. "Me too. Ed, let's go public with our marriage. I want everybody to know."

"How about we talk about it tomorrow on the way to Missoula? Grace'll be in her car, so we'll have plenty of privacy."

"It's a plan. Let's—"

Suddenly, the receptionist's voice cut in. "Andi, 9-1-1 call. Shots fired."

"Oh, man, I gotta go. Shots fired."

She heard Ed yell, "Be *safe*," as she hit *End*. She grabbed her outer vest and started putting it on as she rushed out to Reception. She passed Marla without slowing. "How many shots?"

"Two. Caller said it sounded like a handgun."

Andi kept moving toward the parking lot door. Over her shoulder, she yelled, "Where?"

Marla called after her, "206 East Cedar Street. The call came from the house next door."

"Radio Xavier. Tell him to meet me there and . . ." She shivered. "And to wear his armor."

She ran out to the lot. Just before flicking on her siren and lights, she heard Xav's siren fire up north of town. *Good. He's close*, she thought. She finished adjusting the vest as she drove. Four minutes after the call, she swerved around the corner onto East Cedar Street, Xavier's siren close behind.

Shots fired, she thought. "Be careful what you wish for," she whispered. The dashboard clock read *9:41*.

2

Ed pocketed his phone, uneasy. *Shots fired?* His worst fear was losing Andi in a violent confrontation. "Let it go," he said to himself. "She'll be okay."

Grace walked past him, carrying another box. "Who'll be okay, Northrup?"

He picked up the box he'd set down to answer the phone, following her out. "Andi just got a call at work. Shots fired."

"Shots? My God, where?"

"In town, I suppose. But I don't know for sure. I'm just hoping she'll be okay."

"She will. Andi can take care of herself."

"Right." He carried the box of Grace's things out to his pickup, still jumpy. The last shots fired in Jefferson were the ones that almost killed Andi four years ago. He tried to dredge up that reverend's name, the one who'd started it all.

Grace's car, a used pink Volvo she'd immediately named the Pink Vulva, groaned with her belongings jammed into every corner. When Ed dropped the box onto the tailgate of his pickup, she called, "Careful with that, Northrup."

"How'd you accumulate all this junk in just four years?" He snugged the box into the last open spot in the bed of the truck and raised the tailgate.

She studied him for a moment, calculation in her eyes. "I've been yours only three years and eight months."

"Then it's even more amazing you have so much junk."

"Jen's folks rented a whole trailer for, as you call it, her *junk*." She sniffed. "I prefer to think of all this—" She pointed at the PV and then at his pickup. "—as beloved possessions."

"Any more beloved possessions in the cabin?"

"Uh-uh. But would you consider letting me take a few bottles of that wine you and Andi drink so much of?"

"Ah. Would you consider first turning twenty-one?"

"Come on, Northrup. Please? I can't buy wine for three more years. Having some in my dorm room would be a nice ice-breaker for those new friends I'm about to make." She gave a coy smile. "Work with me here. I'm on the threshold of my new life."

Ed took that in. *Her new life.* It felt too soon, after three years and eight months. "All right. One bottle for breaking the ice."

"You're grits and gravy, Northrup," she sang as she dashed up the porch steps and into the house.

Ed smiled to himself: free "dad points," and no harm done—she'd never remember the corkscrew.

He followed Grace up the porch steps, wondering who, if anybody, had been shot. In his head, he listed his patients. None of them were likely to take up arms against their particular slings and arrows, or to invite someone else to do so. Even Beatrice John, as broken and wounded as she was, wouldn't shoot anybody. Except maybe herself. He pushed the thought away and concentrated on Andi's shooting four years ago and the reverend who'd caused it all. As he opened the screen door, the name rushed back to him, riding a jolt of anger: Crane. The. Reverend. Loyd. Crane.

3

Andi pulled up at 206 East Cedar Street, lights flashing, siren screaming. Xavier's squad sailed around the corner just behind. As her tires screeched, braking in front of the darkened house, she switched off her siren. Xavier pulled up fast, his own tires squealing. His siren died. Both flashers stayed on, spraying red and blue lights around the dark neighborhood. Scanning the shadows, she made sure her body armor was secure and, cautiously opening her door, stood behind it. Jefferson had never put streetlights in its neighborhoods, but the flashing lights illuminated a figure in the deep shadows near the house. No lights inside. She drew her weapon as Xavier climbed out of his squad, staying behind his door, gun drawn.

"Identify yourself," she demanded of the shadowed figure.

Raising its hands to shoulder height, then higher, the figure replied, "I'm Daniel Essex." His voice carried on the cooling air. "This is my home."

"Did you hear shots?"

"Of course. I fired them."

What the hell? she thought.

"Mr. Essex, I want you to keep your hands where they are. I'm going to approach, and my weapon is drawn. I will not shoot unless you move suddenly. My partner will come toward you from the side. Are you good with that?"

"Sure, Officers. Come on."

She glanced at Xav. He nodded and moved off to the side, flanking her.

As she approached Daniel Essex, she said, "Are you alone?"

"I am."

Coming closer, her eyes adjusted to the dark, and the red-and-blue flashes from the squad cars showed a bulge at Essex's hip. "Mr. Essex, are you armed?"

"Of course, Officer." He started to lower his hands.

"Freeze, sir." *Oh, man. Don't make me shoot.* She was ten feet from him. A few feet to her left and a bit behind, Xavier had his weapon trained on Daniel Essex, but that didn't slow her racing heart. Essex froze, hands high.

"Sir, please turn around slowly, keeping your hands in the air. Don't do anything fast."

"Sure. Whatever you say, Officer." His tone was cool, almost friendly. When he turned, Andi approached, saying, "I'm going to disarm you, so please be still." She patted him down, found the gun, and took it. She stepped back. "Do you have any other weapons on your person, sir?"

"Just that one." His voice sounded less friendly. "And I want it back."

She moved a step back, holding out the weapon grip-first to Xavier, who took custody of it. "One thing at a time, sir," she said. "You'll get it back once we straighten all this out." *Which could be a long time.* "You can turn around, but please don't make any sudden moves."

"I won't hurt you, Officer."

"Glad to hear it. And please, call me 'deputy.'" *The guy must be new to the valley,* she thought. Doesn't know we're *deputies*, not *officers*. "Sir, you fired the shots a few moments ago?"

"Like I said, yes."

Andi noted that his voice remained friendly, but his words were clipped, exact.

"Why did you fire, sir?"

He pointed toward the open garage. "He's in there."

"Who is?"

"The intruder who invaded my home. I stopped him."

Andi's chest tightened. She said, "Is he all right?"

"I doubt it, Officer. I'm a good shot."

She moved toward the open garage. "Mr. Essex, Deputy Contrerez will wait with you while I look in the garage."

When Essex nodded, she glanced at Xavier. He nodded. "Go."

She holstered her weapon and moved toward the garage.

She heard Essex say to Xavier, "Contrerez? Name like that, you must be Mexican." He no longer sounded friendly.

She smiled faintly as she heard Xavier say, politely, "No, sir. Born and raised in Billings."

4

The garage door was up, the interior dark. The open door of a refrigerator against the back wall spilled light into the space. The door rested against the hip of a man on his stomach, the back of his sweater dark with blood. His head was twisted, wedged at a hard angle against the lowest shelf. He'd fallen part-way into the fridge. Above him, Andi saw nothing but rows of beer cans on the refrigerator shelves, a few on their sides. She hurried to the body, noting the blood that had soaked through the back of his sweater. She stooped, pressed two fingers against the neck. No pulse. She felt the other side of his neck, still feeling no pulse. She gazed at his face, then stood, hollowed out, her stomach tight. A boy.

Dead. Unexpectedly, hanging in the dark air above the body, another boy's face flashed. She jerked back, but as swiftly as she'd seen it, it vanished. She was left with a nagging feeling: *Someone I knew.*

She shook herself, pulled out her cell, called the station. "Marla, I need EMTs to 206 East Cedar, fast. We've got a shooting and I can't get a pulse. And call DCI and get their mobile crime scene here from Missoula a.s.a.p. Also, call Ben and tell him what's happening." She almost signed off, then added, "Oh, and call Doc Runge. He'll want to meet the EMTs at the emergency room." Runge was the retired doctor who acted as the county's medical examiner.

She leaned closer to the boy's face, twisted up to the side where his head had struck the shelf. Chin and forehead sprinkled with acne and unshaven young-man whiskers. Short hair under a Seattle Mariners ball cap, knocked askew by the shelf. A Jefferson High School sweater. In the back of the sweater, two holes surrounded by dark bloodstains. She leaned closer, unclipping her flashlight and switching it on. The edges of the holes looked sharp, no protruding threads. *Shot in the back.* His left arm was folded under his body. Beside his right hand, a can of Bud Light lay on the floor, dented, but unopened. It had either fallen there when his face crashed against the shelf, or he'd dropped it when he was shot. She ran her eyes farther down the body. Wrangler jeans, creased in the back, maybe in front too. Crocs on his feet. No socks. *A kid. Killed for stealing cheap beer.*

She tried again for a pulse, got none, spent a couple more minutes closely watching him for signs of breathing, holding her fingers in front of his nose. There was no movement, no breath. She stood, looked methodically in widening circles from the body, memorizing the layout of the garage and the location of things in relation to the body. On the long workbench beside the refrigerator sat a twelve-pack of a craft beer she recognized from Bitterroot Brewery in Hamilton, unopened. *Pricey beer.* But nothing else caught her eye. She looked down at the boy, felt an urge to move his head into a more comfortable position. *No. He doesn't need it.*

She went outside and approached Essex. In the distance, a siren wailed. *EMTs on the way.* "Mr. Essex, why did you shoot him?"

His answer rocked her. "He invaded my home. I was protecting myself."

"Looks like he was breaking into your beer refrigerator, sir."

"I have a right to stand my ground."

Against a kid stealing your damn beer? She steeled herself. The trial would come soon enough. She held her voice steady. "Yes, sir. Where was he when you fired?"

"In the garage. Where do you think?" In the dark, his voice took on a whine.

"And where were you when you fired?"

Essex pointed at his car, parked in the driveway. Andi said, "Show me."

Essex walked around the front of the car and stood on the passenger side, over the right front wheel. "Thank you, sir," she said. "Please demonstrate how you fired at him."

Essex crouched, almost resting the sides of both hands on the hood of the car, as if steadying a gun. She cautioned him, "Don't touch the hood, please." She heard quiet voices behind them. After the sheriff's vehicles had arrived, neighbors had begun gathering across the street, watching and murmuring to one another. Andi decided not to spend much more time out here.

The ambulance pulled onto Cedar Street, lights and siren wild. As they pulled up behind the squads, the siren died. Both Andi and Essex watched for a moment. Two men jumped from the ambulance, moving fast. "Where's the vic?" the first one called.

She pointed to the garage. "He's dead."

The two men slowed down. The driver went back to the rig and shut down the flashers.

Andi turned to Essex. "I have one more question here. Did you warn the young man before you shot him?"

Essex stepped away from the car. His eyes narrowed, but he smiled. "The castle doctrine doesn't require me to issue a warning, Deputy."

Xavier, who'd followed them, grunted. For the moment, she ignored Essex's non-answer and turned to Xavier. "I've called Marla. The EMTs are here, and DCI should be here in three hours or so." She glanced across the street at the growing crowd. "I caught the call, so I'm lead on this. After I go, put up a police line around the scene. The EMTs can secure everything until DCI arrives. Talk to the neighbors, particularly the one who called it in, get the details. I'll take Mr. Essex to the station for his statement."

Essex, turning sinister, his features distorted by shadows cast by the dim refrigerator light and the flashing squads, snarled. "Take me to the station? What the hell's that about?" He took a step toward her.

Andi rested her hand on her gun. "Sir, I need you to step back."

He stopped, but didn't step back. "Deputy, I was standing my ground. You're violating my Second Amendment rights. I demand my firearm back." His voice had lost any softness, edging toward anger.

"Sir, your weapon is evidence in a homicide investigation. I need your cooperation."

"Homicide?" His voice rose. "You're fucking with me, right?"

"No, sir, I'm not. When someone kills someone else, we arrest them and investigate, to determine what the charges will be."

"Arrest? Charges? Damn it, this punk invaded my goddamn garage. It's my right to kill someone who threatens me." Again, he stepped toward Andi. Xavier, to the side, swiftly drew his weapon. "Freeze, man. Don't make this worse."

Essex stopped, and the deputies watched him a moment. Andi said, "Deputy Contrerez and I are going to put you in the squad car until I'm done with your garage. Then we'll go to the station."

"Am I under arrest?"

"Yes, sir, you are." She pulled the Miranda card from her pocket and read him his rights.

At the part about an attorney being appointed if he couldn't afford his own, he snarled. "The hell with this, *Deputy*. I can afford my own goddamn attorney. And I'm not stupid. You can't arrest me in my own home without a warrant."

"You're not in your home. You're in a public space." She rested her hand on the butt of her gun. "I need you in the squad, now."

For a moment, Essex glared at her, then shrugged. "Whatever." She took his elbow, and Xavier his other arm. They walked him to Andi's squad, where Xavier searched him. Finding nothing, they settled him in the back seat.

As he sat, he said, "I'll have your job over this, *Deputy*."

Andi looked at him. "No, sir, you won't."

5

On the way back to the garage, Andi said, "The vic's a kid. High school age, I'm guessing."

Xavier said nothing. Andi knew his two daughters attended Jefferson High. Inside the garage, the EMT who'd driven the rig said, "Confirming, Andi. He's gone."

"DCI's been called. They should be here in three hours or less. You guys mind waiting till they do their thing?"

The driver shook his head. "No problem, unless we get another call. If we do, we'll come back." The other fellow said, "We'll wait in the truck."

Andi and Xavier pulled on latex gloves. Andi flipped the switch, and light flooded the space. While Xavier examined the boy's pockets, Andi said, "Xav, is your squad's camera charged?"

"Sad to say, no," he said, retrieving the boy's wallet.

"Okay. Use the camera in my vehicle. You do the photos." She divided the garage into mental gridlines, starting closest to the body.

Xavier straightened, rubbing his lower back. He opened the wallet. "Name's Bernardo Cirilo. Fourteen. Lives across town. High school ID and a couple dollars is all he had." He folded the wallet and dropped it, along with two crumpled bills, into an evidence bag. "Fourteen." He sighed. "Hardly old enough to jack off."

Grief pierced her. *Fourteen.* For a swift moment, she felt like offering a prayer, but nothing came to mind. *Don't pray*, she thought. *Solve this.*

Xavier went to Andi's squad for the camera. When he opened the front door, Essex barked, "This is bullshit, Mendez. I have a right to call my lawyer."

Xavier retrieved the camera. "Yes, you do. That'll happen after Deputy Pelton books you at the station. And the name's Contrerez." He slammed the door.

Andi refocused on the garage. Beside the body, oil stained the cement floor. The oil stain looked roughly three feet in diameter, and thick. She touched it in the center: wet. Pulling her flashlight again, she went out, knelt at the front bumper, flicked on the light, peered under the engine. A few drops of fresh oil lay on the cement, not enough to make a stain yet, but over time, it would build.

She stood and backed against the hood, studying the garage, thinking. *What went on here?*

Xavier returned, prepping the camera. "Xav, before you start, let's talk a minute."

He joined her beside the car.

"Tell me what you think. The kid comes into the garage, garage-hopping's my guess, looking for a beer refrigerator to raid. He opens the fridge, grabs a beer in his right hand. Essex somehow moves to this point—" She gestured toward the right front wheel well. "Without drawing the kid's attention, shoots him in the back. The kid falls into the fridge, his face hits the shelf, a few cans fall over, the door bumps against his hip and stays open. Sound right to you?"

"Fits what I see. The open fridge door says garage-hopping to me." He sighed. "You want me to inform the parents?"

"I'd rather you stick around here, talk to the neighbors. I'll talk to the parents after I take Essex's statement."

"Right." He waved toward the garage. "Man, this leaves a lot of questions."

"Yeah. Like, why's this car out here?" She pointed at the oil stain in the garage. "That stain tells me the car is ordinarily parked inside, not out here. Grab a picture of that one—" She pointed to the garage floor beside Bernardo Cirilo's body. "And take another one under the car—there's just a few drops out here, another reason to think the car is typically parked inside."

Xavier flicked on his own flashlight and peered under the car. "You're right." He turned on the camera and snapped pictures of the oil drops, front and side.

"Essex said he fired from out here, so the garage door must've been up."

"What if it was down when Bernardo entered?"

Andi squinted. "Well, he wouldn't have raised it himself, would he? Drawn attention to himself?"

Xavier nodded. "Yeah, that's too dumb even for a beer-hungry fourteen-year-old boy."

"And if it was down and Essex raised it—" She pointed to the keypad on the outside door frame. "Wouldn't the kid run when it started going up? He'd have been out that side door before the big door was high enough for Essex to see inside and shoot. Or at least he'd get far enough toward the side door that his body wouldn't fall into the fridge."

"It had to be up."

"Or another possibility: The door's down and Essex enters from the house and shoots from *inside* the garage."

"He lied?"

"Always a possibility."

Xavier shook his head. "Naw, he didn't shoot from inside." He pointed toward both side doors at the back corners of the garage. One led outside, the other into the house. "If the garage door's down, no way Essex gets in through either door without the kid seeing him. He'd maybe turn and face Essex, maybe run, but either way, his body wouldn't fall into the fridge the way it did. And the bullet holes are in his back, not his side."

"All right. Door's up, car's out here, Essex shoots from the car—or maybe just inside the garage—and hits Bernardo in the back. We agreed?"

"We're agreed. And pissed," Xavier muttered.

"Got that right." Andi went back into the garage and peered over the body into the fridge, counting. She called over her shoulder, "I've got forty-seven cans of beer in here—Kokanee, Bud Light. Plus the one on the floor. Forty-eight."

Xavier came up beside her. "Four twelve-packs." He snapped a couple of photos.

She looked closer at the twelve-pack on the workbench butting up against the side of the refrigerator. "Bitterroot Single-Hop Ale." She turned to Xavier. "Cheap beer cold in the fridge, a good craft beer warm on the workbench. Mean anything?"

Xavier took two pictures of the twelve-pack on the bench, from two angles, to establish its position. "Maybe he just bought the good stuff and hadn't stocked it in yet."

"Could be." She went over to the side door and turned the handle. Unlocked. She examined the frame for signs of damage or forced entry. Found none. "The kid could've come in this way," she called to Xavier.

Xavier said, "Or through the big door, if it was up."

"We're assuming the door was up."

"Question is, why?"

"Maybe Essex left it up by mistake. Or meant to come out later and move the car in and close it."

"More questions."

Andi pulled her notebook out and jotted all these questions down. "Okay. You finish up here. Ask the guys to watch the body. See what the neighbors have to say." She put the notebook back in her pocket. "Oh, and when DCI gets here, give me a call. When I'm done with Essex, I'll go see the parents. I'm thinking we'll end up wanting a warrant to search the house, so I'll write it up before I come back."

As she started toward the car where Essex waited, she shuddered. "Xav, could there be somebody inside the house?"

"Let me raise hell with the doorbell. See if anybody answers." While he banged on the door and kept pressing the doorbell, Andi went to the door in the garage that opened into the house and pounded there as well. Xavier called to her, "No answer yet. I'll keep checking while you take him to the station." Andi beat the door again, as loudly as she could. No answer from inside.

As she went back out to Xavier, he said, "I gotta say, Andi. This looks cold-blooded to me, shooting the kid in the back."

She let out a long breath. The rush of rage she'd felt pounding on the door was dissipating. All she said was, "Yeah."

6

Arriving at the station, Essex cursing her all the way, Andi got out and opened the back door six inches. "We can do this one of two ways, Mr. Essex. You cooperate, and I won't handcuff you. Keep your mouth running, and I will."

"Fuck you, Officer."

"It's *deputy*, not *officer*. You really want to do this the hard way?"

He pushed sharply on the door. "You're not the one to stop me. *Deputy*."

She jumped back and drew her weapon. "Okay, the hard way it'll be. Get out, face the car, and put your hands behind your back."

Without moving, he glared at her. She thought, *God, no, suicide by cop?*

But he shrugged, turned his back to her, and held his hands behind his back. She cuffed him.

When she'd deposited him in the interrogation room and locked him in, she went out to Reception. Marla's shift done, Kris Erikson had taken over. She was reading a paperback. "Hi, Andi. That the shooter you brought in?"

"It is. Has Ben indicated what he wants us to do?"

"He's on his way. Marla called DCI, and they'll be here in a couple hours."

"Good. I'll be in interrogation." She went back and let herself in.

Essex was pacing. "You're making a big mistake, Deputy. I was following the castle doctrine. The asshole invaded my property, and I'm within my legal rights to protect myself."

"Yes, sir. The castle doctrine's a defense against a charge of homicide. It's not for the police to decide, it's the court's business. If we charge you with murder, your attorney will help you make that defense, but it doesn't stop our investigation. Please, sit down."

He didn't. "I demand to know why I'm under arrest." He moved sideways, as if to come around the table.

Is he that stupid? "Sir, stay where you are." She rested her hand on her weapon, but didn't draw it. "You're under arrest because you told Deputy Contrerez and me that you shot the young man in your garage. He's dead, so it's very likely your shooting resulted in a homicide, which is why we're here. We need to discuss what happened in detail so I can make a determination what to charge you with. Now please sit down."

He glared a long moment, but then sat. She relaxed and felt for the *Record* button under the table. "Mr. Essex, I'm recording this conversation." She repeated the Miranda warning. "Do you understand those rights?" She held her breath, assuming he'd clam up and demand his lawyer.

"Of course I do. I'm not an idiot."

She wondered. *Will his arrogance make him talk?* "Okay, then. Start at the beginning and tell me what happened." Maybe he'd be too eager to make the news and wouldn't demand his lawyer. Yet.

Essex narrowed his eyes. Andi thought, *Damn, lawyering up.* But after a moment, he said, "Okay. I was watching TV when I heard a noise in my garage. I had a burglary three weeks ago, so I knew the fucker was back."

Andi, relieved that he'd started, made a note about the burglary. "How did you know it was the same person, Mr. Essex?"

"It had to be. What are the odds?"

"What was taken in the first burglary?"

"Beer."

"Beer. Anything else?"

He leered at her.

"Okay, just beer. So, you heard the noise. What did you do?"

"I went to get my gun—which I want back—and went outside. To see if it was him."

"When we arrived, maybe no more than five minutes after the shooting, your weapon was holstered. Did you put on your holster when you went to get your gun, or after the shooting?"

Essex didn't answer for a moment. "I don't . . . I guess when I got the gun. Yeah. I grabbed the belt and put it on while I went outside."

She jotted it down. "Had you seen the burglar on the previous occasion?"

"What's that supposed to mean?"

"You said, 'to see if it was him.' How would you know it was a male, unless you'd seen him before?"

"When was the last time you heard of a girl stealing beer?" His eyes challenged her.

Andi just stared back.

He looked down, then back at her. "Okay, maybe I didn't know who it was, but he was in my home."

"Your garage."

"It's my property. And I have the right to defend my property."

"Yes, sir, you do. But let's leave that to the lawyers, okay? You got your gun. What happened next?"

"I went out. I saw him, leaning into my refrigerator, stealing again. I yelled at him."

Andi pretended confusion. "At the scene, you said you didn't issue a warning." She knew that wasn't what he'd said.

Essex smirked. "No, I didn't. I said the castle doctrine doesn't require that I issue a warning."

"Huh." She smiled. "Got me on that one." *Let him think so.* "So, what did you yell?"

"'Come out, prick, with your hands up.'"

"Did you yell it loud?"

"What does 'yell' mean where you're from?"

"Okay," she nodded. "Loud. Go on." *He thinks he's smarter than me. Good.*

"The little prick jumps up and makes this huge roaring noise and comes running at me. I could tell he was going to kill me if he could. I shot him."

Not in the back? "What happened then?"

"What the hell do you think happened, *Deputy*? He dropped like a stone. I'm a very good shot."

Andi looked at him for a moment. "Sir, the body was facing the refrigerator, *away* from the car where you were standing. I'm certain the medical examiner will confirm that he was shot in the back. How do you explain that?"

Daniel Essex looked over Andi's shoulder. The door was opening. Andi turned. Ben Stewart poked his head in, pointed to Andi. "Talk to you a minute?"

"Sure, Sheriff." She left the room with Ben, locked the door behind them.

7

"Fill me in," the sheriff said. He looked gray, tired, his eyes dark. Since his heart attack last year, he'd been exercising, eating well, and generally looking and acting healthier—and happier—than he had since his wife left him. Tonight, he seemed tired. "You all right, Ben?"

"Fit as a fiddle, for midnight. Fill me in."

She rehashed the facts, and outlined her questions from the scene.

"So, we got us a shooter claimin' stand-your-ground, but you don't see any threat to him? Or his family?"

Andi flinched. "Family? Xav and I pounded on both doors to the house, nobody came out. I don't think there's family. But maybe I should call Xav, send him inside."

"I'll call him," Ben said. "You go back in there." He rubbed his forehead, hard. "Crap on toast, Andi. We've had us a few shootings over the years, but this stand-your-ground crap busts my butt." He almost panted. "Maybe I'm gettin' too old for this job." He started down the hallway, then turned back to her. "After I talk to Xav, I'll be behind the mirror. Eat the bastard alive."

She returned to interrogation. "Let's pick up where we left off, sir. The body is facing into the refrigerator, but you say you shot him charging toward you. Explain for me."

"Elementary, *Deputy*. Don't you watch *Chicago Blue*?" He chuckled. "After I shot him, the kid crawled back toward the refrigerator and collapsed. I suppose he wanted to grab another beer." He grinned.

She ignored her anger, and his lie. "How close had he gotten to you before you shot him, sir?"

Essex, elbows on the table, steepled his fingers, then raised his eyes to the ceiling. "Oh, maybe ten feet away? I'm no good with distances."

"Ten feet from your position, which you showed me at the scene, would have put him, say, out of the garage when you fired?"

"I suppose."

"How many feet, sir?"

"All right, damn it. Ten goddamn feet."

Andi thought about the size of the garage and the blood trail Bernardo would have left as he crawled ten or twelve feet back to the refrigerator. She remembered no such blood trail, just the blood soaking the back of the sweater. It might be possible he'd been shot in front, she supposed. She wrote, *Shot in front?* She changed the subject. "Okay. You mentioned an earlier burglary. Can you give me the date, please?"

"About three, four weeks ago. I don't remember the date."

She pushed him, asking for details—what had he been doing when he discovered the burglary, what had he done earlier that day, had the garage been open or locked? He seemed to remember nothing. "How about the name of the deputy who responded?"

"No."

"Huh." *He's upset enough about the first burglary to be on guard against a second one, but he remembers hardly anything about it.* She adopted a skeptical look, waited.

He noticed. "The intrusion traumatized me, damn it. Trauma makes memory unreliable."

She arched an eyebrow. "Yes, it can, Mr. Essex. Your memory for tonight's shooting seems clear, though. A funny thing, memory."

"Can I go now?"

"No, sir." She pretended to study her notes. "When the victim was crawling back toward the refrigerator, you shot him again, right?"

"No."

"How many shots did you fire?"

"Two. They dropped him. That was my objective."

"The evidence suggests the young man was shot in the back. Can you explain that?"

"Exit wounds." He looked smug.

Andi debated: Confront his bullshit, or move on? The medical examiner would make the determination. She decided to let it go for now. "I understand. When he was crawling away from you, did you do anything to help him?"

"Help him? Are you nuts? He might've been armed."

"Did you observe any weapons on his person?"

Essex did not answer immediately. He looked again at the ceiling. Then he said, "No, I guess not."

"Did you call 9-1-1?"

"Uh, no."

"Why not?"

"I was, uh, shaking too much. By the time I'd calmed down, I heard your siren coming. A neighbor must've called."

She visualized the dashboard clock in her squad. *9:41.* "Odd. I arrived at the scene four minutes after the call came in. You were very calm when Deputy Contrerez and I arrived. You weren't shaking at all." She glanced at her notes, changed focus, hoping he'd slip. "What was the sound you heard in the garage?"

"I heard the refrigerator door opening."

Really? "You were inside the house?"

"I already told you I was, damn it."

"When you heard the refrigerator door open, was your garage door up or down?"

He looked up at the ceiling. "I don't remember. No, wait. Down. It's always down. I'm very careful about that."

"Okay. So. When you got your weapon, what did you do next?"

"What the hell do you think I did? I went outside."

"Why didn't you go to the garage through the kitchen door?"

For a moment, Essex looked perplexed. Then he nodded to himself. "I was right next to the front door and I wanted to get out there as fast as I could."

"I see. So, when you went outside, the garage door was closed."

Essex narrowed his eyes, said nothing for a moment. "Uh, actually, it was open."

Without the car inside. "But it's always closed, you said."

He stared at her, silent.

"So, how do you explain it being open when you went outside?"

"The kid must've opened it."

"Did you hear the door go up?"

"Yeah, now that you mention it, yeah. I did. A rumble."

"A rumble. Okay, good. Excuse me." She took out her cell phone and tapped a number. "Xav," she said after a moment, when her partner answered. "Look, when DCI gets there, be sure to have them dust the garage door switch. The boy's prints should be on it." She watched Essex's face pale as she said that.

Xavier answered, "I doubt it."

"Mr. Essex says the boy raised the garage door."

"Ah. Gotcha. I'm on it, Andi."

"Good," she said, watching Essex. He glared back at her.

She put the phone away. "Do you often leave your car outside with the garage door down?"

"What?" His eyes narrowed.

"Your car is sitting outside the garage. You said the door was down and you heard a rumble when the victim raised it. So, I'm asking if you ordinarily leave the car outside with the door down."

Andi watched his eyes quivering side to side: *Thinking how to answer,* she thought.

"No, it's almost always inside. I must've forgot."

"You forgot to put your car in the garage?"

"Quit repeating what I say. This isn't a therapy session."

Andi pondered him a moment. "No, sir, you're right. This is your initial statement in a murder investigation." She smiled. "Moving on, after you shot him and he crawled back to the refrigerator, somehow he rose up and then fell into it. Can you explain how that happened?"

He waited. When she said nothing more, he grunted. "I don't recall." Paused again. "I want to talk to my lawyer."

She pretended she wasn't annoyed that he'd clammed up. "You can call him or her when we're done."

"I'm not answering any more questions."

She shrugged. "Well, thank you, Mr. Essex." She slipped it in: "Is there anything you'd like to add at this time?"

"Yeah, damn it. I want the record to show you're depriving me of my rights. You've confiscated my weapon against the Second Amendment."

"Noted." She stood. "I'm going to talk next steps with the sheriff, and then I'll be back."

As she left the room and locked it behind her, Essex was swearing at her. Ben met her in the hall. "Jesus in a Jeep," he grunted.

"Deliberate homicide?"

"Good God, yes. Let his lawyer jawbone about stand-your-ground."

"Got it, boss." Andi saw Ben put a hand to his side, heard him gasp. "You okay?"

"Peachy. Go book the jerk."

<h1 style="text-align:center">8</h1>

Ed and Grace sat on the porch, waiting for Andi to come home. The evening was pleasantly cool; the sweet smell of wood smoke from a stove somewhere in the night wafted on the soft breeze through the yard. A little after midnight, Grace yawned. "She's late. Didn't her shift end at eleven?"

As if on cue, his cell phone rang. Ed looked at the screen. "It's her." He touched *Talk*. "Hey, kid."

"We've had a homicide and I caught it, so I don't think I'll be home tonight. Gotta go see the victim's parents, then back to the scene. And I doubt I can go with you guys to Missoula in the morning."

"Did you say parents? Was it a kid?"

"Yeah. Fourteen years old."

"Oh, man, that sucks. Bad enough it's a murder, but a kid . . . You're gonna be up all night?"

"A good bit of it, anyway. Look, would you give Grace the phone? I want to say goodbye before this place gets crazy."

Ed handed the phone to Grace. "For you."

He waited while Grace listened, and heard her gasp. "What's his name?" she said, then nodded at whatever Andi was saying. Her eyes blurred with tears. She whispered, "It's awful, Andi."

Andi said something else. Then Grace said, "Absolutely." Then, after a momentary silence, she added, "Get the guy who killed him, Andi."

After they ended the call, Grace wiped her eyes. "Andi says you should give me a hug for her."

"Good idea." He moved toward her.

She held up her hand, stopping him. "Northrup, I think I'll know the kid who died. Andi said he was wearing a Jefferson High sweater." Her voice caught, and she cleared her throat. "God, Northrup, what a shitty thing."

On the night before you start your new life. "That it is," he said, and reached for her. This time, she let him hold her. He felt her rapid breathing against his chest, then heard a small sob. After a moment, she pulled away. They both gazed wordlessly at the sky, the stars a thick road overhead. *Beauty and ugliness.* Ed heard another catch in her breathing, and rested his hand on her far shoulder. She moved closer under his arm, and her shoulders heaved.

She whispered, "All of a sudden, I'm scared, Northrup."

SUNDAY, AUGUST 26, VERY EARLY

1

A little before two in the morning, Bernardo Cirilo's father, Emilio, slowly opened the door after Andi's quiet knock. "*¿Sí?*"

"Mr. Cirilo, I'm Deputy Andi Pelton. Is your wife awake?"

As she said it, a small dark-haired woman came into the living room. "Emilio? Who is it?"

"*Policía,*" he said, his eyes terrified.

Her eyes locked on Andi's, the woman said, "The police. Where is my Bernardo? He is not home."

"May I come in?" she answered.

"*Sí*, of course," Mr. Cirilo opened wide the door and Andi went into the living room. She asked the couple to sit, and delivered the news as gently as she could. The woman fell back against the couch, clutching her husband's arm. She exhaled, a long "Aaahh," then no more sound, though her eyes welled and tears coursed down her cheeks.

Mr. Cirilo's face had lost all color. "Always," he whispered, "I have been . . ." His haunted eyes sought his wife. "*¿Asustado?*"

"Afraid," she whispered through tears.

"*Sí.* Afraid one day this would come." His eyes filled with tears. He brushed them away. "*¿Sabes quién* . . . You know who?"

"Yes, Mr. Cirilo. We've arrested the man who shot him."

Mrs. Cirilo growled, "I will see him."

"There will be a trial, ma'am. You will see him there."

The mother's eyes narrowed, but then she nodded.

The remainder of Andi's stay was painful for everyone—three girls, all younger than Bernardo, stumbled into the living room, wakened by the conversation, and began wailing when their father told them. Andi waited until they had quieted.

Mr. Cirilo said, "*¿Que* . . . what was *mi hijo* doing in the garage?"

Andi explained the garage-hopping theory. As she did, the oldest sister shook her head. "'Nardo wouldn't steal beer. It can't be true."

Andi considered which would be worse for the Cirilo family, hearing it from her now or hearing it on the street or at work or in school? "You're right, we don't know for a fact what he was doing. But we found him in front of a refrigerator full of beer, and there was one can on the floor beside his hand." The sister's eyes filled. Andi murmured, "I'm sorry."

Mr. Cirilo said to his daughter, "*No importa, hijita*. It doesn't matter now."

Andi stood, and gave him her business card. "I will call you when they release Bernardo's body, so you can bury him."

The Cirilos were all weeping again as she let herself out.

2

Back at the station, she yawned as she unlocked the door to the cellblock and closed it behind herself. In his cell, Essex jumped up from his bunk, furious. "I want my lawyer. Now."

Andi said, "You made that quite clear." During his booking, Essex had twice tried to leave the station, and Andi had been forced to use her gun to control him. He'd then demanded, and gotten, his phone call. "It's two forty-five in the morning, so I assume your lawyer will drive over from Missoula when she is ready to. That's not my worry."

"She said she'd come in the morning. I want you to call her, tell her to come now."

"Mr. Essex, you're talking to the wrong woman. It's not my job, and not many lawyers work on Sundays, so if she's coming later today, you're luckier than most."

"Then you need to let me go home and get some clean clothes."

"No, sir, I don't. You're under arrest for murder, and you'll be staying here until your arraignment."

Essex slammed his hands against the cell bar. "When the fuck is that?"

"I don't know. I'll talk to the DA in the morning and see what he says, but judges seldom work on Sunday, either. I'll let you know what I find out." It felt petty, but she said it anyway: "Well, no. I'll let your lawyer know. She can tell you whenever you see her."

"That was a fucking cheap shot."

"Mr. Essex, I couldn't care less." She didn't add, *Not as cheap as the shot you took at Bernardo Cirilo.*

3

After Andi let herself out of the cellblock, she stood still a moment, facing the door and listening to Daniel Essex swearing on the other side. She grimaced and turned toward the squad room, and jumped. Brad Ordrew had come up behind her without a sound. "Damn it, Brad—don't sneak up like that."

She moved around him. "What are you doing here, anyway? You're not on duty till morning."

"I want this case," he answered, the anger in his voice thinly contained. "Tell Ben you want off so I can take over."

He followed her into the deputies' squad room. "The call came in on your day off, Brad. You know how things work here." She sat down in her cubicle.

He leaned over the wall. "Or don't work."

Her annoyance with Essex spilled over onto him. "What the hell's that mean?"

"It's called procedures. You people are way too casual about procedures. Last year, with that Jared Hansen kid, hiding him at your boyfriend's—"

Andi bristled. "Brad, that's crap. You know damn well Ed was trying to diagnose him and that'd never happen in a jail cell. And knock it off with the you vs. us stuff—you're not all that new here, you're one of us." She glared at him. Ordrew'd joined the department twenty months ago, after leaving the LAPD, and he'd acted hostile, primarily toward Andi and Xavier Contrerez, from the day he arrived. She had no idea why.

"Who authorized your booking the shooter?"

Off guard, she hesitated. *Where's he going with this?* "I was the one caught the call, so I—"

"The manual says bookings have to be authorized by the officer's supervisor. Did you get Stewart's approval?"

Her mind blanked: Fatigue, and the stress of the night. Had she notified Ben? Wait, they'd talked a half-hour ago, but she couldn't recall what he'd said. Had he authorized . . .? A gut-deep gust of irritation flooded her. "Damn it, Brad, it's the middle of the night. Ben was here and we talked, so I know he was okay with it. I didn't need—"

"—to follow the rules?" His face bore a sour look. "That's your problem around here." He leaned in close. Too close. "Tell Ben to give me this case."

"Back off, Brad. You want this case because I can't remember if Ben authorized me to book a guy who shot a kid in the back? Seriously?"

"And because I have ten times the homicide experience you and Contrerez have, and—"

"This conversation is over. If Ben wants to switch me off, that's his call, but it's between you and him. I'm not calling him."

His voice abruptly turned confidential. "Contrerez says the guy's claiming stand-your-ground."

His abrupt change of tone threw her off. "Uh, yeah, he is. Castle doctrine all the way. But there're too many inconsistencies, and he's not answering our questions convincingly."

"You sure you're asking them right?"

Exasperated, she turned away. "Give it a rest, Brad. It's my case unless Ben takes me off."

Ordrew's smirk turned into a glare, his tone again rude. "Shouldn't be. When I'm sheriff, you'll be gone."

Andi snapped alert. "You're running against Ben?" Ordrew had threatened this last year, but she'd figured it was empty talk, and he hadn't mentioned it since.

He turned to his desk and picked up the phone. "You don't read your goddamn mail?" He started tapping the phone's keys, then looked at her again. "Start interviewing for another job."

4

Before she could ask what he meant about the mail, Andi's desk phone buzzed. She punched the flashing button. "Visitor, Andi. DCI's here." As she hung up, she heard Ordrew's intense but low-pitched voice from his cube across the squad room. Who was he calling at this hour? But eagerness to meet the DCI investigator and start digging into the murder trumped her curiosity. In Reception, she saw Phil Oxendine, who'd helped them last year on the Warriors of Yahweh case. "Ox," she called, delighted.

"Andi, hello. You have caught this case?"

"Sure did. Right at the end of my shift, too." She pointed to the conference room. "Let me fill you in on what we've got so far."

"Wait. I prefer letting the scene speak to me first."

"Got it." She enjoyed Oxendine's formal grammar—he spoke with the deliberation and precision of a man who learned his English late in childhood. Never a contraction, never a wrong word. Oxendine was a Cree from near Havre.

On the way to Cedar Street, he asked, "Have you any news on the Warriors of Yahweh case?"

"Not much since the trial. Mike Payne's doing ten years in Deer Lodge for the aiding-and-abetting charge. Last I heard, Scopus is at Big Sandy, in Kentucky." Richard E. Scopus had been the leader of the sex-trafficking cult the "Warriors of Yahweh," and it had turned out that Mike Payne, a deputy in Carlton County, had been a secret member of his group. When Scopus was arrested, Payne had broken him out of the Carlton County jail.

"I am told that Payne testified effectively against Scopus."

"He did. But I think it was testimony by the woman that Scopus almost burned in the crematory that nailed him."

"What was her name, again?"

"Beatrice John. She's Ed's client now."

For a moment, he was quiet. Then, "I wish her well." He changed the subject. "I assume your scene has been secured."

"Done. Xavier Contrerez is there."

"Good. The Mobile Crime Scene team should be here promptly. They left the lab fifteen minutes behind me."

Cedar Street was dark under the tall cottonwoods. Light poured out of the garage at 206, in front of which Xavier's squad and the ambulance continued splashing blue and red light against the walls of the houses. The EMTs stood beside it, arms folded, looking bored. On the other side of the street, in the darkness, a group of neighbors huddled close together, watching, murmuring. *Murder's big news in a small town*, Andi thought. A couple of cigarettes flared every few moments, fireflies in the soft dark air.

Andi introduced Oxendine to Xavier, who pointed to the EMTs. "Those guys want to get the body to the morgue, but I reminded them you need to release the body."

"I am appreciative, Deputy. Have you taken photos?"

"I did." He grabbed the camera from his squad and turned it on and handed it to the agent, who scrolled through the photos. "These are excellent. You have done this before?"

"Eight years military police. Plenty of practice."

Oxendine nodded. "Very well, then. It is time that I look."

He moved to the front of the garage, ducked under the yellow tape, and stood a long time, his back against the tape, hands on his hips, surveying. After a couple of minutes, he walked slowly toward the body, stood above it, looking intensely. He squatted and touched the sweater beside the two holes. Without standing or looking back, he said, "Have you found a weapon?"

Andi nodded. "Smith & Wesson M&P. .40 caliber. He surrendered it. No ballistics yet, of course."

"We will take care of that. Who is the shooter?"

"Name's Daniel Essex, lives here, I think alone." She glanced at Xavier, who nodded.

Andi said, "Essex lives alone."

Oxendine was still squatting beside the body, patting the boy's rear pockets. "Have you got his ID, or is he without one?"

Xavier said, "I have it. It's in an evidence bag in my squad. Name's Bernardo Cirilo, fourteen. High school freshman. Two dollars in his wallet, high school ID."

"A child." Oxendine stood and backed away, still studying the details of the body and its close surroundings. "To me, it appears he was shot from behind and fell forward into the refrigerator." He put on Latex gloves, leaned down, tenderly turned the boy's head. He inspected the ugly slice where his cheek had struck the shelf. "There is no bleeding from the cut. This tells me his heart had already stopped before he collided with the shelf." He stood up straight. "The beer can beside his hand says he had already grabbed it before he was shot. My team will dust it. If the boy's prints are on the can, we will consider that he might have been stealing it." He gingerly placed the can in an evidence bag. "Did you find anything else in his pockets?"

Xavier shook his head. "Just the wallet, a couple dollar bills, and seventy-eight cents in change."

"I am going to look at his front. Please help me." Andi and Xavier gently rolled Bernardo Cirilo half-way up on his side. "This is good," Ox whispered. "Hold him while I look." He peered at the body's front, then patted his shirt under the sweater. "I see no frontal bleeding or exit holes in his clothes, and can feel no bullets inside his clothes. So, we can conclude they remain inside his body, which an autopsy will establish. Put him down." They guided the body to resume its position, softly cradling his head onto the cement.

Next, the agent pulled blue painter's tape out of his pack and laid a crooked line on the floor in the shape of the body. He turned to Xavier. "You may let the EMTs take him now."

When the crew lifted Bernardo Cirilo's body onto the gurney, Andi watched the refrigerator door drift slowly shut. Oxendine opened it and stood peering into the refrigerator. "There is nothing but beer in here." He stooped, pointed at the bottom shelf. Three cans jutted out an inch or so from the others, all the rest of which were aligned in neat rows.

Andi said, "Jostled when his face hit the shelf?"

Ox straightened. "Perhaps, but we will look." He removed the misaligned cans. From behind them, he drew out a device. White, rounded at the top, a small grill-like grid on its face, and below the grid an on-off button, switched to *On*. A hatch for batteries on the bottom. Nothing else.

"What the hell?" Andi muttered. Ox studied it, equally mystified.

Xavier came back into the garage. "It's a baby monitor transmitter."

Ox said, "And what is that?"

"It's a miniature radio, real cute. You put the transmitter in the crib with your *niñita* and keep the receiver with you in the living room or your own bedroom or wherever. If the kid cries, you hear it." He chuckled. "'Strella loved the damn thing. I hated it."

Andi, childless, had had no idea such things existed. "Damn. We just figured out how Essex heard a noise in the garage."

As if he were changing the subject, Oxendine mused, "I saw two entry holes in the boy's sweater."

Andi said, "I saw them too."

"Xavier," said Oxendine, "please check your photos to be sure you got that."

"I got it," he said, turning on the camera again. In a moment, he added, "Got the entry holes in his sweater, big as life." He held the camera out.

"Good," said Oxendine, after taking it and studying the photo. "Your ME will have to make the final call, but it looks clear to me: Mr. Cirilo was shot in the back." Disgust laced his voice. "For a can of beer."

He slipped the transmitter into an evidence baggie. "We will have to learn what this was doing in the refrigerator, where there is no baby."

5

After about five minutes of more silent and intense observation, Oxendine joined Andi and Xavier at the car. "So, run it down for me. I am ready for the story."

Andi told him what Essex had told them, and what they thought, had happened. Their version and Essex's did not much agree.

Oxendine listened, his head tilted thoughtfully, taking in what they said. As they finished, he squinted. "Essex told you the boy charged him and he fired in self-defense. I cannot see it."

Xavier said, "No blood on the floor."

"Yeah." They went back in the garage and examined the floor. "Had he been shot frontally, he would bleed in front. We found no wounds in the front and no smear of blood from the door of the garage backwards." Oxendine's voice was quiet.

Oxendine studied the large oil stain. He looked out into the dark driveway at the car. As Andi had, he shone his flashlight on the cement beneath the engine. They went out.

Andi crouched beside him, leaned down, peered under. "Hardly any more than when I checked, maybe four hours ago, but if this car sat out every night, there'd be a lot more."

Just then, the Mobile Crime Scene unit pulled onto the block, lights flashing. When the team started climbing out, Andi went toward them. "Let's turn off the flashers so the neighbors can get some sleep." She switched both county squads' lights off, and the driver turned off the unit's. The silence of the night pulsed with darkness.

Ox made the introductions; the techs were Jane and Will. Then he said, "Good. Let us take this place apart."

Andi said, "Ox, something about the car and the garage bothers me."

"Oh?" He turned to face her, leaned a little toward her. "Speak to me."

"Judging from the oil leak, I'd say it's normally parked inside. There's no big oil stain out here, just those fresh drops. So, I think the car being out here is unusual. We'll ask the neighbors, of course. And when I first examined the scene, which was maybe six or seven minutes from the time the 9-1-1 call came in, I found that the side door to the garage was unlocked, and the garage door itself was up. I can't figure out when it could have been raised during the encounter without changing the outcome."

"How do you envision that?"

"So, Essex admitted it was up when he first went outside, before shooting the kid. That fits with the scene, Essex firing from outside through the open door. If I suppose it had been down, either Bernardo raised it or Essex raised it. I can't see Bernardo doing it—drawing attention to himself. But if Essex raised it, Bernardo would've heard and started to run. Either he'd have escaped out the side door, or he'd have been closer to the door when Essex shot him, not right by the fridge."

"You are thinking Essex must have left it up?"

"Yeah, though he claims the kid raised it."

Oxendine turned toward the open garage and was still for a short time. "Which you believe means the victim would have died in another position." He peered into the garage. "I can see no reason to disagree with your conclusion. And I also agree with your thoughts about the oil. So, we wonder why the car was outside, and why the door was left up." He took out his notebook again and made a note.

She yawned. "Sorry. Long day. I wish the neighbors were still out. I'd like to ask them about the car and the door."

"I talked to them about that," Xavier said. "They all agreed that his car's been out the last three nights, with the garage door up. They say that's never happened before."

"Thanks. That helps, but let's do the neighborhood thing and talk to them again and anybody not out here tonight."

Xavier chuckled. "Tomorrow's another day."

"No, tomorrow's today."

6

A few minutes after three a.m., Andi came in to the silence of the house. She crawled in beside Ed, and he roused. "You're home," he mumbled.

"Shh. Go back to sleep. I've got to be back at six-thirty." As she listened to Ed's quiet breathing, Bernardo Cirilo's acne-scarred face, sliced by the refrigerator shelf, haunted her. *For a damn beer.* Sleepless, at six a.m., she showered in a stupor, then drove into the station for morning report with her eyes at half-staff. Xavier was already at the table, holding a cup of thick coffee against his chin. "Breathing the fumes. You sleep?"

"Dozed, maybe. You?"

"'Strella said I climbed into bed with my uniform on, gun belt and all. She had to unbuckle it and roll me over to get it off. Can't remember a thing, but I woke up in uniform, which hasn't happened since Afghanistan."

The other on-duty deputies started filing in. Chip Coleman took the chair beside her. Andi mumbled a greeting.

"Long night, eh?"

"You heard about the shooting?"

"Sure. We all heard. Did you see the flyer in the mail?"

"Flyer?"

Before Chip could answer, Ben walked slowly in and sat heavily in his chair at the head of the table. Unusual for a Sunday report, when only the working deputies were required to attend.

He looked terrible, ashen, eyes dull.

Andi slid her chair near his. "You all right, Ben?" she whispered.

"Didn't sleep a goddamn wink. Ordrew called me around two a.m., demanding to take over your case. I said no, he said you're incompetent, I told him to give it a rest or I'll give him a rest, and he told me he's runnin' against me." Color returned to his face as anger flushed out the fatigue.

Just then, Brad Ordrew came in. Instead of taking a seat at the table, he leaned against the doorframe, hands in his pockets, scowling. Ben squinted at him, but said nothing.

Ordrew's threat to fire her popped into her mind. Annoyance flared. She ignored it. Instead, she wondered if Phil Oxendine and the crime scene team were finished, then decided they weren't. Ox would've left her a message, but nothing had been on her phone or in her inbox. Email? Not for the first assessment; they'd do it by phone. When her turn came, she gave her report, updating everyone on what they knew. She mentioned the apparent contradictions between the evidence at the scene and Essex's story.

She finished. "Xav, anything else?"

He nodded. "I spoke with a group of neighbors, and they agreed that for the last three nights, he'd been parking his car in the driveway and leaving the garage door open. They said he'd never done that before. A couple of neighbors also said he'd told them his home was burglarized."

Andi looked around. "That's in his statement too. Who handled that burglary? At 206 East Cedar Street?"

Heads shook. No one volunteered.

Xavier stood. "I'll go get the burglary reports for, what, the last month?"

"Good idea. Essex said it was about three weeks ago." She rubbed her eyes. "Let's be on the safe side. Check the reports going back six weeks."

Ordrew moved away from the doorframe and snarled, "Why aren't we talking about the kid? Why was he in Essex's garage, for God's sake? Stand-your-ground gives Essex the right to defend himself and his property, and you can be damn sure his attorney will be taking that line."

Andi slowed herself down. Tired enough to say something she'd regret, she tuned out her irritation. "The boy is dead, so we can't know his motive for being in the garage. But the body's position suggests he wasn't posing any threat to Mr. Essex. We think he wanted to steal some beer. Castle doctrine law requires a real threat. It doesn't give Essex *carte blanche*, Brad."

"The law's clear. Essex has the right to defend his property." He stood away from the doorframe, his face reddening.

Andi disagreed. "Essex needs to have perceived a serious threat to himself and to have believed only the use of deadly force would prevent the threat to him. So far, we can't see how he was threatened, or that he had any reason to believe he was being threatened. Come on. The kid was shot *in the back*." She wished she'd censored the disgust in her voice.

"I suppose you didn't tell the sheriff how you violated the manual, never got his authorization for the booking." He again shook his head.

The other deputies rustled, shifting uncomfortably in their seats. Ben lifted his hand. "Drop it, Bradley. This here's a damn murder investigation. It ain't a political campaign. And you're runnin' against me, not against Andi." His hand dropped as if weighted, slapped the table.

The door opened. Everyone looked. Xavier, returning with a sheaf of paper. "Maybe I missed it, but there's no burglary report on East Cedar in the last six weeks." He tossed the pages on the table.

Andi pulled them to her place, thumbed through them. "Nothing. He didn't report it."

Ordrew snorted. "Or you guys lost the damn report."

7

As the deputies filed out, a couple glared at Ordrew as they passed. For a moment, he flinched inwardly, but kept his frown. Andi picked up her jacket. "Ben, I'm going back to the scene. Anything else you need me for today?"

"Go. We'll take care of business here."

Ordrew hung back and followed Ben to his office. "A minute, Sheriff?"

"Didn't appreciate your call in the middle of the night, Bradley. And that crap in the meeting was uncalled for."

Ordrew ignored that. "I feel strongly that you should replace Pelton with me. I've got—"

"Ain't how we do business here. Deputy catches a call and leads the investigation, unless there's a good reason to change."

"I've got two good reasons. One, I've investigated ten times the murders Pelton's even seen. Two, she's not following procedures."

Ben narrowed his eyes. "That's serious talk, Bradley."

Ordrew wondered if Ben might listen this time. "Procedures *are* serious, Sheriff. The manual says she was supposed to call you last night, first to notify you of the homicide, and second to get your authorization to book him. She didn't remember doing either one."

"Wrong, both counts. She told Marla to call me right at the start, then after she took his initial statement, I told her to book the guy."

Shit. Ordrew wanted to swear, but stifled it. "Fine. But I've got way more experience with homicide than she's got, and—"

"And you know that how?"

Ordrew snorted. "How many murders have you had here, Sheriff? I investigated dozens down in LA."

"This ain't about dick size, Bradley. Andi's been here goin' on six years, and before that she worked twenty years for Cook County. She's handled plenty."

His jaw clenched. *Cook fucking County?* "She's biased."

"Biased?"

"Yeah. She as much as told me the shooter's stand-your-ground defense isn't valid."

"I ain't heard her say no such thing."

"Sheriff, I've seen it and I know you've seen it. Officers who break protocol and don't follow the manual slip up. She's not right for this investigation. You can't trust her."

Ben's big fist hit the table. "She followed the damn manual, and she's a fine cop." Ben shook his head. "Arguin' with you tires me out, Bradley. Andi's on this case, end of story. Go argue philosophy with somebody who gives a good goddamn."

"You think procedures and protocol are a matter of *philosophy*?"

"What I think, Bradley, is with you they're a *religion*."

8

Grace pounded on Ed's bedroom door shortly after Andi left. "Up and at 'em, Northrup. Let's rise and shine. I'm going to college."

Through the wispy fog of an abrupt awakening, he chuckled at her enthusiasm. During the four years, wait, three years and eight months, since he'd adopted her, he could recall precisely zero Sunday mornings when Grace had risen before noon. Today, though, was her big day. *Her new life.* "I'm awake, thank you," he called. "Go make coffee."

Over breakfast, she said, "I gotta see Jared one last time before we leave."

Grace's friend Jared Hansen had not recovered well from his brain surgery. After much of the year spent in a rehab facility in Missoula, he'd returned to Jefferson three weeks ago. The surgery had removed not just the tumor, but also much that made Jared who he'd been. During his time in Missoula, Ed and Grace had visited him twice a month. The time at home, Ed knew, was for the parents to say goodbye, because Jared would not survive much longer.

"Okay. It won't be good."

"I know, but I promised him I'd come before I leave."

"Did he understand you?"

Her eyes clouded. "No. I know he's not really Jared any more. But I promised."

"And promises should be kept." He looked at the clock above the stove. "How about we leave in twenty minutes."

"Why not leave right now?"

He smiled. "You need to do the breakfast dishes."

"Geez, Northrup. Why?"

"For old time's sake."

9

Grace followed Ed's pickup in the PV and parked behind him in front of Jared's home. Ed watched her walk up the drive to the house, sad that she had this burden, proud of her bearing it. Marie Hansen opened the screen door and Grace stepped inside. Ed waited in his pickup, mulling his brief but packed relationship with her. *Three years and eight months.* How could time have flown so fast? He smiled at himself: A typical dad, moping over his little girl leaving for college.

Grace's mother—Mara Ellenson, Ed's long-ago ex-wife—had brought her to the valley and abandoned her. When the sheriff's department ultimately located Mara, she was dying in a Las Vegas hospital. Grace's only living relative, her father, was a few years into a life sentence for his third drug conviction. In her will, Mara had left a small fortune in trust for Grace, on condition that Ed adopt her and serve as trustee. He'd done it, and it had changed him. *Saved me,* he thought. Before Grace, he'd been a burned-out case.

•   •   •

Jared's mom took Grace into her arms. They'd grown close over the year, more so in the few weeks Jared had been home and Grace had visited him every couple of days.

"It's your big day, Grace."

"Sure is, Mrs. Hansen." Grace imagined that Marie Hansen was thinking *her* son's big day would never come. "I'm here to say goodbye to Jared."

"You know," Mrs. Hansen said, her voice catching, "he won't be with us much longer."

Grace didn't trust her voice. She nodded, a thickening sadness in her throat.

Marie touched her arm. "He's in the living room."

Jared was sitting in his wheelchair, facing out the front window. Grace moved into his field of vision, but his eyes didn't focus on her. "I'm going to college today, Jared."

He continued staring out the window.

"I'll come back for Homecoming. I'll bring you some college stuff."

"Oh." His eyes were blank.

"Are you doing your exercises?"

"No."

"You have to do them, Jared. They're good for you." Six months ago, she'd stopped telling him the exercises would help him get better. They wouldn't.

His head slowly turned toward her, but he said nothing, then stared out the window again.

"I'll be back to see you soon." It was all she could manage before her grief closed her throat.

His lips twitched. Without looking at her, he whispered, almost too low for her to hear, "Who are you?"

She fought against the tears that rose. "I'm Grace, Jared." She bent over and kissed his forehead. When she was at the archway into the hall, she turned back and looked at him. He was staring at the window.

Mrs. Hansen leaned against the kitchen sink, wiping her eyes. They held a long, deep embrace, then Marie Hansen said, "Go start your new life, dear."

•   •   •

Ed watched the screen door open and Grace walk slowly toward their vehicles, head low. She came over to his window. He lowered it. "God, Northrup, it's so sad."

He nodded. "You okay?"

"He didn't know me." Her eyes welled over, tears falling down her face.

He reached through the window and touched her arm. She pulled in a deep shuddering breath. "Yeah, I know."

10

A few minutes before eight, when Andi got back to Cedar Street, the techs were stowing gear in their van. Phil Oxendine was in the garage, writing in a notebook he'd rested on the workbench. He turned when she came in.

"Essex says there was a burglary here sometime in the past month," she told him. "One of the neighbors said that he told her there was a burglary here three weeks ago, but we have no report of one. In his statement, he said there'd been a burglary, but had no memory of the details. He said he was traumatized. Neighbors also tell us he's left his car out and the garage door up the last three nights, which apparently has never happened before. He always puts the car away at night."

"Which prompts me to wonder why."

"Me, too."

"We processed the car. We found nothing that helps explains its being left outside, but there were two puzzling things. First, the entire vehicle is uncommonly clean. Also, there are prints we assume must be the owner's in some places—you should send us copies of his fingerprints so we can be sure the ones we found are his. The other oddity is that there are no prints on the steering wheel. He must have wiped it down."

"Or wears driving gloves. We'll email Essex's prints to you."

"Good. Come and look at something." He led the way to the car in the driveway. "We found something curious, here." He pointed with his pen to a spot on the hood, above the right tire, just beside the printing powder.

She bent down and studied the spot he'd indicated: two scratches, about a quarter-inch long, parallel, apparently fresh—no rust. She straightened and said, "He told me he fired from this position." She demonstrated him steadying both hands on the hood.

"Hmm. This is speculative, but if the butt of his gun touched the hood, perhaps the scratches were caused by the two recoils."

As she was thinking about this, her phone buzzed. *Ben Stewart* came up on the screen.

"Excuse me," she said. "What's up, Ben?"

"Doc Runge just called with some preliminary stuff to pass on to you and DCI. First thing, he confirms the boy was shot from behind. Also, he took two slugs from the body. He'll send 'em here for ballistics. Tell DCI to pick 'em up."

".40 caliber?"

"Nope, nine millimeters."

She felt her jaw drop. "Damn. Okay, Ben." She tried to process this, couldn't. "I'll pass that on."

When she told Ox, he paled. "What?"

She nodded. "The weapon he surrendered was .40 caliber, not a nine mil."

"So, the gun you confiscated is not the murder weapon."

Anger focused her. "The guy's jerking us around. We'll need a search warrant for the house. Can you guys stay and help?"

Oxendine looked thoughtful. "Certainly. But I have a question: How long between the shots and your arrival?"

Andi thought back to her car clock. *4:21.* "Figuring conservatively, I'd say I was on my way no more than sixty seconds after we got the call. Add a minute for the caller to get his phone and dial in, another two minutes between here and the station, so what's that? Four minutes, five max. He was standing on the lawn."

"Out of breath?"

"Not at all. Very cool, very calm. Even friendly. At first."

"Very well," Oxendine said, eyes hard. "Either the murder weapon will be inside the house, or we will find it not far away. Five minutes does not give him time to run very far, ditch the gun, return here, and catch his breath. Can you get some deputies searching the alleys and garbage cans and such? Maybe inside a three-hundred-yard radius?"

"Already on the agenda." She pulled out her phone. "I'm calling about the search warrant."

Oxendine said, "When you get the warrant, include his computer and cell phone, if he has them."

"Sure. Because?"

"All that you have told me, first. Then, his giving you the misleading gun, second. This does not pass my smell test. Computers can often tell us things." He yawned. Jane, the tech, walked up, also yawning. "It's contagious," she mumbled.

Andi smiled. "Check in at the Jefferson House motel and get a few hours' sleep. I'll get the warrant and start the search, and a crew of deputies will be out looking for the weapon outside the house. Maybe we all meet here at noon?"

Jane looked to Oxendine. "What's up? Thought we were done."

Andi explained about the gun and the search. Jane sighed. "Sleep's a righteous idea."

Ox rubbed his hands. "Right, then. Andi, you will lower the overhead door and we can all go rest our weary brains." He smiled at her. "Except you."

LATER THAT MORNING

1

Andi was typing up the paperwork for the warrant when her desk phone buzzed. "Mr. Essex's attorney's here from Missoula, Andi."

Andi glanced at her watch: *10:18* a.m. *Must've left Missoula at seven,* she thought. *On a Sunday. A bulldog.*

At the reception desk, her briefcase resting open on the counter, stood a trim woman, five-eight, Andi's height, graying hair cropped close to her head, broad shoulders. Andi thought, *Bet she's a swimmer.* Charcoal-gray pantsuit, expensive leather briefcase. She saw Andi come in, snapped the briefcase shut, and approached her. Andi thought of a bull's charge. "Angela Norton, Deputy. I'd like to see my client, please."

Andi remembered her. Jared Hansen's parents had retained her when Jared's case still looked criminal, before the brain cancer had been discovered. "You took the Jared Hansen case last year, didn't you?"

"Sad case, wasn't it? How is he?" Something in her eyes softened.

"Not well, I'm afraid. Recovery's, ah, poor."

A mask settled over Angela Norton's face. "I'm sorry, Deputy, but I need to see my client, Mr. Essex."

"Of course." *I was right: A bulldog.* She showed the attorney to the conference room. "I'll bring Mr. Essex."

Angela Norton said, "I assume this room is secure and not bugged? That you people respect the attorney-client privilege?"

Andi paused a beat before answering. "Of course. Our recording equipment is nowhere but the interrogation room." *No use fighting yet.*

"I called your district attorney, but he hasn't returned my call yet. I'd like to have the arraignment while I'm here."

"I can understand that. But Judge Flure isn't going to agree to a hearing on Sunday."

"Hmmm. You people work banker's hours, I take it?"

"If bankers work double shifts till three in the morning. But Judge Flure's a stickler for observing the Lord's Day . . ." She was about to add something about the DA's hours, but the look on the attorney's face stopped her. *Don't piss her off. Yet.* She said, "I'll give Irv Jackson a call, see what he can work out."

Norton's face eased. A bit. "Thank you. I'd appreciate that."

Andi enlisted Chip Coleman and together they entered the cellblock to get Essex. His night in the cell hadn't cooled his temper. "When the fuck's my attorney coming? I called her last night."

She stifled a smile. "Most attorneys I know don't appreciate nighttime calls on Saturday night. But you're lucky. She's here."

"The hell I'm lucky. I had to spend the night in this hell-hole."

"Mr. Essex, please step away from the cell door and turn around and put your hands behind your back."

"What the fuck?"

Chip said, "We're taking you to talk with your lawyer. Our procedure is to use handcuffs when we move people. Deputy Pelton and I are going to do that."

"No way, José. No cuffs."

"Name's Chip, not José."

Andi said, "If you won't cooperate, we'll bring your lawyer in here. And my guess is that'll get you off on a very bad foot."

Essex started to react, then muttered, "Fuck all." He faced away and stuck his hands behind his back. Chip entered the cell while Andi watched with her hand on her gun, cuffed him, then took his elbow. "Let's go, buddy."

Essex pulled his arm away. "I'm not your buddy, asshole."

Andi kept her hand on her weapon. "Take it easy, Mr. Essex. Don't make this worse for yourself."

They ushered him down the hall from the cellblock to the conference room. Inside, Angela Norton was standing by the table. Andi took Essex to the chair. "I'll remove the handcuffs now, Mr. Essex." Angela Norton waited. When the cuffs were off, she extended her hand. "Daniel, sorry we meet like this. I came as soon as I could."

Essex didn't take her hand. "Get me the hell out of here. I'm innocent. I was defending my home. They—"

Norton interrupted. "Stop, Daniel. From this minute on, your mouth stays shut so tight you'll suffocate if I pinch your nose. You talk only when I tell you to." She turned to Andi, who stifled her smile. "Thank you, Deputy. That'll be all."

Andi nodded to the attorney and pointed to a wall phone. "When you're done, just dial 0, and they'll find me so I can interview your client." Essex looked about to burst, but Norton's glare stopped him.

Andi left, and let the door slam.

2

While she waited for Norton to finish her interview with Daniel Essex, Andi dialed Judge Richard Flure's home number. After he growled "Who is it?" she said, "Sir, it's Deputy Pelton. I need a warrant to search a house for a murder weapon and a couple of other items."

The judge, muted anger in his voice, said, "What murder?"

She told him about it. "The shooter's talking with his lawyer now."

"On the Lord's Day? Who's the lawyer, Jerry Francis?"

"No, sir, it's Angela Norton from Missoula. So, may I bring the warrant over for your signature?"

"The man is in custody?"

"Of course, sir." She grimaced. Dickie Flure was going to be difficult. She said nothing. Ben Stewart had taught her well: "Wait 'em out," he'd once told her. "Judges and crooks, they ain't no different: Both gotta fill dead air with the sound of their voice." Andi prepared to beg, knowing if the warrant waited till tomorrow, Phil Oxendine's team would be gone and she and Xavier would need to do the search alone.

After a moment, Judge Flure groaned. "Bring it. But be prepared to answer my questions."

"Thank you, sir." Pressing her luck, Andi asked, "Any chance of a probable cause hearing sometime today, sir? His attorney is asking."

"No way on God's green earth, Deputy. Bad enough *you* ask me to work on the Lord's Day."

"Sorry, sir. I'll call Irv Jackson and he'll be in touch. Tomorrow."

Hanging up, she went down the hall to the conference room and knocked. Hearing Norton's voice say, "Just a moment," she stepped back. The door opened.

"What is it, Deputy?"

"Ma'am, I need to get a search warrant signed a.s.a.p. Will you be much longer with Mr. Essex?"

"Another half-hour."

"Perfect. More than enough time. Then I can interview him—in your presence, of course."

Angela Norton said, "Have you spoken to the DA about arraigning my client this afternoon?"

"Spoke with the judge himself. He said, 'No way on God's green earth.'"

Norton sighed. "Judges." She closed the door.

Andi grabbed the warrant application and ran to her car.

3

When she came back, Callie Martin, the weekday dispatcher, was chatting with Gen Winter, the day shift dispatcher on weekends. Gen saw Andi first. "There she is."

Callie turned. "Mornin', gal. Gen's fillin' me in on the murder. What're you up to?"

Andi waved her folder. "Got a search warrant for the house signed and sealed. The shooter's with his lawyer as we speak. What brings you around on your day off?"

"Bill and I are having brunch across the street at the Angler, so I thought I'd see if you were in. You remember you're hosting the Ladies' Fishing Society this Wednesday?"

"Oh, man, good thing you came by. I totally forgot." She put the warrant into the copy machine to make a bunch of copies for the parties involved. "This investigation is going to keep me pretty busy. I might not have a lot of time to prep *hors d'oeuvres.*"

Last year, Callie had invited Andi to join the Ladies' Fishing Society, and she'd demurred. "I don't fish, Callie."

Callie had laughed. "Neither do we, darlin'." What the Ladies' Fishing Society did was meet to share gourmet *hors d'oeuvres* and gossip. Before she joined the group, these were things Andi would have said bore no interest for her, but over the year, she'd found she enjoyed the meetings. And her growing friendships with the "ladies." The term, she thought, was wrong. Her friends weren't "ladies," they were tough and resilient women of the valley, and one of the "ladies" was Lane Martin, the gay co-owner and chef of the Angler Bar and Restaurant across the street. Before joining the Ladies' Fishing Society, her life with Ed and

Grace had been her main non-work relationships—or more accurately, her *only* non-work relationships. After joining, she could say she had friends outside her family.

The copies were done and she slipped them in the folder. Callie said, "If you need help with the food, tell me Tuesday and Bernie and I'll pitch in."

Andi smiled. Before she could say thanks, Gen's phone rang. She listened, then pointed at Andi. "Your lawyer's finished. She says to come do your interview."

4

Andi cuffed Essex and walked him to the interrogation room, Angela Norton on his other side. On the way, she wondered why Norton was allowing this interview at all. Most defense attorneys, in this situation, would instruct their clients not to waive Miranda.

When they were seated, Andi gestured to the video camera and the one-way mirror. "This interview is being recorded," she said, reaching for the *Record* button. Before pressing it, she said, "I'm curious, Ms. Norton. You're allowing this interview?"

"My client insisted on it," Norton answered tartly.

"Damn right," Essex snarled. "I have a right to be heard."

She engaged *Record*. "Mr. Essex, just in case we weren't clear last night, you're under arrest for the murder of Bernardo Cirilo." She started to repeat the Miranda warning.

Essex interrupted. "Get on with it. I know my goddamn rights."

Angela Norton put a hand on his arm. To Andi, she said, "Can you give me the name again?" She opened her pen and jotted it on her notepad as Andi spelled it for her, then finished reading his rights. He rolled his eyes.

"I have some questions, and I'd appreciate hearing what you can tell me about them. You told us that you experienced a burglary recently, but we're unable to find any report of a burglary at your address. Ever. Can you help me with that?"

To Norton, he said, "Can I answer that?" She nodded. "Damn right I can. You people are a bunch of incompetent idiots. You—"

Norton snapped, "Stop, Daniel. Just tell what happened."

Andi watched him trying to settle himself. After a moment, he said, "I didn't report it."

"Why is that, sir?"

Again, he looked to Norton for the okay, who nodded, but moved her hand closer to his arm. He said, "The bastard took ten damn beers. What would you people do about ten beers? Don't bother bullshitting me, you wouldn't do squat. I don't trust cops."

"Have you had experiences that have led to that lack of trust?"

Norton raised her hand. "What has that to do with the alleged murder of . . ." She glanced down. "Of Bernardo Cirilo?"

"That's what I'd like to find out."

"In which case, Deputy, I'm instructing my client not to answer that question."

Andi nodded, watching Essex's face. He grinned.

"Please tell me what happened in that burglary."

Norton again raised her hand. "Relevance?"

"Mr. Essex shot a young boy who was in his garage, perhaps stealing some beer, although we don't know the boy's intent." She caught the slight lift of Norton's eyebrows, thought, *She's surprised I know it isn't burglary if there's no intent to commit a crime.* "Your client told me earlier that because of that burglary, he was sure another would happen, and that he believed he had to protect his property. *He* claims relevance, and so we need to know the circumstances of that first burglary."

Norton nodded. She said, "I'm advising my client—"

Essex interrupted her. "I want to tell her."

"Against my advice?"

Essex nodded. Norton gave a slight shake of her head. "Let the record show my client is disregarding my advice about this matter." To Essex, she said, "Just the facts."

He nodded. "It was about ten o'clock. I heard a noise in the garage, and before I got there to check it out, the side door slammed. I flipped on the light and saw that the refrigerator door was wide open and ten beers were gone."

"Ten. How did you know that?"

"I know what's in my refrigerator, Deputy. Afterwards, I counted them. I was ten short."

"Okay. When you saw the refrigerator door was open, what did you do?" As she waited for his answer, Andi flashed on the door drifting shut when Bernardo Cirilo's body had been taken away. She jotted a note to check whether the door would stay open with nothing blocking it.

"I ran out the side door after him, but he was gone. There was a beer can on the grass next to the sidewalk. I guess he dropped it."

"Did you see this person at any point?"

"No. Just heard the door slam and saw cans were missing."

"You've referred to the person as *he* a couple of times. How do you know it was a male?"

Norton shook her head. "Really, Deputy?"

She nodded. "Really. But I'll change the question. After you chased the burglar but didn't find him or her, what did you do next?"

"I went back into the garage to see what else he stole from me."

"Did you find anything else missing?"

He hesitated, then said, "No. Nothing. Just beer. That's why I didn't report it."

She checked the note she'd just written. "Did I understand correctly that when you initially checked the garage, you saw the refrigerator door was open?"

"That's what I said."

"Thank you." She paused a moment, making another note. "I'm sorry you didn't report it to us, Mr. Essex, because we could have found other ways for you to protect yourself." She didn't add, *Without having to kill a kid.* "Was there any damage to the side door?"

To Norton, he asked, "Do I have to answer that?"

For the first time, she looked puzzled. "Yes, unfortunately. You waived Miranda on the subject of the first burglary."

"Fuck all. I refuse to answer."

Andi smiled. "Okay. Are you refusing to answer about the door, or about the first burglary as a whole?"

"The burglary thing, damn it."

Andi knew she could push it, since he'd already waived his right to silence. "On what grounds, sir?"

Essex looked at his lawyer. "Tell me the right answer."

Norton looked intently at Andi, who knew that at this point she needed to read Essex his rights again, and this time he'd clam up.

"Deputy Pelton will get a court order forcing you to answer about the burglary. That will delay everything, including getting you out of here."

Essex growled, "I'll answer."

"You do have the right to remain silent, and anything you say can be used against you in court. You understand that?"

"Damn it, yes."

"All right." She looked at her notes again. "Where was your car parked the night of the first burglary?"

"In the garage, where else would it be parked?" Before Andi could follow up, he said, "Oh, last night it was in the driveway, so you think maybe it was that first night. No. I never leave the car outside. It invites trouble."

"Other than last night, you've never left it in the driveway?"

"Nope, never."

"That's odd. When we talked with your neighbors, they told us that for the past three nights, instead of parking your car in the garage as you typically do, you left it outside, in the driveway. They also said you left the garage door open, which surprised us. Why, Mr. Essex? Why leave the car outside with the garage open?"

Norton held up her hand. "Don't answer that."

Andi realized she'd asked it wrong; he hadn't admitted leaving the garage door up, only that it was up. She took a moment, then said, "Please tell me why you left your car in the driveway last night."

He looked to Norton again; the attorney nodded. "I don't know. Must've forgot."

Same answer as before. "Forgot." Andi jotted it down, as if it were important. "Last night when I looked around your garage, I saw that the side door was also unlocked. Do you leave that door unlocked ordinarily, or just last night?" She doubted Norton would let that get by, but was surprised.

"No. I always lock it."

"Except last night?"

"No. I locked it last night."

"I see. How did it get unlocked, then? Did you unlock it after shooting Bernardo Cirilo?"

Angela Norton shook her head. "Don't answer, Daniel." To Andi she said, "We're done here. I'm instructing my client to refuse to answer any further questions."

Andi hid her smile. It was a good start. "I'm not done, Ms. Norton."

"Yes, you are, dear."

5

After collecting the recorded DVD and writing up her notes of the half-frustrating, half-pleasing interview, Andi grabbed the original search warrant—she'd given copies to Norton and Essex—and drove to the scene. She was hardly out of the parking lot when Gen's voice crackled on the radio.

Static. "EMTs, unconscious male at Russell Fork Road, number 77."

Andi knew the address: Ben Stewart's log house on a fork of the Monastery River. Memories of his first heart attack—at this same time last year—flooded back. She sped up, and pulled fast around the corner of Cedar Street, skidded to a stop behind Phil Oxendine's vehicle. She ran across the grass toward Oxendine, standing in the garage.

"I've got the warrant, but I think my sheriff just had another heart attack. EMTs were called to his house. He lives there alone, so it has to be him. Do you need me—?"

"Go," he said. "My team is finishing breakfast, they will be here in a few minutes. We will do the search, top to bottom."

She ran back to her squad and yanked open the door. Oxendine called after her, "The warrant. I need the warrant."

She stopped. *Settle yourself. Being rattled helps nobody.* She forced herself to walk back across the lawn, breathing hard, and handed him the warrant. "You've got my cell number. Call when you find anything. I'll get back soon as I can."

He took the warrant. "Take care of your boss."

●   ●   ●

Pete Peterson, senior deputy, was already at the emergency room door when she got there. "How . . .?" she started to ask.

"Genevieve called me," he said.

"Ben inside?"

Pete looked toward Division Street. "Any minute." They heard the siren.

"You sure it's him?" she asked.

"Who else lives at 77 Russell Fork Road?"

She flinched, as if punched in the chest. She'd almost talked herself into thinking she'd misheard the address. Then, something rocked her again. "Pete, Gen's dispatch said 'unconscious male.' Ben lives alone, so if it's him that's unconscious, who called 911?"

Before Pete could answer, they heard the siren shut down as the ambulance roared into the ER bay. They moved off to the side. Dashing around to the back, the driver swung open the door. His partner, inside, pushed the gurney out and the driver held his end, letting its legs drop to the asphalt. Under a red blanket pulled up to his chin, Ben Stewart lay, eyes closed, face grayer than his hair. Andi felt a stab of fear. He looked dead.

They followed the gurney inside, then turned into the waiting room. Pete paced, Andi sat. After five minutes, a woman came into the area. Andi did a double-take. "Bernie?" Bernadette O'Reilly was one of her friends in the Ladies' Fishing Society.

Bernie's face was fierce. Andi thought of a mother bear separated from her cub.

"Andi," Bernie growled. "You heard?"

"Yeah." She'd heard over the first-responder radio. "How did *you* hear?"

"I called it in."

"You did? How . . .?"

"Ben's my neighbor."

"I know. But I mean, how'd *you* know?"

Bernie looked around, nodded a sad greeting to Pete. She lowered her voice even further. "You can keep a secret?"

"Uh-huh."

Bernie rubbed her upper lip. "Hon, Ben and I, we're having an affair. I was beside him in bed." Tears gathered in her eyes. She coughed roughly and rubbed them away.

Andi whipsawed between her fear for Ben and delight in her friend's news. She'd suspected something for a while—Ben's casual mentions of Bernie had grown more frequent and fervent, and were almost always accompanied by a shy grin.

"Ben has seemed a lot happier lately," she told Bernie. "Happier than he's been since Marlene left." She smiled. "Must be you."

"Hell's bells, he's like a kid." She blushed. "Well, a teenager." She blushed more. "I guess you can say the same for me. Never knew sex'd come back at this age . . ." She stopped.

"Why didn't you tell us?"

"The Ladies? Hells bells, I'd've told you, but I'm of an age you don't want the gossip to last longer'n the sex. I told Ben we could blab about it when we're sure it's real and it'll last." Her head bowed toward her lap.

When she looked up, her eyes were again full. "It's real, all right. But that part about lasting . . .?" She wiped her eyes again. When she could speak, her voice was so soft, so far away, Andi had to turn her head to hear. "I love that man. I couldn't bear to see him die."

A vice gripped Andi's chest. "Damn it, he's not going to die."

Bernie straightened her back. "Hell, no, sweetness, that's the truth. And if praying can help, well, I'll be on my damn knees till God brings that man home to me or tells me why not."

"Atta girl." Andi touched Bernie's arm, said, "Excuse me, I've got to talk to Pete."

"Girl, you'll keep it quiet?"

"Sure, Bernie."

"Good. It's just, well, I don't want to put the news out till Ben says it's okay."

"Of course. I'm good."

"Figured you'd be, child. You go, now," Bernie said firmly. "I've got a few things to say to Himself."

6

Andi joined Pete, who was staring out the window at the mountains. "Pete, you have to call the Commissioners and get yourself named acting sheriff again."

He ran his fingers through his hair, then faced her. "I don't want that burden again, Andi." During Ben's first heart attack and recovery last year, Pete had been appointed to take his place. "Last year, I hated it, every minute."

49

"I know, but you're senior deputy, and you're experienced. Think about it: Ordrew tried to get himself the job last time, and came close. What if he gets there first?"

"Andi, you're the one. They'll appoint you in a heartbeat."

Her breath caught. *Never.* She ignored how hard breathing had become. "Come on, Pete. You've been around for twenty years; I've been here less than six. Besides, I'm not real sure the commissioners are ready for a woman sheriff. Even an Acting."

Pete turned back to the window and stared out. She told herself he wasn't avoiding her. *Looking for a line of escape.* Her heart, though beating frantically, went out to him. After a minute, his shoulders slumped and he nodded slowly. "You're right, I've got to do it. But Andi?"

Before he could finish, Doc Keeley emerged from the ER, his eyes weary. "Andi, Pete?" He glanced at Bernie O'Reilly, and moved the deputies to the far corner, lowering his voice. But Bernie jumped up and followed them. "Doc, I found him. Ben's my . . ." Her voice caught. She glanced at Andi. "My neighbor, and he's got no family."

Doc nodded. "Join us. So, he's had a massive coronary. He's unconscious, but the signs suggest he hasn't had a stroke on top of it. It's touch-and-go right now." He hesitated. "It's possible he might not make it, though we've done everything we can at the moment." Doc's voice thickened with emotion. His eyes, Andi realized, weren't fatigued: They were drenched with sorrow.

Bernie shook her head. "I say we fly him to Missoula."

Doc looked pained. "We've done everything they'd do, at this point, and I don't want to stress his body if I can avoid it."

"So, what *can* we do? I have to do something."

Doc touched her arm. "Wait. And if you do it, pray." He started to turn away, then said, "He's on his way to the ICU, but I can't allow any visitors. If he makes it through the night, we'll see what's up in the morning. Sorry for the bad news." Doc took a halting breath, then turned and left. Bernie went back to her chair in the corner and closed her eyes.

Andi shivered. *If he makes it through the night.* She looked at Pete.

His eyes were narrow, thoughtful. "That just upped the ante, didn't it? If Ordrew's Acting Sheriff, he'll have an advantage in the election—assuming Ben recovers."

"You've got to call the commissioners, Pete."

He rubbed his eyes. "Yep, I do." He pulled his cell phone out and dialed. "Gen? Pete here. Ben's had a serious heart attack." He waited a moment. "No, we don't know any more than that. But I need Jack Conrad's number. After a moment, he took out his pencil and jotted the number on a newspaper. "Thanks, Gen."

He started to dial, then stopped. "Andi?"

"What?"

"I'm going to need your help for this one. Lots of it."

She felt it all, then, her fear and her sorrow and her anger and her resolve. She put her arms around her friend, and for a moment they both held on. Then Pete stepped back, and continued dialing his cell phone. Bernie O'Reilly was already in her chair, her lips moving without a sound.

Andi wished she knew a prayer. Or believed that it would help.

LATER THAT MORNING

1

When she joined Phil Oxendine in the spare bedroom of Daniel Essex's house, he was sitting behind the desk, searching a drawer. He looked up. "How is your sheriff?"

"Not good. We'll know more in the morning." She refocused. "Find the gun?"

"No nine-millimeter yet. He has an armory of others, though, mostly in his basement gun locker, but a number in the garage too. And a couple in his car. The guy is a one-man army."

"But no nine-mil?"

"Not one."

"Damn."

"If it is here, we will find it. Jane and Will are still taking the basement apart. I did his bedroom and bathroom, and we have not started on the other rooms. And I want to go over the garage again."

"I'll start in the kitchen. My dad was a Chicago cop. He told me mobsters hide their weapons in the freezer." She pulled on latex gloves on her way to the refrigerator and emptied everything out of the freezer. No weapon. She peered into the refrigerator itself—not much there. Eggs, veggies, two packages of ground beef, a six-pack of Coke, milk, a loaf of bread. Two empty shelves. Condiments in the door.

Thirty-five minutes later, as she was finishing the last kitchen drawer, Jane called up from the basement gent, "Found the gun." Andi went down fast, followed by Oxendine.

"What is it?"

"Glock 19, looks like generation 4."

"Fantastic," Andi said, excited. "Better dust it."

Jane nodded. "Already on it."

Oxendine said, "And I found a ream of print-outs from various websites dedicated to stand-your-ground laws and propaganda. Ugly stuff."

Xavier Contrerez's voice sounded above them. "Anybody home?"

"Down here, Xav."

He joined them. "You hear about Ben?"

Andi stiffened. "Yeah. It's not good." She pointed. "Jane found the murder weapon." Caught herself. "Assuming it prints out as Essex's."

Xavier looked hesitant. "Ben's . . . going to be all right?"

Everyone looked at her. She sighed. "Don't know. It's bad. We'll learn more in the morning." *Change the subject.* "What've you found out?"

"First thing, me and Lannie and Chip scoured the neighborhood and didn't find a nine-mil anyplace. I talked to more of Essex's neighbors and they all confirm what we heard before: two shots. All of them agreed Essex *never* leaves his car outside, until three nights ago, and he's obsessive about keeping his garage door closed and locked. One of the men said Essex talks all the time about thieves, and about how he'll kill any intruder that invades his home."

Oxendine frowned. "He appears to have meant it."

"Anything else?" Andi asked.

Xavier nodded. "I ran his prints. Seems our boy has three priors for assault, all in Massachusetts."

Andi caught her breath. "Home intruders?"

"No. One ex-wife, two ex-girlfriends."

Jane, dusting the Glock on a workbench in the corner, looked up. "A genuine asshole's asshole."

"Where in Massachusetts?"

"Brookline." Andi's cell phone buzzed in her pocket. *Ben?*

No. *Peterson.* "Andi, Jack Conrad just called. The commissioners are going to meet at four o'clock this afternoon. Turns out Ordrew got to them and demanded to be considered. They're going to interview both of us and decide after that."

"Damn. You get any sense from Jack what they'll do?"

"Not really. He was careful not to take sides. I did notice that he called Brad by his last name, and called me Pete. Which could mean squat."

"Four o'clock, huh?" She looked at her watch. "Oh, man," she groaned. "Two hours."

Pete didn't say anything.

"Okay, Pete. Call me when you know."

2

Ed and Grace arrived on campus at 11:45. New student orientation was scheduled for noon, beginning with a lunch in the cafeteria. Grace and Ed sat with another family, whose son maneuvered himself into the chair beside Grace. Ed, getting acquainted with the parents, watched Grace laughing with him, then talking seriously about something he couldn't hear, then mock-slapping him on the shoulder for some remark. After a dozen minutes of this—they'd just met—Ed thought, *Flirting.* He grinned.

The mom smiled too. "Looks like Garth and your daughter are hitting it off already."

"I noticed," Ed said. "She's never been shy."

The mom chuckled. "Garth's shy, but she seems to bring out the . . ." She turned to her husband. "What's the word I want?"

"Lust."

"Stop." She blushed. "I'm sorry, Ed."

He waved it off. "Don't worry. That sword cuts two ways." They laughed.

Later, as they walked to the auditorium for the president's welcome speech, he said to Grace, "Garth's a nice guy?"

"He thinks I'm cute."

Ed's eyebrows lifted. "And how do you know that?"

She rolled her eyes. "Northrup, we women know these things."

"Ah."

•　　　•　　　•

After the speech, they found their orientation group and toured the library. When they were shown the reference section, with its rows of computers, Grace raised her hand.

"Yes?" said their tour guide, a senior.

"Don't most of the students have their own computers?"

The guide looked surprised. "Well, sure. I mean, everybody has one, right? At least a tablet."

Grace nodded. "I have a friend who told me—he's a professor—it would be great if libraries could spend more money on books, so we could do our Internet research in our rooms and then come and study the primary sources here. I don't know if he's right."

The tour guide looked at her. "You know, nobody's ever asked that before. But the faculty always tell us to check primary sources, so maybe your friend's got a point."

Ed looked at his daughter, surprised—Grace had never talked about the computers-vs-books issue before. Then it hit him: Merwin. Her "friend" was his grad school buddy and life-long friend, Charley Merwin, enthroned as a professor of clinical psychology at the University of Minnesota. He knew Merwin took rich and deep pleasure in pontificating about students doing research in journals and books, not on the Internet. Grace must've listened.

As they left the library, he said, "You've been talking with Merwin about more than schools."

She hooked her arm in his, a gesture she'd never, not once, done before. "I talk to lots of people."

He smiled. "Cool." In talking to Merwin about her future, Grace couldn't have chosen anyone about whom Ed felt better. "Picking Merwin was a good choice. What led you to call him?"

"When he was here on vacation a couple years ago, he gave me his number and said I could call any time I needed an independent opinion." She glanced at him.

"Independent from mine?" He was tickled. Merwin would do that.

"Yeah. He said a girl needs a second father figure to balance her dad's bias."

"Does he? Balance me?"

She stopped strolling and let go of his arm, turned to face him. "That's what's funny, Northrup. Merwin always ends up telling me the same things you do."

•　　　•　　　•

A little after four, they finished loading all Grace's things into her dorm room and putting everything in its place. The room looked almost lived-in when Ed dropped the last box onto her bed.

He was huffing. "Let's go . . . have dinner."

Grace emerged from her far-too-small closet, where she'd buried herself, arranging her clothes. "I love my room, Northrup. What did you say?"

"Dinner? I'm bushed."

She looked stricken. "Sorry, Northrup, but I've got a date for dinner."

"A date? Zach's not here, is he?" Her boyfriend from Jefferson High was a year older, and wouldn't be coming to campus for another week.

"Not Zach, Garth." She pushed into her closet again, straightening the hangers so they hung precisely in a row. Her voice came out muffled. "He asked me to dinner in the Commons."

Ed felt a rush of unexpected emotions, disappointment leading the parade. "I thought, our last night and all . . ."

Her face registered her recognition that she'd hurt him. "Geez, I'm a klutz, Northrup. I was so ready to be on my own, I didn't think about you. Let me text Garth." She grabbed her phone from her little desk.

Ed pocketed his disappointment. "No, no. I'm fine. You go have dinner with him. I'll get my motel and call Andi." He wondered if he should ask the next question. Decided he should. "How will Zach feel about you dating somebody else?"

"He'll be fine. And I'm not dating Garth, I'm having dinner with a guy I think I could be friends with. And Zach said it himself—college is for making friends, not for getting married."

"Got it. So . . ."

"So, all good things come to an end."

"Meaning?"

"I'd love to have dinner with you, but . . ."

"You'd love dinner with Garth more." He put a smile behind it. "A little more."

"That's right, Northrup, just a *little* more." The look on her face said she meant it.

"We still on for breakfast before I drive back to Jeff?"

"Yeah, but how about brunch? Noonish?"

"Starting college life right, eh?"

"Northrup, truer words were never spoken."

"Well, no, sweetie. You get dinner with Garth, I get *breakfast* with you. *Quid pro quo.* I'll pick you up at eight."

She pouted briefly, then grinned. "It's college life. Sometimes you get an eight o'clock class."

●　　　●　　　●

When he put his backpack down and sat on the motel bed, grief blew through him like a squall. He let it take him. "It's too soon," he whispered. "I've only had her four years." He lay back on the bed.

After a few more minutes, he sat up, blew his nose, wiped his eyes. Remembered: *Three years and eight months.*

3

When they finished the search of Essex's house, Andi said, "Thanks for all your help, Ox. I'm running on fumes."

"Yes, my team and I had a few hours of sleep you never got. I am not authorized to seal this scene, though."

"Right. Xav and I can do it. I just want you to know I appreciate the extra help."

"Not a problem. We will be getting back to Missoula and I will be in touch as we sort through all this evidence. I hope your boss will be well."

When the crime scene team drove off, Andi waved, then glanced at her watch: 4:45. The commissioners' meeting should be ending soon, if it hadn't already. For a moment, she breathed in the sweet afternoon air, trying to drive away her tension. *If Ordrew's acting sheriff . . .*

Xavier came out of the house. "Seal 'er up again?" he asked, holding up an evidence bag with the house keys inside.

"Yeah. You lock the doors, I'll put the tape up."

Just as they finished, Andi's cell phone buzzed. The screen read *P. Peterson.*

"Meeting's over, Andi." Pete said. "They named me Acting."

Relief collided with fatigue. She called to Xavier, who was locking the front door. "Pete's the Acting." To Pete, she said, "How'd the meeting go?"

"Smarmy. Ordrew couldn't have been more charming. Get this: He told the commissioners that naming him would be 'historic.'"

"Historic? Give me a break."

"Commissioner Conrad laughed out loud at that. Anyway, all three voted for me." He was quiet a moment. "I suppose I should be glad, but . . ." Another pause. "You'll have my back, Andi?"

"All the way." She yawned. "Look, I'm sorry I pushed you to take this on, but we need you in the job. And I need me in the sack. I'm dead."

Pete said, "Right. You've been on since yesterday. Go home. I'm going over to the hospital."

"I'll nap for two or three hours, then I'll be there too."

"Nothing we can do tonight, Andi. Just sleep."

"Maybe nothing we can do, but I'll be there anyway."

4

After a worthless two-hour nap, Andi woke with a sick ache in her gut. As she flushed water on her face in the bathroom, she saw that Ed had forgotten his razor. She picked it up, felt its heft, laid it down. She put both hands on the sink and leaned toward the mirror, resting her forehead on the cool glass. The house was silent around her. *I need Ed.* After a moment, she straightened up and gazed in the mirror. Her eyes were red. She dried her face, left the house, and drove to the hospital.

Callie Martin and Gen Winters, daytime dispatchers, sat close in one corner, whispering together. Pete was opposite them, working on papers on his lap. He looked up. "Hey," he greeted her. "Thought you'd be sleeping."

"Couldn't. Any news?"

"Not about Ben. Most of the guys were here for a while, but there's nothing we can do. Why don't you go home and get some real sack time?"

"Ed and Grace are in Missoula. The house feels too lonely after a day like today," she said. "You working?"

"Uh-huh. Acting sheriff baloney."

"Can I help?"

"Nope. Not with this stuff, anyway."

"Okay." Andi walked over and sat beside Bernie.

"You been here all day?"

Bernie nodded. "Except for dinner. And I'm staying here till we know."

"Know?"

"How this ends."

In Andi's pocket, her cell phone vibrated. "Excuse me, Bernie." She'd turned the ringer off when she entered the hospital. She stood and moved to an empty corner, thinking, *What the hell's next?* Ed's name came up on the screen.

His voice was playful. "Up for a little phone sex?"

"Ed, hold on a minute." She spoke urgently. "Ben's had another heart attack. Serious." She stepped outside the waiting area. "Doc doesn't know if he'll, uh, make it through the night."

"Oh, man." All the laughter left his voice.

"Yeah. I'm at the hospital now."

A pause. "Huh. Okay, soon as I find Grace to say goodbye, I'm on my way."

Andi took a breath, realizing she hadn't thought of Grace's move to college once during the last twenty-two hours. "How'd orientation go?"

"Good," Ed said. "I'll fill you in when I get back. Once I find Grace, I'll be on my way. Three hours."

"Text her. She'll answer." Andi felt her throat tighten, as if gripped in a large hand. "Hold on a second." She stepped into the empty lobby. "Ed? I'm a wreck."

"Sure you are. I'll be a wreck too, soon as this sinks in. We both love him."

"It's more than that." She hesitated. "I'm not just scared for Ben. I'm pissed too. If Ben can't run, Ordrew's unopposed. Him being sheriff will make life hell. I shouldn't . . ." She paused, torn. *Shouldn't think that way.*

"I don't think—"

She cut him off. "I know, it's selfish to even think it, but remember? He said he'd fire me if he becomes sheriff."

Silence. "Ah. I forgot that. Well, it won't happen tonight. We'll deal with Ordrew. I'm on my way."

She returned to the waiting room. *Maybe we'll deal with him. Or maybe we won't.*

•　　　•　　　•

An hour later, everyone had gone but Andi and Bernie.

"Why don't you head home, Bernie? You look beat."

At first, Bernie didn't answer. After a moment, she said, "Girl, I'm not leaving Ben alone. Comes with loving the man."

Andi thought of Ed's razor on the sink. "I know what you mean." Without warning, an ache of loneliness filled her. "Funny," she said, "Ed just took Grace off to college—I miss them both."

Bernie laid her hand on Andi's arm. "Not to mention you got that murder to deal with. When I went home for dinner—hospital food's not my cup of tea. Sorry, my metaphors are as jangled as my brain. Anyway, I stopped at Art's Fine Foods for something to cook up, and the place was buzzing. People are shocked and scared. Who got killed?"

"A high school kid. Bernardo Cirilo."

"High school? Good God in heaven. Who killed him?"

"Guy named Daniel Essex. Just moved to the valley last spring."

"Don't know him, and don't know the family either." Bernie looked at the sky outside the window, yellow with late August heat. "Well, they've got it worse than me."

"How's that?"

"They got no hope their boy might live. I still do."

Andi felt a rumbling in her belly. "God I'm starved," she said. "Mind if I head to the cafeteria for something?"

"Sweetness, you go do that." As Andi stood, Bernie added, "Hey, did you see that bombshell in yesterday's mail? With Ben sick, I forgot about it."

"I was hardly home a couple hours, to sleep. Never saw the mail. What bombshell?"

Bernie paled. "So, you haven't seen this." She fished a folded paper from her purse, and handed it to Andi, who took it, started reading, and gasped.

5

Splashed across the page waved the American flag, so vivid it seemed to ripple in the wind. Superimposed on the flag, in bold dark blue, the title leapt off the page.

"A Patriot's Campaign."

Below, in full color, a picture of a smiling Brad Ordrew. Then the text, also in blue:

Ben Stewart—old, out of touch, and out of date.
Bring the Adams County Sheriff's Office into the 21st Century.
Vote Brad Ordrew, your next Sheriff.
Effective. Efficient.

A Patriot.

Below, centered, "Invest in Your Future in Adams County," a phone number, a website address.

In a cloud of emotions, but closing in on rage, she handed the flyer back to Bernie, who refused it. "Keep it. Makes me too frickin' mad."

Andi folded the flyer and put it in her chest pocket, then pulled out her phone and brought up the website. Scrolling down the page, she read a similar attack on Ben: old, weak, no longer up to date. There were threatening implications in the words—hints that Monastery Valley was poorly protected, that the policing was substandard, that Ben tolerated lax performance.

Buried in the vague, insulting language was a single line that stole Andi's breath. *"Policing is serious, dangerous work. It is no place for the gentle sex or minorities who despise our way of life."*

"Hell," she said under her breath, handing the phone to Bernie, who scanned the page. Her eyes widened, and she teared up. "Hon, you think he might have something? Could Ben not be up to the job anymore? You know, with his heart?"

Reining in her anger, Andi said, "If this came yesterday, it must've gone out Friday. Ben wasn't sick then. No, it's a personal attack, and this just makes it more plausible."

"What's with that 'gentle sex' crack—what's he think, we wear corsets and petticoats?"

"No, it's aimed right at me. And the bit about minorities is aimed at Xav Contrerez."

Bernie had dried her eyes; now she snorted. "Hell's bells, if Xavier's a minority, so's Babe Ruth."

"Well, it looks like Ordrew's going all out to replace Ben."

Bernie handed back her phone. "Girl, all I care about is my man pulls through. Ordrew can have the sheriff job if he wants it that bad."

Sitting back down, hunger forgotten, Andi muttered, "Over my dead body."

6

An hour or so later, Andi couldn't bring herself to leave Bernie alone, so she pulled chairs together, found a couple of blankets and pillows, and improvised beds for them both. Within minutes, she was asleep.

And then, a distant voice was calling her name, caressing her shoulder. "Andi. Andi."

She jerked awake. *Doc Keeley? A nurse?*

It was Ed. She reached up to him. They embraced, Ed leaning down, Andi pulling herself up to him. She held her face against his chest, feeling his heart beating against her cheek. After a moment, he whispered, "How is he?"

She clambered out of the makeshift chair-bed, almost stumbled. Ed grabbed her elbow. She grunted, said, "Last I checked, around nine, he was still unconscious." She choked back a rush of emotion, forced herself to say it. "I don't think he's dead. Yet. They'd tell us."

Ed grimaced. "That bad?"

She nodded, not trusting her voice.

"I'm going to talk to the nurse."

"Give me a minute . . . to wake up all the way." She yawned. "I'll go with you."

But nothing had changed.

On the way back to the waiting room, Ed said, "Let me stay with Bernie. You have to work in the morning. Get some sleep."

Andi thought about the murder case, then about Ordrew's "patriot's campaign." *Two assassinations: one of Bernardo Cirilo, one of Ben—both flying the "patriot" flag.* She took the flyer out of her pocket. "Have you seen this?"

He unfolded it, read silently, his eyebrows lifting a couple of times. "Hell, this is ugly." He handed the flyer back. "Even if Ben recovers in time, Ordrew'll add 'sick' to the 'old-and-out-of-touch' crap."

"Don't I know it."

"What's your plan?"

Andi felt her fatigue give way to anxiety. She tightened her fists. "For what?"

"For getting a man who's just had a bad heart attack re-elected sheriff."

MONDAY, AUGUST 27

1

Seven a.m. The report room crackled with tension. Andi had managed three hours' sleep for the second night running, and "on edge" did no justice to how she felt. Like everyone in the valley, all the deputies had gotten Brad Ordrew's campaign flyer in their mail, and they murmured among themselves, waiting for him to appear. The valley people would be buzzing—on top of a murder in sleepy Jefferson, Ben Stewart hadn't been opposed in an election since 1988. Thirty years. The deputies quieted when Pete came in and took his usual seat. Uncomfortably, everyone shot glances at Ben's empty chair beside Pete.

Ordrew came into the conference room but didn't sit. Once again, he propped himself against the doorframe, the half-smile stiff on his face.

Andi felt the bite of anger, but stifled it. She gripped the arm of her chair, hard—then wondered why his arrogance so bothered her.

Pete, annoyance flaring in his eyes, said, "Sit down, Brad. You're not sheriff yet."

Ordrew said nothing, moved nothing, kept his pose.

Chipper Coleman's voice came hard and low. "Don't piss off your friends, Bradley. We spread the word that we don't want you as sheriff, it'll hurt."

Ordrew looked at Coleman a long moment, then shrugged and moved toward his usual chair. "Making public statements like that would be unprofessional. Which of course I'd expect of you all."

Andi rolled her eyes, looked at Pete. "Let's do this," she said to him.

Pete nodded. "I called Doc Keeley a few minutes ago. Ben's still unconscious, but seems to have stabilized. It was a massive heart attack, and he may have suffered another one just after being admitted to ICU." He paused, cleared his throat, and glanced up. "Doc wants you guys to know, Ben won't be coming back to the station anytime soon." Another pause. "Which means, if you pray, Ben can use your prayers."

Andi felt as if a hand had scooped out her heart. Briefly, she considered which frightened her more: Ben dying or Ordrew running the department. Ben's dying, hands down.

Pete sighed, then rustled through papers on the table in front of him. "Okay. Business." He read off the patrol assignments for the morning and afternoon, reminded them of several ongoing issues in the valley, and before the end, turned to Andi. "Fill us in on our murder investigation, would you?"

Andi nodded and addressed the team. "I asked Phil Oxendine, the DCI agent on the case to join us by speaker phone, so he should be calling any minute. Let me give you the background." She started at the beginning, with Daniel Essex's nonchalant claim of the stand-your-ground defense. Much of this ground had been covered, but she repeated it anyway. She said, "The trouble with that is, there are a number of discrepancies in his story."

Ordrew shook his head. "Discrepancies?" His voice was acid. "May I assume you're planning to sort them out sometime? Like soon?"

The phone rang before Andi could answer, which was a relief. She wanted to avoid a confrontation with Ordrew. One was inevitable, eventually, but not now.

Pete picked up the phone, nodded, said, "Will do." He pushed the speaker button on the phone. "Acting Sheriff Peterson here."

Phil Oxendine introduced himself. Andi took over. "I asked Agent Oxendine to join me to make the report. I spent a lot of time at the hospital yesterday, so he graciously agreed to make this call. He'll report on what was found in the house search."

Ordrew said, "Good. A report from an officer with forensic experience."

Andi ignored him, said, "Go ahead, Ox."

"Andi told me that you know what we knew as of yesterday morning's report, so let me start with what we learned later in the day. The first item was a surprise. Mr. Essex surrendered a Smith and Wesson M&P forty-caliber, and led us to believe it was the gun he fired at the victim. However, the victim was killed with nine-millimeter bullets, so we obtained a search warrant and eventually found a Glock

19 Gen4 that had been hidden in his basement. We are doing the ballistics this morning, so we will know more later today."

Lannie McAlister leaned toward the speaker phone. "So, you're thinking the Glock's the murder weapon?"

"I consider it probable, yes, although we need to wait for the ballistics. We found only that one nine-millimeter. Of course, it is possible he stashed another weapon somewhere nearby—he had . . ." His voice paused. "Andi, refresh my memory. What was your response time?"

"Four-and-a-half to five minutes."

Ox went on, "So, it is doubtful that he would have had time enough to get the gun away from the house."

Ordrew frowned. "*Doubtful*?" He turned to Andi. "Is this one of your *discrepancies*? It's pure speculation."

"Not speculation at all, Brad," said Xavier. "Chipper, Lannie, and I searched the neighborhood thoroughly, every damn garbage can and hedge, and found *nada*, zilch, nothing."

Ox, on the phone, added, "In any case, the ballistics report will settle the matter. If the Glock is not the murder weapon, we will be back. Wherever Mr. Essex may have hidden it, we will find it."

Ordrew barked at the speaker phone, "You people keep calling it a 'murder weapon.' The man was protecting his home from a violent intruder, for God's sake. He was perfectly within his rights."

Andi kept her voice even. "So far, there's no evidence the intruder acted violently or exhibited any violent intent toward Mr. Essex. In fact, the evidence suggests he may never have known Mr. Essex was there."

"What evidence?" Ordrew demanded.

Ox said, "Our view, and I believe it is the view of your medical examiner, is that the victim was shot in the back. Twice."

Andi saw Ordrew's face pale. But his voice was hard. "Your *view*? You call that *evidence*?"

For a moment, the speaker was silent. Andi almost said something, but Oxendine spoke first. "With whom am I speaking?"

"I'm Deputy Brad Ordrew."

"Thank you. Our *view*, Deputy Ordrew, is *based* on evidence, which I am told was outlined yesterday morning. You may have missed it. The position of the body suggests either that the victim was standing and fell face first into the refrigerator when he was shot, or that he was on his knees, again with his back to the shooter. The sweater's thread arrangement at the sites of entry point inward. The *view* of the medical examiner is based on his physical observation of the entry wounds in the back, and the fact that there are no wounds in the front. And we have photos, thanks to Deputy Contrerez."

"You're not taking into account that the intruder was in Essex's garage, damn it. And that's a threat." But his voice had lost its edge.

Andi broke in. "With his back to Essex, who was *outside* his garage when he fired."

"There are a couple of other findings we do not yet understand," Oxendine added. "One is that neighbors have told us that, contrary to his usual practice, Mr. Essex left his car parked in his driveway for three nights prior to and including the night of the shooting. They also tell us that he left his garage door open, which hadn't happened before."

Ordrew shook his head. "So, what? Who gives a damn where Essex parked his car?"

"I do," Andi said, keeping her voice calm. "For one thing, I want to know why he broke his long-standing habit. He claimed he'd suffered a burglary two or three weeks before, but he never reported it to us. If he'd had a previous burglary, why leave his car outside and the garage wide open?"

Oxendine's voice overlapped hers. "Deputy Ordrew, I examined the car. On the hood I found two quarter-inch scratches. They pointed in the direction of the spot where we found the body. In addition, the Glock we found had some paint on its base, the same color as the car. It's being analyzed as we speak."

"Which could mean squat, right?" Ordrew said. "Cars get scratched."

Chipper Coleman tilted his head at Ordrew, but turned instead to Andi. "Sounds like you're thinking the shooter rested his gun on the hood."

Andi nodded. "He told me that he did."

On the phone, Ox put in, "The recoils from two shots could account for the scratches." He paused. "Andi, gentlemen, I have another meeting to attend."

Pete thanked him and ended the call and the meeting. Ordrew stood up and went to the door. "I don't approve of your trying to shoot down his defense from the outset, but I guess you're right to be cautious of the

. . . *discrepancies."* His voice sounded strained, as if allowing even that much was an effort.

Andi pondered that small concession. "We're continuing to talk to Mr. Essex about all this. His attorney, I believe, will be coming over from Missoula either this afternoon or tomorrow for the arraignment hearing. I'm going to interview him again when she's here." She looked at Pete. "Xav's off today. Can you second me?"

Pete grimaced. "No can do. Meeting all afternoon with the commissioners about this acting sheriff job. Tomorrow, I'm off to Helena for a Homeland Security briefing."

Ordrew jumped in. "I'll be second."

Looking like he was swallowing a bad egg, Pete nodded. "Okay. Brad's in the interview, whenever it happens."

Andi swallowed hard. If Ordrew's concession was genuine, perhaps his being second would be all right. Perhaps.

The meeting broke up, and Andi started out the door. Ordrew braced his arm across the doorframe, preventing her from leaving. "A minute?"

She wanted to say no, but decided to test whether his concession was real. "Sure."

Ordrew waited a moment as the last deputies filed out. Then he said, "You see my campaign announcement?"

"I did."

"You remember my promise?"

"I do."

"Good. Count on me keeping it when I win."

She turned away. *Damning me with faint praise. But why?*

2

Around noon, Ed munched on a tuna fish sandwich at his desk, torn. He'd been to the hospital early, but Ben remained unconscious. He'd wanted to stay, but he needed to work out his strategy for tomorrow morning's session with Beatrice John, or, more likely, with the part of Beatrice named Protector. Today, he'd planned to be in Missoula with Grace, so his usual Monday patients weren't coming. He had time to think more deeply about Protector and what he should do with her. She was a mystery. And a profound frustration. He swallowed the last of the sandwich and gulped some water. Time to call Merwin.

"Eddie, old son. How's that delightful daughter of yours?"

"Thanks to you, she's at Montana. First day of orientation."

"She's a sweet kid, Eddie. Smart as a whip and old beyond her years. We've had some excellent conversations."

"She told me." He tapped Beatrice/Protector's folder. "Look, I need a consultation about that multiple personality case I've told you about."

"The one who was part of the sex trafficking gang?"

"Yeah. An unwilling part. We've been working together ten months now, and I'm stuck, no progress. The alter personality I'm allowed to talk to is named Protector, and I don't know whether to push harder, accept things as they are, or stop."

"Question: Is 'Protector' his name or his role?"

"Both name and role. Protector's a she. Lately, she's been hinting I might be allowed to speak with the child alter she protects, but nothing's moving."

"Such hints qualify as progress, Eddie. Do you know anything about this child part?"

"Just that her name is Connie and I suspect she might have been the main object of early abuse."

"Aha. I counsel you to bank on that. You have an impending breakthrough, my dear, a chance to meet the child alter. And your problem is?"

"Suppose Protector lets me speak with Connie and it disrupts the balance in the personality system? I'd be making the situation worse than it already is."

"Or, old man, you will set this poor woman on a new road that sports a chance, however slim, of healing. Before I render an opinion, answer me three questions. How extensive a support system has she? Friends, family, work associates?"

"Just me."

"That bodes ill. Second question: How strong are Protector's coping skills—her ability to handle daily life?"

"Limited but sufficient. She's able to manage hygiene, groceries, cleaning her apartment, managing her bills. For the life she lives, she has the necessary self-control and coping ability. The greatest danger to her, now, is from within."

"From within? Elaborate."

"There apparently is an alter who wants to kill Connie."

"Indeed? Your interpretation?"

"Standard theory would suggest it might be a second protector—killing Connie to protect her from more abuse. I'd label it love, of a kind. Delusional, of course, and extremely dangerous, but a twisted kind of love."

"I concur—it's dangerous, but potentially helpful, provided you can make an alliance with this murderous protector. Which leads me to my third question: May I assume that this Protector protects the child from the internal killer—or are there external threats as well?"

"Until she came here to Jefferson, both. Now, it's the internal one who wants to kill the child. Protector refers to him as 'the One.' Capital 'O'."

"And your assessment? If you do nothing additional and refuse to meet this child alter, what do you believe will happen?"

"Protector's wearying, and needs my help with Connie. My fear is that eventually 'the One' will break Protector and get access to Connie."

"If you do not help, it's foreseeable, no? And if he gets to Connie?"

"He'll kill her. Which would be suicide, unless it's imaginary." Ed looked out the window at the mountains. He didn't want another suicide on his conscience.

The line went silent. Merwin was thinking, Ed knew, so he waited. Then, "Eddie, allow me to summarize my thoughts. You name two outcomes—on one side, destabilization, possibly suicide: not good. On the other, more effective protection of the child: good." Merwin took a moment to answer. "Consider, old son: If you can help this child part, and if you are correct that 'the One' may in fact care for Connie, eventually you may win the trust of this 'One.' I do not fear destabilization in these multiple personality cases; it goes with the territory, and should it transpire, we can handle it. What I do fear is the fact that if you don't intervene, suicide seems probable."

"So, I should work toward meeting the child, Connie?"

"In my humble opinion, you should. No, let me say it differently: In my opinion, you should offer her the love of which you are capable and which she so much needs."

Ed's emotion caught him off guard. For a moment he said nothing. Then, "Thanks, Merwin. That I can do. And will."

3

Ed hung up, grateful for his friend's kindness. When the phone rang a few seconds later, he considered letting it go through to the voice mail. But it was Grace's number on the screen.

She launched. "Northrup, I'm coming home."

"Whoa," he said. "What happened?"

"Sheriff Ben's what happened. I've been thinking since you told me last night. I have to be there. He helped me lots of times, you know."

"I do know that."

"Yeah. So, now I gotta help him."

Ed felt a soft tug in his chest. He hadn't raised Grace, had only adopted her—*three years and eight months ago.* She'd always been, people said, feisty. But from the start, she'd shown a prodigious loyalty to people who cared for her, and she was turning out to be a compassionate young woman. He couldn't take credit for that, but her leaving college was on his watch. Should he block it? Loyalty and compassion were good things, but not so good you give up university for them. He cleared his throat.

"Don't clear your throat at me, Northrup," she said. "You always do that when you want to lay down rules. But I'm at college, so I make the rules now." A pause. "Right?"

He heard a veiled smile in her voice. She was expecting him to pull rank. He smiled into the phone. "You're at college, but you're saying you're leaving college. Can't have it both ways, kiddo."

The line went silent for a moment. "Hmm. That sounds logical. My Intro to Philosophy prof says logic is the key to a successful life. But I'm coming home anyway. Sheriff Ben's sick, and Jared is dying, so I need to be there."

"You're homesick, Grace. I had that too when I went away to college. It's hard, but the way to cure it is to stick it out. A few days, a few weeks, you'll be glad you stayed in Missoula." He remembered his father's method of handling this, and wouldn't repeat it: *Homesick? Homeshit. Keep your ass there at that money-pit school you wanted so damn much to go to. I already turned your room into my TV den.*

"Whatever *homesick* is, I'm not. I *want* to stay here. I've already got a couple of new friends. But I feel like . . . like Sheriff Ben might need me."

He heard a quiet emotion in her voice, and considered what to say. "Grace, seriously. There's nothing you or I or anyone other than his doctors can do for Ben at this point. Maybe if . . ." He gulped. "I mean, *when* he comes home, we can talk about it then. But stay at school for now. Get started in your classes and keep making friends, and I will call you every day to let you know what's happening here."

Another long silence. Then, "Northrup? What if Sheriff Ben dies and I'm not there?" A soft sound choked off her question.

He reconsidered, remembering his father. "I don't know, Grace. You're right, it's your call, not mine. Here's my advice: Stay in Missoula, start your college life, and I'll notify you right away if Ben, uh, gets worse." He swallowed. "But if you think it's better to come home now, your bedroom is warm and waiting."

Grace didn't answer for a moment. Then, "Okay. I'll stay for now, but you call me every day." She paused. "Northrup?"

"What?"

"Growing up sucks."

4

Three in the afternoon. Andi, with Brad Ordrew beside her, sat facing Daniel Essex and Angela Norton. The preliminaries were done, Miranda repeated. Essex had indicated he would answer questions. Andi said, "Mr. Essex, some questions have arisen, and I will appreciate your helping us with them."

"My client is not here to help you, Deputy."

Andi forced a smile. *Already pissing on my territory.* "I understand." She glanced down at her notes. "Mr. Essex, do you own a Glock 19 Gen4?"

Norton nodded even before he looked for permission. He said, "I don't."

"A Glock 19 Gen4 was found in your basement. It has your fingerprints on it, and no one else's."

He folded his arms. "I don't remember. Maybe I do. I own lots of guns."

Ordrew spoke before Andi could frame her next question. "Why did you shoot the intruder?"

Andi, shocked, glared at him, as Angela Norton shook her head. "Don't answer that."

But Essex disregarded her advice. "I was standing my ground. I had been burglarized, and I wasn't going to risk getting killed."

Norton stood up. "I want a moment with my client, Deputies. And I expect the recording systems to be turned off. And that you will not listen behind that." She pointed to the mirror. "If I don't have your word on it, I require a private room with no eavesdropping capabilities."

Ordrew said. "Of course. We'll turn the system off."

Andi said, "No. The system stays on. If you wish to confer, you can use our conference room. There are no recording devices there."

Norton protested, but Andi held firm. After they'd escorted Essex and his lawyer to the conference room and closed the door, Ordrew said, his voice low, but fierce. "What the shit? You overrode me in there."

"Think about it, Brad. We leave them in that room with an active recorder and a one-way mirror, anything Norton doesn't like out of this interview she can claim violates lawyer-client privilege."

Ordrew snarled, "That's why we turn them *off*, damn it."

"Sure, we *say* we turned them off. But Norton can use it as a distraction at trial, subpoena our tapes, you name it. I'm not going to give her anything to use against us."

Ordrew said nothing.

She wondered if he'd taken her point, and was about to ask when her cell phone buzzed. It was Phil Oxendine, with the ballistics report.

•　　•　　•

They reconvened.

Norton said, "I've instructed my client that he should not answer until I give him permission."

"Thank you, counselor," Andi said. "For the record, Mr. Essex, you told me on Saturday night that you shot Bernardo Cirilo, and repeated it later. Am I correct?"

Essex looked at Norton, who nodded. "Damn right."

Andi locked eyes with the lawyer. "I'm informing you and your client that the ballistics examination by the DCI shows that a Glock 19, with your client's fingerprints on it . . ." She turned to Essex. ". . . and not the Smith & Wesson you surrendered, is the weapon used to murder Bernardo Cirilo."

No one spoke for a moment. Then, the attorney said, "Perhaps we could use less prejudicial language, Deputy. My client is charged with homicide."

Andi decided to challenge it. "Ms. Norton, your client is charged with deliberate homicide. Deliberate homicide *is* murder."

Norton narrowed her eyes, but forced a smile. "Thank you for the legal lesson, Deputy."

Nice try, counselor, Andi thought, looking at her partner. He gave a very slight nod. *What's that mean?* Andi turned back to Essex. "Sir, you informed us that you shot Mr. Cirilo to protect yourself?"

Angela Norton touched Essex's arm, shaking her head.

"Let the record show that Mr. Essex's attorney instructed him not to answer." She reviewed her notes. "And are the notes my partner took that night correct in saying he *heard* you tell me you shot him to protect yourself and your home?"

Angela Norton looked startled.

Andi pulled out her file of Xavier's notes. She spread them on the table. "Here they are."

The attorney read them, quickly, the pushed them aside. "These could have been written by anyone, anytime, Deputy. I'm instructing my client not to answer."

Andi nodded. "They *could* have been written by anyone, but they weren't. They are Deputy Contrerez's account. If you wish, we can have a forensic handwriting expert testify to the identity of the writer."

Norton frowned. "It'll come to that." Her fingers drummed on the table. "I can't see the use of this, Deputy. You will ask your questions, I will instruct my client not to answer anything that might violate his Fifth Amendment rights, and we'll all get frustrated. Let's not and say we did, shall we?"

Ordrew interrupted. "Sorry, counselor. We have our job to do, you have yours. Let's do them, *then* say we did."

Andi was shocked: Ordrew had backed her.

"Mr. Essex," Ordrew went on, "you've stated your belief that you were standing your ground when you shot Mr. Cirilo. Please tell us your understanding of the stand-your-ground law."

Norton's eyes narrowed, and Andi glanced at Ordrew. *What the hell?* Was he giving Essex a chance to formulate his defense? Andi watched Norton struggling to find a reason to tell Essex not to answer, and failing. Grimacing, the attorney said, "Go ahead."

Essex's eyes widened. He looked back at Ordrew. "I don't know what you want."

"I want you to tell me what you think the stand-your-ground defense means."

"I'm no lawyer. You'll have to ask her," he said, nodding toward Norton.

Andi saw the opening, wondered if Brad had set it up intentionally. "And yet, you've repeatedly said you shot Bernardo Cirilo because you were 'standing your ground,' and that it was your right. You apparently were willing to shoot, and kill, another human being based on your understanding of the law in Montana. Deputy Ordrew and I would like to know what your understanding *is*."

"I've got nothing more to say," Essex said.

"That's it, deputies." Norton stood. "We're finished."

"You know, Ms. Norton," Andi put out. "Your client, with your permission, has waived his Miranda rights. We can ask for a court order to continue."

Norton's eyes were hard. "Get your order, Deputy. You can call me in Missoula, and I'll be back when I get the time."

5

As Norton stood, someone knocked on the door. Ordrew opened it. Lannie McAlister stood outside. "Sorry to interrupt, but Judge Flure moved the arraignment up. We got us ten minutes, is all. I need to get the prisoner to court."

Cuffing and marching Essex to the squad car, his lawyer beside him, took two minutes. After they drove off, Andi went back inside. Ordrew followed her.

Inside, she turned to him. "You surprised me in there. I couldn't tell if you were on our side or Essex's." She hesitated, but then went on,

"After your campaign flyer, I'm thinking you're not on our side. And I know you don't like me."

Ordrew frowned, scratched his neck with a finger. "It's not about you, Andi, it's about high quality policing."

"Haven't we been through all that? I got my start in Chicago, Cook County. I've been shot twice." He looked shocked. She touched the notch in her right ear, the product of a bullet, though not the one that practically killed her. "I've made my share of good busts. We both understand the big city job, and we're both here in the small-town world. We're on the same side, man. I just don't get . . ."

"Same side? Maybe, maybe not. You ever get betrayed by a partner?"

"Betrayed?"

"I had a tough call a few years back, a motel domestic, we were told. Turned out, there were bad guys in *two* motel rooms. We knocked, they all let loose with automatics firing through the doors, and my partner, a rookie girl, ran behind our truck instead of taking out the second room. I took three slugs—thank God for armor." He scratched his neck again. "You go through that, you going to trust a woman after?"

She considered her answer. "I was shot too—my armor didn't stop the bullet. I almost died. I don't blame my partners."

"Did they run and hide like my partner did?"

"Of course not." Exasperation simmered. "Damn it, Brad, I'm not that woman."

Ordrew looked momentarily sad. "Yeah, well." His eyes hardened. "I'm that man."

6

At her desk, writing notes to accompany the recording of the Essex interview, Andi thought about what Ordrew had said. It riled her to be tarred with the same brush as his rookie partner; and that he'd injected it into his campaign was a step too far. She sighed. *Gotta talk to Pete about whether to get a court order to compel Essex to talk.* She saw the red light blink on her phone, then heard the buzz. She picked up.

Callie said, "Line 2, Andi. It's Irving Jackson."

Andi thought, *DA.* She picked up. "Hey, Irv, Andi here. How'd the arraignment go?"

"Well. Xavier's testimony was superb. We're going with deliberate homicide. Dickie Flure set bail at two hundred thousand, and when Essex's attorney informed him he'd have to put up ten percent, he went apeshit and rushed the bench. The bailiff tackled him, after which Dickie changed his mind and rescinded bail. 'Your client's a danger,' Dickie told Norton."

"Holy shit. So, he's on his way back here?"

"Any minute now. Trial's scheduled for the last week in October. So, you guys get the pleasure of his company for a couple of months." Andi heard a rustle of paper. "Oh, I asked Dickie for a court order forcing Essex to talk despite Miranda. On the blanket order, he turned us down—said the importance of Miranda was, and I quote, 'sacrosanct.'" Irv chuckled. "Anyway, he did order that you Mirandize him for each interview, so he can waive on a time-by-time basis."

"Huh. Well, could've been worse. He could've let Essex's current Miranda refusal stand permanently. What'd you think of Angela Norton?"

Irv chuckled. "Don't give my wife her business card."

7

Andi was leaving the squad room when Callie buzzed her. "What's up, Callie?"

"Doc Runge left a message. You can tell the family he's releasing Bernardo's body tomorrow morning at nine."

Andi's sadness welled. This would almost as hard a visit to make as the first one. She sighed and drove to the Cirilos'.

Met at the door by Mrs. Cirilo, she gave her the news and added, "Ma'am, if you'd like my advice, let the funeral home pick him up. Mr. Bayless will do a nice job and make Bernardo look good, like he's sleeping. He won't look that way at the morgue."

Bernardo's mother nodded, ignoring the tears in her eyes. "I was afraid to see him."

"Would you like me to call Mr. Bayless and arrange it?"

"*Sí*. Thank you."

"He'll get in touch with you about what he'll need from you and when you can see your son."

"You mean, when *mi corazón* will break all the way through."

8

After talking with Merwin and then Grace, at loose ends, Ed had spent a couple of hours reading journals and jotting notes about his strategy with Protector tomorrow. Around four, he'd drifted over to the hospital, where Ben's condition was unchanged. At the ICU nurses' desk, he asked if Doc Keeley were still in the house. The nurse said, "Let me page him."

"Ed," Doc said, coming down the hall after being paged. "Not much to tell you."

"Which tells us something, doesn't it."

Doc nodded. "Every hour he stays unconscious is an hour we've lost something. We won't know how much till he wakes up."

Ed hesitated, then added it. "Or he doesn't."

"Or he doesn't." Doc sighed. "Strange thing is, he's been stable, if unconscious . . ." He glanced up at the clock above the nurse's station. ". . . twenty-eight hours now."

Ed looked out the ICU's window. The forests climbing the mountainsides were still a dusty green; in six weeks, there'd be broad sweeps of yellow brushed across the canvas of the mountains. And then, three or four weeks after the gold, they'd be white. *Life goes on*, he thought. *When do you let go?* He turned to Doc. "You on duty long?"

Doc glanced at his watch. "Been here since four in the morning. That's, what, twelve-plus hours. Reckon I can go home till the next emergency."

"A beer at the Angler?"

"My lord, that's the gate of paradise."

• • •

Ed took his usual stool at Ted Coldry's bar, The Angler, and Doc sat on the stool where Ben always sat, on the corner. For twenty-nine years, Ed had joined Ben most Wednesday evenings after work, talking valley business or gossip, sometimes bandying hypotheticals about problems Ben had with a case, most often just having a beer with his friend. That Doc sat beside him, while Ben lay in ICU, desolated him.

Behind the bar, Ted was obviously upset. After pouring and coastering their beers, he'd been pacing, glancing anxiously at them, or more particularly at Doc. In a moment, he stopped in front of him. "I'm sorry to interrupt, John. I'm a wreck about Benjamin. Is he, ah, going to . . .?"

Doc took a sip of his beer. "You know, Ted, we just don't know yet. He's on the edge."

Ted looked hard at him. "The edge of . . . what?"

Doc tried a commiserative smile. "Life. Or death."

Ted's eyes clouded, then brimmed with tears. Grabbing a bar cloth, he dabbed at them. "Since Lane and I bought the Angler, Benjamin has come in here five nights a week. Right there." He pointed at Doc's stool. "On that corner he keeps tabs on the valley's business and . . ." He stopped. "Some months, I spent as much time with Benjamin as I spent with my beloved Lane." He straightened his shoulders, and his eyes filled again. "Edward, I am bereft."

Ed nodded. "Yeah, Ted, we all are."

Ted waited a moment, then turned to the back bar and pulled down a bottle of Glenlivet. "Edward, John, what the barman drinks is his lifelong secret." He poured himself a tall two fingers. "You both must carry this to your graves."

Ed smiled. "Bad choice of words, my friend."

"Oh, my God, it is." He gave a sudden sob. He slammed back the single-malt. And poured himself another.

9

Andi, sitting alone on the porch swing, was watching the evening lengthen, savoring the long black shadows reaching down from the peaks of the Monastery range and the tinges of purple edging on the high clouds. Tired as she felt, perplexed by Daniel Essex, brimming with worry for Ben, she took comfort in the honeyed evening air and the pastel sunset and the prospect of seeing Ed. *Being married to him anchors me.* She hugged herself.

Ed's truck came crunching up the long gravel drive, and she delighted in a chill of pleasure. When he climbed the steps to the porch, they kissed.

"You smell like beer," she said.

"Not too remarkable, considering I just had one with Doc and Ted."

"One?"

"Two. What're you thinking about?"

"About getting married last year, and how happy I am we did it."

"You're the one who made it happen," he said, smiling. After the horrors of the Warriors of Yahweh case last fall, Andi had invited Ed for an autumnal hike up the Coliseum, the glacial cirque at the southern end of the valley. She'd asked Ed's good friend, Jim Hamilton, to meet them in the summit meadow—without telling Ed. Jim, a former priest, performed a wedding ceremony there, high enough to touch the sky.

Jim, though, reminded them he was a *former* priest. "You realize," he'd told Andi, "it's not official. Consider your marriage bond an IOU." Even though they felt it was all the ceremony they needed to become husband and wife, they agreed to keep their "marriage" a secret and to stage an official ceremony this fall.

Andi said, "You want a glass of wine to top off that beer?"

"I don't think so."

She said, "Be right back." After a moment inside, she called out to him, "Where's the corkscrew?"

He went in and pawed through the silverware drawer. "It's always right here." Nowhere. He straightened up. "Damn."

"What's wrong?"

"Grace took my corkscrew to college."

"Why?"

He looked sheepish. "I . . . let her take a bottle of wine. An icebreaker, she called it. I figured she'd forget the corkscrew, so it wouldn't hurt."

Andi chuckled. "Sometimes I think you grew up locked in a closet. You don't actually think a college kid can't open a bottle of wine without a corkscrew, do you?"

He shrugged. "I guess, now that you mention it . . ."

"Well, anyway, I'll skip the wine."

"My lady wants wine, she gets wine." He lifted a finger. "A moment." In the mudroom, Ed rummaged, found his Swiss Army knife in the tool kit, said, "Voilà." He opened out the small corkscrew. "Always prepared."

Andi smiled, held out her glass. Out on the porch again, she said, "We haven't talked about our public wedding at all."

"Funny. I'm the one who bugged you to get married, but once we did it up on the mountain, I don't feel a need to make it official."

She leaned against him. "Me neither, I guess. What do you think?"

Ed's forehead crinkled. "Maybe a small glass won't hurt." He went inside.

He returned with his wine and sat beside her. She tried to read his face. Calm, at least. "Your thoughts?" she asked.

He sighed and sipped his wine. "I don't know. Seems like a bad time. With Ben down, could be hard to . . . uh, enjoy ourselves."

"True."

They both watched the descending sun backlight the serrated ridge of the Monasteries. After a long quiet, she said, "I love you, Ed. And I love being married to you, even if it's unofficial and secret. So, don't take this wrong, okay?"

"You're thinking we shouldn't?" That it wouldn't matter surprised him.

"No. I'm thinking we should postpone it." She glanced at him, gauging his reaction. "Spring might be a better time."

Another long silence stretched out, while the long ribbons of cloud glowed gold and red above the valley. At last, Ed said, "Yeah, spring. Long enough so Ben'll have time to recover."

Superstitiously, Andi didn't want to say it, but she forced herself. "Or for us to get past losing him."

TUESDAY, AUGUST 28

1

Before sunrise, Andi got up and went back out on the porch. Lacy fabrics of cloud lit by the coming sun streaked the soft morning sky. The fields and trees on the valley floor were still dark. End-of-summer smells graced the air, dry grass and dusty leaves, a tinge of sweet smoke from wood stoves lit against the late-August night-time chill. Andi folded her arms and took in the moment, putting off the problems waiting at the station.

Behind her, Ed came out in his running gear and, from behind, wrapped his arms around her. "Still okay about putting the wedding off?" he murmured into her hair.

She nodded and leaned back against him. "I dreamed we eloped. Didn't tell anybody, just went off and did the deed, all proper and alone."

"Huh. That's pretty much what we did." He let her go. "Nice morning. Come run with me."

Still leaning back against him, she said, "Can't. The day from hell starts in thirty minutes."

"Worried about Ben?"

She nodded. "Sure. And this shooting. And Brad Ordrew's 'patriotic campaign.'"

"What a joke." He released her, and started toward the steps.

"He's not joking."

"You're right." Ed went down the steps, stopped, turned. "I forgot to tell you, Grace called last night. She wants to come home. I talked her into staying at school for now, but I'm guessing we'll hear more of that. Ben's like her grandpa."

Andi nodded. "There's nothing she can do here."

"That ever stop *you* from trying to do something anyway?"

"Good answer." She paused. "I miss her, but staying in school's the right thing."

"Speaking of Ben, I have a little good news. Once we got talking about the wedding, I forgot. On my way home yesterday, after the beers with Doc Keeley at the Angler, I stopped at the hospital, and the night nurse told me he's showing signs of consciousness."

She stiffened, alert. "He's awake?"

"No, but apparently he's making eye movements when they say his name, and moving his fingers a bit."

"Good God," she whispered. "Just eye and finger movements? That's not good."

"It's a step."

"Not a big enough one."

"You're worried about Ordrew's threat to fire you, if he wins the election?"

"Yep. Monday's Labor Day, so the election's in two months. If Ben doesn't recover, he can't run, Brad wins, and when he does, he'll try to fire me." She looked out over the western valley. The sun hadn't touched the mountain tops yet, but the sky was alight. "If that happens, I'll maybe have to leave for another job."

"What the hell? Eight hours after we decide to make our marriage official in the spring, you start talking about leaving?"

"Cut me some slack. We can still do it, but damn it, Ed, I'm a cop. It's what I do. My dad was a cop, my granddad was a cop, and I've wanted to be a cop since I was a kid. There aren't any other cop jobs in Jefferson."

Ed looked as hurt as she'd ever seen him, and she knew he had the right to be. Last night, talking about a spring wedding, she'd managed to forget about Ordrew's threat, but it was lurking in the soft morning. She ran her fingers through her hair. "Ed, please, don't be hurt. I'm trying to think my way through this."

"Look, I'm not interested in a commuter marriage. It just . . . ." He stopped. "Okay, but think hard. I'm not letting you go."

She felt rotten enough, but that angered her. "'Letting me go'?" She shut her mouth. *Now's not the time for an argument.*

Ed started to say something, stopped, then turned away and ran down the drive toward the highway.

2

On the way into town, Andi's gloom deepened. She said aloud, "I like life here, damn it."

As she pulled into the parking lot behind the station, she sat behind the wheel, looking at the sky. The sun had crested the Washington Mountains, and the Monasteries were rose-brushed, their gray granite glowing in the light. She tried to let the beauty lift her. Failed.

She sighed and left her SUV. Time to face the day. And to find a way to turn this around.

After report—Ordrew had sat at the far end of the table, looking smug but saying nothing—she booted up her computer and brought up her file on the Essex case. The case troubled her, but the why eluded her. After a few fruitless minutes, she decided to go back to Essex's garage and prowl around. The search warrant was still good. She went to the evidence room and checked out the house keys. A few minutes later, she parked at the curb fronting Essex's house. East Cedar Street was quiet.

After pulling on her gloves, she let herself in by the side door and flipped on the overhead light. Her eyes roved randomly around the room, saw the dark black of the oil stain. The closed refrigerator door. Essex claimed it had stayed open after the first burglar had run. She opened it, then let go without any pressure: It drifted shut. She opened it again, and again it slowly drifted shut. She took out her cell phone and made a video of it doing so, and then a second, and a third. *Evidence, Ordrew,* she thought. She emailed one of the videos to her computer and Xavier's.

Next, she counted the cans of beer. Forty-five in the refrigerator, twelve on the workbench. For a moment, she felt confused: She and Xav had counted forty-eight in the fridge, before. Ah. Oxendine had taken the one beside Bernardo's hand and the techs must have taken two more from the refrigerator for analysis. She wasn't quite sure the analysis of what. Fingerprints? Looking at the remaining cans, she had the same thought she'd had earlier: cheap beer. She studied the twelve-pack of Bitterroot Single Hop Ale, still on the high workbench. Craft beer. *Expensive* beer. So, why was the expensive beer out in the warm garage, not in the fridge?

She let herself out. Essex's car, still parked on the drive, had been examined thoroughly, and Andi'd gotten the report: The paint on the butt of the Glock 19 matched the paint on the hood. As Essex had told her, he'd rested the gun on the hood to steady his aim. *At a kid stealing a few beers from his refrigerator.* She bent down and looked under the car. A small stain of oil had begun to gather on the driveway. She stood up, glad Xav had gotten a photo of the few drops on the first night.

She went back into the garage, walked over to the door opener switch, flicked it on. She checked her watch as the door lumbered up, creaking. Eleven seconds to reach waist-high. Plenty of time for the kid to have run out the side door. She repeated the experiment and video'd it as well. *The door was open already, like the neighbors said.*

Essex was lying.

One by one, she opened the cupboards lining the walls. The lab crew had gone through these minutely, but . . . After she'd taken everything out and examined it all, nothing had set her mind on fire. She put everything back, frustrated.

She stood a long moment, emptying her mind. She calmed her breathing and simply looked. At first, she saw nothing they hadn't registered on the weekend. She stepped outside. Saw the garbage can against the garage wall. Opened it, flinched at the smell. No doubt it had been searched already. She was putting the cover back when something caught her eye.

A sales receipt, partly concealed by a white garbage bag. She lifted the bag, brought out the slip. "Art's Fine Foods," it read, over a list of grocery items. Half-way down, she read:

"Kokanee-12pk.Qty:2."

"BudLite-12pk.Qty:2."

"Bitterroot-SglHop-12pk. Qty:1."

She found the sales date: "Mon 07.16.2018."

She pulled up the calendar app on her phone and checked the dates. Six weeks before the shooting. Puzzling. In the fridge, before three had been taken to the lab, there'd been forty-seven cans, plus one beside Bernardo Cirilo's right hand. Forty-eight. And twelve on the bench: the same number he'd bought on July 16. Hadn't Essex drunk any beer this summer? Wait. Ten were stolen three weeks ago.

He must've replaced them.

She wrinkled her nose at the garbage smell, but opened the bag anyway and poked through the mess, looking for another slip. When she got to the bottom, growing more nauseous by the second, she'd found none. If he wanted to replace ten, wouldn't he have had to buy another twelve-pack? Or could he get individual cans?

"One way to find out." She called Laurie Swenson, the manager at Art's Fine Foods. Before Art Masters died, Laurie managed Magnus Anderssen's StreamSide Lodge, and when Magnus bought Art's from the estate to protect the staff's jobs, she moved over to manage the grocery and beer and wine operation.

Laurie picked up on the second ring. "Art's Fine Foods, Laurie speaking."

"Hi, Laurie, Andi Pelton here. I've got a question about beer."

"Shoot."

Andi grimaced at the word. "Do Kokanee and Bud Light come in individual cans, or only in six-packs or twelve-packs?'

"We carry sixes and twelves. To tell you the truth, I don't know if they're sold individually, but not in our store. If you'd like, I can call my distributor and find out."

"That'd be great. It's for a case I'm working on."

"The shooting?"

"Yeah."

"People say he shot the kid in self-defense. That right?"

She grimaced. "I can't talk about an active investigation. Sorry."

"Oh, I understand. I'll make the call right away and get back to you. This your cell number?"

"It is. Thanks a bunch, Laurie."

"No problem. Talk to you in a few."

While she waited for Laurie to call back, Andi collected her thoughts. If they don't sell singles, and if he'd replaced the ten stolen cans with a six-pack, they'd have found forty-four in the fridge, not forty-eight. If he bought a new twelve-pack, they'd have found fifty-two, unless he drank four. She wondered too why keep the cheap stuff cold while a good craft beer sits on the bench? Maybe a gift for a friend?

Her cell buzzed. "Hi, Laurie. What'd you find?"

"Kokanee sells sixes, twelves, and twenty-four packs, no singles. Bud Light can be purchased in single cans, but our distributor doesn't know anyone in southwestern Montana who sells them in singles, only fours, sixes, eights, twelves, eighteens, twenty-fours, thirties, and thirty-sixes. Oh, you can get fours and eights online."

Andi thought about that. "Online orders require use of a credit card, don't they?"

"Yeah."

I should get Essex's credit card statements.

"Very helpful, Laurie. Thanks again."

He buys another twelve-pack to replace the ten stolen cans. Now he's got sixty-two beers, so he—or somebody—drinks just *two*, and leaves sixty untouched? She'd never known a guy who'd let so much beer sit half the summer, untouched.

But then, she'd never known a guy who'd shoot a kid for stealing one.

3

As always, Protector arrived at the stroke of ten, her appointed time. Ed surmised that arriving with not a minute to spare freed her from sitting in the waiting room—and perhaps meeting another patient.

"Morning, Protector," Ed greeted her. She had the stern look coupled with the graceful movements he'd come to know her by. Last year, when he'd known her as Beatrice John, it had been Protector who came to sessions and talked with him. Eventually, she'd acknowledged her name, and told him that Beatrice no longer "came outside" since escaping being burned alive by her tormentor, the Bishop.

"Come on in," he said, gesturing toward his office. As always, Protector said, "You first." She did not like him being behind her.

Once they were settled, she stared at him. She always sat in silence, insisting that he speak first. He preferred that patients bring up whatever was bothering them, but he'd turned her refusal to speak first to his advantage: He could follow the thread of the previous sessions by bringing it up at the start of the new one, a luxury. She never balked once he brought something up.

He smiled. "So, we agreed last week that we might talk about letting Connie meet me. Are you still willing to talk about that?"

She nodded. "I have asked the others. Some disapprove. Others believe it is time."

"And you? You're Connie's Protector. How do you feel about it?"

"She spoke to you once, when we first met last year. I am unsure if allowing her out is safe."

In their very first session, Connie had emerged without warning and exclaimed, "Bishop burned the lady in the fire." That mysterious sentence had been key in helping Andi solve the brutal sex trafficking murder.

This time, Protector sighed. "I failed in my work when she told you that."

"Scopus is in federal prison. You're safe now." Scopus had been the leader of the gang, and had kept Protector prisoner. He'd tried to cremate her alive.

Protector shook her head. "Connie does not believe it. She fears he will capture us." She set her lips primly, then squinted.

How drained she looked. "You look very tired, Protector."

The woman nodded. "Connie is weaker now, and the One who wants her to die grows stronger. I must watch all the time."

Ed shivered. "Will you tell me about the One who wants her to die?"

Protector stiffened. "I am forbidden to talk about Him."

Don't push. "Okay. How can I help you protect Connie?"

For a moment, Protector sat in silence, but Ed could see her eyes narrow, and her fingers tapping on her leg, signs he'd learned that she was pondering. "*Can* you help me protect the child?"

"I could answer that better if I knew more about the One. I know you can't talk about him, but if I say what I think about him, can you tell me whether I am right or wrong?"

She closed her eyes. *Consulting,* he thought. In a moment, she opened them and nodded. "I am permitted."

Be careful, man. "He believes that the best way to protect Connie from being hurt again is for her to die."

Protector's eyes widened, then narrowed. He caught the barest movement of her head, a slight nod. "Go on," she whispered.

"He wants Connie not to suffer any more."

Again, she looked surprised, then closed her eyes. This time, when she opened them, she said, her voice wavering, "He spoke to me. He has never spoken to me before."

"Can you tell me what he said?"

"Wait." She closed her eyes, then in a moment opened them. "Yes. He says, 'We are both protectors. You—' He means me," Protector said, her voice pitched lower than usual, almost as if she were mimicking the

One's voice. "'You protect by concealing her from me and outsiders, I protect her by ending her suffering.' Then he said, 'Ask your doctor if he can help us protect Connie.' So, I must ask: Can you help me, uh, help us protect Connie?"

Merwin was right. We're close to a breakthrough. He calmed himself, then said, "To hear that both you and the One want to protect Connie from suffering gives me confidence that I can help, Protector. I'd need an agreement from the One that he won't try to kill her while I offer my help."

She jerked in her chair, her body rigid. "Impossible. If He takes control of the body, He may not give it up. Connie could lose her life."

"I can communicate with him without you needing to give up control of your body. I'll teach you."

"It is not my body." But her eyes told him that perhaps she was ready. "What is this way?" she asked.

He explained.

When he was finished, Protector said, "I must think on this."

"Of course. I can teach you next time we meet, and then start, if you're willing. But think it over. If you can, discuss it with the One."

"This way of yours will allow you to help me protect Connie, without endangering her?"

"You *and* the One who has his own way of protecting. I believe I can, Protector."

"I have no such faith," she said. But her eyes looked haunted. "I have no faith at all, but I have little strength left. She is going to die if you cannot help me." Her face registered surprise. "Us. He says he needs your help as well."

Ed thought about that. "I think that the One does not want to kill Connie, if we can find another way."

Protector's body jerked, almost like a seizure, and then she peered at him with clouded, moist eyes. Her eyebrows arched in surprise. "He says you are right. And He is weeping."

Hoping he wouldn't upset the moment, Ed spoke in his gentlest tone. "So, next time? We start?"

Protector sagged back in her chair. "Next time. If she lives till then."

4

Through the remainder of the morning and over lunch, Andi re-interviewed all of Essex's neighbors she found at home. The neighbors on Cedar Street added nothing new, so she went around the block to Larch Street and rang doorbells at the three houses closest behind Essex's. At two, no answer. But in the house right behind Essex's, a young woman came to the door. She looked nervously at Andi's badge, then down to her gun. "You're with the sheriff's office?"

"I am, ma'am. My name's Andi Pelton, and we're following up on the shooting Saturday night. May I come in?"

The woman looked more nervous, glanced back into the house. "It's a mess, really . . ."

"Would you prefer to talk out here?"

"No," she said, sharply, then blushed. "I'm sorry. You surprised me, is all."

"I'll be quick. I've just got a few questions we're following up on."

"All right. Come in."

The woman hadn't exaggerated—the house was a mess. From the couch, she crushed a pile of laundry into her arms and dumped it on the dining room table, already covered with stacks of paper, books, and dirty dishes. "I'm totally embarrassed," she said, brushing a lock of hair out of her eye. "I've been a wreck since the shooting."

Andi surveyed the disarray she could see. *More stuff here than just two days' worth*, she thought. "It's always upsetting to have something like that happen close to home. Do you know Mr. Essex?"

The woman flinched. "I'm sorry, Ms. Pelton. I never introduced myself. I'm Brenda Cantor."

"Hi, Brenda. And please, call me Andi." Andi waited a moment to give her time to answer the question. When she didn't, Andi asked again.

Her eyes reminded Andi of a caged animal. "Uh, I'm afraid I do. Too well."

Andi hid the energy that jolted her. "Can you tell me about that?"

Brenda pointed to the open space on the couch. "Please, sit down." After lifting off a stack of newspapers from the chair at the end of the couch onto the floor, she sank down onto it, looking sadly at the newspapers. "Daniel and I had an affair."

Andi took a quick breath. "Had? You're not still together?"

Brenda shook her head. "No."

"When did it end?"

"Two weeks ago."

"Just after the earlier burglary?"

Brenda looked puzzled. "What earlier burglary?"

Andi tensed. "Mr. Essex told us he'd been burglarized about three weeks ago."

"No, there wasn't any burglary, not when we were together. I stayed over there . . ." She paused, gestured toward the Essex house. ". . . almost every night since we started, um, our thing."

No burglary? "Which was when, Brenda?"

"I remember. April first." She paused, looked down. "Guess I was the April Fool."

"You said you spent evenings at his house."

She nodded. "He hated coming over here—I'm a terrible housekeeper, and he's real anal." She tried to smile, but managed to look only more embarrassed. "And it wasn't just evenings. Daniel insisted I sleep with him. Every night, all night. He got upset if I said I wanted to sleep in my own bed."

"Upset? Why?"

"He wanted to have me to himself?" Her face had reddened and she shrank back into the chair. "No, it was worse than that. Once we started having sex, he tried to control me completely. He wanted me dependent on him."

"Men like that don't often let their girlfriends get away. Who broke it off?"

"Uh, I did."

"How'd he react?"

Brenda sighed. "At first, seriously angry, you know? I was, like, terrified." Her shoulders twitched. "He's a big believer in open carry, you know? He wears his gun all the time, even around the house. Unless he was naked—" Her face reddened.

"Unless he was naked?"

"Yeah, then he took the gun off." She blushed again. "Sometimes I thought he'd wear it to bed if he could've got his pants off. Anyway, when he was yelling about me leaving, he started waving his gun around. I was terrified he was going to shoot me. Then out of nowhere, he just grinned, this weird, scary grin, and said, 'Yeah, you're right. Get outta my life.' I left right away and didn't go back. He's still got all my stuff over there."

"Has he bothered you since then?"

"At first, I was scared he'd come over, but . . . no." She looked around the house. "Maybe that's why I haven't tidied up. He hated my messes, you know? He's totally anal about neatness."

"You're thinking he avoided coming over because your house wasn't up to his standards?"

"I guess so, yeah."

Andi tried to remember precisely what Essex had said about the first burglary. *Three weeks ago.* "Could the burglary have happened after you left?"

"I suppose it could've." She stopped, looking thoughtful. "It's strange, though, you asking that. Daniel was always talking about being burglarized, like it had happened many times before. He called it *intrusions.* That's one reason he wore the gun, you know?"

"He told you that?"

She nodded, nervously. "He said the next time he wouldn't be made a fool of." Brenda sighed again. "Do you mind if we stop now? Talking about him kind of freaks me out."

"Of course." Andi wanted to learn more, but Brenda's eyes were red, and her breathing heavy. *She looks like she's seeing a ghost,* Andi thought. She stood and handed Brenda her card. "Call me if anything comes to mind, no matter how unconnected it seems. Let me be the judge whether it fits into the case, all right?"

Brenda looked at the card, then nodded.

"Do you mind if we talk again, maybe in a day or two?"

Brenda looked at Andi without speaking, then shook her head. "I guess so. Is Daniel in jail?"

"Yes. The judge refused bail, although I expect his lawyer will try again in a few days. If he makes bail, I'll call to let you know he's getting out."

"Thanks, Andi. I'd appreciate that." She wrapped her arms around herself. "I'm scared to death of him."

5

After dinner that evening, Ed and Andi sat, silent, on the porch, watching the sun setting over the Monasteries. Andi glanced at her watch: the evenings were darkening earlier. She smelled a tang in the breeze, saw the air above the mountains bathed with soft golden light. The days were still warm, but now the lucid evening air cooled quickly as the slant of light leaned to the south. After a few quiet minutes, Ed said, "So, have you figured out whether you're staying or going? If Ordrew becomes sheriff?"

"I didn't like what you said, about not letting me go."

"And I didn't like your threat to go."

"Can we not argue about this now? I have enough on my plate with the murder and Ordrew's campaign."

"If not now, when? It feels to me like we just get to a good point, and you pull back."

She stood up and went to the railing, looked out at the night. "Ordrew's serious, Ed. He doesn't like female cops, and he wants to get rid of me. How would *you* feel if Montana stripped you of your license?"

He didn't answer. She turned and looked at him.

"Okay, I understand," he said, his voice tense. "But don't just default to moving away. We can fight it. He can't fire you without cause. And there are other things we can do."

She sat down again, beside him, and laid her hand on his leg. "You're right, I'm doing my usual thing—if I can't control things, I run. But give me some time to figure out what to do. If he wins, I'm the one who has to deal with it."

"Not alone. We both have to deal with it."

"We?"

"We. Ordrew fires you, our life here changes."

"Meaning?"

"You go, I go with you."

"Ah. I didn't think of that." She sighed, her eyes focusing into the far distance, where the evening light bathed the mountains. "I love this time of year. Not fall yet, but you can feel it in the air." She turned and kissed Ed on the shoulder.

"Me too." After a moment, he said, "So, the election."

She sighed. "I suppose we have to ruin a perfectly nice evening and talk about it."

Ed pulled the flyer out of his pocket. They studied it together.

Andi said, "He's making Ben's fitness the issue for the campaign. I can't see him losing on that, now."

They sat, unspeaking, for a few minutes. Andi broke the silence. "You're right about one thing. There are rules, and if there's anything he's big on, it's rules. He can't fire me without due process."

"That's good, but we need a plan to beat him in November, not let him win and then find a way to fight him."

"I'm hoping Ben can run, from his bed if he has to, while he recovers." She thought a moment, feeling more convinced it could happen. "The guys and I can do all the work, give speeches and all. He'd win. Everybody trusts him."

Ed studied her a long moment. "Andi, Ben's still unconscious. No way he'll run for sheriff."

The breath went out of her, as if an iron fist had reached into her chest and clutched her lungs.

For a moment, she tried leaning against Ed's body, as if feeling his bones and muscle could ease her. She jumped up. "God. I'm suffocating." She went down the porch steps into the yard and leaned against her SUV.

Ed followed her. "What's going on? Talk to me."

"Talk? What the hell will *talking* do? If Ben's too sick to run, Ordrew's sheriff and I'm toast."

"Wow, Andi. We just decided we'd figure a way to stop that, and now, just like that—" He snapped his fingers. "—you're back to square one."

His finger snapping pissed her off, his anger fueling hers. "Glad you're so confident we can stop it, but don't forget, it's my goddamn career that's on the line here." She felt her face flush.

"And our goddamn life together is on the line right beside it."

Andi caught herself. Every muscle in her body wanted to run, to escape this clawing tightness in her chest, but he was right. They'd just agreed to solve this together; she didn't need to do it all alone—or run. She forced a few long, calming breaths, and the pain in her chest began to ease. "I'm sorry. You're right. But if Ben's out, Ordrew's going to win."

Ed waited a moment. "Ben can't run, but you could."

She felt her knees buckle, and put a hand on the SUV to steady herself. "God, no. I'm no sheriff."

Ed started to say something, but Andi interrupted. "No, Ed. Don't say anything else. I need to walk."

"Okay. Let's walk." He turned toward the road.

"No. I need . . ."

Ed waited a moment, but she didn't finish. "What do you need, Andi?" His voice was gentle, which helped her.

She forced a smile. "I need to walk. And think. Alone."

"We're going to figure it out together."

"We will. When I'm back."

6

Ed's gravel drive curved a quarter mile down to the highway. As the darkness fell across the valley, Andi walked fast, close to running. She panted, this time from effort, not fear. By the time she reached the highway and turned onto the shoulder, sweat beaded her forehead. Along the road, August-parched grasses rustled, stirred by the breeze or night animals. Ahead, the blue-black mountain ridges were blurring into the darkening sky. Her panic had ebbed, but walking hadn't generated any helpful thinking.

Headlights approached, so she stepped off the shoulder into the weeds. As the wave of wind from the car hit, the realization stunned her. Ben wasn't going to be her boss. Ordrew was, unless . . . She stood still in the weeds, feeling the evening breeze against her face. *Ben's unconscious. Maybe he won't recover. And he won't be my sheriff.* She made herself let that in.

In the dark, below the swarm of stars hanging above her head, she realized her cheeks were wet with tears. She let them fall, standing in the dry grass, the breeze caressing the moisture on her face.

"All right," she said to herself. "Enough." She gave a quick decisive nod, turned back toward Ed's drive, and looked up the long rise to his cabin, its windows lit yellow, warm in the night, welcoming. Surprising herself, she felt a longing to pray, to wrest by sheer desire Ben's life from the death ensnaring him. She wanted to find God up in those stars and beg, plead, demand. But the stars were silent, and she found no words in herself, or faith enough to make them. To the darkness, she whispered, fiercely, "He'll wake up."

Halfway up the drive, she stopped, said aloud, "But he'll never run again." She wondered if she'd ever be able to say those words without this surge of grief.

PART TWO

Elections are like crimes: An order is upended, lives are disrupted, the normal course of events is suspended. But they are also different: The suspense of a crime comes after it's been committed; an election's suspense comes before.

Anonymous

WEDNESDAY, AUGUST 29

1

Andi stood a moment at the nurses' desk in the ICU. Joni Filer looked up, smiled. "Morning, Andi. We've got good news."

Her heart jumped. "Tell me."

"Ben woke up last evening. Doc's moving him to a regular room later today, if it looks like he'll handle it."

The rush of relief startled her, and she wiped her eyes. "God, that's good. Is he awake now?"

Joni shook her head. "Sleeping, but it's just sleep, thank God." Joni crossed herself.

Andi breathed deeply, letting the news settle in. Maybe . . . She stopped herself. One step at a time.

As she was walking out, Doc Keeley came out of the doctor's lounge. She waved. "Talk to you a minute?"

Doc looked rumpled and rough; the usual dark bags under his eyes looked more like balloons this morning. "Sure," he said, yawning. "Sorry. Long night."

"You look tired, Doc. I was hoping you could tell me about Ben, but if this is a bad time . . ."

"Ben." He looked confused a moment. "Sorry. Brain fart." In a moment, his eyes focused. "No, I'm okay. He woke up about eight-thirty last evening." He yawned again. "In fact, he was in better shape than I expected." He rubbed his forehead. "Tell you the truth, Andi, I didn't expect him to wake, but we must've got him stabilized fast enough. We'll see. If he looks good, I'll move him to a regular room later today."

"I'm sure it's too early to tell, but what are his chances for recovering?"

Doc shook his head. "Mickey Barnes came over Monday morning and examined him, and—"

"I'm sorry: Mickey Barnes?"

"Oh, he's my go-to cardiologist in Missoula. Anyway, Mickey thinks his ejection fraction is around thirty-five percent, which is very serious."

"Ejection fraction?"

"The amount of blood pushed out of the left ventricle at each heartbeat. Normal is between fifty-five and seventy percent. So, he's at risk, and assuming he survives, recovery will be slow. And partial. We still have tests to do to determine *how* partial."

"Will he stay in the hospital long?"

Doc shook his head. "Typically, they go home three to five days after a heart attack, but we'll be running those tests, and when he's conscious we'll evaluate whether there was any brain damage resulting from the heart attack. I'd guess maybe another week?"

Andi hesitated, unsure she wanted to ask this. "What about his re-election campaign?"

Doc shook his head. Andi felt her chest tighten even before he said it. "Andi, Ben's campaigning days are over."

2

She went from the hospital to morning report. There, she relayed the good news, and the mood in the room lightened, except for Brad Ordrew's. He frowned. But the last thing Doc had said, she kept to herself. The news that Ben couldn't run was none of Ordrew's business. No, that wasn't it: She dreaded the smirk she'd see on his face.

Xavier Contrerez chuckled when she finished. "Hey, Bradley, watch your back now. Big Ben's back in town, and those fancy flyers won't do you much good once he's on the trail."

Ordrew said nothing, although the dark look he shot at Xavier required no interpretation: Pure contempt.

After the meeting, Pete called her into Ben's office. "A minute?"

He ran his fingers through his hair. "This'll be quick. Are you getting the support you need in the Essex case? Anything we can do to help you?"

"No, I'm good. Xav's great. Look, I didn't want to say it during report, but just between you and me, Doc Keeley said Ben can't campaign."

Pete grimaced. "Bad news." He picked up his briefcase. "Well, I gotta go. Damn meeting in Helena with FEMA."

Not enough time. I'll catch him later. "You go, Pete. We'll handle things here."

3

She set aside her fret about the election and joined Xavier in the conference room. As they spread out their Essex case files on the table, she related her conversation with Brenda Cantor.

Xavier stopped her. "He talked about intruders a lot?"

"Uh-huh. And she said he wore his gun around the house so . . ." She consulted her notes. "Brenda said, 'the next time he wouldn't be made a fool of.'"

"Like he expected intrusion."

"Yeah, that's the feeling I got."

Xavier rested his chin in his hand. "Well, that's the purpose of the castle doctrine, right? To allow people to protect themselves."

"But wearing his gun around the house? Brenda said about the only time he took it off was when he was naked. Remember how he said when he heard the noise he went and got his gun? If he wears it around the house all the time, that doesn't square."

"Unless he was naked at the time." He grinned.

"Why would he be naked if Brenda had already ended their affair? We know the house was empty the night of the shooting."

He smiled. "Just joking, Andi."

"Ah. I'm too serious, eh?" She waited a moment, then shared her thinking about the number of beer cans. "Seems odd to have so much beer and not drink any of it—or a mere four cans."

"Maybe it's not for him. Maybe he's got a buddy who drinks beer."

"Hmm. So, maybe the buddy drank the missing beers sometime between the burglary and the shooting." Another thought occurred to her. "Let's think about this: He hears the noise while he's inside. Then he comes out the *front* door and goes around the car and rests his gun on the hood before firing. He says he used the front door to be as fast as he could, but why didn't the kid hear him and bolt out the side door?"

Xavier grinned again. "In an earlier life, Essex was a cat burglar."

Andi chuckled. "Who shoots other burglars? Professional disloyalty." She cocked her head. "You gave me an idea, though. Let's go look at his shoes."

They let themselves into the cell block. Essex was sleeping. Beside the cot, his shoes lined up neatly, side by side.

Andi whispered, "Rubber soles."

Xavier nodded. "Real *quiet* rubber soles."

Back in the conference room, Andi said, "If you heard an intruder in your garage, would you sneak out so quietly he couldn't hear you?"

Xavier laughed. "Naw, I'd make more noise than kids banging a *piñata*."

"Unless you *wanted* to fire a shot. With the gun you wear around the house."

"Except when you're naked."

4

About four in the afternoon, as Andi was walking through Reception to leave the station, Callie, at the reception desk, said casually, "What you got on the menu for the Ladies' tonight, Andi?"

Damn. She'd completely forgotten the Ladies' Fishing Society. "You'll just have to wait and see."

"You haven't bought 'em yet, have you?"

Mock-offended, she said, "Of course I have. They're my dad's favorites, so I'm keeping them a secret till we meet. It's at six, right?"

"You forgot the whole schmear."

"I won't dignify that with—"

"—an honest answer." Callie grinned widely.

"You're enjoying this."

"I am."

5

Cottonwoods towered over the wide green pasture where Magnus's fireworks show would go off on Monday, Labor Day, his annual celebration of summer's end. His crews were mowing, preparing the field for Monday's show. As Andi drove along the dusty road bordering the field, she listened to the drone of their engines. She nosed her SUV into the shade under the big trees along the river and lugged the cooler and a thermal bag filled with her appetizers to the grassy clearing on the shadowed riverbank. This late in the summer, the river was running no more than a foot deep, bubbling gently over rocks and backing up into small pools behind wind-fallen trees, then pouring over the natural dams in elf-sized waterfalls. She set the cooler down on the grass and went back for the blankets and her folding chair.

Her *hors d'oeuvres* waited in the thermal bag. The fancy French phrase didn't seem to apply to her offerings; even "appetizers" seemed too snooty. After she'd hurried to buy them at the deli of Art's Fine Foods and dumped them in an insulated bag, she'd bought a bag of ice to chill two bottles of wine in the cooler. Each of the Ladies would bring a bottle, so with her two, they'd have five. One for each—and one extra—way too much. They seldom drained more than two, sometimes three, bottles, but they kept bringing five. Tradition mattered.

The first Lady to arrive was Lane Martin, carrying his wine and a lawn chair. Andi pretended not to feel sheepish—Lane's *hors d'oeuvres* were gourmet class, often exquisite—and her offerings? Well, her *dad* had liked them. But the Ladies would be polite. As Lane walked toward her, she rehearsed her plan, then stopped herself. *Tonight's not for politics.* "Hey, Lane. Great evening, isn't it?"

Lane smiled. "The finest time of day in the finest season of the year," he said. She gave him a hug and he kissed her on the cheek. He said, "So sorry about Ben, Andi. You must be beside yourself."

"Well, the news today is good. He'll be getting out of ICU, maybe already is. And Doc thinks he's not as bad as they feared."

"Wonderful. I'm delighted." His eyes drifted to the flowing water. "My daddy died of a heart attack when he was thirty-seven. I was ten." For a moment, he watched the shallow river, then looked back at her. "I sincerely hope that we're not deprived of Ben's presence. He's a pillar here in the valley."

They heard vehicle doors slamming, and looked toward the field. Bernie had ridden with Callie. When they got to the clearing, there were hugs and greetings and pours of wine into plastic glasses, and they'd just sat down to some serious gossip and sipping when Maggie Sobstak drove in.

Callie stood up. "You remember today's her one-year checkup for the cancer?" As Maggie came into the clearing, she said, "So, girl, how are you?"

Maggie grinned. "Clean as a whistle." Everyone cheered, although Andi noticed that Bernie's cheer was subdued. She caught Bernie's eye and lifted her eyebrows. *Do you know?* Bernie looked sad; maybe she hadn't heard. Andi said, "There's more good news. Have you all heard about Ben?"

Bernie nodded, as did Callie, but Maggie said, "No. Tell us." She leaned forward. "I haven't heard."

She repeated what Doc had told her. Another round of cheers, this time joined more heartily by Bernie. "It's not all good news, though. Doc says Ben's campaigning days are over."

Callie's mouth opened, then shut. Maggie said, "He won't be sheriff?"

"What Doc says." She hesitated, then decided to ask their advice about her plan. "I need some—"

Bernie interrupted. "Sweetness, I need to be more than usually rude . . ." She stood up, her face working. She walked to the riverbank, stared into the trickling water. "Hell's bells, I got something I gotta get off my chest."

Andi knew: *Bernie's going public.*

"Damnation, this is hard." Bernie turned, came back to the circle, dabbed her eyes with the sleeve of her shirt. "Lemme just say it. Ben Stewart and me, we've been having an affair."

6

No one moved or spoke. Up in the canopy of cottonwoods, a squirrel chirped angrily at them, the sound echoing from the dry tops of rocks in the soft burble and twinkle of the river. Lane cleared his throat.

"Bernadette, you win the prize for the biggest surprise in the history of this Society."

Callie's eyebrows hadn't yet descended. "Hell, in the history of the valley," she said, then stood up and enfolded Bernie in a long, deep hug. "Sister, no wonder you been hanging out at that hospital looking sad as a basset hound. Your ol' heart must be in shreds."

Bernie shook her head. "Naw, I got my prayers and I've been roughing God up since it happened. My heart'll be just fine. It's Benji's I'm worried about."

No one spoke. After a moment, Bernie said, "Do me and Benji a favor?"

"Of course," said Maggie, and the others nodded.

Bernie said, "Can we keep this among ourselves? Till Benji comes home."

For a moment no one spoke, then Maggie, again, said, "No problem. The word stops here."

Callie nodded. "Goes without sayin'. But I got two questions." She turned to Andi. "First one, you bring hot horse-dovers?"

"I did," Andi said, reaching for the thermal bag. "Here we go." Her plan could wait.

Bernie looked at the three plastic trays. "Child, what've we got here?"

"My dad loved these. Little weiners in BBQ sauce, pigs in a blanket with Kraft mustard, and cream cheese on RyKrisp."

Lane, the gourmet chef, put on a brave smile. Andi thought he'd gone a little gray.

Callie clapped her hands. "Good God, I never thought I'd get cop food in this bunch. About time."

Bernie turned to her. "Hon, what's your second question?"

Callie gulped a little weiner, then addressed Bernie. "*Benji?*"

FRIDAY, AUGUST 31

1

Outside his bathroom window, the eastern sky was dim. Brad Ordrew kept the bathroom lights off while he peed, then flicked them on and yawned. He ruffled his fingers through his hair, smoothing down the stick-ups from sleep. "Jesus, I'm looking old," he said, half aloud. He ran the hot water and lathered his face, and ran his razor over the right cheek. As he rinsed, his cell phone rang back in the bedroom. He swore, but went to grab the phone. He muttered, "Something's fucked up at the station, they're calling us in early."

No. He didn't know this voice, robust and ripe. *A radio voice*, he thought. Seductive. "Deputy, thank you for picking up. I apologize for the early hour, but I needed to reach you at home."

"Who is this?"

"Who I am is immaterial unless you accept my proposal."

"What proposal?"

"The proposal I'm about to make. May I have a moment of your time?"

"You've already had a moment. I've got to get to work."

"Or course, Deputy. I'll be brief. I am offering to help your campaign for sheriff."

A donor. Ordrew softened his tone. "I'm all ears. How much can you give?"

A slight chuckle. "Money is not the most important thing you need, although I will provide plenty of that. No, I'm offering a better kind of help."

Money and more? His heart raced. "Such as?"

"Patience, Deputy. We'll come to that. But to show my good faith, I'd like to offer you some advice."

He strode back into the bathroom, switching the phone to *Speaker* mode, and picked up his razor. "Look, Mister Whoever-You-Are, I don't need—"

"Yes, you do, Deputy. I read your announcement flyer. It's a good foundation, but that's as far as it goes, a mere foundation. You need much more than that for decent campaign messaging."

Ordrew bristled. "What makes you think—"

"Your message is that Sheriff Stewart is old and sick and out of touch, while you're young, healthy, and up to date. Am I correct?"

"Yes. Your point?"

"What happens to that message if Sheriff Stewart recovers and runs vigorously against you?"

Ordrew swallowed, feeling foolish. He hated being wrong. He glanced in the mirror—half his face was still lathered, unshaven. He rested the phone on the sink and resumed shaving. "If that happens, I'll deal with it."

"Or if the younger and still strong Deputies Peterson or Pelton run against you?"

The razor jerked in his hand, and he felt the sting of the cut. In the mirror, he saw the thin line of blood. He cursed inside. "Look, make your point. I can handle them."

"All due respect, Deputy, no, you can't. To *handle* them, you need a set of issues that doesn't require a sick Sheriff Stewart as your opponent, and you don't have any."

Ordrew snatched a tissue and pressed it against the cut. "I sure do have other issues. They'll come out in due time."

"I beg to differ. Your campaign needs at least three issues at its launch, and you haven't spelled them out."

"And you're going to tell me what they are, I suppose."

"I am. Gratis. No charge."

Ordrew realized the man was right, but hated to acknowledge it. "I have to get to work, mister."

"I'll be brief. You need three issues. I'll take them in order. Tell me some evidence that Stewart's department is 'out of touch.'"

"Evidence?" Ordrew gingerly finished shaving, watching the mirror.

"Examples, Deputy. Facts, if you please, that demonstrate your claim."

"I know what you mean." He paused, thinking. "Okay. Our riot gear dates back to the 80s. Our riot shields wouldn't stop a rock. We've got no tear gas. No armored vehicles. No batons."

"Well said. So, by 'out of touch,' you mean unprepared for mass civil disorder, correct?"

"That's absolutely what I mean."

"Rioting crowds, angry Blacks."

"I still don't see what—"

"Your phrase 'out of touch' conveys nothing of that, Deputy, but your department's unreadiness to control civil unrest and restore law and order is your first issue. It goes far beyond the sheriff's health or age or being out of touch."

Ordrew removed the tissue from the cut, which welled blood again. *Damn it, he's right.* He said, "The fact is, there won't be any riots here. Compared to Los Angeles—"

"Where you're from."

"Yeah." *This guy's done some homework.* "Anyway, compared to LA, Adams County's quiet as a nursing home. Nobody's the rioting type."

"Grow up, Deputy. The *facts* are irrelevant. A political campaign isn't about facts, it's about the fears and hopes of your constituents. Whether riots will actually happen does not matter. What matters is whether the voters *fear* that riots might happen. Your first issue is to *make* them afraid and *keep* them afraid, and assure them that under your watch, the sheriff's office will protect them. Do you fathom the difference, Deputy?"

With a sickening certainty, like a slug to the gut, Ordrew understood. He had never thought that through.

"Deputy?"

"All right, I get what you're saying."

"So, tell me, who are your constituents?"

"Everybody. I want every vote I can get."

"Admirable, I'm sure. But naïve. What group in Adams County might fear civil unrest? The liberals?"

Ordrew thought immediately of Andi Pelton. "Of course not."

"Your target voter is the Second Amendment crowd."

Ordrew grimaced. "Obviously. The second sentence of my flyer is about the Second Amendment."

"A nice touch, by the way. That subset of your population lives in terror that a mob of Blacks or Hispanics or, God help us, Muslims will destroy their comfortable way of life, and that's your first issue: You will upgrade the department so that you can maintain law and order. And your second issue is that Sheriff Stewart has created a department that is ready to repeal the Second Amendment and confiscate their guns."

Ordrew laughed, then felt a stab of annoyance. "That's nonsense. Stewart's old, but he's not—"

"Stop. Never use that word 'old' again. *Unprepared for civil disorder* is what you must say. Your Second Amendment constituents will hear clearly what you mean."

"Fine and good, but nobody in the department's against the Second Amendment. I'm just—"

"Deputy, I hope to God you're brighter than you're sounding. Perhaps it's the early hour. I'll say this again: It matters not at all that no one is against the amendment. What counts is that your voters *fear* that they are. Your job is to maximize that fear and to show them you will ensure that no one takes away their guns."

Ordrew shook his head into the mirror. "That's lying. I don't lie." He used a washcloth to remove the flecks of shaving cream from his ears and neck, then started running a brush through his short hair. He inspected the brush for dandruff. Clean. *Good.*

"Of course you lie. Everyone lies. Everyone expects politicians to lie, and it doesn't matter, as long as the lie reinforces what your constituents already fear." The sonorous voice took a beat, like the pulpit voices Ordrew remembered from his childhood, rich arching voices poised to hammer home hard truths. "If you insist on not lying, Deputy, you will lose."

Once more, Ordrew felt the punch to his gut.

The voice turned intimate, soft. "Brad, you're a decent man. A good officer. I understand that embellishing the truth goes against the grain. But this campaign is in the service of a truth greater than the simple facts."

"Sounds like a load to me. The truth is—"

"Tell me, which is more important to the future of Adams County: That the department is not factually out to repeal the Second Amendment or that your voters, if you succeed in giving them hope and a sense of security, will be less troubled and therefore less prone to *creating* trouble?"

Ordrew wrinkled his nose, staring at the mirror, trying to grab what smelled wrong with that, but missing it. "I suppose, if you put it that way, security and hope."

"Well said. Call that the Greater Truth. Which brings me to the third issue of your campaign."

"Good," Ordrew said. "I have to get to work. Keep talking, but you're on speaker while I put on my uniform."

"I'll be brief."

Speaking of lying, Ordrew thought.

"Tell me, what *other* group, besides Blacks and the government, does your constituent group fear?"

Ordrew stepped into his pants, thinking. *Druggies? Gangs?* Then he got it. "Immigrants."

"Indeed. And that's your third issue."

Ordrew couldn't stop his laugh. There were maybe a couple dozen Mexican families in the valley, most legal and working on the ranches, except the illegals on Magnus Anderssen's ranch, who was above the damn law. "That's not an issue around here."

For once, the voice did not respond. After a moment, Ordrew, taking a uniform shirt off its hanger, said, "Are you there?"

"I'm here, but I believe I'm wasting my time."

He realized what he'd said. "No, I'm sorry. What I said was wrong, from your perspective. It doesn't matter that we don't have an immigrant problem here. What matters is that my people are afraid immigrants will come in and take their jobs." He buttoned the shirt and reached for his cap and gun belt. "Look, morning report's coming up. I've got to get going. You said you have a proposal."

"I do. But I'm not sure you're interested."

Am I? "No, I am. I appreciate your advice and I'll take it seriously. What's your proposal?"

"I want you to watch the six o'clock news on Channel 13 from Missoula. Watch the first commercial block, at about ten or eleven minutes. You'll see what I am offering to do for your campaign if you choose to follow my advice."

Ordrew went out to the kitchen and grabbed the go-cup of coffee he'd prepared fifteen minutes ago. *Cold already.* "You're running a commercial for me?"

"No. For your campaign, Deputy."

He parsed that. "What do you want from me?"

"Watch the ad. Consider it a favor from an admirer. After the ad runs, I'll call you. Take the call, and I'll make my proposal then."

Ordrew stood in the doorway, his finger poised over the *End* button. "Look, I need to know who you are and what you—"

He heard three beeps, and the line went dead.

2

On the steps of his porch, Ordrew hesitated, shaken by the call. *Greater truth versus the facts? What the hell's that mean?* The first sunlight fingered the upper heights of the mountains. When he'd arrived in the valley, they'd frightened him, the rugged Monastery Range to the west the most. Too high, looming, not like the friendlier slopes of the Santa Monicas or the Simi Hills, covered in sage and valley oak. He'd felt hemmed in here, surrounded by mountains, not like Los Angeles, where even when you faced the ranges, the open sea was at your back. Over time, though, his reaction to these mountains had changed. The immovable rock, the daily presence of unchanging contours, the peaks and canyons born a hundred million years ago, spoke to him: Mountains, like principles, don't change. They girded Monastery Valley in a way the sea never could contain Los Angeles.

Sometimes, watching eagles or osprey soar high on mountain thermals, or seeing the cobalt sky outlined against the sierra, he'd almost felt free, thrilled with emotions of flight, of exaltation. He saw himself as sheriff, rescuing the county from . . .

Or sometimes not. Sometimes, the mountains dwarfed him, mocked his ambition. The phone call had left him unsettled, like the mountains' sometimes confusing stimulations—on one hand the caller had promised victory, had offered powerful support for his bid for the sheriff's job; on the other hand, he'd challenged Ordrew's need for honesty, for well-established procedures, for protocols. The voice had said, "If you insist on not lying, Deputy, you will lose." Could he lie to win the election? He wasn't sure. But could he let his squeamishness about honesty cause his loss? Could he bear knowing he'd dropped the key to success when it was placed within his grasp?

This morning, the mountains frowned. Ordrew ducked into his vehicle. "Screw this," he muttered, angrily jamming the key into the ignition. "I've gotta get to work."

3

Ed had waited, patient. In the chair opposite, Protector's face was stony, her eyes dark. Her back was stiff. Ed smiled, hoping to put her more at ease, but she did not loosen a notch. He began the conversation. "You look troubled, Protector. Are you concerned about my helping you protect Connie?"

For a moment she stared at him. "I am afraid. I am not certain allowing you to talk to Connie or the One is wise. If I allow either to come out, they may take control."

"Has either of them threatened to do that?"

"The One who wishes to kill Connie." She hesitated. "I have always known the One as male. But she revealed herself to me after our last session."

"The One who wants Connie to die is female? Didn't you say 'he' spoke to you last time?"

"She makes her voice sound deep."

"Ah, so she's a female protector like you, with a different approach."

"Yes. But I still fear that if I permit her to take control, she may not give it up."

"Shall I tell you about the way I can talk with the One or with Connie without you losing control?"

She nodded, though the obvious fear in her eyes pierced him.

"I'm going to teach you about finger signals."

"What does that mean?"

"I'll teach you—and the One and Connie or anyone inside—how to answer my questions by using fingers instead of coming out to use the voice."

Protector closed her eyes; the body went slack. Ed waited, familiar now with the signs of her conferring with other parts inside. In a moment, the eyes opened. "The One says it must be like sign language."

"Yes and no. It is like talking with the fingers, but I ask questions that can be answered only four ways, and we assign one finger for each answer. It's very simple."

"But if you ask questions of the One, She will come out."

"Coming out means you take temporary charge of the whole body, right? So, you can talk and walk and get things done. But in the finger signals—"

She interrupted. "Sometimes whoever is out is controlled by someone inside."

He nodded. "Yes, I've seen that happen, haven't I? But with the finger signals, the one who's answering doesn't take control of the whole body, just of the four fingers we assign answers to."

Protector was silent, but looked at him suspiciously. "Tell me the four answers."

"They are 'Yes,' 'No,' 'I don't know,' or 'I don't want to know.'"

"What if you ask a forbidden question? If I were answering, none of those questions allow me to refuse without lying."

Ed took a moment. No one had ever asked that before. *No one had forbidden questions before.* "You're right. So, we can set up five answers— the fifth one will be *I cannot answer that*. And when I see the finger that means you cannot answer, I'll know I shouldn't ask that question again."

Again, she waited a long time, and then, although she looked skeptical, she sagged in her chair. "Very well. You may begin."

He slowly induced a good relaxed state. When her face was calm and her hands had relaxed, he said, "Please put your hands on your knees where I can see them."

She moved her hands slowly to her knees.

"Thank you. That's perfect. Please lift the index finger on your right hand."

As she did so, he said, "This finger means 'Yes.' You can lower the finger now." It lowered. "Now, if I ask you a question that you want to answer *Yes* to, show me the finger you will use."

She lifted the right index finger. *She's working with me,* he thought.

Using the same approach, he set up four more fingers, one for *No*, another for *I don't know*, the fourth for *I don't want to know*, and the thumb for *I cannot answer that*. They practiced with non-threatening questions about the weather.

When he was confident that she was ready, he said, "Please have Connie nearby, but staying inside to listen. I will wait a few moments, then I will ask my first question. Are you ready?"

The *Yes* finger rose, hesitantly.

"Good. Now I'll wait." He counted to thirty, then said, "Is Connie near you?"

The *Yes* finger rose, this time more firmly.

"Wonderful. And do you feel relaxed and safe?"

Again, *Yes*, but it wavered.

"Can Connie hear me?"

I-don't-know.

"Is Connie listening now?"

Yes.

"Is Connie afraid?"

Yes.

"And is Connie afraid of me?"

A long pause. *No* rose.

"I'm happy she isn't afraid of me. Is she afraid of someone else?"

Yes rose fast.

"Is she afraid of the One?"

At first, *Yes* twitched, but after a moment's indecision, *I-don't-want-to-know* went up.

Ed doubted that was true, but decided to move on. Today, forging a safe connection with Connie and the One mattered more than charting the politics of the inner world. "I want Connie to know that I will not allow anyone to harm her when you're all here with me. Does she know that?"

A pause, then *I-don't-know* moved a little. Then, *Yes* rose, slowly.

"I'm glad. And does Connie know that if she ever wants to talk to me, I will sit still in my chair and won't do anything to scare her?"

No.

"I promise that if she ever wants to talk to me, I will sit still in my chair and I won't do anything to scare her." He paused. "Does Connie know she never needs to come out with me if she doesn't want to? Even if I ask her to?"

No came up, fast, insistent.

"Connie never needs to come out if she does not want to. Ever." He waited, but no finger moved. *Stupid move*, he thought. *Ask a question.* "Did Connie hear me?"

Yes.

"Does Connie believe me?"

Both hands were very still. Ed waited, watching the fingers.

I-don't-know quivered, then lowered. After many seconds, *Yes* quivered, lowered, then went up.

"That's good. I'm happy she believes me. Is everyone feeling safe at the moment?"

All the fingers started waving, and Ed realized he'd asked an impossible question. He had no idea how many "others" there were in the system, and no doubt there were a lot of mixed and contradictory feelings. He hastened to say, "I'm sorry, I asked a stupid question. Don't try to answer it."

The fingers settled down.

"Does Connie think she might ever want to talk to me, not just through the fingers?"

I-don't-know waved vigorously. Ed took that as a positive signal.

"Does Connie think maybe she'd like to talk to me now?"

At that, Protector's eyes jerked open and she sat up, on high alert. "I will not allow it. I told you. It is too dangerous." She stood, then staggered.

Ed knew he'd overstepped, but saw her swaying. *Blood pressure dropping.* He said, "It'll pass if you sit for a moment, Protector." She fell back into the chair. "I'm sorry I upset you. You and Connie were doing very well. Shall we try some more?"

Protector shook her head. "Not today. Perhaps Tuesday. But you must not ask her to come out."

He nodded.

"No, not a nod. I need your word on it."

"I will not ask her to come out without your permission. You have my word." He smiled. Protector was hard, but his respect for her was growing with every meeting. She was a woman toughened by desperation. He wondered if his care would be enough to soften that.

4

A few minutes before ten-thirty a.m., Andi parked in the lot beside St. Bernard's Catholic church. The Bayless Funeral Home hearse stood at the curb before the church; Rick Bayless and six men in ill-fitting suits stood on the sidewalk, smoking and talking in low voices, heads bowed. The funeral would begin in a few minutes. It moved her that the church bore the name of the boy they would bury.

She went inside and took a pew in the back. A few people sat closer, murmuring in Spanish. She saw Mrs. Cirilo and her three daughters in the front row. The doors opened beside her, and the six men, including Mr. Cirilo, carried the casket slowly up the aisle and laid it on a waiting bier. Rick Bayless moved two large candlesticks into place beside it. The priest had come in—Andi recognized young Father Anselm from the monastery. He stood calmly at the head of the casket while Rick draped a white cloth over it.

The Mass was over in thirty-five minutes. Andi waited in the back pew as the family followed Bernardo's casket toward the back. As they approached, she moved to the aisle, and when Mrs. Cirilo passed, Andi touched her shoulder. They embraced. And then the family and Bernardo were gone.

5

When Brenda Cantor opened her front door, Andi saw immediately the transformation. All the piles of clothes and papers and other stuff had disappeared. The place looked attractive. "Your house is amazing," Andi said. "What happened?"

"After we talked, I got pissed and started cleaning." She looked around. "I don't think I've ever had it this nice. Oh, and I changed the locks, so Daniel can't get in."

"He has your house key?"

"Yeah, he put it on his own ring."

Andi smiled. "Your lucky day. We've got his keys, so after the trial, you can get it back. Of course, with your new locks, it's not worth much."

"I'm just glad he can't get in. Excuse me a moment."

Brenda went into the kitchen and returned carrying a pot and two coffee cups. She put them on the dining room table. "We can sit here to talk."

Andi sat down. "I appreciate your seeing me on your lunch hour. I need to go over some things you told me. You said Daniel talked a lot about being burglarized. Was there anything else like that?"

Brenda poured the coffee. "That he talked about a lot? Oh, sure. He was always going on about a man's home is his castle, and how he moved to Montana because it has a good stand-your-ground law. I'll bet he brought it up every time they mentioned guns on Fox News, which was a lot." She handed a cup to Andi.

Andi took a sip. "Daniel moved here for our stand-your-ground law?"

"Seriously. He complained about where he lived not having stand-your-ground."

"Where was he from?"

"Massachusetts."

"Ah, I knew that. He's right. In Massachusetts, you're required to withdraw from a threatening situation unless it's impossible without resorting to deadly force."

"That totally pissed him off. He thought it was idiotic."

"Are you sure he didn't move here for his work?"

"I don't think so. He works at home, on the Internet. He said a few times he wanted to live in a stand-your-ground state."

"Huh. Tell me again when he moved here."

"I remember clearly. It was the first evening of last Passover, March 30. I remember because my folks had driven from Missoula for the Seder dinner and we had just sat down and started the prayers when he came to the door and said he needed to use my phone. He was rude. He called somebody and yelled about something the movers broke, took maybe ten minutes. Mom and Dad and I just sat there, waiting for him to be done swearing. He never thanked us, just walked out."

"*Rude* sums that up, all right. Did he say anything about interrupting your prayers?"

"I doubt he knew what we were doing." She pointed to an old-fashioned phone on a table in the living room. "He used that phone and never came in here where we were." She looked thoughtful. "Truth to tell, that's the reason I broke up with him. My being Jewish never came up, until right at the end. He wanted us to go to Boston the weekend of Yom Kippur, and I said no, I was Jewish. He got all red in the face and yelled, 'You're effing with me.' 'No,' I said, 'it's true.' He went nuts, just raving about the Jews this and the Jews that. I hadn't challenged him on the other things, the gun and the stand-your-ground talk or the control, but I told him to stop with the anti-Semitic crap. When he didn't, I said, 'We're done here,' and got up to leave. That's when he started waving the gun."

"Scary. Besides waving it, did he threaten you, like pointing it at you?"

"No, just waved it around. Then, like I told you, he just gave this weird grin and said, 'Get outta my life.'"

"So, you left. Did he bother you after that?"

Brenda shook her head.

Andi looked at her notes. "Didn't you tell me your affair started on April first? That's only two days after March thirtieth."

"Yeah. He came over again, this time real nice and told me he'd like to take me to dinner. I thought, what the heck, and we had a real nice time. That's when it started."

"Okay, changing the subject, where did Daniel generally park his car?"

"Omigod. Always in the garage. And *always* locked. I mean, he locked the garage doors and then he locked the car, too. He was fanatic about it. One time, I had to run over here for something." She paused. "I said I'd be right back—I always used the side garage door, it was the quickest way between our houses. When I got back, he started yelling at me for leaving the side door unlocked. I almost left him then."

"But you didn't. Why not?"

Brenda lips quivered, and her face reddened. "I was lonely? I've got a good job and all, and some friends since I moved here, but nobody special, you know? When he asked me out the first time, we had a real nice time. For the first couple of months, when he wasn't talking crazy or being mad, we had a lot of fun. Good conversations." She looked down, shy, then brushed aside hair that had fallen over her eyes. "And the sex was pretty good. At first, anyway. When everything started getting weird, I got scared if I left, he'd do something to me. But the anti-Semitism was the last straw."

"Good for you. You said it started getting weird. What do you mean?"

"It's kinda embarrassing, and it has nothing to do with your case, okay? Can I take a pass on that one?"

Andi hesitated. Should she push it now, or come back to it later? She decided to push. "Uh, can I nag you a little? The more we know who Daniel is, what he's really like, the better case we can send to the DA. And whatever turned weird, it might be part of a bigger picture that'll help us make the right charges."

Brenda looked down at the table's surface, her coffee cup clutched with both hands. The cup was shaking. She looked up. "Who else will hear about it?"

"It depends on what it is. If you're right and it's unrelated to the case, nobody else but me, and I'll respect your privacy. If in fact it's relevant, though, it'll go in my report, which will be seen by the DA, Essex's lawyer, the court officers, and anyone with access to our police reports. It could come up at trial."

Brenda put down her cup. "That's a lot of people." She ran her hand through her hair. "I need to think about it, Andi. I've got a good job at the hospital, but if this ever got out, I'd have to leave."

Andi felt a rush of sympathy: She could understand not wanting to leave the valley. She wondered whether Essex's weirdness could be something criminal. "I get that. Okay, consider it. How about I call you tomorrow or Sunday, and we can talk again?"

"Yeah. That'd be good. I'll think it over."

Andi put away her notebook and pen and stood up. "You've been helpful, Brenda. And I love your house."

Brenda looked around. "Yeah, it's nice, isn't it?" But her voice was weak.

6

When Andi left Brenda's and climbed into the squad car, she double-checked the search warrant's expiration date: September fourth. *Good.* She drove around the block to Essex's house, put the gloves on, grabbed his keys, which she'd checked out of the evidence locker, and let herself into the garage. She opened the fridge: Two shelves, all stocked with beer. Counted the cans again: Forty-five. Plus the twelve on the bench. And three in DCI's lab.

She let herself into the kitchen through the garage. Brenda's belongings had been left in the house, although Andi couldn't recall any mention of women's clothing or toiletries in the inventory after the search.

She opened the bathroom vanity and the medicine chest. Nothing remotely female-friendly. Looked in the drawers. Nothing. She went into the master bedroom and opened the closets—there were two large closets, almost walk-in size, but both were lined with men's clothing.

Nothing for a woman. She studied the clothes. Expensive, grouped by type—dress shirts with dress shirts, casual shirts together, slacks neatly hung side by side, T-shirts with T-shirts, shorts and jeans with shorts and jeans. She pulled out a T-shirt—it had been ironed, and like all the others, hung on a hanger. The second closet was filled with suits. She counted nine. More dress shirts. A rack of belts and another of ties. On the floor, thirty-six pairs of shoes, lined up perfectly.

The guy's a clothes horse, but he works from home, she thought. *And Brenda's right: Anal.* But he hadn't kept her clothes, or at least any place she'd looked. The bedside table's drawers held porn, lube, condoms, but nothing unique for a woman. In the dresser, underwear, socks, handkerchiefs—all men's and all folded and carefully stacked. She looked under the bed. Nothing. Not even dust bunnies. *Is this guy for real?*

She checked the spare bedroom, then the cabinets in the second bathroom. Nothing that only a woman would use. But the cupboards were meticulously, scrupulously tidy. Even the over-the-counter medicine bottles all faced out, displaying their names. In the kitchen, she opened the cabinet above the sink: Lined up tidily and all facing front, fourteen bottles of single-malt Scotch. Macallan, Glenfiddich, Glenmorangie, and four Andi had never heard of. *Not just a clothes horse,* she thought. *The guy's got expensive taste in alcohol.*

She went out to the squad for her cell phone and dialed Phil Oxendine's number. No answer. She left a message. "Ox, Andi Pelton. Did you or your crew find any evidence that a woman might have been staying with Essex? Anything at all? Let me know one way or the other."

Very strange. Why would Essex dispose of Brenda's things?

Another question occurred to her. She returned to the kitchen and opened the refrigerator. *Like I remembered.* No beer. *Pricey Scotch in the cupboard, cheap beer in the garage. What's up?* She took another photo of the kitchen fridge. To record what? Something missing.

7

After dinner, Ed told Andi, "We're in for some cooler weather. I'm going to chop some firewood."

"Want company?"

"Sure."

"Okay. I'll clean up these dishes and join you."

Andi was finishing the dishes when the landline rang. She answered it.

"Andi, did you see it?" It was Grace, breathless.

"See what?"

"The ad."

"What ad?"

"For that creep Ordrew. It's against Sheriff Stewart."

"Damn," she muttered.

Ed, who'd come in when he heard the phone ring, looked a question at her. She cupped the phone. "It's Grace. She said there's an ad for Ordrew on TV."

She went back to Grace. "What channel?" She'd felt a cool calm come over her. No. A chill.

"Wait, we were taping the news—it's an assignment for my Intro to Philosophy class, we're supposed to analyze the reporters' use of language. Anyway, me and Zach, I mean Zach and I were taping the news with my phone, so we got the ad too. I'll text it to your phone."

"Do it. And thanks, girl."

Grace didn't answer for a minute. "Andi, I want to come home. I know Northrup told me Sheriff Ben's showing good signs, but I feel like I should be there."

"Hold on, he's right here." Andi handed the phone to Ed. "She said Ordrew's got an ad on TV attacking Ben. And she's talking about coming home."

He raised his eyebrows at Andi, then said, "Hey, kid. What's up? Besides the ad?"

Listening, Ed pondered what he wanted to say. "Ben would want you to get your education." After a moment, he said, "It's good news— he came awake this morning. Look, just stay there till we know what's happening. I promise, if he gets worse, I'll tell you. Besides, we need your good eyes on the TV in case there are more ads."

He laughed as he ended the call.

Andi asked him, "She say something funny?"

He grinned. "Yeah. When I told her we need her good eyes on the TV, she said, 'I get it: I'm your eyes, you're my moneybags.'"

Andi grabbed her cell phone. "She said she'd text me the video they made."

They waited until the text signal beeped. She opened it, and tapped the *Play* button. In a moment, Brad Ordrew appeared on the screen, smiling, in uniform, in three-quarter profile; he seemed unaware of the camera. His weapon was conspicuous on his hip.

They watched the ad unfold.

FADE TO BLACK. LONG ESTABLISHING SHOT of HUNTERS' PEAK. CUT TO SILENT LONG SHOT OF MONASTERY VALLEY FROM ATOP THE COLISEUM, THEN SLOW ZOOM TO MONASTERY RIVER LOOPING ACROSS THE VALLEY. THEN:

VOICEOVER: *We live in a beautiful place.*

CUT TO SHOT OF HIGH SCHOOL FOOTBALL GAME, PAN THE CROWD. CUT TO COWBOYS BRANDING A CALF. CUT TO SHOT OF PEOPLE EXITING ST BERNARD'S CATHOLIC CHURCH. THEN:

VOICEOVER: *We are good people.*

CUT TO SILENT SLOW ZOOM TOWARD JEFFERSON, THEN QUICK SHOT OF DIVISION STREET, THEN ESTABLISHING SHOT OF SHERIFF'S DEPARTMENT BUILDING. THEN:

VOICEOVER: *We deserve the very best government services.*

CUT TO CUBICLE CURTAINS, EMERGENCY ROOM IN ADAMS COUNTY GENERAL HOSPITAL, WHILE:

VOICEOVER: *How can a man who lies unconscious in the ICU lead our sheriff's department and keep us safe?*

CUT TO SHOT OF ICU NURSES' STATION, WHILE:

VOICEOVER: *Criminals,   terrorists,   illegal immigrants—shall we leave our protection from these elements in our society in the hands of a sick old man?*

SILENT SOFT SHOT OF RESIDENTIAL STREETS, SLOW ZOOM IN:

VOICEOVER: *Brad Ordrew has the experience, the skills, the knowledge, and the love of country to lead the sheriff's office in the 21st century.*

LONG SHOT OF THE VALLEY, SLOW RISE UP THE FLANKS OF THE MONASTERIES, TO HUNTERS' PEAK: HOLD. THEN:

VOICEOVER: *On November 6, vote for Brad Ordrew for Sheriff. This is a patriot's campaign.*

CUT TO SHOT OF AMERICAN FLAG RIPPLING IN WIND. FADE TO BLACK. THEN: WHITE TEXT ON BLACK: *FRIENDS OF A PATRIOT'S CAMPAIGN.*

VOICEOVER: *I'm Brad Ordrew, and I approve this message.*

Andi frowned. "That isn't Brad's voice. Not at all. But, man, it sounds familiar."

Ed swore. "Jesus Christ, that's obscene."

"How the hell did the hospital allow him to take that footage?"

Ed grabbed his phone, dialed. After a moment, he said, "Doc, Ed Northrup. Look, have you seen Brad Ordrew's ad on TV? . . . How'd he get into the hospital to take that footage? . . . . What? That's damn dishonest— . . . Yeah, I will. Take care."

"What?" Andi said as soon as he hung up.

"A film company talked to the board, said they were making a documentary about small-town hospitals, and offered a large donation for permission to film. All that happened over the weekend and the film crew was there Monday morning."

"A *film* company? Does Ordrew have that kind of money?"

"I wouldn't think so. I don't know much about video, but it looked good. Beautiful, even."

"This is big trouble." Andi shivered. "I'm going to talk to Ben."

"And say what?"

"That he's got to run. From bed if need be."

Ed studied her a moment. "What if it kills him?"

She glared at him. "Thanks for the support." She turned. "Where are my keys? This scares the crap out of me and I need to see Ben."

"Andi, stay. Please. Let's talk this out."

"All right, but I'm freaked. First thing in the morning, I talk with Ben."

8

Ordrew'd planned not to watch the ad, but he had. He'd planned not to answer the phone afterward. All day, he'd muttered to himself, *This guy wants me to lie, and I don't lie.* But now, in his living room, his chest was throbbing as the ad finished, his throat full. He had no words, just an enveloping thrill. Within seconds, his phone rang, and he grabbed it off the side table and hit *Talk.* "Ordrew."

"Your first thoughts, Deputy."

"It's awesome. My heart's thumping like a flat tire at 70. That was beautiful." He didn't mention the tears that had filled his eyes. Since he'd been a kid, enduring his father's beatings, he'd dreamed of being top dog, not the poor dope getting the shit kicked out of him. The ad told him his dream had just gotten possible.

He heard a chuckle at the other end. "Yes, it was, wasn't it? I can provide you more like it, Deputy. Can you?"

Ordrew's excitement ebbed. He'd budgeted ten thousand dollars for the campaign, money from his already emaciated 401(k). "I have no idea what an ad like that would set me back."

An outright laugh. "Your saying that tells me that you truly cannot afford a campaign that is guaranteed to win. Am I wrong?"

Ordrew gritted his teeth. No way he'd answer that. "Look, I'm appreciative. The ad will help me, and I suppose I'd have a hard time affording many more like that." *Or even one.* He took a deep breath. "So, what are we talking about here?"

"I'm prepared to offer the following. First, four additional ads of similar quality, on all four Missoula stations that broadcast in your valley, as well as a couple of cable news channels. Also, we'll place the voiceover portion in radio ads on all the stations that play across Adams County. Three of the ads will address one of the issues we discussed this morning, and the fourth will attack any opponent who runs against you."

Thrilled again, Ordrew asked, "What if I'm unopposed?"

"You are never unopposed. On all three of your issues, people will bring up the facts, the lesser truth. People who won't like your platform are not stupid. For instance, on civil unrest. Despite the fears of your target voters, other people understand that it is improbable in Monastery Valley. They'll argue about it in the bars, at church, in the cafe. They'll talk about facts and demographics. Those *facts* are your opponent, and we'll create an ad that will attack that opponent. If a human being happens to become spokesman for those facts, our ad will attack him. Or her."

"The greater truth against the lesser truth."

"Precisely, Deputy. Precisely."

Who is this guy? Something about this man revolted Ordrew, but he felt a strange compulsion to listen. *Whoever the hell he is, he's going to win me this election.*

"Second," the man said, "I will underwrite a mass mailing to every valley resident. It will attack your opponent."

"The lesser truth."

"Indeed. Third, you'll need polling, including exit polling on election day, to inform us how you're doing. Last, I will arrange and pay for a victory celebration, with a hosted bar. Your constituents will appreciate that."

Ordrew was overwhelmed. But that last point bothered him. "Sir, you're making a generous offer, and I don't even know you. But I'm a cop. I don't like using booze to manipulate people. No hosted bar. A cash bar, maybe."

The line was quiet. After a moment, "Very well. That is unimportant. But it's true I am being quite generous here."

"I know, and I'm grateful." Ordrew hesitated. *Don't look a gift horse in the mouth,* his old man always said when he took a bribe. He grunted. "What's the other side? What do you want from me?"

"Ah, yes. Your *quo* for my *quid*. I'm planning certain, ah, projects in Monastery Valley, projects devoted to the greater truth we discussed this morning." He cleared his throat. "As sheriff, you'll be in position to help me in my projects, or at least to turn a blind eye to any conflict between my projects and small-minded legalisms of the lesser truth."

Ordrew flinched. He'd suspected as much. He could feel his face reddening and was glad they were doing this over the phone. His anger kindled swiftly when he felt his integrity challenged. He breathed hard through his nose, which often helped in moments of anger that he did not want to indulge. He closed his eyes and replayed the lovely images of the ad. *There'll be more like that*, he reminded himself.

"Deputy Ordrew? Are you there?"

"I am," he answered. "Sir, I've been called many things, but corrupt isn't one of them." It was ironic. He'd been railroaded out of the LAPD for being *too* honest a cop, a stickler for procedure, outspoken against police brutality in a very brutal police force. He'd refused to blur the edges, and was hated for it. Now this bastard was offering to buy him off, to purchase his "blind eye" to whatever the guy wanted to do for "the greater truth."

Ordrew held the phone away, whispered, "Greater truth my ass."

"Deputy? What did you say? I'm not asking you to violate your conscience. I'm proposing a joint venture for the safety and security of your constituents."

Ordrew had calmed himself. "Give me an idea of this project of yours."

"Gladly. Sensible tax-code reform, based on the authority of the county sheriff—which will be you. It's an old and venerable tradition, Deputy."

"Taxes aren't the business of sheriffs, sir."

"That's my project, Sheriff, er, excuse me, *Deputy*. Our movement believes the Constitution implies that the county sheriff is the highest authority in the land, and all I'm proposing is that, as sheriff, you allow us to make our Constitutional case to the people."

Ordrew thought about that. Posse Comitatus boilerplate, that anti-government, anti-Semitic, white supremacist movement from the 1960s. No way he should associate with that. On the other hand, ads, polling, mailings. Money. He could almost feel the sheriff's badge on his chest. Even as he spoke, he grimaced. "If I'm sheriff, you're welcome to state your views in the county. It's the First Amendment. But if those views turn into illegal acts, I can't promise to ignore it."

"Perhaps we'll discuss this at a later date. There's one more thing I'll ask of you. A trifle, actually."

"What's that?" Ordrew's suspicion jumped to high-alert.

"As I say, a trifle. If Deputy Pelton should ask you if you're being supported by anyone, tell her my name."

Ordrew frowned. "Which is?"

"The Reverend Loyd Crane. One L. She'll recognize it." He paused, then said, "Now, however, it is six twenty-three p.m. I need your answer, yes or no, now. I need to set the program in motion."

Ordrew sighed and pressed his forehead against the archway of his living room. Silent images flickered across the TV screen. The ad had stirred him. If it had endorsed anyone else, he would passionately support and vote for the candidate it portrayed. This Reverend Loyd Crane had already given him the three issues his poor-ass flyer had failed to spell out. His eyes grew moist. The words *The Greater Truth* had resonance. Emotional power.

Still, he was wary. He'd never taken a bribe, not a line of coke or a quick blow job in an alley when he was working vice, not a glass of beer or an envelope of money when he walked the beat. Unlike his dad. But what if this guy was right? What if politics was different from policing? What if there *were* greater and lesser truths? Could that greater truth justify blurring the hard edges and black-and-white boundaries that the lesser truth depended on? That he'd built his career around? He rubbed his eyes. *I'm a cop, not a fucking philosopher.*

Reverend Crane interrupted his thoughts. "Deputy, you have one minute to make up your mind. May I remind you, I came to you with valuable advice and a free TV ad—very expensive gifts, I might add—because your flyer, for all its faults and weakness, promised a true patriot's campaign. In turn, I ask your support for *my* patriot's campaign, construe it as you will. You have sixty seconds, Deputy."

Ordrew's back stiffened, just as it always had when his father had dangled the long black belt he'd just pulled from around his fat waist and growled, "You'll pay for your refusal to follow my rules, boy. I'll have your apology in the next ten seconds, or you'll have a bloody ass." And when Ordrew's back stiffened, his mouth shut tight. Afterward, his mother, seeing the bloodied underwear, would mumble, "Ah, those darn hemorrhoids of yours."

Ordrew wrenched himself out of the memory, and relaxed his back. He'd spent his adult life being different from his old man. He couldn't let all that go to hell in the blink of an eye. "I need time to answer that." Added, "Sir."

After a long pause: "Very well. Take a pencil and write this number. Are you ready?"

"Yes, sir. Go ahead."

Reverend Crane dictated a phone number. "At ten o'clock tonight, call this number. At ten minutes after ten, my offer expires. You'll get a recorded message. When it ends, follow the instructions. Your answer can be one word only: 'Yes' or 'No.' No argument, no reasons, no explanations. 'Yes' or 'No,' one word. Then hang up."

Ordrew felt a thrill. No belt had slashed him, no blood would soil him. Crane had backed down. *I have till ten.* "And if I decline?"

"If you accept my offer, you will be the next sheriff of Adams County. The patriots' sheriff."

"Yes, sir. Thank you. And if I decline?"

"Then, Deputy, you will indeed decline."

9

Brad Ordrew despised the trembling of his finger as he touched the keypad.

After Crane's call, he'd sat on his front steps, immobile as the mountains, mulling his decision. To become sheriff, to take control and wrestle this department into shape had become a desire he could no longer defer. Whoever the hell the Reverend Loyd, one L, Crane was, he would ensure it.

But to lie? To expose himself to the stench of corruption? Would Crane bring his crazy ideas to the valley and expect him to turn a blind eye? Of course, he would. No one spends big money without demanding a return. His father had taught him that.

After sunset, Ordrew had looked up at the sky, a dull wash of pale color in thin clouds. The Monastery Range brooded. He felt its looming presence. Still he'd sat, oddly chilled despite the warmth of the late August night. Gradually, the mountains had faded, a blacker silhouette against the black sky. He went inside. Paced.

His mind churned—corruption, perhaps, but victory. Being beholden, perhaps, but being sheriff. At one point, he'd prepped some food, but had forgotten to eat.

A most uncomfortable image pierced him: Andi Pelton getting the news of his bargain with the Reverend Crane. He saw the look of disgust on her face, the pity in her eyes.

Then, startling him, the alarm he'd set went off. The clock on the wall above the kitchen table read ten. *I have ten minutes*, he thought. For a moment, he had held the phone immobile in his hand, which is when he saw his fingers trembling.

Annoyed with himself, he pressed in the number. Listened to the rings, then the recorded message. It was not Crane's sonorous voice he'd heard, but another man's, a cold, cruel voice.

"At ten-ten p.m., the Reverend's offer and this message will expire. If you intend to answer him, wait for the first tone. After the tone, press '1.' When you hear the second tone, give your answer in one word, *Yes* or *No*. Then hang up. If you answer yes, you will be contacted. Regardless of your answer, do not call this number again." He heard the first tone.

Ordrew held his breath, pressed '1.'

He heard the second tone. He took a long, shaky breath. Said, "Yes."

SUNDAY, SEPTEMBER 2

1

Still reverberating from Ordrew's ad, Andi drove to the hospital. The last couple of days when she'd visited Ben, he'd looked half-alive, his face ashen and furrowed, the stubble on his chin and cheeks gray. This morning, despite the narrow green tubing draped from his ears delivering oxygen to his nose and two IV tubes entering his arms, he looked better. Electronics above his bed read out numbers, and the jagged mountains and canyons of his heart beat. "You sleep well, Ben?"

"Like a sheepherder in lambing season."

"How do sheepherders sleep?"

"Don't. You look like somethin's chewin' on you."

She described Ordrew's ad.

"So, I'm a sick old man, eh? Ain't sick enough I can't fire his ass. I ain't gonna quit bein' sheriff till January."

So, Doc had already given him the bad news. "You've talked to Doc about your campaign."

He nodded. "The campaign that ain't."

To Andi, he didn't look as disheartened as she'd expected. "You're not upset?"

"Sure as hell I'm upset, but a heart attack makes a guy think. Bein' sheriff's the main thing that's mattered to me since 1984." He looked almost happy. "Now I got me other some things that matter."

"Bernie O'Reilly?"

"She told you?"

"And the Ladies' Fishing Society, who all swore secrecy."

"Well, good. It ain't like we're ashamed of ourselves."

"Ben, I need your advice about something."

"What?"

But before she could ask it, an orderly came in with a wheelchair. "Hey, Sheriff, time for your MRI. Check and see if you still got a brain."

Andi gulped. *Hurry up and wait again. Damn.*

Ben seemed to pick up her feeling. He stretched out his hand and engulfed hers with it. His grip was stronger than she expected. "Me not runnin' ain't the end of the world, Andi. You'll figure somethin' out."

She nodded. It could be the end of *her* world.

2

Andi called Ed. "Hi, you," he said. "You flew out of here early."

"I wanted to talk to Ben before morning briefing. Didn't work out."

Ed was quiet for a moment. "What happened?"

"I wanted to get his advice about my idea for the campaign—but they took him for an MRI before I could tell him about it."

He said, "You planning on telling me that idea?" He paused. "I'm sorry, that sounded pouty. Want to talk now?"

"No, Ed. I want us to climb the Coliseum. I need to think this through."

Without a moment's hesitation, he came back, "Great. I'll throw water and some trail food in the backpack. Meet you in town in twenty minutes."

"Best thing I've heard all morning."

"Huh. And it's only eight-fifteen."

3

At the southern end of Monastery Valley, high up Mount Adams, the Coliseum, a glacial cirque, loomed thirteen hundred feet above St. Brendan's Monastery on Lake St. Mary's western shore, itself eight-thousand feet above the valley floor. Generations ago, the valley settlers had decided the glacial cirque resembled the Roman gladiators' arena, though at the time there was fierce debate about how to spell the name. Telling the story, Magnus Anderssen always capped it with "My great-great-grandpa Günter's camp lost *that* spelling bee. Politics were a little tamer in those days."

Folks hiked the Coliseum's trails for recreation, or for hunting, or for those encounters with solitude that are the parent of wisdom. Ed, walking a few yards behind Andi, knew she was seeking the last.

Halfway up the trail, where it verged close to a granite ledge, she stopped. "Ed, I'm going to stand on the edge. My brain's running a mile a minute—I need to feel the silence."

Ed grimaced. Four years ago, before Grace, up here during the bitter winter of his depression, he'd contemplated stepping off into the void. Andi's moving toward the brink unnerved him. He told himself his apprehension didn't apply here, was a hangover from his own *black dog*. There'd be no suicide today on the Coliseum. He clamped down on his nerves and chose a boulder to sit on. "I'll just wait here."

Andi dropped her pack, moved to the edge, her body stilled. Ed watched her, talking to himself: Andi wasn't suicidal, just upset about something. If she'd meant to kill herself, she'd have come alone, would have brought her gun. *Shut up.* He slowed his breath. Waited. The breeze ascending the cliff face rippled Andi's sleeves. As they hiked, he let himself enjoy the stillness of her body etched against the blue sky. *My wife, in my mind. And come spring, in reality.*

After ten minutes, Andi turned toward him, and Ed stood. "Got what you needed?"

"Some. I'm a little quieter inside."

"How about we talk about it?"

"Not ready."

They continued up the trail. After another hundred yards or so, steep switchbacks replaced the easier upward trail. Andi kept the lead; behind, Ed admired her steady gait. And the muscular ripple of her legs. And the snug fit of her shorts. His intuition was that she was grappling with Ordrew's running unopposed, but she'd voiced that issue before. *Why not now?* Maybe he was wrong. When they topped the last switchback, they entered a dense, cool cedar grove, and stood for a few minutes, catching their breaths, drinking water. He watched her. She smiled. "Those switchbacks always clear out my brain."

"Yeah. Feels good in here."

The trail out of the grove angled up again, curving across a long rising meadow, then through a stand of alpine fir, and emerged onto the meadow above the cirque. Andi went out to the lip, where the grass gave way to bare rock, and lowered her pack to the ground. She stood approximately where Ed had almost stepped off, that hard day four years ago. He sat on the grass behind her, watching.

For a long time, she stared out over the tiny lake beside the miniature red-roofed monastery below, out to the long north reach of Monastery Valley, out over the river running its lingering westerly arc. *She'll talk when her time's right.* He lay back in the meadow grass, enjoying the sun's warmth on his face. He replayed the memory of Jim's "marrying" them last fall, in this same meadow. Above, an eagle circled, black against the blue. He dozed.

A shadow darkened his closed eyes. He looked up. Andi stood above him, an aura of sunlight haloing her. Her face was resolved. "I know what to do."

MONDAY, SEPTEMBER 3, LABOR DAY

1

Despite its being Labor Day, the on-duty crew was drifting in for morning report. Catching Pete outside the conference room a few minutes early, Andi said, "Can we talk? In the office?"

Pete said, "Sure, but quick. The guys'll be waiting."

He closed the office door. "What's up?"

"The election. Ben made it clear he's not running, and I can't stand the thought of Brad running unopposed. He's as much as told me I'll be fired if he's sheriff. I—"

Pete interrupted. "The sheriff can't just fire a deputy, Andi. You know that. Due process. He needs cause."

"If he wants to find cause, he will. So, I'm thinking you ought to run, and I'll work for your campaign."

He laughed a quick, short laugh. "Not a chance, Andi. I'm not cut out to be the boss. I was telling Lucy last night, I hate this Acting Sheriff job. I'm a born deputy." He chuckled again.

She ignored the stab of anxiety, forced herself back to the calm certainty she'd felt yesterday on the Coliseum. "Come on, Pete, you'd make a great sheriff. You've got the skills, you've been around a long time, and the people respect you." She saw she was losing him. "I'm sorry to be so pushy. But we can't let Brad just waltz into office."

Pete shook his head. "I don't want Brad to be boss any more than you do, but I'm not the guy for that job."

Andi turned away in exasperation, but then wheeled back. "Pete, name one deputy who's got any more experience in this department than you. You're the senior deputy, and you've got acting sheriff experience. You're the—."

Pete lifted his hand. "I said no, Andi. And you're as experienced in police work as I am."

Andi felt hollow. "Even if it means Brad takes over?"

Pete hesitated, then rubbed his forehead. "Run against him, Andi. You'd win. You have more to lose than I do."

Her breath caught. "God, no." She scrambled to subdue the sudden burst of fear. "I'm not interested in administration." It felt feeble. It *was* feeble. "I dislike meetings as much as you do. More."

"Hell, you know as well as I do Callie runs this shop. Ben lets her do all that admin stuff, and I do too. You'd still be a cop."

She shivered, shook her head.

Pete asked, "What?"

"You'd be a better sheriff than I would." Her smile, forced, hid her anxiety. "Back to work, eh?"

Pete stood and held out his hand; Andi shook it. "I'm sorry, Andi. I know this is tough for you. But you're the one."

For the moment, she felt touched. But her realization grew: *I can't do this job.* Turning to leave, captive to her sense of failure, she missed seeing the worry in Pete's eyes.

2

Churning inside, she walked into report ahead of Pete. As he read the assignments for this evening's fireworks at Magnus Anderssen's Double-A Ranch, she half-listened, scanning the men in the room. The idea that she couldn't do the job had rattled her—when had she failed a job before? So absorbed was she in the speculation, she was caught off guard when he said, "Andi, fill us in about the Essex case."

She hesitated a moment, trying to shift her thoughts onto the case. "We're continuing to investigate, Pete. There are still discrepancies in Mr. Essex's story that we're trying to sort out." *Lame. Might as well say the dog ate my homework.*

A thin smile formed on Brad Ordrew's lips. He lifted a hand. "Question?"

Wary, she nodded.

"Can you actually name some of these, uh, *discrepancies*?" he said, his sarcasm venomous. Andi felt stung.

She gathered herself. Xav looked at her, then started to speak. Andi interrupted him. "Thanks, Xav, I've got it." She focused on Ordrew. "The guy claims the kid attacked and he shot him in the front, but he

133

shot the vic in the back. He mislead us into thinking the gun we confiscated was the murder weapon, but he'd hidden the actual weapon in his house. He claimed he'd gone to get his weapon and put on the belt as he went out, but we have information that he wore his gun around the house. He said he always, make that *always*, put his car in the garage and lowered the door, but the car was out on the drive and the door was up. And on and on."

"'And on and on.' What kind of evidence is 'and on and on'?" Ordrew looked around, as if looking for agreement. No one spoke. "There are protocols for detective work, and 'on and on' doesn't appear in them." He stood, frowning. "Well, I've got patrol this morning, so I'm outta here." He stood.

Pete's voice was soft, but granite-hard. "Brad."

"Pete?"

"I think Andi deserves an apology."

Ordrew narrowed his dark eyes. "Well then, Pete, why don't you give her one?" He turned and left the room.

When he'd left, Pete said, "I'm sorry about that, Andi."

Andi let her anger put some steel in her voice. "Not your problem, Pete. Thanks for the support, though."

"Don't pay Ordrew any attention, Andi," Chip Coleman said. "He'll ease up when Ben beats his ass." The others chuckled.

Andi formed her words carefully. "Well, that's what worries me." Took a breath. "Ben's not going to run, which leaves Brad unopposed."

"Whoa. What's that mean?" The other deputies, the ones who hadn't known, looked around at one another, then at Andi.

"Doc says he's too sick to run."

Pete lifted a hand, warning. "Guys, until Ben goes public with this, let's keep it among ourselves."

The deputies in the room looked at one another, but no one spoke. Andi watched as a shadow eclipsed Chip's momentary optimism.

Lannie McAllister looked shocked. He asked, "So, Ben won't be sheriff?"

She wondered if she should bring in her personal stake in the election. *No. Too much self-pity. An Ordrew win puts us all in the same boat.* "That's right. Unless somebody steps up, Bradley's our next boss."

Loren Sanders grinned. "You're the one, Andi. You'd be a great sheriff. We'd all be behind you." Heads nodded, two or three voices agreed.

She felt the knife edge of her fear inching close. "I've been here, what, going on six years—everybody but Brad's been here longer."

Loren laughed. "That don't mean nothing," he said. "You're the best-known deputy on the force. Everybody in the valley knows about, uh, what happened." Ballplayers don't mention their pitcher's no-hitter, and cops don't use the word "shot" about a partner.

"Not me," she said. "Adams County's not liberal enough for a female sheriff. And I'm not the sheriff type."

Chipper Coleman's eyebrows arched. "You never know if you don't try."

She thought, *And I won't prove it by blowing the job.*

3

A little before noon, Ed called Grace, who, he realized when her phone rolled over to voicemail, was probably still asleep. To the machine he said, "Hi, kiddo, just calling to see how you're doing. Give me a ring." Early yesterday morning, before he and Andi hiked the Coliseum, Grace had called, half-crying and half-angry because Zach had broken up with her with no warning, because she'd had dinner with Garth. "He's acting like a jerk," he'd told her.

An hour later, when she called, her voice sparkled. "'Give me a ring'? You set your cell to buzz, Northrup. What's this 'ring' business?"

He smiled. "An expression."

"Yeah, from the Middle Ages."

"So, how'd your talk with Zach go yesterday?" When she'd called about Zach's break-up text, Ed had encouraged her to confront him.

"Not so good at first. He got all jealous at me about Garth and then he started to brag about this new girl he's found."

"Nice," Ed said.

"Yeah, real nice. I got pissed and told him to stuff it. He looked real surprised. Then I told him you said he was being a jerk."

"Doubt he took that well."

"He shut up. He respects you a lot, you know. Anyway, I told him mature adults talk about hurt feelings, they don't just trade in their girlfriend."

He waited a moment. "And then?"

"You were right, Northrup. It worked. He got all sad and told me he thought he was losing me. I told him that was silly, Garth's just a friend I met at orientation. I said, 'I'm your girlfriend, damn it, Zach.'"

"I'm guessing Zach didn't get himself a new girlfriend. I'll bet he said that to make you jealous."

Grace was silent a moment. "Wow, Northrup. You're right, that's what he said. I'm surprised."

"About what?"

She waited a beat. "That a guy as old as you knows this stuff."

4

Hoping it would help her shake her lousy mood, Andi dialed Brenda Cantor's number. Answering how her relationship with Daniel Essex turned "weird" might drag some of the unknowns into the daylight.

"It's been a couple days since we talked, and I wonder if we could meet . . ."

Brenda said nothing, so Andi waited. "It's Labor Day, Andi. A holiday."

Andi hated pushing her, and intruding on a holiday didn't make it easier. "Ten minutes. Fifteen. Just fill me in on how Daniel got weird." She took a breath. "Please, Brenda. I need all the information we can get to help us at trial."

After another long silence, Brenda sighed. "All right. If I have to."

Andi noticed she made no promise of coffee this time. This talk could be tougher.

•   •   •

When Andi sat at the still-clean table, Brenda surprised her. "I made coffee. Want some?"

Andi nodded, relieved. "Thanks. That'll hit the spot."

Brenda set two steaming cups on the table and sat across from her. "I'm sorry if I seemed uncooperative, Andi. This is . . . hard. Real hard."

"I understand, Brenda. I promise you, if this isn't relevant to the shooting, it'll never see the light of day."

Brenda lifted her cup toward her lips, then put it down without taking a sip. "Look, if what we did is illegal, do you have to arrest me?"

Andi considered that. "There's all kinds of illegal. How about this: If this weirdness involved hurting somebody else, yeah, I'll have to do something about it."

"We didn't hurt anybody else." Across her cheeks, a red flush had spread.

"Okay, then. If you and Daniel *plotted* to harm somebody else, I have to do something, but if you help me, I'll do everything I can to make sure it's on him, not you." Andi shifted uncomfortably. She couldn't guarantee anything except how hard she'd work to make that true.

"No, no plot." She breathed a shaky rattling breath, then lifted her cup to her lips. This time, sipped. Andi thought, *Buying time.*

After a long moment, Brenda looked at the table, said, "He made me watch pornography with him. On his computer." Her face blushed. She kept her eyes down.

"Were children involved?"

"No." Brenda looked shocked.

Andi relaxed. It didn't bring her any closer to Daniel Essex the shooter, but it didn't hurt Brenda either. "Girl, porn's disgusting, but there's nothing illegal about watching it, as long as it wasn't under-age kids."

"It *is* disgusting. So, you don't have to tell anybody?" Brenda's eyes were pleading. Andi remembered from years ago the wide terrified eyes of a thirteen-year-old girl she'd found working West 47th Street in Cook County. Andi had taken her to Project Freedom, where they tried to save these kids who'd been trafficked into prostitution. And, seething with rage so deep she didn't even comprehend it, she swiftly went out on the street to find the pimp, whom she wanted to pistol whip.

"No, I don't. Not ever, Brenda." Andi felt deflated—Essex watching porn with his girlfriend gave no support to her intuition that Daniel Essex wasn't merely "standing his ground." She sensed something, somewhere close; she couldn't pin it down, but she'd caught a hint of something foul.

As she stood to leave, Brenda looked up at her, eyes pleading. "You're sure Daniel will never know I told you?"

Andi put her hand on Brenda's shoulder. "Positive. I've got your back on that."

5

Pete had assigned four deputies to work Magnus Anderssen's fireworks this evening. Andi was the fourth. The deputies roamed the newly mown pasture while the families were gathering, setting up lawn chairs, opening coolers of food. The field lay along the Monastery River, a small part of Magnus's enormous Double-A Ranch, near where the Ladies' Fishing Society met in the summer. Andi meandered casually, greeting people, smiling, but preoccupied. Mostly she was stewing about Pete's refusal to run. He was near the river with Lucy, his wife, comfortable in their lawn chairs, each holding a can of beer. *Beer*. She had an intuition about Essex's refrigerator, but she couldn't craft it into words.

Maybe Xavier? He'd been in the department more than fifteen years and was universally liked and respected, except by the valley's white supremacists—and hardly a dozen of those were known to the department. She surveyed the families scattered over the fragrant green grass. Everyone looked happy. Bursts of laughing punctuated the murmuring conversations.

The walkie-talkie clipped to her shoulder pad crackled. She answered, "Pelton."

She'd plugged the earphone in. "Lannie here. How's your area?"

She pitched her voice low. "Couldn't be quieter. Yours?"

"The same. Ordrew's off duty, right? Well, he's here, passing out those campaign flyers like they're candy tossed off a parade float."

Her stomach clenched. "Damn. See if you can get a sense of how people are feeling about them." Her shoulders tightened. She strolled into the cottonwoods lining the riverbank, hoping she looked more casual than she felt. Men, and a few women, stood in small groups at the water's edge. Closer to Magnus's StreamSide Lodge, a hundred yards or so farther into the shoreline trees, Ed was talking with Magnus and Ted. She walked over.

"What're you scoundrels plotting here in the woods?"

"Hi, Andi," said Magnus. Ted Coldry tipped his ball cap. "Andrea, you're stunning in sheriff's brown tonight."

138

She laughed and looked around. Seeing no eyes following her, she leaned up and kissed Ed.

"Whoa," Ed said. "Thought on-duty fraternization is frowned upon."

"Boss's not here to see." The minute she said it, the mood shifted, as sudden as sunlight blocked by a speeding cloud.

Magnus nodded. "I saw Ben this afternoon. Not a happy man. Doc's not going to sign off on him running for re-election. He's disappointed." He reached back and pulled a crumpled page from his hip pocket. Ordrew's flyer. "This piece of crap tells me the valley's got a problem."

Andi nodded. "Lannie said Ordrew's passing those out." She gestured toward the field rapidly filling with families.

Magnus nodded. "It's so. He handed me this one. What're you thinking, Andi?"

"I asked Pete to consider running, but he said no. I'm thinking maybe Xavier would make a good candidate."

Ted said, "I don't know him very well, but I'm sure he would. But what about you, Andrea? You'd—"

She cut him off with a wave of her hand. "Not me. A female sheriff isn't something people are ready for."

Magnus looked at her, his eyes quiet. After a moment, he said, his voice kind, "Or perhaps it's the female sheriff who's not ready."

She caught Ed looking at her quizzically. She knew he wanted to second Magnus's motion, urge her to campaign. Abruptly, she turned away. "Gotta get back to work," she managed.

As she walked back toward the mown field and the gathered families, she forced herself to stop brooding and concentrated her questions on Essex's beer. Why were there sixty if he couldn't replace ten, only six or eight or twelve or some multiple that would leave either more or fewer than sixty? What if he replaced them with a twelve-pack? Wouldn't that mean two extras, or that he drank two—but why only *two*? Or . . . No. That couldn't be . . . Could it?

TUESDAY, SEPTEMBER 4

1

Next morning, before she got to work tracking down Essex's beer purchases, she decided to take a shot at talking Xavier into running for sheriff. He was off duty, so she called and invited herself out. "Sure, Andi. Come over. 'Strella is making sweet tortillas."

Xavier and his family lived on the south edge of Jefferson. Across the street from their house began the northernmost pastures of Magnus Anderssen's Double-A ranch. She sat a moment looking south over the fields. Splotches of yellow-brown, more from late summer dryness than from early autumn, dappled the line of cottonwoods and poplars along the river. Higher up, green forests looked cool and deep. *I love it here,* she thought. She climbed out of her vehicle, breathed in the mountain air, and walked up to the house.

Xavier's wife, Estrella, brought them coffee and the tortillas baked with honey. She started to leave the room, but Andi said, "Estrella, stay. You need to hear what I want to say."

Estrella's eyes widened, but she sat down.

Xavier grinned. "You're here about the election."

Andi managed a laugh. "Word travels. I'm the local recruiter."

"Pete called. He figured you'd be coming."

"So, you've had some time to think about it."

Xavier nodded, took a tortilla, and looked tenderly at his wife, then back to Andi. "We have talked."

"And your decision?"

"We think Pete or you are the best for the job."

Andi pushed through the tightening in her chest. She wondered if the flush she felt across her chest and throat reached her face. "Pete says no, and the valley's not ready for a female sheriff." She smiled at Xavier, but felt a bit guilty at that evasive reason not to run. She wasn't ready to admit she was afraid. "You haven't given me your decision."

He said nothing. After a moment, Estrella, who, like Magnus's wife Luisa and unlike Xavier himself, had been born in Mexico, spoke softly. "Xavier desires it, but he will say no."

"Is that your thinking, Xav?"

"Yeah, I want it. But it's complicated. Being Mexican-American in the valley isn't always easy. Some people doubt our loyalty, even more since Trump. There'd be some ugly things said in the campaign, and I'm not going to put my family through that."

"The department has to be neutral, but the deputies will support you. And Ben will endorse you, loudly and firmly. That would count a lot."

Xavier said nothing for a bit. "Yes, it would. The valley is mostly a good place, but some people here are . . ." He paused. ". . . uncomfortable with Latinos."

"You were born in Billings, for God's sake," she snapped, then reined herself in. "Man, I'm sorry. I know how Ordrew thinks about you. If he wins, you'll have to live with him." She felt cruel pushing him: What he'd said was true enough.

"I know, but it's not just Bradley. There are some folks like him in the valley. Please, understand. I have children. They're doing fine and have good friends, but they still get some criticism at school. I cannot put them through more, Andi."

He didn't need to hit her over the head with it: She didn't have children, no family to worry about. Whatever shit would descend on her would not spill over onto kids.

But onto Grace, her "step-girlfriend"?

She forced a smile. "Well, thanks for considering it, Xav." She stood to go, numb.

Xavier walked her to the door. "It's you, Andi. You're the one to take Ben's place."

She felt a chill. For a moment, she just looked at him, then turned and left. At her vehicle, she waved. He waved back.

Standing there, Andi hardly felt the sun. Despite the cloudless blue of the sky, she felt muddled, obscured. A small corner of her mind, though, wondered what *really* made her afraid to run. And then, she wasn't numb any more. She grabbed her cell phone and angrily touched the number for Art's Fine Foods. *Might as well get some damn work done.*

2

Two minutes before ten, Ed heard his waiting room door open. *Protector*, he thought. *Right on time.* This morning might be his first meeting with the child-part Connie, if he could overcome Protector's reluctance.

If not, they'd stick with the finger signals.

Protector, who had always waited for him to ask the first question, surprised him. Before he'd even sat, she said, "I insist on rules, Doctor."

"Sure, Protector. Let's talk about them."

"First, you will meet with Connie and no one else. I will prevent any of the others, especially the One, from coming."

"Agreed."

"Connie has two rules, which I will tell you in a moment. My rules first. You must remain in your chair."

"Absolutely." *I wouldn't leave it anyway,* He thought. *Safety must be high on her list today.* "What else?"

"You must ask no questions about anything that may have happened to Connie in her life. None whatsoever."

Ed hesitated. "Let me be clear. Are you setting this rule for today's session, or for all sessions?"

Her eyes flashed. "Forever."

Ed considered that. "Well, I will agree with your rule for now, if you'll relax the rule once Connie feels safe with me."

Protector said nothing. Her eyes went dull for a moment, then sharpened. "The rule is forever. But we will allow you to ask to relax it. We may not agree to allow it, though."

Good enough. One step at a time. "I'll accept that, for now." The stakes—Connie's safety—were so high, Ed assumed that all the parts were listening, intent, ready to react if he asked the wrong things, and he wanted to be clear. "But please, you should know, at some point I may *need* to learn more about Connie's experience so I can help you protect her. Do you understand?"

Again, Protector's eyes went dull, then she returned. "We understand."

"Do you have more rules?"

She nodded. "Connie's rules, now. First, you must not look at her."

"I should keep my eyes closed?"

"No. You are to turn your chair around."

"Wow, that's a hard one, Protector. I—"

She interrupted. "Connie insists. If you do not, she will not come to talk to you. And her second rule is that you mustn't get out of your chair."

He disliked the notion of turning his chair. Not being able to gauge a patient's non-verbals robbed him of critical information. *Still, one step at a time.* "Yes. I already told you I wouldn't leave my chair."

"You told me. You did not tell Connie."

"Ah." *How literal dissociated thinking can be.* "Okay. I promise Connie I will turn my chair around and I won't get up while she's with me."

Protector was silent; her face took on the distant stare of her listening within. "Very well. Turn your chair."

"Before I do, I have a rule too. I need Connie to promise me she will not get up or leave my office and that she will go back inside when we're finished."

Protector nodded; Ed thought a sliver of a smile played briefly over her lips. Her eyes closed. Her breathing relaxed. Then, in a minute, she returned. "Connie says no to your rule."

He sighed. "Then I'm afraid we can't meet as we had hoped. Perhaps we can use the finger signals again?"

Protector closed her eyes. In a moment, she opened them. "No."

3

"Laurie, it's Andi Pelton again. You have a minute?"

"Sure. What's cooking?"

"I have two questions. If I needed to see one of your customer's sales receipts, could I do that? With a search warrant, of course."

"With a search warrant? Can't see any reason not."

"Second question, how far back do you keep those receipts?"

"Shoot, they're all on the computer. As far back as the computer system goes."

"Mid-July of this year?"

"Oh, sure."

"Great. I'll be there with the warrant. Within the hour."

•　　　•　　　•

Laurie was near the check-out counters when Andi came in an hour and a half later. "That was quick," she said.

Andi laughed. "Took longer than I expected. Judge Flure gave me a hard time."

"Well, come on up to my office." They climbed the stairs and Laurie pointed at a chair. "Grab a chair and I'll find what you're looking for."

Andi gave her a copy of the warrant, and a slip of paper on which she'd written the credit card account numbers for both of Essex's cards, which she'd copied from the cards in his wallet, in the evidence room. "I didn't know if your sales receipts were filed according to the credit card numbers or names, so I included both."

"We go by account numbers if they use a card. Some people pay cash, and those receipts don't have any name on them. You're wanting slips for . . ." She looked up. "Oh," she said.

Word's out about Essex, Andi thought.

Laurie studied the warrant again. "Daniel Essex's sales receipts. So, this is about the shooting."

"Yeah."

"I heard he's claiming stand-your-ground."

"Uh, Laurie, I—"

"And you can't talk about it."

"Also yeah."

Laurie smiled. "So, you want all his sales receipts since July 16."

"That's right." She thought about it. "No, can I get them from June 1?"

"Sure." Laurie worked the keyboard for a moment, then sat back. After a few seconds, she said, "Got 'em." She hit *Print*, and pages began emerging from the printer. Laurie gave them to Andi.

"Very slick," Andi said. "I appreciate how easy this was." She counted the pages—four, with four receipts on each page. Sixteen. She stood and shook Laurie's hand.

Laurie smiled. "Hope you find what you're looking for."

Andi thought, *I hope I don't.*

•　　　•　　　•

At her desk, Andi studied the receipts. The beer purchases on July 16 she already knew. Otherwise, between June 1 and today, September 4, there had been no additional beer purchases. None. And no receipts for cash at all. She thought about that. With no names on cash receipts, there wouldn't be any. She grabbed a yellow legal pad, jotted notes to make sure she was thinking through this logically.

- *Found: 60 cans—48 in fridge/floor and 12 on bench, all bought July 16*
- *Solo beer purchase 7/16 at Art's; same numbers and brands found in garage*
- *First burglary three weeks b4 shooting—10 cans stolen: leaves 38 + 12 on bench.*
- *But all 60 July 16 cans accounted for—45 in fridge, 12 on workbench, 3 in custody*
- *Conclusion: <u>Had</u> to buy 10 replacements—either 12-pack or could be six- and four singles*
- *If not 6 + 4, what's possible? 2 six-packs or 12-pack—leaves 2 extras—unless he/someone drank 2. But why drink only two?*
- *And why replace any if you don't plan to drink them?*

She double-checked Essex's credit card numbers. Both were bank VISA cards, one a Massachusetts bank, the second from Wells Fargo Montana. She was glad she'd written the warrant to include getting those account statements. If he'd bought replacement cans elsewhere, odds were it'd most be in another grocery store or C-store, either in town or elsewhere. The credit card statements could show her where purchases were made, so she could search for receipts there.

If there were no beer purchases on credit, he could have used cash. She drummed her fingers on the desktop. *Damn.* How to track that? Cash receipts don't carry a customer name. *First things first,* she thought. Time to send a copy of the warrant to VISA legal.

Once she'd sent it off, she returned to the problem of tracking cash. She needed to talk it over with somebody. She tapped Ed's cell phone number. No answer.

She called a couple of the deputies. *No answers, everybody's busy.*

Brad Ordrew came into the deputies' room and sauntered past her cubicle.

She thought, *Why not?*

4

"Brad, I have a problem with the Essex case I could use your help with."

He stopped. *She wants* my *help? What's with that?* He stepped into Chip Coleman's cube, which faced hers, sat on the edge of Chip's desk, and folded his arms, curious, wary. "What's the problem?"

"I'm thinking my way through a situation with the shooting and I'd appreciate some help with my logic."

Where's this heading? He kept his face neutral. "Go."

She laid it out, following the notes she'd just written.

"You're wondering where the replacement beers are."

"Not quite. I know where *they* are—in his garage. What I don't get is if he replaced them with a twelve-pack, he must've drunk two, but why only two in here weeks? And if he replaced the ten with a six-pack and singles, why didn't he drink any? Why buy them if you don't intend to drink them?"

That stopped him. *Didn't catch that.* "Good questions," he allowed.

"A couple other things. I'm confused—he buys sixty beers, puts forty-eight cheap ones in the fridge, and leaves a pricey microbrew twelve-pack on the workbench. During the heat of summer. Would you do that?"

He smiled. "Not in a month of Sundays." He thought a moment. "Maybe the guy likes cheap beer?"

"Maybe. But then why the expensive microbrew?"

He shrugged again. "Another good question." *Damn, she's thinking like a real cop.*

"Here's another thing I don't get. Let's say he likes the cheap stuff. He loses ten to a burglar. So, he replaces them. Laurie Swenson at Art's tells me they don't sell singles or ten-packs, just sixes and twelves. So, he buys a twelve, or two sixes, which leaves him with two extras. But on the night Bernardo was shot, the extras aren't in either the garage fridge or his kitchen fridge. In two or three weeks, from the burglary till the shooting, he only drinks *two* beers? I don't think so."

Ordrew looked at her a moment, then nodded. *She's right.* "Beer drinkers," he said, "the guys who buy four or five twelve-packs at one time, *drink* their beer, they don't leave it sitting in the garage."

"Okay. So, here's my idea: I just requested his VISA statements for the whole summer. They'll tell me if he shopped any place other than Art's that can sell beer. Then I get his sales receipts from those stores and see if he bought any." She tilted her head. "Logic? Am I missing something?"

That's what I'd do. "Not that I can see. I think you're on the right track. It gets tougher if your VISA search turns up lots of purchases in other groceries or C-stores."

Andi sighed. "True. That's a cop's life, though. Tedious." She looked thoughtful. "What reason would he have to buy outside of Jeff? Nobody knew he'd lost the beers. Why would he hide buying replacements?"

"Maybe he was on a business trip and remembered he had to replace them?"

"Daniel works from home. Some computer job."

"What if he paid cash?"

"That's the hard one. I can talk to all the checkouts at Art's and at the Conoco C-store, show them his picture. Any ideas?"

"There are a lot of grocery stores in Montana."

"You're right." She rubbed her eyes. "I sure as hell can't carry his picture around the whole state of Montana." She sat upright. "Wait. I can get on the horn with the surrounding sheriffs and fax them the photo and ask them to see if they can find anyone remembers selling Essex beer for cash."

Hell, I'd never think of that. "My money's on him doing the obvious—buying them here."

"What if he wanted to hide the purchase from us?"

Ordrew looked at her. "Why would he want to do that?"

She held her hands open, palms up. "Can't see a reason. We didn't know there'd been a burglary."

He stood up from the edge of the desk. "Me, neither. But if he used cash, you're back to zero."

Andi shrank a bit. "Yeah. That's the snake under the rock, isn't it?"

That's one hell of an image, he thought.

5

Ordrew sat stony at his own desk. Much as he wanted to, he couldn't find fault with her thinking. His contempt for her felt weakened, like it was seeping out of him. In fact, he had to admit she'd surprised him a couple of times. One was when she mentioned Essex's drinking two beers all summer. That was a good catch. Or the one about contacting all the surrounding sheriffs. *I've got to start thinking small town—these guys work together more than departments in LAPD.* That thought pissed him off. *Why the hell should I have to learn something from a damn woman?*

After a moment's brood, he muttered to himself, "Okay, maybe for now she's thinking about this case the way a cop should think." Then thought, *But she'll break the rules eventually, like she did with that Hansen kid last spring.*

Ed Northrup, Pelton's boyfriend, had concealed Jared Hansen, who'd planned a school shooting, hoping to diagnose the boy's erratic behavior and paranoid thinking. Andi had learned of Ed's move, and kept it to herself for a couple of days. Ordrew had uncovered the deception, which confirmed his contempt—female cops don't follow the rules.

He thought of Reverend Loyd Crane. *Why'd Crane tell me to give Pelton his name?* How was she involved with him? Maybe Pelton was corrupt after all?

His contempt crept back in.

6

That evening, Ed sat on the porch alone, savoring the quiet. Andi was in town, and Grace was doing something with her girls. Over the Monastery Range, where the sun had just set, the clouds were jumbled, askew, so red he thought of blood. There was no evening breeze. He wondered why the child-alter Connie had said "No" to his rule. Had he pushed too fast?

The phone rang inside. He jumped up to answer it.

It was Ben Stewart. "Hi, Ben, something wrong?"

"Ain't nothin' wrong, bud, somethin's right for a change. I'm goin' home soon as Bernie picks me up." Ben had taken the news that the valley knew about his affair with a heavy dose of uncaring. He'd never mentioned it, and when Ed had brought it up, he'd retorted, "If a young buck can shoot a kid for stealin' a beer, I figure an old guy can have a damn love life."

Now, he went on, "Doc Keeley says no work for a month and I gotta walk three miles a day." Ed knew Ben's basic attitude toward exercise: It happened on planets Ben would never visit. But after last year's first heart attack, he'd come to enjoy his walks—not to mention that walking every morning with the ladies of his neighborhood had led to his affair with Bernie.

"Anyway, I ain't callin' you. Your lady home?"

"No, she's out and about."

"That'd be why her cell phone's off. Tell her to give me a call in the mornin'. I'm thinkin' she's gotta run."

"Something bothers her about that. I think she's afraid of it."

"Hell's bells. Everybody's afraid to run. You get over it real quick. Just have her call me."

"Will do." Ed thought he was about to hang up, but Ben added, "Better yet, tell her I'll see her in the mornin'. At the station."

"Ben? Doc said no work for a month, didn't he?"

Ben hung up with a snort.

WEDNESDAY, SEPTEMBER 5

1

Preoccupied with the question of Essex's motive, Andi tucked copies of his booking photo in her pocket and walked fast down Division Street to Art's Fine Foods. She found Laurie Swenson. "Hi, Laurie. I wonder if you'd let me show a photo to your checkout clerks?"

"Don't see why not. Is it still about the murder?"

"Yeah. We've got a question I think they can help answer."

But none of the three checkout clerks recalled Daniel Essex buying beer with cash. All three wanted to talk about the murder. "I think it's horrible," Jonna Erickson said. "His mom must be a wreck." She handed the photo back to Andi. "He never pays cash. Never. Will he get off?"

"I don't know, Jonna. That's for a jury to decide." She thanked Jonna and moved to the next aisle.

When Andi gave her the photo, Karla Randall asked, "Is he for real claiming the kid attacked him?"

How the hell do these things get out? She made an uncomfortable sound. "I'm sorry, Karla, but I'm not free to talk about the case. Tell me, though—he ever pay cash for beer that you know of?"

"Uh-uh. No way. I seen his wallet a couple times when he was getting his credit card, and I never saw no cash in it."

"Thanks, Karla. That helps."

At her register, Ella Parks said, "I ain't never seen him pay cash. But one time, something he did struck me strange. The customer 'fore him leaves her change on the counter. I calls after her but she don't hear. I ain't allowed to leave my till unattended, so I says to him, 'You mind taking her change to her?' Get this, he turns real pale, and he's like, 'No, I don't touch money. It's invested.' Or some word like that."

Andi's radar was working. "Might he have said 'infested'?"

"That's it, yeah."

Andi made a note. "He said he doesn't touch money?"

Ella nodded.

"Thanks, that might help a lot. Would you be willing to testify to that?"

Ella looked like she'd won the lottery. "In a heartbeat, Andi. Anything to help nail that creep. Killing a kid over beer." She made a spitting sound.

Andi returned to Laurie Swenson's office. "Thanks, Laurie. You've got more checkers than this, right?"

"You bet. I'll show his picture to the others and I'll call you if we hit the jackpot."

"Call me either way, okay?"

She left Art's and walked farther south on Division Street to the Conoco station C-store at the edge of town. Emily Reston was behind the counter.

Andi asked about getting the sales receipts for Essex's VISA accounts.

"You'll have to talk to Marv on that, Andi. He's manager now. He'll be in at four."

"Okay. I'll come back." She showed her Essex's photo.

Emily looked at the photo. "This is the Essex jerk. Never seen him buy anything here, but he's always coming in after he pumps his gas to pay me."

"He doesn't pay at the pump?"

"Nope. He comes in and stares at my tits while I'm running his card. Every time I look at him, I expect to see drool on his chin." Emily was in her mid-twenties, slender and busty.

"Jerks come in all flavors, don't they?"

"I'll say. Oh, there's something else strange about him. When I hand his card back, he always wipes it with his hanky."

"Really?" *Now that's anal*, she thought. It backed up what Ella Parks had said. *He doesn't touch money. It's infested.*

"Yeah. Grosses me out."

"So, on your shifts, he buys nothing but gas, and he always comes in with his credit card."

"And his filthy mind."

Andi wrinkled her forehead, thinking. "How many clerks work here? I know you and Marv. I'm trying to remember the others."

"There's two others, Becky Albright and Johanna Fall. I open at seven and Marv takes over till close, weekdays. Becky does days on the weekends and Johanna's nights."

"Look, if I leave the photo and my card, could you have the other clerks call me if anyone remembers Mr. Essex buying beer with cash? I'd sure appreciate it. And tell Marv I'll be coming in for the sales slips."

"No problem, Andi."

2

She got back to the station at one-twenty p.m. She called Brenda Cantor. "Hey, Brenda. Andi here. Any chance we could talk for a few minutes? Got a few things to follow-up on and I could use your help."

Brenda didn't answer.

Andi didn't wait. "I have some evidence that Daniel's not being honest about this shooting, and I'm getting closer to being able to prove that. Any answers you can give me will help a lot."

"I . . . I've told you everything I remember."

"Something new has come out that I'd like to get your reaction to."

"I suppose. I . . . I'm just nervous, I guess. Can we meet after work today?"

"Sure. When?"

"I get off at three-thirty. Meet me at my house?"

"You got it. See you then."

3

Opening her front door, Brenda looked apprehensive. They sat in the living room. Andi began, "There's something I forgot to tell you last time we talked. When I searched Essex's house after we talked the second time, I didn't find any sign of your clothes or possessions. Are you sure they were left there?"

Brenda stiffened. Offended at the implication? Or upset that her possessions were gone? Andi waited.

"You're kidding," Brenda muttered. "That bastard," was all she said before a long pause. Then, "I'll bet he burned everything, then fumigated the house."

Andi lifted her eyebrows. *"Fumigated?"*

"Daniel's a germaphobe. He's always washing his hands, and he bleaches his sinks and countertops every day. When he stops to gas up, he washes the windshield, but then he washes the steering wheel and the gearshift. He won't touch money or public things for anything. After he washes the steering wheel, he takes his credit card into the station for them to run it."

And to stare at Emily Reston's breasts. Andi felt a thrill. What Brenda described fit with Oxendine's findings about the car and her impression of his house. And it fit with what Ella Parks and Emily Reston had said. "He won't touch money? You mean cash?"

"Yeah," she nodded. "Says it's infested with microbes."

Same word. Ed would have a name for diagnosis. Andi offered, "I got the impression he was, uh, very tidy."

Brenda made a sound that, if she hadn't looked so disgusted, might have been a giggle. "'Tidy'? Daniel is to 'tidy' like a razor is to 'sharp.'"

"So, he didn't touch money? Ever? Isn't it possible he might have paid cash for something, at some point?"

Brenda disagreed firmly. "Not anytime when I was with him. He refuses to carry money. One time, we were out for dinner and I paid for mine with cash. He wouldn't let me in his car unless I washed my hands."

Andi made a note to that effect in her notebook. She looked up. "This could prove to be very important, Brenda. If it comes to that, will you testify to what you just told me?"

Brenda went still. She looked, Andi thought, like a rabbit in the sudden shadow of a swooping owl. After a moment, she whispered, "Testify? In court?"

Andi nodded. "It could be the thing that proves he's been lying to us about the shooting."

"I don't see how . . ."

"And I can't explain it at this point. But it's very important."

"Well, can I think about it?"

"Of course." Andi smiled. "Don't worry. We'll talk about it later." She thought about the beer problem. "Okay if I change the subject?" At Brenda's nod, she continued, "What kind of beer does Daniel drink?"

Brenda's eyes lifted, surprised. "Beer? Daniel doesn't drink beer."

"His garage refrigerator was full of beer." As she said it, Andi remembered: But not his kitchen fridge or cupboards.

"Really? No, he drinks Scotch. We had cocktails a couple nights a week—well, I did. Daniel drank every night, always two shots, and always single-malt Scotch. I'd drink vodka sours, and he always teased me about having a 'girlie drink.' He buys the best brands of Scotch and drinks a different one each evening. He says it's how 'educated' drinkers do it."

"Hmm." Andi jotted a note, remembering the expensive Scotches in his cupboard. "So. He won't use cash and he doesn't drink beer." She looked up at Brenda. "So, why's he stocking his garage with beer?"

Brenda looked blank. "I don't have any idea, Andi."

Andi thought, *I do.*

4

Later, as they were leaving afternoon report, Andi took Xavier aside. "Got a minute?"

His eyebrows went up. "Uh, sure. What's up?"

"I need to run something by you I just learned about Essex."

"Oh." His face relaxed. "Good, yeah. I was afraid you were going to ask me to run again."

"Wish I could, but I understand your situation, Xav." She briefed him about Brenda's information that Essex refused to touch cash and didn't drink beer. She buttressed that with Ella's and Emily's comments.

Xavier's face reddened. "Shoot, I forgot that about him and money. When I was doing the booking inventory, his wallet held no cash, just two credit cards. I asked him if he had any money in his pockets. He glared at me like I just swam the Rio Grande, and then he snapped. 'Cash carries disease. I refuse to handle it. And wash your fucking hands before you touch my things.'"

"Hmm. I don't remember that in the file."

He smiled weakly. "That's because I forgot to put it in. I'm sorry."

"No problem. Just get it in, soon as you can, okay?"

He looked at her, his eyes sympathetic. "Sure." He paused. "Andi, I felt terrible saying no yesterday, but I can't run. It's got to be you." He looked down. "I hope you're not pissed, but I called the guys, Pete, Lannie, Chip, all the others. Except Bradley, of course. We all think it's got to be you. And we're all behind you."

His words emptied her out. She leaned back against the wall, two fingers touching her lips. Magnus's gentle remark at the fireworks came back. *Maybe it's the female sheriff who's not ready.* He'd been right.

5

Another perfect September evening, the sky graying already at seven-thirty, the high forests rose-colored, the thin clouds above the ridges bluing in the last light. The air smelled sweet with the lingering fragrance of mown hay, ranchers up and down the valley putting up their autumn bales. Andi sat beside Ed on the porch, oblivious to the tranquility. Xavier's and Pete's refusals had rocked her harder than she'd expected. She had a decision to make.

Other than Pete, and maybe Xavier, no one else had a reasonable chance to beat Ordrew. Just her. And she didn't want it. *Why not, damn it?* Time to dig into this.

Instead, she told Ed what she'd learned from Brenda and observed in Essex's house. The suits, the matched shirts, the military order of his pill bottles. No dust bunnies under the beds. The refusal to touch money. Calling it "infested."

"Obsessive-compulsive. I'm surprised. Obsessive-compulsives aren't predisposed to shoot kids. Far too messy."

"He won't touch cash."

"You said that. Is it important?"

"He didn't use a credit card to buy beer at Art's or the gas station, so either he went somewhere else and used a card, or he forced himself to use cash."

Ed nodded. "Got it. If he's got a cash phobia, it's unlikely he'd touch it. I'd assume he used a card somewhere else."

"That's the loose end I need to tie up."

"Why? What's it got to do with the shooting?"

"Think about it. If he didn't replace the beers, he never lost them."

"He lied about the first burglary?"

"Yep. And get this: He doesn't even drink beer. He drinks single-malt Scotch, expensive stuff."

Ed cocked his head at her. "Which makes you think what?"

"That there's no obvious reason for him to have five twelve-packs of beer in his garage."

Grinning, he said, "I bet you've got a non-obvious reason."

She nodded. "Garage-hopping kids are typically sniffing for beer."

Ed's smile shut down. "That's a very ugly thought, Andi."

"It is. The beer might've been bait." She sighed. "Sometimes when you're not watching, this job turns real dark."

They sat, wordless, watching the slow darkening of the valley.

Ed stirred. "Something's missing."

Andi nodded in the dim light. "Yeah. A motive."

"Right. If he used beer as bait, why? Did he *want* to shoot somebody?"

"Brenda made it sound that way. Wearing his gun around the house, obsessing about intrusions, moving to Montana because we have a stand-your-ground law."

"Boy howdy, proving that could be hard."

"Tell me about it."

6

They fell into another silence. Andi's thoughts slipped to Ordrew's campaign. She tried to ignore her growing dismay, but after failing to dismiss it, she swallowed hard, turned toward Ed. "Xav said no."

He didn't answer.

After a moment, she said, "I'm not ready for this, Ed."

"Running for sheriff?"

"Yeah. No. Being sheriff."

Ed's voice was very soft, almost caressing. "Remember what Mack said, on Labor Day?"

"Maybe he's right. I don't think I can do the job."

"You afraid of it?"

"No, damn it." Her arms folded, guarding her heart: He'd seen into her. After a moment, she blew out a long, shuddery breath. "Okay, yeah. I'm afraid of it. It's one thing to work with the guys, earn their respect by doing the job. But being their boss? I don't know anything about that."

He said nothing. Andi's tension twisted tighter. He spoke kindly. "How many sheriffs have you worked for, besides Ben?"

At first, his question confused her. "What's that got to do—?"

"Humor me, okay? How many sheriffs?"

She shrugged. "In Cook County, my bosses were sergeants and captains. I'm guessing I worked for, oh, seven or eight over the years. Tell me why."

"Any of them particularly bad?"

She snorted. "Two come to mind." She narrowed her eyes at Ed, verging on annoyance. "Come on, why?"

"Stick with me. Any of your sergeants particularly *good* bosses?"

Okay. He's trying to help. She sat back, unfolding her arms. "Yeah, one special one. Larry Nichols. I don't think I know any deputy who didn't want to work for Larry." She smiled. "He was a lot like Ben, come to think of it."

"So, you know how *not* to be a boss, and you know how to be a good one. Ben Stewart and Larry Nichols are your models."

Her arms folded again. "But what if I can't do it right?" It came out whiney, weak. "Hell. Disregard the whimpering."

"Do it *right*: What's that mean?"

"Forget I said that."

"No, Andi. What did you mean?"

She sighed, teetering between irritation at Ed's pushing and, admit it, curious. *What* did *I mean?* Something surfaced, something rough. "Sergeant Nichols had this program for teens where they'd come into the station. They'd do ride-alongs, get coaching on how to avoid drugs, learn gun safety, and get a half-hour shooting on the practice range once a month. We called it 'Cops and Kids.'"

She paused, unexpectedly short of breath. "The program was popular." Her throat tightened. "Larry put me in charge of it. My first real leadership." She felt her face flushing, her ears hot. Shame flooded her. "Within six months, the program was dead."

"Nichols blamed you?"

She didn't answer right away. Then, "Didn't have to. I blamed myself."

"You decided you failed?"

"No *deciding* about it, Ed. I failed. The program was deep-sixed by the brass."

Ed didn't say anything for a while. Then, "Could blaming yourself let you avoid something else?"

"Fuck the psychology crap, Ed, I—" But she knew it, knew it like you know a pain in the chest. Her mouth hung open, words impossible for a moment. When she could, she said, "I was a *woman*. They wanted a guy to run their program." She heard the defeat in her voice, felt it in her chest, knew its truth. "I'm a woman. And I couldn't lead."

"If they had wanted a guy, they would've just reassigned you and put a guy in charge and—"

"No way," she barked fast. Then realized, *Too fast.* "Maybe so. I don't know." Ed said nothing while she wrestled with the memory of Cops and Kids. "I loved it at the start, because it reminded me of the patrol ride-alongs my dad arranged for me when I was fourteen. The whole idea thrilled me. We were helping the kids see the good side of police work."

And then she remembered Albert. A foul feeling sickened her.

Albert had been a skinny Haitian kid about fourteen. He'd come to every activity, listened to every word, and the light in his eyes had touched her. She opened her mouth to tell Ed about Albert, but she felt herself too close to an edge of something dark, a grief like a black well, words hovering in her mind: *I couldn't hold on to him.*

Full night had fallen. Ed waited beside her, his hand resting on her forearm.

She cleared her throat.

"What is it?" he asked.

"Not sure I can talk about it. Not yet." She laid her own hand atop Ed's, on her arm. "Thanks for pushing, then not pushing. I think I understand why I'm afraid to run, but I need to work it out."

"Any clues?"

She turned to him. His head, backlit by the soft yellow lamplight from inside the cabin, comforted her. "Oh, yeah. A kid back in Chicago. A kid I lost."

THURSDAY, SEPTEMBER 6

1

Andi hadn't been ready to talk before work this morning, so they each went to work. On her lunch break, she went across the hall and stuck her head into his office. "Got a minute?"

"For you, a lifetime of them." Standing up, he dropped the sandwich on his desk and opened his arms. She felt his heart beating. She leaned back and searched his eyes.

"You look roughed up, kid," he said.

I am. "I need to talk."

"Shoot," Ed said.

She took a long quivery breath. "So, this is about Cops and Kids. You remember how I blamed myself for its failure?"

"Because you were a woman."

"Yeah. Well, you were right. Blaming myself helped me avoid something. They made a budget decision that didn't have a damn thing to do with me. But I told myself it was because I was a woman, that the budget excuse was just a pretext to avoid a Title VII complaint." She looked down, shut her mouth.

He mistook her silence. "That's understandable. Women in a man's profession don't—"

"Uh-uh, Ed, that's not it. I blamed myself because I couldn't face something else." She heard the thickening in her voice, took deep breaths to stay in control. After a few seconds, she whispered, "Can we sit down?"

"Sure." He pointed to the chairs.

"Okay, here goes." The quivering in her voice hadn't gone, but she ignored it. "There was this kid. Albert. He came every week. Fourteen, Haitian, the sweetest round eyes. He loved Cops and Kids, did everything I asked. He was short for his age, but when the bigger guys pushed him around, he always pushed back just enough to stand his ground. After a while, even the toughest boys liked him, or at least left him alone." Her voice caught, and she forced herself to breathe until she could speak. Then, "One day, Albert said he loved me." This time, her voice cracked.

Andi's eyes closed, picturing that afternoon, and Albert's shy eyes.

She came back, focusing her own eyes on Ed. "When I had to tell the kids that Cops and Kids was shutting down, they were all mad, except Albert. He looked like I'd just shot his puppy. He didn't say a word, just stood up and walked out and never came back, even though I'd told them we had another month. Six months later, Albert killed another gangbanger-wannabe in a firefight. They tried him as an adult. He's doing life." She had to brush her eyes to see.

"The kid you loved . . ."

"And who loved me. I lost him." She looked down at her hands. "I felt the same thing when my mom died. Like it was my fault. I lost her by, I don't know, not being helpful enough around the house." She felt a bolt of anger. "Fuck it, I don't know."

Ed said nothing. She felt grateful for that. She looked up at him, as if he could throw her a lifeline. He smiled, which was what she needed.

"When I first saw the boy's body in Essex's garage, for a second I had this weird flashback: I saw Albert's face." She needed to finish this, say it all. She steadied herself. "After his heart attack, I knew I was going to lose Ben. Because I love him."

Tears came, fell. She ignored them. *Say it,* she told herself. "I love this department Ben wants me to lead. Ed, I *lose* the ones I love."

FRIDAY, SEPTEMBER 7

1

As always, at ten a.m. on the dot, Protector came into Ed's office and, following him in, took her usual chair. Surprising him again, she spoke first. "We are not enthusiastic."

"Are you concerned about something specific, Protector? Or has something happened?"

Protector shook her head. "But you must remember the rules."

"I do. How about Connie? On Tuesday, you told me Connie does not agree to my rule to not leave and to go back inside when we're done. Has that changed?"

"Yes. She agrees to your rule." Her eyes drifted for a moment, then sharpened again, pinning him. "She just said you should turn your chair around now, so she can see."

Ed tensed. Being blind to his patient worried him, but he knew Connie believed she could be safe only by hiding, so he understood that his seeing her would be terrifying. He stood and reversed his chair, setting it between Protector and the office door. As he sat, he realized *he* was feeling vulnerable now. "I'm ready," he said.

There was no reply. He was tempted to turn and look, but didn't. After a few moments, he heard shallow breathing. Then, a child-like voice: "Your hair has a hole on the back of your head." He thought maybe he heard a giggle.

"Yes, it does," he said. "It's called a bald spot."

"It's silly." The voice sounded young, maybe five, six. He recognized the little voice: Last year, she had said to him, "Bishop burned the lady," which turned out to be key to stopping the gang of sex traffickers Andi was investigating. He said, "Is my chair okay?"

"Don't turn around."

"I won't. I promised."

"We have to keep promises," the little voice said. "Or bad things happen."

He started to ask about that, stopped. Against the rules. Instead, he said, "I am happy you decided to talk to me, Connie."

A long silence. "How come you know me?"

"Protector has told me about you."

"Protector's mean."

"Really?"

"She makes me stay inside. And she has lots of rules."

How to respond to that? Would building rapport with Connie offend Protector? Might he disrupt the internal balance of power that protects Connie from the One who wants her dead? He took a breath. "People make rules when they're worried."

No answer. Had she taken it as a rebuke, implied Connie caused worry for Protector? He ached to turn, but kept himself still. After a minute, he said, "When I was little, I didn't like rules either."

Again, a long silence. Then, in a trembling voice he strained to hear, she asked, "You were little?"

"Yes, a long time ago."

"Who hurt you when you were little?"

Ah. For a moment he couldn't speak. He was trying to frame an answer, when Protector's sterner voice said, "She is within. You may turn your chair."

He did. Her face did not look as displeased as he'd expected. Rather, her eyes were as soft as he'd ever seen them. "How is she, Protector?"

"She is unharmed."

"And she won't be harmed, right?"

"Not if she does what I teach her."

"What is that?"

"She must ask no questions."

He sighed. "Questions are how children learn, aren't they?"

Protector's eyes softened further. *Sorrow,* Ed thought, *or longing.* She said, "Some children, perhaps. But for others, questions bring pain."

He nodded, profoundly sad. "I appreciate your taking care of her, Protector."

She looked startled, then puzzled. "Why? It is my purpose."

2

A little past noon, Andi sat at her computer, writing up a report on a traffic crash she'd handled during the morning. Words turned out misspelled, some sentences never found their verbs. Yesterday's talk with Ed about Albert had released an ancient sorrow, and she was filled with it. She closed the file and sat, thinking, at her desk. Her belief—*I lose the ones I love*—was irrational, she knew that. *But sometimes, you survive things by being irrational.*

Her email notice dinged. She opened her inbox. The message read, "From: VISA LEGAL." Her heart jumped. *About time.* She'd emailed the search warrant on Tuesday.

She opened the message. All it said was, *For security reasons, the records described in your search warrant, Case Number PG 04-9881 G-05, have been forwarded to the Adams County Sheriff's Department by special courier. They are scheduled for delivery at approximately 4:30 p.m. today, September 7. Please ensure that Deputy Andrea Pelton or her authorized representative is available to sign for the documents when delivered.*

She glanced up at the big Howard Miller clock. 2:30. Two hours. *Wish it were here now.* But anticipation shouldered aside her grief over Albert, and she was grateful for that. For the first time today, she felt her thinking sharpening, focusing. She was ready to drive another nail into the coffin of Daniel Essex's stand-your-ground defense.

·　　·　　·

The courier arrived a little before four, and Andi signed for the package. To avoid interruptions, she turned off her cell phone and asked Callie to hold any calls. Inside the parcel were six statements, three for each of Essex's accounts, June, July, and August. His Montana account closed on the fourth of every month, Massachusetts on the second. If there weren't any new grocery or C-store purchases on the statements, she could argue that Essex hadn't bought any replacement beer. What she wasn't confident about was what that could imply. Setting aside her doubt, she started her examination, studying each purchased item.

Forty minutes later, she had found two possibilities, both in Missoula—a Valu-One Groceries and a Gas-and-Groceries convenience store. Both were on Reserve Street, a break. She looked in Pete's office, but the lights were off, so she went out to reception. "Callie, can you find Pete for me?"

"Can Eric Clapton find a C-chord on his guitar?"

Andi laughed. "I need to talk to him."

"Eric Clapton?"

"Good one. No, Pete."

"Left ten minutes ago. He's home by now."

"Damn." She looked up at the clock. "This can't wait. I'll call." She dialed Pete's number.

"Hey, Andi, what's up?"

"Hi, Pete, sorry I missed you before you left. Will you authorize me driving over to Missoula tomorrow? It's for the Essex case."

"Fill me in."

After she told him about the missing replacement beers, he nodded. "Okay, you're good to go. We'll cover your shift."

"Thanks, man. I may be close to wrapping this one up."

After hanging up, Andi had a thought. She pulled up Grace's contact on her phone and tapped the number. After a few rings, it rolled over to voicemail. "Hey, step-girlfriend, it's me. I'm coming to Missoula tomorrow. You up for dinner? Call me."

It wasn't a call that came back later. It was a text. All it said was, "Awesome."

SATURDAY, SEPTEMBER 8

1

Gas-and-Groceries posed no problem; the store manager read the warrant, turned to her computer, and after a moment, said, "I've got two receipts; let me print them for you." A moment later, Andi had read each receipt, and found no beer purchases on either one.

Valu-One Groceries was a different story. The cashier, a kid who looked about fifteen, a stud through each nostril, wore a name badge that read, "I'm Barry, Proud to Serve!"

Andi asked to speak with the manager.

Barry said, "She's not here today. It's just me."

Damn. She said, "I have a search warrant to check your sales receipts." She handed him a copy of the warrant. Barry studied it, looked up, asked what this was about. When Andi answered, "An investigation," he shrugged.

"Barry, can you get me those receipts?"

He shrugged. "Don't know. Never did it before." He turned without saying anything more and walked toward the back of the store. Andi followed. In a back office, he sat in front of a computer and typed a few commands. Fingers poised above the keys, he said, "Okay. Read me the name and the credit card numbers."

She did, slowly. After maybe two minutes watching his computer screen go dim while it searched, he looked up and shrugged again. "It says, 'Contact IT Department.'"

"How do I do that?"

Another shrug. Barry's shoulders seemed the most communicative part of him. "Don't know. I just started here."

"Where's your IT department."

He shrugged. "Boise?"

"Boise, Idaho?"

Barry shrugged. "I guess."

After extracting the IT department's phone number, she started tapping in the numbers on her phone. Barry said, "Gotta get back on the floor."

She put on her cop face and glared. "Stay right here. I'm going to need you."

He looked shocked, then a bit scared, and sat back down.

The IT guy, when they ultimately located him, got by on fewer syllables than Barry did. After she explained what she needed, and added that she had a search warrant, he said, "Shoot it over."

"Look, this is a murder case." Barry's eyes went wide. "And we have some urgency. What I'd like to do is have Barry, the store manager here in Missoula, get on this phone and assure you he's seen my search warrant. Then I want you to run a search on sales receipts for two VISA account numbers I'll give you. If you find sales receipts, just say yes, and I'll courier the search warrant to you, so you can then send the sales receipts back to me. Got it?"

"If not?"

"If not what?"

"Not any receipts."

Andi tried not to sigh. "Just say no."

"I'll ask my boss."

Despite her frustration, Andi appreciated the full sentence. Barry, restless, said, "Can I at least check to make sure nobody's stealing everything? My manager . . ."

"Okay, but come right back here. I need you."

As Barry came back and was sitting down, a woman on the phone said, "Deputy? This is Qing Jiang. I'm manager of IT here at Valu-One. What can I do for you?"

Andi went through the situation again. Barry's right leg was bouncing. After she finished, Qing Jiang said, "That sounds reasonable. You just want a yes or no as to whether there are sales receipts for this person in one of our stores."

Not quite, Andi thought, but said, "Yeah, that's the gist. But if the answer's yes, I'll ask you to email the receipts to the computer in this store. Can you do that?"

Qing Jiang was quiet. After a moment, she said, "I think I should see the search warrant."

"Ms. Jiang, this is a murder investigation, and time is precious. Maybe I can fax it to you?" She looked at Barry. He shrugged. She whispered, "A fax?"

He shrugged. "Don't think so. What's a fax?"

Andi just looked at him. *Is he for real?* She said to Qing Jiang. "How about I take a photo of the warrant with my phone and text it to you? I'll still courier a hard copy to you later if there are sales receipts."

Qing Jiang was quiet a moment, then spoke slowly. "A murder investigation? . . . Under the circumstances, I suppose so."

She breathed out her tension. "Thank you. I'll hang up now and send you the photo. Can you give me your cell phone number so I can text it and then call you back?"

It took her two minutes to get a good photo of the warrant, and a half-minute to text it to Qing Jiang. She waited three minutes to tap in Qing Jiang's phone number. The call went over to voicemail. She gritted her teeth. "This is Deputy Andi Pelton calling back. I assume you're reading, or waiting for, the search warrant. Please call me when you're ready." She gave her number and touched *End*. She decided to wait five minutes before calling back.

Her phone buzzed sooner than that. "Pelton here."

"Deputy, yes, Qing Jiang. I have read the search warrant."

"Probably hard to do on a small screen."

"My phone synchs with my computer monitor. It's no problem. I see two requests: For credit card account statements for two numbered accounts, and for sales receipts. I don't have access to credit card statements."

"Yes, I'm looking for sales receipts. I already have the VISA statements. I need to find out if the person in question has made certain purchases."

"Very well. I can search for them using both his name and his credit card numbers. I will put you on hold, if you don't mind."

Andi waited. A couple minutes later, Qing Jiang came back on the line and said, "There's one receipt."

Andi said, "Thanks. Can you email it now? I'll fax a hard copy of the warrant later today."

They ended the call, and in a couple of minutes, Barry's computer beeped. Andi called him back in. "Open your email for me, please. There should be one from corporate IT."

He shrugged. When the account was on the screen, Andi pointed at the most recent, marked "IT@Value-One.com." "That's it." She pointed at the printer. "Print it for me, please."

"Then can I go back to work?"

"Yeah. Just print it."

Barry typed in the *print* command, then scooted out to the store. In a minute, the paper dropped into the tray. Andi grabbed it and read each item slowly.

No beer purchases.

She sat very still in Barry's chair, re-reading the page, searching for anything she'd missed. Nothing.

No beer purchases could mean no burglary, she thought. *No burglary means he lied to justify shooting the boy. So, what the hell's his real motive?*

2

Before dinner, Andi and Grace strolled along the Clark Fork River, downtown. Creamy yellow-white horsetail cirrus clouds stretched across the blue sky. "It'll be autumn pretty soon," Andi said, mostly to herself. More and more, the word "autumn" translated to "election." She was thinking of Ordrew's campaign.

"Andi, can I ask you something?" Grace's voice was hesitant, sober.

Instantly alert, Andi stopped walking and said, "Anything."

Grace stopped with her. "Are you guys telling me the truth about Sheriff Ben? Is he going to be all right?"

Andi considered that. Losing his job as sheriff—would that be *all right*? "Physically, he's doing very well. He's in the office almost every day, and he's almost his old self—although he's thirty pounds skinnier."

"Northrup told me he can't run for re-election."

"That's right. He's not recovered enough."

"So, does that mean he won't be sheriff?"

"It does."

"How do you feel about that?" Grace asked. Andi heard tears somewhere behind the girl's voice.

"Oh, wow," Andi said. "For starters, I'm sad for Ben. This is no way to end his career."

"What else?" Grace's frown clued Andi that something serious lurked in her question.

"To tell you the truth, I'm a bit worried about it. Brad Ordrew's running unopposed. He's not going to be easy to work for." She decided not to add Ordrew's promise to fire her. "People are telling me I should run, and that scares me."

"Really? Andi, you're the bravest woman I know. What are you afraid of?"

That's the question. She thought of Albert. Taking Grace's arm, they pivoted back onto the trail and their walk. "Thanks for saying that." She told Grace about Albert, and what she'd concluded—that she loses the ones she loves. She added her new resolve not to think that way. They walked that way, arm in arm, for a couple of silent minutes. Then Andi said, "That's not the whole story, though."

Grace's serious concern steadied her. Grace believed in her and, more than anything, she wanted to rise to that belief. She said, "Politics is totally new to me. I'm unsure of myself."

"Uh-huh. Like me in college."

Andi looked at her. "You scared here?"

Grace nodded. "A little. But I think of you, though. I want to be brave, like you. Sometimes I can't do it."

Her words stirred Andi. "I think courage is doing something even though you're afraid. So, I guess I should run, shouldn't I?"

Grace didn't respond.

Andi made a quick decision. "How about we get a motel room and stay together tonight? We'll have a girls' night."

Grace's eyes shone. "Oh, man, step-girlfriend, that'd be sweet."

3

After checking in to the Double Tree Inn, right on the river, they ate dinner in the restaurant, then returned to the room. Andi ordered a bottle of Pinot Noir from room service, and when it arrived, she poured two glasses. Grace grinned. "For me?"

"Girls' night. Enjoy."

They watched a movie, then at ten Andi switched on the news. At the first commercial break, they saw it. Or rather, heard it: The voice saying, "I'm Brad Ordrew, and I approve of this message."

But it wasn't Ordrew's voice. Andi sat up, heart pounding. Until the final words "of this message," the screen had been black. Then all at once, this:

FOOTAGE OF AFRICAN AMERICANS CONFRONTING POLICE, SHOUTING ANGRILY, SHAKING THEIR FISTS. PAN CROWD. CUT TO WIDE SHOT OF POLICE LINE, IN FULL RIOT GEAR.

VOICEOVER: *The Adams County Sheriff's Department is unprepared for civil disorder and unrest.*

CUT TO SHOT OF POLICE HELMETS, VISORS DOWN. REFLECTION OF FLAMES GLINT ON THE VISORS.

VOICEOVER: *The Department has riot helmets made twenty years ago. And those helmets have visors that may not protect the officers' faces.*

CUT TO SHOT OF SHIELDS. PAN DOWN POLICE LINE, FOCUSED ON SHIELDS, BATONS HELD ACROSS THEM.

VOICEOVER: *The same for our shields. They are outdated and would not protect the officers . . .*

CUT BACK TO THE ANGRY MOB. FOCUS IN ON ANGRY, HATE-FILLED, SCREAMING FACES. BLACK FACES, WHITE TEETH GNASHING.

VOICEOVER: *. . . against confrontation by an armed and angry mob.*

CUT TO IMAGE OF ADAMS COUNTY HOSPITAL.

VOICEOVER: *How can a man who lies mortally ill in the hospital lead our sheriff's department?*

CUT TO SHOT OF BURNING BUILDINGS IN BACKGROUND, FOREGROUND POLICE DISPERSING A CROWD WITH TEAR GAS.

VOICEOVER: *Tear gas reserves are low, almost too little to control a single incident.*

LONG SHOT OF THE VALLEY, FROM HIGH ON THE COLISEUM. MORNING SUN GLINTS ON THE ROOFTOPS OF JEFFERSON UP IN THE CENTER OF THE VALLEY. THE RIVER CURVES EAST TO WEST, REFLECTING GOLD.

VOICEOVER: *Our beautiful valley looks peaceful now, and the Sheriff's Department believes we are prepared. But . .*

CUT TO SIMILAR SCENE OF SMALL TOWN, BUT THIS TIME, TOWN IS BURNING.

VOICEOVER: *When the day comes, will you be glad you accepted their ideas? Brad Ordrew has the experience, the skills, the knowledge, and the love of our country to lead the sheriff's office in the 21st century.*

LONG SHOT OF THE VALLEY, SLOW RISE UP THE FLANKS OF THE MONASTERY RANGE, TO HUNTERS' PEAK: HOLD. THEN:

VOICEOVER: *On November 6, vote for Brad Ordrew for sheriff. This is a patriot's campaign.*

CUT TO SHOT OF AMERICAN FLAG RIPPLING IN WIND. THEN: CUT TO RED TEXT ON BLACK: *A PATRIOT'S CAMPAIGN.*

VOICEOVER: *Paid for by Friends of Brad Ordrew for Sheriff.*

They sat, stunned. After a moment, Andi cursed. "Damn that man."

Grace's eyes blazed. "That was awful. Those pictures were from big cities." She turned to Andi. "That's called video-deception. We talked about that in philosophy class."

Andi's cell buzzed. *Ed.*

She answered, "You saw the ad?"

"Hell, yes. I'm shifting from shocked to pissed. I recognized the burning town. It was Lac Magantic, that town in Quebec where the oil train derailed and exploded. Not a riot at all."

"Hell, Ed, even if it was a riot, that's not our valley. Grace called it video-deception. Perfect term for it."

"Andi, you've got to fight this guy."

In her mind, she replayed the images of armored, shielded, visored, helmeted police tapping their batons against their shields. She felt almost ill. Was this what Ordrew wanted for the department?

On the phone, Ed was asking, "Andi? You there?"

"Uh-huh. Here. You're right, I've got to do something." *God help me. Am I ready?*

Grace said, "That's more like it, Andi."

SUNDAY, SEPTEMBER 9

1

At breakfast, Grace said, "I'm coming home with you."

"Homesick?"

"No. I want to help fight Ordrew."

"I bet you do. Wanting to get back at him for how he treated you about Jared?" When Jared was having his wild swings between being one of the nicest kids in the high school and threatening to shoot his class, Ordrew had put Grace through a brutal interview, hoping to get her to admit Jared used drugs, which she refused to do—even when he threatened her—because it wasn't true.

"Well, yeah, that and these horrible ads."

"I'm thinking you're better off here. We'll handle Ordrew. You concentrate on getting your education and building your future."

"Which old people think is important, right?"

Andi lifted an eyebrow. "*Old* people?"

Grace stifled a grin. "Old*er* people." When Andi smiled, she added, "Okay, I stay. But call me when you need me, okay?"

Andi heard the *when*.

• • •

A little over three hours after she dropped Grace at her dorm, Andi parked behind the Adams County sheriff's building and went inside. She knew Ordrew was on duty and hoped he'd be in on a slow Sunday afternoon. He was, feet up on his desk, reading a paperback. Andi roughly swiveled him around to face her. His feet slammed to the floor. "What the—?" he snarled.

"What the hell was that commercial for?"

His anger palpably dimmed; he lowered his eyes. "For my campaign, obviously, and the truth. We're, uh, not prepared for civil unrest."

"What that commercial showed was big-city riots and a burning oil train. That's not here, and it's dishonest as hell."

"Your opinion," Ordrew said. He avoided her eyes, but Andi detected hesitance in his voice.

Damn. She got it. "You didn't approve that ad, did you?"

"Doesn't matter. Just say, I'm not in control of it."

"So, who is?"

"He said to tell you, if you asked, his name's the Reverend Loyd Crane."

Andi went cold, backed against the cubicle wall, bracing herself. She opened her mouth, closed it, and left the squad room without a word.

•　　•　　•

Still at his desk, Ordrew puzzled about what connected Crane and Pelton. Hard as it was to acknowledge, the closer he observed her, the more integrity he saw — what would a woman like that have to do with Crane, a piece of dishonest shit? For a moment, he felt degraded to be taking Crane's help. But he shook it off. If Pelton or Peterson decided to run, he had a hell of a head start. *Still, you gotta watch out. Don't let Crane corrupt you.* He thought about it. *And don't let Pelton get under your skin.*

2

Walking three times around the parking lot didn't settle her. Trembling with fury, she jumped in her vehicle and drove out to the cabin, fast. Way too fast.

When she came inside, Ed got up from the couch, smiling. "Hey. How's our college girl?"

"I've got horrible news."

He paled. "Grace?"

"No. Guess who's behind Ordrew's ads?"

"No idea. Who?"

"Loyd Crane."

"Sweet Jesus." Ed looked as shocked as she'd felt. "How'd you find that out?"

"Ordrew himself. I'm pissed."

"Why the hell would Loyd Crane want to get involved in this election?"

"Revenge? Hell, I don't know, maybe—" With no warning, the ugly memory roared back:

Crane's anti-tax conspiracy gathered in the Jefferson House motel. Vic Sobstak, Maggie's husband, wearing a wire to record Crane's pitch. Crane's henchman finds Vic's microphone, a fight erupts, Ben Stewart orders them in: "Go, go, go!" Pete kicks the door, Andi's in first, Crane's guy fires, takes her down. Falling, she fires back, killing him.

Shivering, she shoved the memory aside, felt the muscles of her jaw clench.

Ed touched her cheek. "You okay?"

"Yeah. No. Remembering the shooting." She caught her breath. "I just got it. The voice."

Ed looked puzzled. "The voice?"

"That voice in the ads that says 'I'm Brad Ordrew, and I approve this message.' Remember how I said it wasn't Ordrew's voice? It's Crane's. I remember hearing it on the radio when Vic was in the meeting."

"Hmm. Could Crane be behind Ordrew's threat to fire you?"

She thought about it. "I suppose he could be. But here's something else: When I confronted Ordrew about the ads, he seemed embarrassed, like he's not totally on board with them. He said he's not in control of them."

"What if Crane's been involved with Ordrew longer than just now? What if they're working at something else together?"

Andi moved closer to Ed, and he put his arms around her. "Then this just got scarier."

Ed held her. "You know, you have to face this."

She pulled out of his arms. "I know I have to face it, but I sure as hell don't have to like it."

TUESDAY, SEPTEMBER 11

1

Andi's cell phone buzzed insistently on the bedside table. Ed woke first, recognized it was hers, and nudged her. "It's yours."

She could hardly rouse herself. "My God. What, uh, time is it?"

Ed craned his neck to the clock. "Six-fifteen."

"What day?"

"Tuesday."

"Ah, man," she said. "It never ends," she groused as she reached for the phone. Too late. It had stopped buzzing. She checked *Missed Calls*, said, "It was Callie. At this hour? Damn, I'm not on till three."

She sat up, the blanket and sheet falling away from her breasts. She called back. Callie answered, "Andi? I'm sitting in my kitchen with coffee and my paper. You see the morning paper?"

"I haven't seen the *morning* yet."

Callie laughed. "Forgot you're on evenings. Anyway, Ordrew's got an ad in the paper—he's going to give a Patriot's Day speech tonight at the Foreign Legion post. You should go."

Andi shook her head, then remembered she was on the phone. She glanced at Ed, whose eyes were closed. *Guess he doesn't mind me talking.* Or was pretending not to mind. "Why would I go?"

"So you know what he's saying."

"I know what he's saying, and it's not him saying it."

"What?"

"Do you remember Loyd Crane?"

"That reverend whose goon shot you?"

"The same. He's behind the ads." She got caught by a huge yawn. "Sorry. In fact, I think it's Crane's voice saying he's Ordrew and approves the message."

"Hell, all the more reason for you to go."

"Can't. I'm on duty tonight, remember?"

Ed stirred. He rolled toward her, a question in his eyes. She held up a finger.

Callie was not a woman long lost for words. "Right. Sounds like a job for the Ladies' Fishing Society." She paused. "Ordrew'll know I'm not on his side, so how about I ask Bernie and Lane and Maggie to go?"

A realization broke over her: *They're waiting for me to decide to run.* She said, "Well, yeah. If Maggie and Lane can go, that'll be good." She hesitated, then added, "I haven't decided to run, Callie."

"I'll be in touch," Callie said.

As Andi tapped *End,* she realized she felt torn, her anger about the ads and Ordrew's threats on one side, and her fear on the other. *No place like dead center to paralyze a girl,* she thought.

Ed said, "What's going on?"

"Ordrew's giving a Patriot's Day speech tonight. Callie wants somebody to eavesdrop." She sat very still.

"Ah, Patriot's Day." An annual right-wing shindig, built on the ashes of the Twin Towers. He rolled toward her and put a hand on her exposed breast. "You want me to go?"

She pushed his hand away.

He put it back. "Let's make a deal."

She laughed and climbed out of bed. "Tell you what, Romeo. You go to his speech and I'll have sex with you."

"When I get home?"

She shrugged and pulled on her t-shirt. "No. But someday."

2

Twenty minutes past her appointment time, Beatrice John called. Her voice sounded strained. "I know we are supposed to be there, but we cannot."

"Am I speaking with Protector?"

"You are."

"What's the matter, Protector?"

She took a moment. Then, "Connie is upset with you."

"May I ask what she's upset about?"

Again, silence. He waited. In time, as if a committee had debated and allowed Protector to speak, she said, "When you did not answer her question, she felt you were angry with her."

Ed grimaced. *So many traps in this work.* "She's thinking I was angry? I'm so sorry. I was searching for the best words to answer her."

"She's a child. When adults do not act as she hopes, she assumes, always, that they are angry."

"Will you let her know that I'm sorry I frightened her, Protector? I'd like to see you all again."

Again, a silence greeted that. He didn't intrude on her pondering, or perhaps her consulting with others within. At last, she said, "We will be there on Friday. At the usual time."

"I'm glad. Very glad."

But the line was already dead.

3

Although her shift didn't start till three, Andi drove in to the station at noon, to talk with Xavier about the credit card statements and the sales receipts and what she thought they meant.

"I need ten minutes to finish this report, Andi," he said from his cubicle. "How about lunch at Alice's?"

"You're on." She went to the evidence locker—in reality, a good-sized room—to collect the evidence bag holding the sales receipts and credit card statements. When she got back to her cubicle, her voicemail light was blinking. Two messages. The first, from Laurie Swenson at Art's Fine Foods, said, *I spoke with all the clerks and no one saw Daniel Essex buy beer with cash.* Second, Emily Reston's call from the Conoco store, same message. She took a few minutes to call the managers at Missoula's Valu-One and Gas-and-Go. They confirmed: None of their clerks saw Daniel Essex pay cash for beer. She was another step closer to breaking this open.

Her theory about what she'd learned—no beer purchases—was outrageous, and she didn't want to promote it without Xavier's support. He was just finishing his report when she knocked again on his cubicle door frame. "Xav, I'm not sure I want to take evidence to Alice's, and I need you to look it over with me. How about Cokes in the conference room. We can take a lunch break later."

"No problem." They got Cokes and went into the conference room, where Andi laid out the statements and the receipts in front of him.

Before getting into the case, she said, "Xav, can I ask for an honest opinion?"

He smiled. "You're going to run?"

"I'm thinking about it. Do you honestly think the department's ready for a woman sheriff?"

"You're asking just about the department, right? Not the valley as a whole?"

She nodded.

"Andi, like I said, I talked to everybody, except Bradley, of course. And all of them support you."

She ignored the now-familiar twinge of failure-fear. "They'll work for me?"

"And *with* you. If Ben can't be our sheriff, we want you." He looked so earnest, Andi almost smiled.

"Okay, then. I'll let you know my decision soon."

"Run, Andi. We need you."

"Thanks, man." She took a deep breath. "Okay, the case. I've learned some things about Essex that make the case look clearer to me, but I need your eyes on it too." She began with the information that Essex didn't drink beer.

"Not at all?"

"Not according to Brenda Cantor. His drink is single malt Scotch, period. His cupboard's full of bottles. He calls himself an 'educated drinker' and subscribes to a magazine about fine whiskeys. And I tracked down his credit card statements—" She slid them in front of Xav. "—and found the places that sell beer." She'd circled them earlier, and pointed them out now. "And the only sales receipt for beer from any of those places is from Art's on July sixteenth. See if I missed any possibles."

"Stores that sell beer?"

"Yeah." She waited while Xavier went line-by-line down the statements. It took four or five minutes. "Nope," Xavier said, "just Art's."

"Good. We know that at Art's, from the sales receipt in his garbage ..." She placed that atop the statements. "... he bought what was in the refrigerator the night of the shooting, sixty beers in all." As Xavier peered at the receipt, which he'd studied three times, she explained the dates, the absence of any additional beer purchases within the past two-plus months. She put the other sales receipts—from Emily's Conoco C-store and the two stores in Missoula—with the one from Art's, and Xavier studied them.

"Okay, no beer at any store other than the original purchase. But maybe he used cash someplace else?"

"He's germ phobic, remember? Never touches cash. And none of the clerks at either Art's or the C-store here or the stores in Missoula saw him buy beer with cash. Oh, and another thing, I talked it over with Brad and we agreed it didn't make sense for Essex to go to some distant town just to buy replacement beers."

Xavier nodded, rubbing his jaw. "So, you're thinking what?"

"I'm thinking he never replaced any beers."

"What if he has a buddy who drinks beer while he drinks Scotch? Maybe the buddy replaced the beers."

"Good catch." She reached for her phone, tapped Brenda's number. When she answered, Andi said, "Brenda, sorry to call you at work, but—" She listened. "Oh, good. I just have a quick question: Does Essex have a friend he drinks with, somebody who drinks his beer, while Daniel drinks Scotch?" She listened again. "Not once? Wow. Okay, Brenda, thanks. It helps." She ended the call and said to Xavier, "During the entire time they were together, she never met any friends of Essex, not one. And remember, he'd only moved into the valley two days before they started their affair. He never went out with anybody else. Just Brenda and Daniel, a cozy little twosome, all by themselves, all the time."

"So, either a Good Samaritan replaced the stolen beers, or—" He narrowed his eyes.

"Or they weren't replaced because they weren't stolen in the first place."

"Bite me."

"Think about it: What are garage-hoppers almost always looking for?"

"Beer. Or money for beer." He squinted again, as if trying to peer into a dark distance.

"Correct. And Bernardo had a can near his hand, which tells us what he was after."

"*Jesucristo.*" His face registered something between anger and disgust. "We gotta be sure about this. Are you—"

"As sure as I can be from the evidence."

Xavier rubbed his eyes. "So, you're thinking Essex was luring kids in." He stood, began pacing around the conference table.

"Using beer as bait."

"And the open garage doors—making it easy for somebody to get in."

"And the baby monitor in the refrigerator."

"You're thinking he *wanted* an intruder." Xavier stopped his pacing. "My God, Andi. That means he *wanted* to shoot somebody."

She had lifted the Coke to her lips, but set it back down without drinking. "I'm taking this to Pete, and then to Irv Jackson. He *planned* to shoot somebody."

"So now we gotta find out why."

4

After conferring with Xavier, Andi declined his invitation to lunch, wanting to get going on motive, even though she was off-duty. She scanned her notes, trying to remember where Essex had lived in Massachusetts. Found it: Brookline. She re-read the report to refresh her memory: He'd had three prior convictions for assault, one on his ex-wife and two on ex-girlfriends. She wrote herself a note: *Motive for the assaults?*

She buzzed Callie. "Callie, I need the number of the Brookline Massachusetts police department."

"Comin' up." Two minutes later, Callie came into the squad room and handed her the number. Andi thanked her, dialed, talked to a receptionist, was forwarded to the detectives' room, and introduced herself to a detective named Ron Sipes.

"Detective Sipes—"

"Ron, please."

"Great. Okay, Ron, we've got a murder here in Adams County, Montana, and the shooter—name's Daniel Essex—recently moved here from Brookline. He has a record of three prior assaults, two on ex-girlfriends and one on his ex-wife. Any chance you know of the cases?"

"Name doesn't ring a bell. Spell it for me and the dates of his convictions, and I'll see who might know something."

She spelled Essex's name and read the dates Xavier had gotten in his background check.

"Okay. You want to sit on hold or have somebody call you back?"

"I'll wait, thanks."

It took eleven minutes before a different voice came on the line. "Deputy Pelton? This is Detective Rick James. I handled the first and second Essex cases, the assaults on his girlfriends, and I know him. Danny was my first case as a rookie investigator. Must be twenty years now. You're looking at him for murder?"

She repeated what she'd told the first detective.

James grunted. "Sounds like Danny. He's been trouble since he was a kid. Spent a year in Juvie Hall for vandalism at fourteen and grand theft auto when he was sixteen. The first assault was on his girlfriend when he was twenty, and the second was another girlfriend three years later. He served twenty-one months for the first, and twenty-seven for the second. He assaulted his wife when he was twenty-nine, damn near killed her. He did thirty-seven months on that one. She divorced him while he was in prison."

"Do you remember what his motives were?"

"Jealousy, jealousy, and jealousy. Danny's an angry, controlling son of a bitch, and prison just made him harder and angrier. He did the girlfriends because he thought they were flirting with other guys. His wife he was mad at because she got pregnant. He wanted her to get an abortion and she wouldn't do it, she was Catholic. So, he tried to beat the pregnancy out of her."

"Did he succeed?"

"I didn't handle that case, but I don't think he did."

"I don't think jealousy is the motive in this case. Is there anything else you can tell me that might help us figure out his motive in this killing? He's claiming stand-your-ground—turns out he moved here to live in a stand-your-ground state. And on top of that, since he got here last March, he's been talking about killing anybody who invades his property. It looks like he baited his garage with beer to attract high school kids who want to steal it. Those facts make us think premeditation, but we haven't found a motive yet."

"You say he baited his garage to catch a *kid*? How old was your vic?"

"Fourteen."

"There you go. Danny claimed he'd been raped by an older boy when he was eleven. We had some evidence it was true, but not enough to win a case. Danny's always had a thing for teenage males. Hates their guts."

"Because of the rape, you think?"

"Like I said, we didn't have enough evidence to charge anything, but the kid he accused ended up raping and killing a gay fellow in the next town, and he's serving life now. So, Danny's claim is plausible, and I suppose it could explain his animosity toward young males. Maybe give you your motive."

Andi was writing as fast as she could. "Okay, Detective, thanks for your help. Can you send me the report about the alleged rape? I'd like to see if I can use it to establish motive."

"I'll round it up. Our archives go back to 1893. We're kinda proud of that."

Andi thanked him, gave him the mailing address, hung up, and sat back in her chair, replaying the conversation. She doubted the judge would allow Essex's criminal history in. *So, how do I talk about a motive so a jury can understand?*

Briefly, she felt a pang of sorrow for Essex. Getting raped at the age of eleven would twist the soul of anyone.

<h1 style="text-align:center">5</h1>

Andi made sure she was in the station around the time Ordrew's speech ended, so she could hear from Ed how the Patriot's Day speech had gone. Around eight-thirty, the heavy station door swung open.

She sighed. *Time for the bad news.* And time to decide.

Ed pushed open the door, then stood aside for Maggie and Lane to come in. Andi'd felt a growing unease all evening, but still managed a smile. "So, is he the next Obama?"

"My horse is easier to listen to," Maggie growled.

"Let's do this in the conference room." Andi led the way. When they got settled, she asked, "So, it's bad, eh?"

"Worse," Lane said. "He came right out and said Ben Stewart's ruined the department and should be removed and his policies thrown out."

Maggie pulled out a notebook. "I took notes." She put on her readers. "Let's see. 'Ben Stewart is sick and old, and he tolerates his deputies depriving a man of his stand-your-ground rights.'"

Andi frowned. "Very cheap shot. He knows damn well stand-your-ground's a defense against a murder charge, not a right."

Maggie nodded. "Tip of the iceberg." She squinted at her notes a moment. "I've got the handwriting of a monkey. He said, and I quote, 'law enforcement in the valley needs to protect the valley's citizens and employers from terrorists and illegal immigrants.'"

"Just like his ads." Andi jumped up and paced a moment, then sat again. "Damn, this pisses me off."

Ed said, "Get this: He said immigrants are the greatest threat to the valley's economy since the Great Depression. Which is more nuts than you'll find on a psych unit."

She jumped up again. "What else did he say?"

Ed again, "He claimed this department is planning to confiscate everyone's guns."

Andi grunted. "That's so dishonest I'd like to fucking . . ." She leaned on the edge of the conference table, settling her breathing. "Okay, what else?"

Maggie grimaced. "Just more crap."

Andi wanted more. "Damn it, tell me. I need to hear it. And I suspect I know what it is."

Maggie looked at Ed. He took the cue. "He said women shouldn't be police officers, and if he's elected sheriff, he'll fire you."

Maggie looked miserable. "And that's not the worst part."

"Oh?" Andi felt the blood rising in her face, as though the inside of her skin were aflame. "What's the worst part?"

"Some people clapped."

WEDNESDAY, SEPTEMBER 12

1

Next morning, on her way to work, after a night tossing between bouts of anger and stretches of shallow sleep upended by nightmares she couldn't remember, Andi dialed Ben's number.

"I'm not here," he growled as he picked up. "I'm grumpy as hell," he said.

"That's two of us grumpy, then," she fired back. "You hear about Ordrew's speech last night?"

"Why I'm grumpy. I feel like drivin' the prick into the ground, only I ain't the one to do it. Doc Keeley's laid down the law."

"Ben, you—"

The sheriff waved her silent. "It's *you*, Andi. You gotta run. For the Department."

"Ben, I'm—" She steadied herself against the bedside table, surprised at the intensity of her reaction. "Don't know if I can do a good job."

"Christ in a Chrysler, girl. Forget that crap. Doin' a good job is down the line. You gotta win the job first. And you ain't got a choice: You know what happens if that jerk wins."

Andi nodded. She knew. "I don't know diddly about running for office, Ben."

"'Bout time you learn. I'll teach you what you need to know. First thing, call Irv Jackson right away and find out how to get on the goddamn ballot."

"Ben, I—" She couldn't finish. Decision or no, another gust of anxiety choked her.

Ben must have sensed. His voice softened. "Andi. I *need* you to do this. My old man built this department, and me, it's been my baby every day for thirty-four years. Don't let that jerk tear it down. Or turn it into a damn Gestapo." Grief laced his voice.

She stood at the window, looked out, drawing a long breath. Mountains rose into a gray, clouded sky, their tops hidden. She took another long, shaky breath. *I've been scared before.* She turned back to Ben. "I'll decide today, Ben. I've got to think. I'll let you know."

"Thinkin' ain't the ticket. Doin' is."

2

After morning report, Andi buried herself in paperwork. She wrote up the evidence she believed supported her theory about Essex luring Bernardo Cirilo into his garage. The weakness in the story, she knew, was Brenda Cantor. Without her, it was all on the beer purchases, and Angela Norton could tear that to shreds. Not using his credit cards proved nothing a good defense attorney couldn't impeach. Lathering on Essex's germ phobia, which also came mostly from Brenda, wouldn't withstand a vigorous cross-examination, although Xavier's notes about Essex's statement would help. She made a note to check that Xavier had gotten Essex's germ comment into the report.

When she had it as laid-out as it was going to get, she called the county attorney's office. Irv Jackson was in.

She outlined the evidence leading to her beer-as-bait idea, including Brenda's contributions. "Your thoughts?" She held her breath and waited for his verdict.

"Tell me about your witness, Andi. How does she know this stuff about Essex?"

"They had an affair, from late in March until a couple weeks before the shooting."

"Who broke it off?"

"She did. She couldn't stand his controlling her or his anti-Semitism."

"Was he abusive?"

"Not physically, but emotionally, definitely. She described several incidents when he yelled at her. He threatened her with his gun when she tried to end it."

"She never reported anything?"

"No."

Irv sighed. "Sweet Lord, what some men will do to their women." Andi could hear papers rustling. "I like your beer-as-bait idea—it hangs together and it's got some evidentiary legs. But your witness could be thin. The defense will smear her as an angry ex-girlfriend. The bait idea just doesn't stretch far enough to neutralize that."

"What if we have Ed examine Essex about the phobia for germs?"

"Is he an expert in this kind of thing? What is it, obstructive-pulmonary disease?"

Andi smiled. "Obsessive-compulsive disorder."

"Well, I got three syllables right." Irv chuckled. "No, if he's not an expert, it won't help. Anyway, his lawyer'll just get her own shrink. It comes back to your lady." He was quiet a moment. "But you trust her?"

"I do."

"Okay, then, I think we've got a case, based on her testimony, Essex's lying, and shooting the boy in the back. Talk to you later."

A sudden rush of energy jolted her. "No, Irv, wait." She took a deep breath. "Look, there's something I need from you. I've decided . . ." *My God, have I really?* ". . . to run for sheriff in Ben Stewart's place. I need to know how to get on the ballot."

"Whoa." He was silent a moment. "Look, I've got no idea. Let me call the Secretary of State. Ben wants you in his place?"

"Yeah. Badly."

"All right. I'll get back to you as soon as I know anything."

"Make it fast, Irv. Before I lose my nerve."

•   •   •

He did. Perhaps two hours after they'd spoken, Andi's phone lit up. Callie, in Reception, called out, "Line 2. Irv Jackson."

Andi punched the button. "Irv?"

"Present and accounted for. Okay, I talked with the Secretary of State's office. There's a glitch—we're way past the filing deadline."

"Damn. So, I can't run?" She blushed at the twinge of relief.

"Considering the circumstances, Ben's heart attack, he says if you're appointed by a qualified party chairman and if Ben and his doctor attest to his illness, he'll let your name go on the ballot. So, step one, you get the county party chair to appoint you to take Ben's place. Are you Democrat or Republican? And don't tell me you're an independent."

"Why not?"

"If you're an independent, you need to collect a pile of verified signatures first. There's not time—he wants you to file no later than Monday noon."

"No, I'm a Democrat. From Chicago, remember?"

"Okay, so you need the Democratic party chair's appointment."

She ignored the anxiety that was creeping back. "Which I get how?"

"Leave it to me." She heard him chuckle. "The chair's my wife. We'll fill out the paperwork. Then, hire Jerry Francis as your campaign counsel, and have him prepare all your filing paperwork. Go over to the county clerk's office this afternoon and pick it up and get it to Jerry, pronto. Tell him to call me, I'll walk him through it."

"That's it?"

"No. Get a letter from Doc about Ben not being able to run and include it with the paperwork. You've got to have all the paper completed and filed at the county clerk's office by noon Monday."

"So, that's all?"

"Well," he chuckled again. "That gets you on the ballot. You still have to do the campaigning, which I'm guessing you're new at."

"Yeah, there's that." She looked out the window, across Division Street to the Angler Bar. *A beer would go down well, just now.* She said to Irv, "Look, thanks for the help. I'll get the paperwork and call Jerry."

"Do that, right away. And Andi? Good luck. I'll be pulling for you, though behind the scenes, of course. If you need anything, I'm just a phone call away."

"Thanks, Irv. A lot."

She hung up, her heart pounding. *What the hell am I doing?* Her fingers were shaking as she maneuvered the keypad to call Ed's number. Even before he answered, though, she felt her mood shift. "Screw it," she said aloud. "I can do this."

When he answered, she cleared her throat. "Ed, I need a favor."

"Hi to you too, beautiful." He chuckled. "Name it."

"I'm picking up some paperwork from the county I need to fill out."

"Hmm. Getting a marriage license?"

She grimaced. "No. That's for spring."

For a moment, he didn't say anything. Then, his voice came matter of fact, "You're running for sheriff."

Time to nail the coffin shut. She flinched at the metaphor, jammed some fortification into her tone. "I am."

"Care to pick up a marriage license while you're there?"

She laughed. "Fuck you, Ed."

"Name the time and place. Anyway, what's the favor? Need a letter of mental fitness?"

Probably wouldn't qualify, she thought. "No, we're going to need an expert witness about Essex's obsessive-compulsive disorder. Can you do that?"

"Nope, sorry. I'm not expert in OCD. Besides, he's not my patient, so I can't even make that diagnosis officially. Irv should get somebody from Missoula. I can call around and find somebody if you'd like."

"I'll tell him. Look, will you come with me Monday morning to file?"

"You betcha, pal."

She half-smiled, partly from relief: The decision was made, the words were in the air instead of echoing in her head. "Well," she said, "we're in it now, big guy."

She heard his laugh. "All the way, kid."

As she ended the call, a shadow moved in her peripheral vision. Standing in the doorframe, arms akimbo, a dark look on his face, was Brad Ordrew.

No time like the present. "I'm running, Brad."

He nodded as he stepped through the door. "May the best man win."

PART THREE

Searching for truth sometimes demands courage, but it always requires doggedness. The truth about a crime—or an election—is buried under an avalanche of lies. Unearth it solely with the brush and trowel of a paleontologist, and with the patience of Job. Beware: The digging may uncover terrible whispers, and awful things can emerge.

Anonymous

THURSDAY, SEPTEMBER 13

1

On her way to work, Andi stopped at Jerry Francis's office to drop off the filing papers she'd collected from the county clerk yesterday. Jerry's delight with her decision boosted her spirit. "They'll be filled out by the end of business today," he said. "Irv called and offered his help filling them out. Should be a piece of cake. Want me to file for you?"

"No, thanks. I'll do it. I need to get my hands dirty." She thanked him and went on to the station. After report, she drove to 77 Russell Fork Road to talk to Ben.

When he opened the door, he growled, "You ain't got a job anymore?"

His weight loss still caught her off guard. "You crabby? I came to see you."

He harrumphed. "I ain't one of the seven wonders of the world."

"You *are* crabby. Look, I need your advice. I'm running against Ordrew."

Ben brightened. "Now you're cookin' with gas. C'mon in, for God's sakes."

He ushered her into his living room, a man's room, leather couches facing each other, books everywhere—Andi had always suspected Ben was better read than he ever let on—amber shades on the lamps, dark wood paneling, a wide picture window looking out through the back porch toward the creek. Russell Fork Creek flowed into the Monastery River

He lowered himself into his chair and pointed at the couch. "Sit. Talk to me."

"You were right, I'm the one, so it's up to me. I need your help."

Ben slapped the arm of his chair. "Knew you'd step up. We ain't lettin' the valley go to hell." He snorted. "That boy wants tanks and howitzers, and we're stoppin' him. What do you need?"

"You tell me. What do I need?"

Ben looked like he was mentally rubbing his hands together. "First thing, you need money. Ask Magnus and Marty Bailey at the bank—"

"Marty? For a loan?"

"Hell, no. Marty's always been good for a couple thou. Tell him I'm bankin' on his, uh, 'support of law enforcement.' Da da, da da. And ask your rich boyfriend. Use their money to buy some ads on the radio to bring in more money from the people. With that, print lawn signs and do more radio spots against What's-His-Name."

"Ordrew."

Ben shook his head. "I know that. We don't use his name any more. He's the enemy. He's just *Him* from now on. When you mention him in public, he's 'My Opponent.' Don't never use his name in public."

"Okay, money and 'My Opponent.' So, what's my campaign about?"

Ben looked thoughtful. "Good question. It's up to you, of course, but it's about beating your opponent. Him. But you gotta have some issue. Decide One Big Idea, capital letters, you think the valley needs from the department, and make it yours. Your opponent wants to fight terrorists and play SWAT games." He grimaced. "Ain't no end to what an asshole that man is. Anyway, One. Big. Idea. If you want my thoughts, ask. I ain't the type to run your show."

Andi almost laughed. Ben was one hundred percent the type to run her show. "That's what I need, Ben. You've been on the corner with people for years. You know what the valley needs. Talk to me. Give me that Big Idea."

He smiled. "Glad you appreciate a 'sick-old-out-of-touch sheriff.' Okay, here. Had dinner with Magnus Anderssen the night before the heart attack, and he was sayin' the Jared Hansen case had him worried. He's thinkin', what if it had turned out the other way and we got us a mass shooting? We got some crazies in the valley, just like everywhere, who'd get everybody feelin' as scared as Ordrew wants 'em. Mack's wonderin' how we could get ahead of that with the high school kids, show 'em government can be a *good* thing, not a problem. Know what I'm sayin'?"

"Ordrew'll say it's not—"

"Shh, shh, shh."

His shushing puzzled her. Then she got it: "Oh. *My opponent* will say it's not police work."

"We could care less what he says. What do *you* say?"

"Our motto is *To Protect and To Serve*. We already do a good job of protecting. This is something we can do to serve the people of the valley, including the next generation."

Ben grinned. "There you go. Now, what would you do to accomplish that?"

Andi without pausing, knew it, full-blown: Cops and Kids, revived. "Programs for teens. Free weapons safety training. Sheriff's department-sponsored competitive firearms competitions. A high school summer internship program. Regularly scheduled ride-alongs. Department sponsorship of kids' baseball and football and soccer teams. Half a dozen ways to get the kids involved on the positive side of weapons and police work. Regular interactions with the high school, positive things like tours of the station for civics classes."

Ben's smile glowed.

She was on a roll. "We could develop a kind of murder-mystery dinner club, like adults have, for kids to solve real-life crimes from real-life clues. Teach them investigative methods by doing investigations— make it like a video game experience, only live."

Ben sparkled. "Whoa, Nellie. Those're *damn* big ideas. You put them into a package you can deliver in three minutes, you got you a winner, girl. SWAT teams versus helpin' kids grow up on the right side of the street. Pitch that to Magnus, and his money'll spill outa your pocket. And plenty more, I'll bet."

"I hate to think of everything in terms of money."

"You got some other terms to think in?"

She laughed. "Guess not. I'm the rookie here." Then she realized she did have another term to think in. "Yeah, I do." She pulled up something she and Grace had talked about, on their girl's night in Missoula. "I'm thinking patriotism's not just talk about threats to our country and fighting enemies. Patriotism's also about making our home community stronger, no, not just stronger, *better* for everybody."

Ben looked at her fondly. "You say it, 'n I see it. You're sayin' your opponent ain't the only patriot in this campaign, and your idea takes his gloomy one—we're weak, gotta make us *stronger*—and adds inspiration: *Make us better*. Doin' for the kids, the next generation—that'll buy you a lot of parents' votes." His voice had thickened at the end. He coughed. "Tell you somethin'?"

She nodded.

"I told your boyfriend once that you were, uh, like the daughter me 'n Marlene never had. Never told you, though."

She smiled. "Ed told me. I can't say you're the dad I never had; my dad was great. But you're like my best uncle. And Grace thinks of you as her grandpa."

His face reddened. After a moment's throat-clearing, he said, "Enough with the Love Boat. Let's get us back to work."

"Got it."

"Okay, third thing. Once you got some start-up money and tighten up your One Big Idea, write a speech. Part One, start out real friendly, give 'em a joke, make 'em laugh. Give 'em somethin' personal to show who you are—your dad bein' a cop might be just the ticket, and maybe that 'make us stronger, and make us better' line." He stroked his chin. "Yeah, I like it. That's your campaign slogan, *Makin' us stronger, makin' us better*. Then after maybe two minutes of intro, switch to Part Two, name two or three things you'd improve in the department. More funding for floods and fires, like. Show 'em you ain't afraid to criticize me. Part Three, tackle any rumors about you that are floatin' around. Take 'em head-on. Don't be afraid to get mad when they're bullshit. Call 'em out. If they're true, admit it and get ahead of it.

"I should say 'bullshit'?"

"Well, no, but find a strong word means the same thing. 'Manure,' maybe. Own up if you made a mistake, jump all over it if somebody's lyin'." He took a breath. "Part Four, no more'n one minute, what's wrong with Ordrew's plan to turn the valley into a war zone. How tear gas and SWAT gear ain't what Monastery Valley is about. Figure out how to say it so it sizzles. Part Five's your Big Idea, wrapped up real clean and clear, no more'n three minutes, four tops. What you'll do when you're elected. Oh, and never say *if*, always say *when* you're elected."

"Not if, just when."

"Right. Then, the last thirty seconds tellin' 'em why you're the one to make the valley better, stronger, and safer. Always end on your slogan. *Makin' us stronger, makin' us better.*"

She was jotting notes. "I'm worried my relationship with Ed will be a problem." She'd told Ben about their secret non-marriage up on the Coliseum, but no one else in the valley knew. "People think we're not married, but everybody knows—"

"That you're sleepin' with him? 'Course they know. And officially, you ain't married. Turn it into a positive, if anybody has the balls to bring it up, which I'm doubtin' they will. You're an independent woman who lives by her principles, and your principles are . . ." He thought a minute. "To be as brave in love as you are in law enforcement, to believe in makin' family even when it ain't the usual sort, and to committin' yourself to upholdin' the law. Hell, if the gays can *get* married, two people like you and Ed oughta be allowed *not* to. Never sound defensive. Be proud of how you live your life. You value love, you value family, you value the law, and ain't nobody gets to say different."

Andi jotted fast.

Ben slapped his blanketed knee. "Ain't felt better since I came home," he said, chuckling. "Guess I'm your campaign manager, huh?"

"You are, Ben. You are." The excitement she'd started feeling as Ben was talking gave way to a sense of weight lowering onto her shoulders. Ben's conviction wasn't contagious. Would Ordrew, no, her *opponent* honestly fire her if he won? Would he be able to turn her relationship with Ed into a scandal that could lose her the election?

Reverend Crane sure might, she thought, with a chill.

And with her next breath, she thought, *Reverend Crane and my opponent can screw themselves.*

2

Andi left Ben's and climbed into a department squad for morning patrol. She'd gotten no more than a mile north of town when the radio crackled. "Andi? Callie here. Got Irv Jackson on the phone, says it's important. Should I patch him through?"

Andi considered. It was either about the campaign, or about the murder charge. She didn't want anybody listening in about either, and a landline phone was more secure than the radio. "No," she radioed back. "I'll come back and call him on the landline. He in his office?"

"Don't know. Let me check."

A moment later, she came back. "Yep, in his office. You got the number?"

"I do."

When she got to her cubicle and dialed, Irv answered right away. "Thanks for getting back, Andi. I've been thinking about the charge. Deliberate homicide's hard in this case. All he's got to do is inject reasonable doubt about the beer-baiting theory or about his planning this. Could be hard for Norton to do, but not impossible, and if she tears Brenda's testimony apart, we could lose."

"What are you thinking?"

"I'm considering mitigated deliberate homicide."

"That's like second-degree murder, right?"

"Well, close. It says he's under mental stress, and knowingly kills Bernardo. Putting together your evidence of his lying with possible obsessive-compulsive disorder, we're in good position to use your beer-as-bait theory, and together they should throw his stand-your-ground defense in the toilet." He paused. "Like I say, deliberate homicide's tricky because he had no specific victim in mind, but I think we can win mitigated deliberate homicide. You okay with that?"

"Not my call, Irv. But I'm good to go on the lesser charge." She was relieved. Deliberate homicide can get the death penalty, and Andi hated the death penalty.

"Good, then. By the way, I talked to Jerry, he's all set."

"Yeah, I talked to him too. Dropped off the papers this morning."

"Okay, then. Later." They ended the call. She went outside and resumed patrolling. Looking for trouble. Like she didn't have enough.

3

Ordrew lifted the phone and pressed the "Talk" button. The voice at the other end was the Reverend Loyd Crane's.

"Your thoughts about the second ad, Deputy?"

Ordrew took a deep breath. "Well, of course I appreciate your help and your intentions. But frankly, I think that ad was dishonest. We don't have—"

Crane broke in. "Dishonest? Deputy, need I keep reminding you that mere facts have little bearing on the greater truth we are fighting for? I know you have few Blacks in Adams County, but that's not the point, is it? Your target voters are *afraid* they're coming. Your campaign has three prongs: The department's unprepared to protect the valley from riots and unrest—which means colored people; the department plans to confiscate everyone's weapons—which your voters will believe in a heartbeat; and the threat of immigrants coming to take their jobs. You need to pitch those points relentlessly."

Ordrew struggled. He knew what Crane was demanding, and he believed it would win him the election, but it rubbed his conscience raw. He chose his words. "I understand, Reverend. And there's nothing I want more than being sheriff in Adams County." It was true. "But do we have to lie? Can't your ads be tailored to real conditions in the valley?"

A silence hung between them. At last, Crane said, "They are not *my* ads, Deputy. They are *your* ads." He was silent for a moment, and Ordrew held his breath. Then, "Allow me a personal statement."

Ordrew frowned. He didn't want to lose this argument about the ads. *What does he want?* "Of course, sir."

"Deputy, I can promise you that whatever it takes to defeat your opponent, I will supply. Andrea Pelton opposes you, I'm told, and I will see to it that she never becomes sheriff of Adams County. But *you* must commit yourself to the greater truth, or believe me, I will bring another candidate into your county who will defeat you both."

Ordrew heard the venom in those words, knew in his gut they were true. But would the valley people elect a stranger, no matter how powerful Crane's ads were or how much money he poured into the campaign? For a moment, he felt a stab of the old resistance to the belt and the bloodied backside. On the other hand, he didn't just want this job, he *craved* it. He ignored the threat. "Reverend, I have my reasons for opposing female police in general, but I don't understand your animosity toward Andi Pelton in particular. Frankly, the longer I know her, the more I find myself respecting her, despite my reservations about female cops. Why are you so adamant against her?"

After a moment, Crane said, "Very well, you are correct to suspect I have a special reason for wanting Pelton removed."

"What's that, sir?"

"Before I answer that, are we on the same page about my support? Are you committed to the greater truth?"

Ordrew swallowed, wanting to say no, but fearful the office would be beyond his grasp without Crane's help. "I am, sir. So, why are you so against Pelton?"

"Ask Pelton yourself. Ask her who the Reverend Loyd Crane is to her."

FRIDAY, SEPTEMBER 14

1

Unlike Tuesday's missed appointment, Protector came through Ed's door right at ten o'clock; at least, he assumed that it was Protector, from the grim set of her face. She replied nothing to his "good morning." When they were seated, he said, "I hope Connie understands that I was not angry with her for asking me her question. I was just thinking of good words to use."

"We have told her what you said, but I do not know if she understands. Adults have always been angry with her."

"I understand. Does she want to try talking with me again?"

After a moment of blinking, Protector's eyes refocused. "Turn your chair around. Repeat your promise not to look and to stay in the chair."

He did, and after repeating the promise, he said, "And will Connie also promise to stay here when she comes out?"

He waited through the long silence. He was about to ask what was happening when he heard a sudden intake of breath, then rapid, agitated almost sob-like gasps. Then, the small child's voice, frantic, squealed, "Make them stop, make them stop." Her voice pitched higher, panicky. "You have to make them stop."

Flushback. Crap. "Who, Connie?"

The woman's body, now directed by this child-self, surged past his chair, moving fast toward the door.

Shocked, Ed forced himself to stay in the chair, but said, firmly, "Connie, stop where you are. You made a promise."

She stopped, her back and shoulders heaving, panting. After a moment, still with her back to him, he heard her say, "Close your eyes."

"I will close my eyes if you will go back and sit down. Like you promised."

"Okay."

When she was seated, he pitched his voice kindly. "I would like to help you, Connie. I don't mean to scare you."

"Why not?"

It caught him off guard. "Why don't I want to scare you? Uh, well, because I . . . I don't like to scare anybody. I like to help them."

"Why?"

Her breathing, he could hear, signaled a return to something closer to high anxiety than to terror, but the mystery of the transient flashback remained. He spoke slowly, careful with his words. "It would be mean not to help people when I can. I try not to be mean."

She said nothing, but her breathing was quickening again. He said, "Connie, would you like me to help you feel safer?"

"Why are you being nice?" Getting agitated again.

"Because I care."

She gave a terrified squeal, then fell silent. Ed waited, on edge. After a long silence, he heard the throat being cleared. Again a moment passed. "You may turn your chair."

He did so, saying, "Protector?"

A nod. "I had to bring her in. She is very upset."

"Do you know what it's about?"

Protector looked away, her eyes almost soft with some emotion Ed couldn't quite pick up. Grief? She nodded. "You said you *care*. That is the word her father used, before he . . ." Her eyes flared. Her head arched back, her mouth gaping, her breaths deep rasps.

"Protector, look at me."

Her head could not lower, but her eyes did, locked on his.

"Are you being stopped from speaking?"

The barest nod. Then, her head lowered slowly and she rubbed her throat. After a moment, she said, "I almost violated the rule against talking about things that . . . have been done to her. I must obey The Silence."

Ed felt a chill creep down his back, and knew that the work had just gotten incomparably harder. "Shall we talk through the fingers again?"

Protector stood. "No, Doctor. I must go. Connie must be controlled."

"Please, stay," he said.

"Connie made a promise, but I have not." She brushed past him and went out the door.

He sat for a time replaying the session in his mind. "Well, I learned one thing, which I suppose is good," he whispered. But he knew it wasn't good. He'd learned the offer of care had preceded something terrible her father had done to Connie. It took little imagining to guess what it was, and it left him sick at heart.

2

When afternoon report was over and her shift done, Andi sat in her cubicle, signing the forms she'd collected from Jerry Francis an hour ago. This evening, she planned to tackle her speech. She'd never much liked public speaking, though both here in the valley and back in Cook County, it came with the job description.

The easiest part of the speech was the Big Idea. She was surprised at how full-blown it seemed to have become since she first dreamed it awake with Ben. In her mind's eye, it was bigger than Bud Nichol's program. Cops and Kids had been a rescue effort, a last-ditch try at saving kids sliding toward being gang-fodder. This Big Idea wasn't about rescue, but about building trust in the department during high schoolers' younger years, trust they could bank for the days they grew into full citizens. She'd gotten that part of the speech into decent shape, talking with Ed last night; after more work on it tonight, she'd take it around to Ben's house and Magnus Anderssen's ranch for their opinions. She'd ask Luisa to weigh in too, get the women's perspective. And the Ladies' Fishing Society's.

She signed the last form and tucked the filing papers into the red folder Jerry had delivered them in.

Her stomach growled. The clock read 4:17. Dinner time soon. Sylvie Holmes, weekday evening shift dispatch, called in from Reception, "Visitor, Andi." She wondered who it was on a Friday afternoon and went out to see.

Grace stood by the reception desk, bouncing up and down on her toes. When Andi came in, she squealed, "Omigod, Andi. I'm *so* excited. When Northrup called to tell me you're running, I just about peed my pants."

Andi stopped. "You're *here*? You're supposed to be at college." But her own smile matched Grace's non-stop grin, and she felt a surge of pleasure.

"That's the best part, Andi. We're still in the drop-add period, so I dropped my other classes and worked out a deal with my Intro to Politics prof. He calls it 'independent study.' I'm going to spend the semester working on your campaign and he'll accept a paper about what I learn about American politics! Can you believe it? He said I can do whatever you need me to, but he wants me to volunteer in the civics class at the high school, maybe see if Lisa McIntyre will let me teach something. I thought I could organize a Town Hall forum for you. Isn't that multigasmic?"

Andi laughed. "Not sure what that means, but I can guess close enough. Come here, girl." She took Grace in her arms. "I'll admit, step-girlfriend, I'm happy to see you here."

After the hug, Andi asked, "What's your dad think about you being here?"

"He doesn't know. I wanted to tell you first."

"Okay. I'm starving. Let's eat at the Angler. Call him and see if he can meet us."

"Awesome. We can talk campaign strategy."

MONDAY, SEPTEMBER 17

1

Ed and Grace were waiting in the county clerk's lobby when Andi arrived with the campaign paperwork. The filing went routinely; she'd missed one signature, which the clerk spotted. Problem solved. "Hope they're all so easy," she said.

The clerk looked at her. "You'll handle 'em, Andi," she said, smiling.

As they left the building, Ed asked, "So, how's it feel?"

"Anti-climactic."

Grace took her arm. "Naw. Think of it as the calm before the storm."

Andi's phone buzzed: *Ben Stewart*. "Got some stuff you need. Come on over."

"It'll have to wait till later in the day, Ben. I've got a day job, remember?"

"This stuff'll keep. But you got a night job now too."

She wondered what he meant, then realized: Giving speeches. And then a thought crashed in that blew her confidence away like paper in a gale. If she was going to give speeches, who would she give them to? And how would people know to come? Shouldn't she make an announcement? She hadn't felt this naïve since she was a rookie cop back in Chicago.

The hell with anti-climax. This campaign business was going to be all climax, all the time.

2

After patrol, Andi skipped lunch and went to Ben's. Bernie was there, in the kitchen. "Have a salad, Andi?"

"I'd love one."

"We have ranch and Caesar."

Ben called out. "Ranch for both of us." He lowered his voice. "She's got me eatin' green stuff every meal, and tiny little bites of chicken or pork with dinner. Feels like life's turnin' into a Weight Watchers meetin'." But his eyes twinkled.

He handed Andi a sheet of paper. "This is for this week. I'm callin' these folks and gettin' you ten or twelve minutes for a speech. Hit 'em all, Andi. It'll be tirin', but you're young. If you get out fast and make a good impression, it'll last."

She was shocked: The list showed five meetings this week. "I didn't know there were this many goings-on in the valley." She looked up. "Should I make some sort of announcement? About running?"

"You file yet?"

"This morning."

"Okay. I wrote you a press release—I'll hustle it over to Bud Groh at the radio station and ask him to get it on the local news. How's your speech comin'?"

"I've got the One Big Idea part written, and . . ." She glanced at her list. ". . . the first meeting's tonight. I'm stumped on the first part, where I tell jokes and make them like me."

Ben scratched his forehead, thinking. "A joke. We got us a political campaign, so we need a sheriff and a politician." He thought for another minute or so. "Try this on for size, my dad used to tell it, won't be many remember it: A famous politician is coming to town to meet with the sheriff. His car goes off the road and crashes into a tree outside a rancher's bunkhouse. One of the cowboys comes out, sees the politician, digs a hole, and buries him. When the politician doesn't show up, the sheriff drives up the highway, and spots the crashed car. He finds the fresh grave, and when the cowboy comes back out of the bunkhouse to investigate, sheriff says, 'You bury this politician?' 'I did.' 'You sure he was dead?' 'Well, he said he wasn't, but you know how them politicians lie.'"

Andi laughed.

Ben nodded. "Good reaction. Go fire up your pencil."

3

As Andi was checking out for the evening, Callie buzzed her. "Can you stop by my desk, Andi?"

When she stopped there, Callie said, "We gotta have us an emergency meeting of the Ladies'."

"We do? Why?" The last "emergency" had been when Maggie Sobstak learned she had breast cancer. "Is Maggie . . .?"

"Naw, nothin' like that. We gotta plan your campaign."

So, the word was out—Ben's press release must've made it on the air. "Man, Callie, I'm giving two speeches tonight."

"When do they start?"

She pulled her list from her pocket. "Tonight's first one's at six, second one's at seven."

"No problem, then. We'll meet in twenty minutes, at five. Gives you plenty of time."

Not to write a speech and get some dinner. She sighed, thinking she may have to use Ben's joke after all. "Okay. Set it up."

"Atta girl."

•　•　•

The Ladies' Fishing Society met in emergency session at the Angler. The others ordered wine, Andi didn't. She wanted to be fresh—though after a long day on the job, *fresh* meant *only partly wilted.*

Callie took charge. "Let's us decide what we're doing for Andi's campaign."

Bernie seconded the motion with a nod. "Sweetness, let me be the first to pat you on the back. If anybody gets to take over for Benji, it's you."

Lane pulled a check from a folder. "Since Callie spread the word this morning, the Ladies and I have been doing some calculating. We'd like to make a start-up contribution to your campaign." He handed her the check.

"Five hundred dollars," she gasped. "My God, that's too much."

He laughed. "Heavens no, you will find that five hundred dollars is but a bubble on a stream, as the Buddhists say."

Bernie said, "Dearie, do what your mother told you. Take the money and say, 'Thank you, and please come again.'"

Maggie walked in. "I see you've gotten started." To Lane, she said, "Give her the check yet?"

"Just did."

Maggie walked up to Andi and enveloped her in a hug. "Me and Vic, we're going to talk to every member of the Cattlemen and Cattlewomen's Associations of Monastery Valley. That's about seventy ranches, so it covers a lot of territory. Vic thinks it'd help us if you could give him and me a few ideas that you're going to run on, so we can be . . . Uh, what do they call those folks go around talking up their candidate?"

Lane said, "I believe the term is 'surrogates.'"

Bernie snorted. "Like we're carrying Andi's baby."

Andi laughed.

Maggie finished, "Yeah, so we can be your surrogates."

Andi was speechless, and upon examination, her backpack was also speechless. When she rummaged for it, to let Maggie look it over, it wasn't there. Momentary panic.

But she remembered her One Big Idea, so that and Ben's joke would have to do. "Sure, I'll type up some ideas for you all. Later, though. I have to get freshened up and get over to St. Bernie's Altar Society for its meeting in . . ." She checked her watch. "Forty minutes. I gotta go."

Callie said, "Just so you know, Bill and I are going to as many of Ordrew's speeches as we can manage—I'm going to pretend I'm on his side, or at least that I can be persuaded. I'll be like a spy."

Andi felt some alarm. "Don't you think he'll be suspicious?"

"You bet he will. That's another reason to do it, make him nervous about what I'm up to. Might throw him off. And I can report back to you all what he's saying so we can counterpunch."

Andi felt a wave of gratitude for her friends. "I'm so glad you invited me to join the Society," she said, unexpectedly emotional, surprising herself. "I . . . ah, just thanks."

"Well, then," said Callie. "Get your little butt out to St. Bernie's and get the Ladies Altar Society to support their Lady Sheriff."

TUESDAY, SEPTEMBER 18

1

"It was very hard for us to come today," Protector said. "We almost could not do it."

Ed nodded. "I'm glad you're here, Protector. Thanks for sticking with this."

"Connie is terrified. She will not come again to talk to you. You used what for her is a bad word."

I care. "I understand." He paused. *Let's just help them calm down.* "Perhaps through the fingers?"

"You may try."

After a brief period of simple relaxation, and Ed's reminding Protector which fingers meant which answers, he asked if Connie could hear him.

Hesitantly, *Yes* wavered, then steadied.

"Good. Are you still frightened of me, Connie?"

Yes leapt up.

"I'm sorry for scaring you. I said I didn't want to, then I did."

Yes went up fast.

"Well, I learned something I should never say, and I won't. Will that help?"

At first, a tentative *No* lifted, then fell, and *Yes* floated up slowly.

Ed watched her breathing, which had been slowing since they started this. "Are you feeling a little calmer?"

Yes.

Mission accomplished. "Good. Maybe that is enough for today. Would you like to stop now?"

Again, *Yes* came up, but slowly. Ed waited. *Yes* stayed in the air.

"That's great, Connie. And everyone. We can be done now."

After a moment, the eyes opened and Protector said, "You were wise to stop when you did."

"She's feeling better?"

Protector shook her head. "'Better' is not something any of us feel, Doctor. She is merely less terrified."

2

It had been a grindingly boring day at work, consumed with calls about the pieces of nothing that fill a deputy's ordinary day—a cow wandering onto a road, a burglary that turned out to be a misplaced checkbook, a fender-bender in the lot at Art's Fine Foods. Andi's evening speech to the Presbyterian choir before rehearsal flopped. She blew the joke; the smiles it drew were in sympathy, not amusement.

A Presbyterian lady had raised her hand. "Deputy, I love your 'Cops and Kids' idea, but do you think a woman who sleeps with a man without being married to him ought to be a role model for our teens?"

She'd given the answer Ben had suggested, about the courage to love and make family in her own way, but the stony faces, especially the sopranos and the altos, spoke silent volumes.

At home, when she told Ed, he quipped, "Well, they're Presbyterians, after all."

"Be serious, damn it. I handled it like Ben told me to, but it didn't work."

"How'd he say to handle it?"

"Say I'm proud of our love, of our little family, even if it's not conventional."

Ed looked unsure. "Hmm. Well, I . . ." He fell silent.

"You what?"

"Well, I suppose not being officially married could cost you support, but I doubt it. This is 2018. If you're worried, though, we could go ahead and get married.

"If we get married now, people could say I did it for votes." She sighed. "I'm getting a glass of Pinot. Want one?"

At his nod, she went to the kitchen, poured, brought them back, sat down. "Okay, what I'm worrying about is money. The Ladies' Fishing Society gave me five hundred, and I called Mack Anderssen. He's giving me a thousand dollars, 'for starters,' he said. He says Ordrew's a danger. Called him a 'bolt.'"

"A bolt?"

"And I quote, 'We've got enough wing-nuts in the valley without giving them a bolt to wind themselves up on.'"

Ed laughed, then rubbed her neck. She moaned. Still rubbing, he said, "Fifteen hundred dollars. That's nowhere near enough."

She stopped purring. "I know, I know." She started to sip her wine, but stopped short and put the glass down. "I hate begging for money."

"You're going to have to, babe. Starting with me. I'm ready to contribute—"

She sat up and shook her head. "No. I don't want your money."

"Why not?"

This time she took a sip. "It's Grace's money. We can't just dip into it."

"Come on, kid. I have money too, and Grace—"

"Drop it, Ed. I said no."

He studied her momentarily, then shrugged. "Suit yourself. So, how *will* you pay for the campaign?"

"My 401(k). Maybe a bank loan." She knew her voice betrayed her worry.

"If you're willing to take a loan, why not borrow it from Grace and me? Our interest rate's better."

"Ed. I said drop it. Grace's money's a damn non-starter, get it?"

He said nothing for a moment, his head shaking almost imperceptibly. He took a sip of wine and looked away. She wished she'd been softer.

After a moment, he nodded. "Got it. Subject's dropped. Look, about our living together, I think you have to—"

Andi pressed her finger to his lips. "Hey, stop, would you? I don't *have* to do anything." Something stiffened inside. "I'm not ashamed of our relationship. I love you, I love Grace, and I love the life we have. End of issue. People don't like that, too bad. Besides, people live together nowadays. It's not the big deal it was in *your* day." She braced herself for his pushback.

He looked surprised, then laughed. "*My day?* As in 'once upon a time'?"

She laughed too.

He said, "Well, sounds like you know your mind."

Surprising them both, Andi eyes welled up.

"I say something wrong?"

"Not at all." She looked fondly at him. "I'm just sure of how I feel. And glad to get it off my chest."

"Good for you." He moved closer to her and looped his arm around her shoulder. He laid, then cupped, his hand tenderly on her breast. "Anything else you'd like to get off your chest?"

She smiled. "Yeah, big guy. Your hand." But she didn't feel like insisting.

3

They said nothing for a few minutes, a friendly silence. Then Ed stood. "I'll have another glass. Want one?"

"No. Maybe some water?"

When he returned with his wine and a glass of water, they sat closer on the couch. She leaned against his shoulder. He shifted, put his arm around her again, and they began a long kiss. Something bumped against the house. Andi, startled, jumped up. Ed joined her and they went to the door, looked out.

"Maybe a bird?" he said.

"No, sounded too big," she answered. She pulled her gun belt from clothes hook and drew the weapon. She opened the door and peered out into the dark. "Nothing out here. Maybe a deer?" She turned on the porch light and went out. She peered into the night.

Ed followed. "Have to be a blind deer." In the darkness, they found no other sign, gave up, went inside. Andi shivered. "Where's Grace, by the way?"

"She's having pizza with a bunch of seniors. She's pitching her Town Hall Forum idea."

"Remind me."

"She's thinking you and Ordrew—"

"My opponent, you mean?"

He grinned. "Yeah. You and your opponent meet with an audience of high school kids and the kids ask questions."

Face-to-face with Ordrew? Andi felt a jab of nerves. "I remember now." She shivered again. "Must be a draft."

Ed got up, checked the door. "Nope, it's closed tight. Anyway, she'll be home around ten."

She moved closer to him on the couch. "Warm me up," she said, pulling his hand back onto her breast.

"That's a nice surprise." They kissed, a long kiss, then Andi pulled away and said, "Let's not let this damn campaign come between us. I think we're already both a little jumpy."

He nodded. "We've got what, four or five more weeks of this?" He kissed her again, deeply.

She came up for breath. "Of which, campaigning, or making out?"

He laughed. "Meetings." They kissed again.

She broke away. "We've got forty-seven days till the election." She leaned back to kiss him again, then stopped, alert. A sound outside the window, then another, someone running down the driveway. She jumped up and pulled open the door, went out, Northrup behind her. Beyond the short reach of the porch light, darkness swallowed everything but the pounding of feet on gravel. Then, out in the night, a door slammed and an engine roared, and a vehicle sprayed rocks speeding away.

FRIDAY, SEPTEMBER 21

1

Brad Ordrew's telephone jangled him awake. Last evening, he'd talked with the Men's Club at St. Bernard's Catholic Church. The meeting was long, and it was unpleasant. He'd stuck to Reverend Crane's three "Greater Truth" campaign points—he'd mentally capitalized them—but the men kept changing the subject back to their smaller concerns. Two men nodded at his ideas, but the rest, eighteen or nineteen, seemed impatient with him. The hardest question had been from the young priest in the back row.

"Deputy, welcome to St. Bernard's. I'm Father Anselm, the interim pastor here, from up at St. Brendan's."

Where? Oh, the monastery on the mountain. "Glad to meet you, Father."

"I would like to ask a question."

"I'll be glad to answer it, Father." He'd always felt a little silly, calling a younger man "Father."

"With all due respect, Deputy, why was your last commercial so, um, racist, if you'll pardon the word."

Stunned into momentary silence, he could think of no answer. Nothing in Crane's Greater Truth bullshit prepared him for this. For a moment he felt a rush of fury, swallowed it. *Am I mad at this kid priest or with Crane?* He didn't know. He did his best to answer. "Well, I suppose racism is in the eye of the beholder. I prefer to think the ad was portraying a sad but common reality in our society that the police need to address." The word, *racist,* hung in the air like a foul smell.

Fr. Anselm mildly said, "All due respect, Deputy, we don't have that kind of social unrest here. We have our problems, obviously, but riots are not one of them."

He heard Crane intoning about The Greater Truth. The priest was focused on the lesser truth, the fact. "It may be so, Father. But many people, as I go around the valley, tell me they're afraid that someday it might be different, and want us to be prepared to protect our community. We can address *that* side of the issue, people's fears, by preparing for the worst, no matter how much we hope it never happens."

Now, at home, his evasiveness annoyed him. *Really? 'A sad but common reality'? Jesus.* Why hadn't he admitted the truth: The damn ad *was* racist. He hated this. His face burned with an unfamiliar feeling: Shame.

He'd opened a beer, flipped on the TV, and had promptly fallen asleep in his chair, until the phone's ugly ring jarred him awake. Groggy, he glanced at his watch: almost midnight. He shook himself awake. The display read *L. Crane.* He sighed. Crane was the last person he wanted to tangle with tonight. He considered letting it go to voicemail, but almost choked at his cowardice, pressed *Talk.* "Hello?"

The radio voice: "Deputy, this is the Reverend Crane."

"Reverend. It's late. What can I do for you?"

"You can start remembering that you are campaigning to be elected to an office. Your answer about the ad being racist missed an excellent opportunity."

Ordrew's breath caught. "How do you know about that?"

"I have representatives at all your speeches—and at all your opponent's too. I know every word you say, particularly the words that betray our cause."

"Well, damn it, Reverend. You made that commercial and to me, it *was* racist. Defending it is hard. So, don't—"

"Deputy, shut up. We're both racist and you know it. I am reminding you that your success depends on following my orders. And my orders are that you attack Pelton, hard. When you're asked about racism, accuse her of it. Not once, not twice, but every speech, every question. In particular, attack her for persecuting Daniel Essex. Hammer home the fact that she is taking away his right to protect himself and his home. Do you understand?"

Ordrew swallowed. This might be a line he could not cross. He didn't answer.

"I'm warning you, Deputy. I expect your cooperation. And watch the news at ten tomorrow night."

Crane hung up. Ordrew's anger wrenched him out of his chair and he flung the phone across the room.

But he recognized a new anger: anger that Crane had pegged him. When Ordrew had seen those raging black faces in the ad, squared off against the police lines, screaming their fury, he'd hated them. *Crane's right. I'm the racist.*

"No," he corrected himself in a whisper. "I don't hate them. I'm terrified of them."

2

Friday morning arrived cold and blustery, autumn's first dawn after the lingering sweetness of summer. Wind had shaken the windows during the night as the cold front moved down the valley. Ed put his coffee cup in the sink and grabbed his heavier jacket. "I'm out of here. Early patient this morning. "

On the way into town, he cranked the heater up to "Max." High above the valley, a veil of new snow dusted Hunters' Peak, but the valley floor was dry and brown.

He worried all the way to his office. What might go wrong this time in Protector's session? Dare he hope he could break through their terror? True, each session wove a strand in their too-thin thread of connection, but the work was so slow. And he had no idea how many alters there might be beyond Connie, Protector, Beatrice herself, and the One. A field strewn with land mines waiting to explode.

The session began well.

Ed helped Protector relax, and as her breathing slowed and her stiff posture softened, he said, "I'm going to ask Connie a question. Are you ready?"

The *Yes* finger lifted tentatively.

"Great. Is Connie listening?"

Again, *Yes.*

"Connie, would you rather stay inside today? We can talk with the fingers?"

Yes.

"Thank you, Connie. I'm glad you came today."

No fingers moved. No question had been asked. *Wake up, Northrup,* he told himself.

"Are you feeling safe now?"

No. Fast, emphatic.

Ed noticed the body was breathing harder, and the eyes were clamped tightly. He made his voice as gentle as he could. "Do you want to stop?"

Abruptly, all the fingers were waving wildly, the eyes started blinking rapidly, and with no warning, Connie burst out. Ed's alarms all went off. *She's escaped Protector's control.* He managed a smile, welcoming her as warmly as he could.

"Stay in your chair," the child-like voice screeched. "Don't hurt me!"

"I won't, Connie. You must want to talk about something very much."

Her eyes bored into him, and he felt the familiar chill on his neck and told himself to relax. She was sitting on the couch, unmoving, staring at him. After a long wait, she said, "Are you a daddy?"

A trap? If daddies abuse their daughters . . . He couldn't wait, though. She wouldn't understand. "Yes, I have a daughter, Grace. She's almost a grown-up."

"Do you hurt her?"

"No, I don't."

"Promise?"

"I promise."

Connie looked anxiously at the door, her face flushing. "My daddy hurts me," she whispered, before stark, naked terror blazed across her face. She opened her mouth in a wide O, then closed her eyes, and her body went limp. After a moment, Protector emerged, her eyes scanning the room rapidly.

"Is she all right?" Ed asked.

"No. She believes her father is still alive and will now punish her for telling you." She looked defeated. "It is as I feared. She cannot come here to see you now. It is too dangerous."

"Protector, actually, this might mean something good. She trusted me enough to say it, right?"

Protector snapped, "Her father, if I cannot control him, *will* punish her. And she is not a child who trusts."

She's not a child, period. But he said, "Her father is not here."

Her face registered a mix of sorrow and frustration. *With my ignorance,* he guessed.

She said, "I have told you: She is the One who wants to kill her."

The father is the One? The father is female? "I'm sorry. I misunderstood you." He considered what to say. "Protector, you and I have worked together now for a year. We both know we've been working so I can help Connie. Help all of you. This is a start."

"You cannot see or hear inside, but the others are restraining Connie now. She is wild with terror. I fear her fright will kill her. And if the One who is the Father inside can get to her, *she* will kill her." Protector stood, slipped her jacket on. "We must leave and get this under control."

"Let me help you calm the situation."

"We know how to *calm the situation*," she said sharply. "We have been calming her all our lives."

She turned and left. Ed sat in his chair, capsized by desolation.

3

By the time Andi and Ed stumbled through the door of his cabin Friday evening, close to ten p.m., she was a wrung-out rag. Since Monday, she'd been door-knocking every evening till almost ten. There'd been a couple speeches—the meetings had been surprisingly stimulating. The people were welcoming, and for the most part, their questions were intelligent and insightful. The hostility she expected hadn't materialized, and she found herself enjoying sparring with Ordrew supporters during the Q & A. But now, she was bushed.

Ed said, "Wine?"

"You have to ask?" She thought he would smile, but he didn't. His eyes were sad.

Except for an occasional suspicious question from a guy convinced Andi had a secret vault into which she planned to hide his guns or somebody scared witless about the immigrant wave about to wash over the county, the most serious drama she'd encountered involved the Essex case. The outrage seemed evenly distributed: Maybe half found Essex's murdering young Bernardo Cirilo horrifying, and a few people went so far as to speak of racism. The other group felt that Andi and the department were "persecuting" him, and a couple of men suggested that the Department was depriving Essex of his constitutional right to kill an intruder. To that, Andi always replied calmly. "The stand-your-ground law offers a legal defense," she'd say. "It's a trial strategy that a jury decides. Our job in the sheriff's department is to investigate and present the facts of the case, not to judge the merits of those facts." This seemed to satisfy most people. But the outrage about the Cirilo murder remained, no matter who became its target. Most valley people, she observed, were horrified, and blaming somebody—Essex or the sheriff's team—seemed to let off some of the steam. Andi got that.

Ed came back with the wine, handed her a glass, said, "We need to talk money. I just ordered lawn signs, and it ate half the fifteen hundred dollars in our kitty."

She sighed. "Let's not talk campaign now. I just want to veg out." She yawned again. "You look kind of down in the mouth. Anything wrong?"

He nodded. "I'm failing with a patient. Beatrice John, the one who calls herself Protector. She's got . . ." He stopped. "I shouldn't talk about her."

"I'm sorry, Ed." She studied his face, saw the sadness in his eyes. "Anything I can do?"

"No. She and I will have to work it out. Somehow." He gripped his glass, but didn't sip.

They sat in an empty silence for a while, then Andi asked, "Where's Grace tonight?"

"Not sure. Earlier, she met with Lisa McIntyre about that town hall she's organizing, and then she planned another pizza party with the junior class to pitch the idea. She called it 'getting buy-in.' Not sure where she is now, though. I'm thinking she's with her girls, acting like grown-ups."

"Ah. Look, Callie said the station's been getting calls about the Essex case from journalists in Missoula. Seems it's caught some traction over there. Let's check the news and see what shows up."

At his nod, Andi clicked it on.

<h2 style="text-align:center">4</h2>

At the first commercial break, they watched another unfamiliar ad come up. Andi tensed.

FADE IN: PRE-DAWN. HUNTERS IN BLAZE-ORANGE JACKETS AND CAPS, THEIR BONFIRE LIGHTING THE DARK, FLICKERING ON THEIR

LAUGHING FACES. DRINKING COFFEE IN A CIRCLE, OBVIOUSLY ABOUT TO BEGIN THEIR HUNT.

"What's this?" asked Andi.
"Trouble," Ed answered.

VOICEOVER: *Owning a firearm, gathering with friends to hunt—these are our rights as Montanans and citizens of Adams County.*

CUT TO SHOT OF MALE CITIZEN ENTERING A STORE, A HANDGUN ON HIS HIP.

VOICEOVER: *The Supreme Court has guaranteed every individual's right to own and carry a gun to protect themselves and their property. Montana has enshrined that right in its Constitution.*

CUT TO IMAGE OF WORDS OF MONTANA CONSTITUTION, WHITE WORDS ON BLACK BACKGROUND, TITLED "ARTICLE II, SECTION 12."

VOICEOVER (DEEP, RESONANT MALE VOICE, READING): *"The right of any person to keep or bear arms in defense of his own home, person, and property shall not be called in question."*

CUT TO SHOT OF SHERIFF'S OFFICE BUILDING, THEN QUICK CUT TO STOCK FOOTAGE OF POLICE RECEIVING WEAPONS FROM PEOPLE.

VOICEOVER: *But under Sheriff Ben Stewart and Deputy Andrea Pelton, your guns and your right to bear them will be taken away.*

CUT BACK TO ADAMS COUNTY SHERIFF'S BUILDING.

VOICEOVER: *Just as in big cities all over America, their plan is to seize your weapons.*

CUT TO IMAGE OF GENERIC HUNTER, AT A DISTANCE, LOOKING LIKE BRAD ORDREW, STANDING WITH HUNTERS' PEAK IN BACKGROUND, LEGS SPREAD, CRADLING A RIFLE IN CROOK OF HIS ARM.

VOICEOVER: *Brad Ordrew will protect and defend your Second Amendment right to keep and bear arms to protect yourself and your family. Stand with him. On Nov. 6, vote Brad Ordrew for Adams County Sheriff.*

CUT TO AMERICAN FLAG RIPPLING IN THE BREEZE. OVER THE IMAGE UNFURL THE WORDS, *BRAD ORDREW FOR SHERIFF: A PATRIOT'S CAMPAIGN.*

VOICEOVER: *Paid for by Friends of Ordrew for Sheriff.*

Mid-way through the ad, Andi, infuriated, had stood and moved closer to the TV. When the commercial ended, she grabbed the remote and shut off the television.

"Damn it, that's bullshit," she snarled. "We don't have any plan to seize firearms, and Ordrew knows it."

"Wasn't that a picture of police collecting weapons?"

"Had to be one of the buy-back programs they did years ago in some of the cities. My God, that's dishonest."

"How're you going to respond?"

"I'm calling Ordrew. He's going to repudiate Crane's support or . . ." She sputtered.

"Or what?"

That almost stopped her. She pondered that for a moment, made a decision. "Or I'll reveal that it's Crane behind these ads. People will remember him." She grabbed the phone and dialed, then waited. Ed watched her. After a moment, she said, "Brad, it's Andi. Your new ad is dishonest and defames our department. I want you to repudiate Loyd Crane publicly and refuse any more support from him. If you—"

Her eyes widened, and she looked shocked. "Well, I appreciate that." She ended the call.

Ed had been watching her face. "What'd he say?"

"He agreed. He'll issue a press release tomorrow repudiating the Friends of Ordrew for Sheriff and setting the record straight about the department's policy on guns." She still looked shocked.

"You believe him?"

"We'll see. If he doesn't follow through, I go public about Crane." She put the phone back in its cradle. "One thing I'm not keen about. He said he wouldn't give Crane's name out, but he said he'd call the bastard tonight and turn down any further support."

"Maybe we're underestimating Ordrew."

"I'm not. He's ugly about women and a hardass about policing, but he says he's not a liar."

"Which could be a lie."

5

Ordrew gripped the phone. His promise to Pelton, renouncing Crane's support, could be political suicide. *I can't stomach losing to a woman, even if she's a halfway decent cop.*

Still, the ad was a bald lie, and sickened him. Or was it repugnance at his own ambition that made his stomach churn?

"The hell with it." He punched the numbers, hard.

The call went to voicemail, which relieved him. Which, in turn, disgusted him. He hated feeling cowed by someone. "Reverend, I disapprove of the latest ad. It goes too far. I no longer want your support, if . . ." He panicked, not sure how to finish that *if*. He stammered, ". . . Uh, if that su-su-support includes dishonesty. Our deal will be off," he started, hesitated, immediately added, "unless future support remains within the truth. And don't call back with your crap about the greater truth." He uncapitalized the words.

After he hung up, he opened his laptop and started writing a press release for the morning, but found he couldn't concentrate. His weakness, his cowardice infusing all those *ifs*, revolted him. Unbidden, the image of Andi Pelton's face formed in his mind. *If she weren't running, I wouldn't need Crane.* He slammed his laptop shut.

"Damn her to hell," he shouted to his empty house.

SATURDAY, SEPTEMBER 22

1

Not long after Andi settled in her cubicle in the deputies' squad room, the second button on her desk phone blinked red. Gen Winters, on the reception desk, called out, "Line 2's yours, Andi."

"Thanks," she called back, and punched the blinking button. "Deputy Pelton speaking."

Bud Groh's German accent growled on the line. "Andi, here is Bud Groh. A press release from your opponent comes, which your comment for the noon news I'd like to get, please."

Andi caught her breath. *So, Ordrew followed through.* "Sure, Bud. Read it to me."

"To read this I will struggle, because full it is of typos and spelling errors. His meaning is clear enough, which now comes." He cleared his throat. "'A recent ad for my campaign, created by a group calling themselves *Friends of Ordrew for Sheriff*, contained inaccuracies. The Adams County Sheriff's Department has no plan to seize the guns of Adams County citizens. We must, of course, remain vigilant in defense of our Second Amendment rights. The *Friends of Ordrew for Sheriff* do not speak for my campaign or for me personally.'" Bud waited a second. "Have you any comment?"

Andi hesitated, partly angry, partly unsure how to respond. *Inaccuracies?* What kind of damn "repudiation" was this? "Bud, can you email me a copy of that? I'd like to talk it over with Ed and get back to you. A half-hour all right?"

"Ja. On the noon news I want to put this out, with your response. Each hour we'll play it with the news. Can you in twenty minutes your response send? A deadline I have to meet."

"Twenty minutes. You got it. Shoot me that email."

In two minutes, her email app dinged. She opened it, and dialed Ed's number.

Grace answered.

Andi said, "Grace, put the phone on speaker and get Ed, would you? I've got something I want to run by you both."

When they were together, Andi read Ordrew's press release. Grace reacted first. "You told him to renounce their support, right? This is a wuss's renunciation."

Andi waited for Ed to chime in. When he didn't, she said, "Ed? Your reaction?"

"Thinking it through. Technically, he's doing two things—setting the record straight about the department, and distancing himself from Crane's group. But I'm with Grace. It's distancing, not renouncing."

"Okay, we agree." She felt relieved. "Bud Groh wants my comment. What if I say I appreciate Ordrew, I mean, my opponent, setting the record straight about the gun issue, but call on him to actively renounce their support?"

Grace said, "You should be stronger than that. Say you're mad, and that you reject dishonesty from any source. Say that unless he publicly renounces the group, he is still accepting their support. And that the people of Adams County deserve better than what Ordrew's dishonest campaign has offered so far."

Andi digested that. "Wow, kid, you're good at this," she said. "Okay, stay by the phone. I'll write it up and call you back."

When she did, they both signed off on her statement, and she dialed the radio station, right at the nineteen-minute mark.

Andi expected a reaction to her statement and she got one. Shortly after the noon news, she got an email from Ordrew: *Harsh statement, Pelton. I did as you asked, and you give me this. Gloves come off now.*

It burned her. She hit *Reply*, and started typing. *You've had the gloves on? Bullshit, Bradley. You said you'd repudiate Crane, but you weaseled. You're hiding your cowardice and ambition behind the tough-guy patriot crap. I'm done with your garbage. Repudiate Crane, today, or I will name him. People in the valley will remember.*

She hovered the cursor over the *Send* icon. Hovered, because she knew she shouldn't send an email written in anger. She clicked on *Save* instead. Which just made her angrier.

TUESDAY, SEPTEMBER 25

1

Rain, steady and cold, had been falling since Saturday night. For the last couple of days, a bleakness had been rising in Ed's mind as the snow line crept lower on the mountains. Driving into town, he tried to convince himself it came from the gray and dismal sky. Failed.

By ten forty-five, Protector had missed her ten o'clock appointment, and more troubling, she hadn't called. Had he pushed too fast? What had he missed? Should he call, intrude on her? No. If Protector felt a need to stay away this morning, he had no business second-guessing her. Or at least not to the point of violating her privacy. Did she fear Connie's power and threat, fear to risk losing control again?

But in the end, he dialed. The degree of risk warranted it. He waited through the early rings, no answer, no voicemail. He let it ring, twenty, twenty-five, thirty times. Hung up.

Now, he faced the deeper intrusion—should he go to her apartment to see if she was all right? Or call the sheriff?

He reviewed the *duty to warn* rules. Did he have serious reason to think she was a suicide risk? The Father-within was said to want to kill Connie, but Protector might be wrong, and he, or rather she—a female "Father"—had agreed not to kill her while Ed tried to help. He picked up the phone again, stiffened, unexpectedly remembering Elizabeth Murphy, his first suicide.

Wait. Protector and maybe other alters seemed to have had things under control for many years. The missed appointment didn't say she was dead, or dying, or even in real peril. So, should he call the sheriff's office? *Yes? No?*

No. He laid the phone in its cradle.

2

Ed and Grace had made a lunch date for noon, and after his eleven o'clock patient left, he walked across the street to the Angler, still worrying about Protector and Connie. Grace's pink Volvo, the PV, angled against the curb outside the bar, under the blue neon fisherman casting his red neon line. The wind bit, and rain stung his eyes. He pulled his collar up higher. Up on the Monasteries, veils of snow drifted like wraiths at the tree line. *Too early*, he thought. *Could be a rough winter coming.*

Grace waited at a table on the restaurant side. "Hey, Northrup. You want to sit in here or over in the bar?"

More playing grown-up, he thought, eased from his worry by Grace's bright smile. "Let's eat here. It's dark enough outside." The bar was dark and cozy, but for such a shadowed day—and such a dimmed mood—it felt too confining. The restaurant of the Angler was all yellow bricks and blond wood, classic big-city elegance. *A light-filled space for a dark day.*

After ordering, Ed said, "How'd your talk to the civics class go?"

"Northrup, tell me something. When I was a senior, did I seem like I didn't want to learn anything?"

"Tough audience, eh?"

"The worst. They were looking at their cell phones before I even started. I asked Ms. McIntyre about it. She said these kids are, and I quote, 'a spectacularly inattentive bunch.' There's a rule against cell phones in class, but Lisa wasn't there and they paid no attention when I asked them to put them away. I'd call them mental empties."

Ed laughed. "What'd you talk about?"

"Whether free speech means you can lie."

"And they didn't get interested in that?"

"You know how I used to get when you talked about rules?"

"Like your brain left for China?"

"Yeah. A classroom of that."

Their food came, and they busied themselves tucking into it. With an almost full mouth, Grace looked at him. "Goddaa dade."

"'Godda dade'? What's that mean?"

She swallowed and laughed at the same time, then choked. When she got past it, she said, "*Got a date* for the Town Hall. The new principal said we can use the auditorium on October 12th."

"That's great, Grace. Gives you some time to build expectations and market it."

"Yeah, that's what I thought." She took another bite of burger and looked meditative. This time she swallowed first. "I'm thinking I should write up a bunch of questions and plant them in the sophomores."

THURSDAY, SEPTEMBER 27

1

Since his first patient wasn't scheduled until ten, and Grace was sleeping in, Ed took his time. A cup of coffee steamed on the counter as he broke two eggs into sputtering bacon grease. Outside, a gusty wind blew sleety rain against the house, rattling the loose window in the living room. He reminded himself to fix that on Saturday.

When the phone rang, Ed grabbed the kitchen extension while he watched the eggs crinkling around the edges. He liked cooking them over a hot flame, crisping the bottoms. "Ed Northrup."

"Tell your bitch to check the mail."

Shaken, he muttered, "I'm sorry, what . . ." but the dial tone interrupted him. Fear for Andi stabbed his chest.

He glanced at his watch. *8:07.* Mail wouldn't reach his post office box till eleven. He dialed Andi.

"Hey," he said when she answered. "I just got a weird phone call. Guy said, 'Tell . . .'" His fear for her censored him. "'Tell your girl to check the mail.'"

"Who's he mean? Grace, or me?"

Her naming Grace chilled him. "Jesus, I have no idea. I figured I should let you know." An urge to tell her the actual word pushed at him. He pushed back against it.

"Well, I won't get time to run to the post office till late. Any idea what I'm looking for?"

She needed to know. "No, but I don't think you're going to like it. The guy's words were, 'Tell your bitch . . .'."

"Huh. That's me. On second thought, I'll run over at lunchtime."

As they ended the call, he smelled the smoke. His eggs were a blackened char.

•   •   •

Before his first patient of the morning, Ed stopped at the post office to get his own mail. He stuck his head into the office itself to say hello to Patty Neal, the postmaster.

Patty looked more harried than usual.

"Busy?"

"These damn direct mail campaigns." She nodded toward the bin of mail she'd clunked on the counter. "Gotta get 'em to every mailbox in the valley in a day. Damn rules." She seemed ready to spit.

"Well, 'neither snow nor rain nor heat nor gloom of night.'"

She shot him a nasty look, softened by a smile. "Or brainless bureaucrats."

Out in the lobby, he opened his box and pulled out the handful of mail. Walking back to his office, he thumbed through the stack. One of the items was a blank envelope, with the words "Resident, Box 33, Jefferson, MT 59763" and the stamp on the front. He tore it open.

Inside was a single sheet, folded in thirds. In 18-point font, with a blurred picture of Andi at the top, the message was plain:

Do you want this killer to be your sheriff?

Four years ago, Andrea Pelton screwed up the motel incident and murdered an innocent man—and she was never investigated, indicted, or tried. Do you want for sheriff a trigger-happy killer who thinks she's above the law?

Rid the valley of this menace: Vote for Brad Ordrew for Sheriff on Nov. 6.

Anger seared him. He slammed his office door and went for the phone. He started to dial Andi's number, then changed to Grace's cell. When she answered, her voice rasped like sand. "Whaaat?"

"Grace. You're talking to the juniors in a couple hours, right?"

"Northrup, I'm sleeping."

"Not any more. Stop by my office on the way to school. You need to read something before you meet with your class. If I'm with a patient, I'll leave an envelope beside the coffee machine with your name on it. You got that?"

She made a huffing noise like a hungry grizzly waking up after a long hibernation. "I heard your words."

"Just do it. You've got to be aware of what's going on before you talk to your class."

"So, what's going on?"

"Another dishonest ad about Andi. A brutal one."

Her voice cleared its sand and radiated anger. "The hell with this, Northrup. I'll be there in fifteen minutes."

2

His ten o'clock hadn't arrived yet when Grace blasted through the waiting room door. "Where's this ad?"

He picked it off the table where he'd placed it for her to find and handed it to her. She read it, her face turning red as her sweater.

"Patty at the post office said it's a direct mail campaign. Going to everybody in the county."

She absorbed that. "I'm, like, totally pissed."

"Me, too. I left Andi a voice message about it, but I haven't heard from her. What're you going to say to the juniors?"

"You know what, Northrup? It's scary. So, far, I'd say the kids at school are split about fifty-fifty about Andi."

Ed swallowed hard. Students' opinions notoriously reflect their parents'. If so, Andi's campaign might be a land-locked *Titanic*. He looked out the window. The week-long cold rain had blanketed the mountains with snow above three thousand feet. On the valley floor, drab ground lay under a shroud of gray, fabrics of fog hanging in the treetops, long swamps of brown water on the fields. A week ago, a dry, sweet fragrance of dying meadow grasses rode like an aftertaste of summer on the cooling air, but now everything smelled of damp and death.

Grace was talking. ". . . are yakking about the ads. They say Andi's as bad as Obama."

"Wow. 'As bad as?'" His chill deepened. Adams County had voted for Obama twice.

"But I just say, 'Don't be stupotic,' and they shut up."

"Stupotic?"

"Stupid and idiotic," she snapped. "Don't you understand English?"

"Not your brand. Look, maybe you want to get past the anger before you talk to the class."

She frowned. "I'm being bitchy, aren't I? I'm sorry. I'm mad for Andi, but that's no reason to take it out on you." She glanced at his clock.

"Class starts in eleven minutes. I'll come up with something on the way over."

"Try reminding them of the truth about that day."

"The day she got shot?"

"Exactly."

3

Andi hadn't gotten to the post office over her lunch break; a sleet-caused crash on the highway had sucked up all her time. She'd just gotten back to the station in time for the shift change at three. Callie gestured her to come up to the Reception desk. "You better take a gander at this." She handed Andi the flyer. She read, and could feel her face reddening, with anger, not fear. Pete came in from his own patrol, dripping, and she handed the letter to him. He moved his lips as he read.

He handed it back. "Repulsive crap."

Andi crumpled it. "This tears it. I'm pissed." She focused her fury, thinking fast. "I want to make a statement on the radio."

Callie, who'd watched this, nodded. "I think you need to. Everybody in the building got the same thing. I'm bettin' it went to the whole darn valley."

Andi turned to Pete, "Can I skip shift report? I want to show this to Ben. I need him to weigh in on what I say."

Pete nodded. "Sure. But keep it quiet. Ordrew'll cry foul if he finds out."

"I don't give a good goddamn what he cries." She turned to Callie, who was releasing her chair to the evening receptionist/dispatcher, Sylvie Holmes. "Can you patch me through to the post office?"

"Faster'n a diarrhea strike," Callie said. To Sylvie, Callie said, "One minute." She turned to her console.

Just then, Chip Coleman walked through Reception on his way to report. "Hey, Andi. My wife called, told me about the bullshit flyer. All the guys got your back."

Andi forced a smile. *That felt good.* "Thanks, Chip."

After a moment, Callie pushed the *Hold* button. "Line two, Andi. It's Patty at the post office. You can use that phone." She gestured toward a handset on the counter, but Andi said, "I'll take it at Pete's desk." She looked to Pete. "That all right? I want privacy."

"Do it."

In Pete's office, she hit the blinking button. "Patty, hi. This is Andi Pelton, and I—" She stopped, listening. Her frown sharpened more. "Everybody in the county? My God, that must have cost a fortune." She was quiet again. "So, who mailed them? . . . Really? Isn't that unusual?" She waited, then said, "Well, yeah, I'm sorry too. . . . Thanks, we could use luck."

She went back to Reception and found Pete, copying notes for the briefing. "Patty says it went out to the whole damn county. Boxes of the envelopes were delivered last night from Missoula's post office, just as the window closed. A guy Patty didn't recognize came by this morning and asked if they'd arrived." She wondered, *Loyd Crane?*

Pete said, "If Patty doesn't know him, he's not from the valley. Did she get an ID?"

"She said it was from a 'George String, LLC.'"

Pete grunted. "G-string. A fake ID."

"The shipment originated in Idaho. All the paperwork was done in Twin Falls." She scrunched up her nose. "Twin Falls was where Loyd Crane's church was. No doubt still is."

"I've got to get to report, Andi. I'll tell the guys you had an emergency. You need to jump on this. Word is, people are starting to buy the bullshit in these ads."

"I'm on it. You coming with me, Pete?"

"I'll join you at the radio station after report."

As Andi gathered her jacket and cap and went through Reception, Sylvie Holmes, now in the chair, said, "Ben called. He's furious. Bernie got a flyer and told him about it. He's on his way in. Should be here in five."

• • •

When he barged into the station, Andi could see Ben's anger, but from the light in his eyes, she sensed he was also almost happy. Maybe this election fight was invigorating him.

Andi expected an explosion, but instead, got, "What's your next move?"

"Do you think I—"

Ben lifted his meaty hand. "Ain't my campaign, Andi. You tell me. I'll advise if I think somethin's better."

"Right," she said, steeling herself. "I'm doing a radio spot. I want to hit back hard."

Ben nodded. "Somebody'll yell the flyer's free speech."

"Libel's not. And fighting back is free speech too."

Ben smiled. "Mailin's like this ain't cheap. Who'd have a lot a money and a grudge against you?"

"Reverend Loyd Crane."

Ben scowled. "You ain't serious. That bastard . . ." He wheezed.

"It's him. Ordrew told me Crane is behind these ads. I'm sure he sent this mailing."

Ben's big face turned even ruddier. "I'm comin' with you to the station."

4

At the radio station, Pete pulled in behind them. The three descended on Bud Groh's tiny office. He hadn't opened his mail, but when he read the mailer Andi'd handed him, he sputtered, *"Gott-im-Himmel.* You I can help. You need what?"

Ben started to answer, then closed his mouth, nodded toward Andi. She said, "I'd like five minutes on the air. Ben starts out, reminding everybody what happened at the motel." She checked with Ben, who nodded. "Then I'll ask folks to support clean campaigning and honesty, and ask the people to exercise their good judgment in reacting. We'll pay for the airtime out of campaign contributions."

Bud shook his head. "For public service announcements I have a budget."

Andi said, "If Ordrew asks for equal time, will you give him a spot?"

"Ja. But just on the mailing to comment, no campaigning."

Pete said, "Bud, give me thirty seconds. I'll announce the Sheriff's Department will be consulting with the county attorney about possible libel charges."

Andi's eyes widened. "Are we?"

"I'm calling Irv Jackson soon's we're done here."

"Won't get far," Ben said. "Irv's skittish about First Amendment stuff."

"You know, Pete," Andi said. "I'm not sure we ought to say that on the radio. I don't want it to look like I'm using the department for my personal benefit. Besides, who do we charge? Later, you have a heart-to-heart with Ordrew—" She glanced at Ben. "With my *opponent*. Warn him to stop these ads because they inappropriately attack a colleague. Something like that."

Pete looked at her a moment, then smiled. "Tough lady. Okay, I'll do it that way." He paused. "You'll make a damn fine boss."

5

Ten minutes later, Ben and Andi sat at black microphones in the station's cramped, dim studio. A Toby Keith song was playing. Sitting at his own microphone about two feet across the narrow table from Andi and Ben, Bud Groh said, "Fifty seconds we've got. When I raise this hand, ten seconds. The last five with my fingers I'll count, five, four, three, two, one, like this. The public service announcement I'll give, and when I point, Sheriff, you start your piece. After, I introduce you—" He nodded toward Andi. "When I point, you start. Do we understand?"

She and Ben nodded, and Andi was surprised she didn't feel nervous: Steady, focused anger. She was ready.

The Toby Keith song ended, Bud raised his right hand, fingers splayed. Then, he started counting off the last five, and then flipped a switch and read from a card, "This program we interrupt for an important public service announcement from the Adams County Sheriff's Department—"

Mistake, Andi thought. This wasn't an official Sheriff's Department spot, it was from her campaign, but she nodded gratefully at Bud. His thumb went up as he continued with the announcement. "—about a mailing today many of you in the county may have received. The first person will be Sheriff Ben Stewart to speak." He pointed at Ben, who looked down at his swiftly jotted notes.

Ben read. "Today each of you got a deceitful piece of mail that lied about what happened in March 2014 during a police operation at the Jefferson House Motel. Let me remind you what actually took place." Ben looked at Andi and pushed his notes back. "You folks'll remember that some tax evasion conspirators were meetin' at the Jeff House. One of our citizens, Victor Sobstak, came to us. He volunteered to go into their meetin' wearin' a hidden microphone, which ain't safe. When the conspirators discovered the wire, they attacked Victor, and I ordered

Deputy Pelton, followed by Deputies Peterson and Coleman, into the room. One of the conspirators fired his weapon, hittin' Deputy Pelton in her shoulder, which damn near took her life." He paused. Andi could see he was shaken by the memory. "Pelton shot back, killin' the man who'd shot her. It was heroic police work in a dangerous and volatile situation. The message we all got in the mail this mornin' is hateful and dishonest, and insults a fine law enforcement officer, not to mention our department. And it insults all of us citizens of Monastery Valley who respect the professionalism and courage of our deputies. I'm askin' each one of you to throw the damn thing in the garbage. Thank you." He sat back, winded and pale.

Andi felt a jolt of worry for him, but he smiled.

Bud Groh said, "Next, from Deputy Andrea Pelton we hear, who is running for sheriff of Adams County." He pointed to Andi.

She leaned in close to the microphone, but Bud waved her back, and when she sat naturally, gave the thumbs-up again.

Andi closed her eyes. "When I saw the message this morning, two things went through my mind. The first was anger. Whoever is sending these messages, both today's letter and the previous TV ads, obviously opposes my being elected sheriff, which is their right. But this is not who we are in the valley, hiding behind anonymous slurs. We can disagree, but let's do it in the open, and do it about issues. I am outraged at these cowardly, anonymous attacks on my character. I challenge whoever is making them to have the courage to face me *in person*, to make their opposition public and open. Whoever is behind these lies, I will debate them, or my opponent, any time, any place.

"The second thing that went through my mind is that in the almost six years I've lived among you and served as a deputy in your sheriff's department, I've come to know you as good, decent, and honest people. I believe that no one in our valley would do this cowardly thing, and I trust that all of you will remember the facts of what happened that day as Sheriff Stewart just reminded us. I expect you to judge me on those facts and on my record, not on the cowardly, uh, bullshit—" She looked guiltily at Bud Groh, then plowed on when Bud smiled. "—that we're being exposed to. Monastery Valley is too great for hate." She sat back.

Bud picked up his card, read, "This concludes the public service announcement. It will be repeated today at five and thirty-five minutes past each hour, until sign-off at midnight. Thank you. To regular programming we now return." Holding his finger to his lips for the others, he reached up and flicked a switch. A Willie Nelson tune started playing through the speakers, and he said, "Well done. All evening and tomorrow it will replay." The phone rang in the outer office. "Your opponent, demanding time, I expect." He rolled his eyes.

As they left the studio, Ben put his big hand on Andi's shoulder. "'The valley's too great for hate,'" he said. His voice cracked. "That won some hearts, not just some votes." His voice thickened. "Sure won mine."

Andi laughed. "I won your heart a long time ago. But it's a sweet thing to say."

Ben harrumphed. "Crap on toast, this heart attack's makin' me mushy."

6

The Cattlewomen's Association meeting was packed. From the crowd size, Andi figured they'd read the flyer and were coming in droves to see how she'd deal with it. She wondered how many had heard her radio response.

Maggie Sobstak, this year's president, introduced her, giving a glowing endorsement whose reception—cool, polite, dark eyes— ratcheted Andi's nerves tight. It wasn't hard to jettison her speech and plunge into the flyer. She skipped over the Big Idea part of her speech, and knew that the Essex stand-your-ground case would be nowhere on the agenda tonight. She detailed what Ben had presented as the history of the shooting, and laid out much of what she'd said on the radio. When a group of women stood and clapped, she had no crowd-counting trouble: They comprised less than half the room. She asked for questions, hoping she'd stay cool.

A rancher raised her hand. "Deputy, Mr. Ordrew said the Friends of Ordrew for Sheriff don't speak for him. You didn't respond to their ad, though, about taking away our Second Amendment rights. We believe in guns here in Montana. How can you plan to seize them?"

Softball, she thought. "As my opponent said, we don't plan to seize any guns, ma'am. Except when they're used to commit crimes." A few women smiled. "As my opponent correctly noted in his statement, I, and the whole department, are staunch supporters of the Constitution in all its articles and amendments, including the Second."

The woman almost growled. "You confiscated the weapons of Mr. Daniel Essex, who was defending his home against an armed burglar. Stand-your-ground is our right, guaranteed by the Constitution."

Surprised, Andi assembled her thoughts, and stepped out from behind the lectern. No softball this time. More like a landmine. "Ma'am, as I'm sure you recognize, I can't talk much about an ongoing investigation, but I can correct misunderstandings. The young man killed was *unarmed*. Stand-your-ground laws are passed by the states, not by the Constitution. It will be up to Mr. Essex and his attorney to prove to a jury that he was standing his ground as Montana law defines it."

The woman stood stock-still. "I heard you took all his weapons, even though just one killed that boy. So, you don't deny you *did* confiscate his weapons. And you *did* imprison him for standing his ground." A small group of women clapped.

Andi felt a flare of anger, returned to the lectern, lifted the water glass she'd left there, and sipped slowly. "Again, I can provide correct information when the facts aren't well enough known. We confiscated the murder weapon and a second gun Mr. Essex suggested had killed the victim, no more. It's police procedure, everywhere in the United States, to confiscate weapons that are used in a shooting. If Mr. Essex is found not guilty and released by the court, he will of course receive his weapons back. And we didn't arrest Mr. Essex for standing his ground. We did so because he killed a 14-year-old boy." She paused, letting the women—most of them mothers—taste that.

From the frowning faces, Andi suspected this audience would not be on her side. "Are there other questions?"

One of the original clappers stood and faced the first questioner. "How can you talk as if Daniel Essex is being picked on by the sheriff's office when he's just done a horrible thing? Don't you have any feeling for that poor boy and his family?"

"'That poor boy' was stealing from Daniel, for God's sake. I heard he tried to attack Daniel."

Andi put up her hand. "Please, there's a lot of misunderstanding about this case. I grant you Bernardo Cirilo might have been stealing beer—although we don't know for sure. But he never attacked. In fact, he was shot from behind and fell face first into the refrigerator. I realize this is shocking and painful and violates everything we value here in Adams County. Everywhere I go in the valley, people are upset about it." She paused. Many of the women were nodding. "Okay, may I have the next question, please?"

Cathy Sound, a rancher Andi knew from a breaking-and-entering last year, stood. "Deputy, what is your plan for making the valley safer? Mr. Ordrew thinks we're in great danger, either from riots or from immigrants."

Another landmine. "Cathy, you know, if we had an urban population living in poverty and simmering with rage, and if we had a large immigrant population who had taken jobs away from those citizens and made them poor, we'd have serious problems and my opponent would be right. But we have neither. Let me ask you all a question: Would any of you here join a rioting mob and attack the police like we saw happening in that ad?" She looked out at the audience.

No one raised a hand.

"That's right, we solve our problems differently here. I'm from Chicago. I know civil unrest and the conditions that generate it. We don't have those conditions here. And you all know better than I do, folks here don't riot when they're unhappy, you get to work to change things. We've got problems, but they're different from those in the big cities. The solutions to our problems are the same solutions you and your parents and your grandparents have relied on for generations: hashing them out with one another, working *together* and not *against* one another, teaching the youngsters the values that have made the valley what it is. That's why I'm proposing . . ."

She recited her Big Idea, and she saw that faces were softening. These women wanted the valley to be the safe, familiar, nurturing place they'd grown up in, and she was offering them that. When she finished, the number standing and applauding had grown. Not as large as she'd hoped, but grown. She sighed behind her smile. *One meeting at a time,* she thought.

FRIDAY, SEPTEMBER 28

1

When ten a.m. once again came and went without Protector showing up for her Friday appointment, Ed's worry escalated, and once again he wrestled with arguments for and against violating her privacy. This time, he called less reluctantly, but again he got no answer. He fretted, her privacy and self-determination against his growing fear that she was losing the battle. What if Connie—or the Father-within—had escaped Protector's control? Hadn't she come out during their last session, against Protector's wishes?

He shuddered: Perhaps his patient had already killed herself—or she'd tried but failed, and God help her, lay at the edge of death even now. He had to intervene, right or wrong. He couldn't bear the thought of her suffering—or dying—alone. Still, for a few minutes, he held back. She was a free human being, entitled to miss an appointment.

Or she was dead.

He dialed Andi's cell phone. When she answered, he said, "I need your help with a patient." He explained the situation and his concern.

"You have reason to believe she might be suicidal?"

"Absolutely, no question. She's missed two straight appointments, and has been actively talking about death."

"Who's the patient?"

"It's Beatrice John." Andi's gasp was palpable. Last fall, Beatrice had saved her when the "bishop" of the sex trafficking cult Andi was investigating had a knife to her throat. Andi owed Beatrice her life.

"Give me the address. I'm on my way."

2

The door to the small house was unlocked, and after three minutes of hard pounding and pushing the doorbell button, Andi let herself in, and knew Beatrice was dead with her first breath. Judging from the smell, she'd been dead a few days. The body wasn't in the kitchen or living room. When Andi pushed open the single bedroom door, the odor of decay blasted out.

She put her handkerchief to her face and went in. Beatrice John lay under the blanket. On the bedside table stood a pill bottle and a quart bottle of Rye whiskey. She read the pill bottle: haloperidol. Both bottles were empty.

She went back outside and called Doc Runge, the medical examiner; Runge promised to get there in twenty minutes. Then she made the harder call.

3

Before Andi's call ended, Ed's eyes burned with tears that gathered, but refused to fall. After she hung up, he stared through a film of grief at the surface of his desk, oblivious to the dial tone droning from the earpiece. After a minute of immobility, he heard the triple tone and a woman's voice. He lifted the phone to his ear, heard, ". . . please hang up and try again."

Paralyzed, he held the receiver above its base, knowing he should hang up, but unable to command his arm. *If I don't hang up, maybe I didn't hear . . .* His hand absently dropped the receiver onto its cradle. A gale of grief swept through him, a wind of anguish he'd felt more than thirty years ago, when young Elizabeth Murphy had hanged herself. His eyes were hot, wet, but empty as his heart. Slowly, he lowered his head to the desk and rested his forehead on his arms.

Twenty minutes later, when his waiting room door opened, he lifted his head. *I can't do it,* he thought. He considered not going out to meet his patient, not even telling her he could not see her this afternoon. *Eventually she'll leave.*

Cold rain drummed against his window. He watched the falling rivulets on the glass. The woman waiting in his outer office was young, seeing him after the SIDS death of her infant daughter. Ed groaned. He couldn't abandon her, as he'd abandoned poor Connie. He covered his eyes.

No, I didn't abandon Connie. Maybe I moved too fast, but I didn't abandon her. He stood and put his hand on the knob of his office door, then paused, taking in a long shuddery breath. *Showtime.* He gathered himself. He opened the door.

MONDAY, OCTOBER 1

1

When Andi came into the station before morning report, Callie gestured her over.

"Something up?" she asked.

"Yeah." Callie picked up the Jefferson *Bee*, the town's twice-weekly paper, and handed it over the counter. She lowered her voice. "The prick's answer to your statement's on page three."

For four days, Brad Ordrew hadn't reacted publicly to Andi's broadcast statement, nor had he demanded equal time. Now, she saw, as she unfolded the paper, he'd bought an inch of column space in this morning's paper:

> The Ordrew for Sheriff Campaign deplores the recent attacks on Deputy Andrea Pelton. We join Deputy Pelton in challenging whoever is attacking her to do so face-to-face.

Most of the deputies were gathered in the conference room before she arrived for the morning report. They were passing the newspaper around and laughing. Through his nose, Chip Coleman whined, "He *deplores*. He deplores the attacks, then says, 'Do it to her face.'" They all laughed. When Ordrew walked in, the laughter stopped abruptly. Xavier said, "Clever shot there, Brad." There were a few chuckles.

Ordrew grimaced. He sat down at the head of the table, in Ben's, and lately Pete's, chair. "Laugh your asses off. When I'm sheriff, things will tighten up around here," he said, but Andi thought his voice sounded almost hurt. The banter stopped, no one spoke. Pete came in. Ordrew stayed in the sheriff's chair, until Pete tapped his shoulder.

"You're not sheriff yet, Brad." Pete waited until Ordrew hooked another chair with his foot and dragged it around to the head of the table, and moved into it. "That good enough, Acting Sheriff?"

Andi watched this, curious. *He's defensive, and covering it up.* That little dab of psychoanalysis gave her a peculiar satisfaction. *He's not immune to me.*

2

The screen of his cell phone read *Lynn Monroe*. Ed sighed. He didn't want to talk to Lynn now. Not to anyone. The weekend had been hell. Awake, he'd been dry-eyed but stunned by grief and guilt. Asleep, he'd been plagued by restless, heartbroken dreams. Andi had been wonderful, offering to cancel her talks to the Methodists and the nursing department at the hospital, and Grace had asked if he'd like her to stay home with him. He'd asked them to stick with their plans. He wanted to be alone, to burrow like a mole into the cave of his grief.

Realizing he'd be of no use to patients, he'd rescheduled today's and tomorrow's for later in the week. But the day had dragged, hours taking days, and now, mid-evening, when he was ready to cocoon himself for the night, trying to talk with Lynn felt almost too heavy, as though his chest were buried in a hundred pounds of sand and words were trapped in it.

He hit *Talk*, tried to inject some energy into his voice. He doubted that he'd succeeded. "Hey, Lynn. What's up?"

"Ed, I heard about your client's suicide. I'm so sorry. I—"

Panic filled him. *Already? A complaint against me?* "How'd you hear?"

"Your daughter, Grace. She called me yesterday and asked if I could come over for a couple of days and cover for you. She thinks you're taking it hard."

Unwept tears reached his eyes. *Grace.* A rush of gratitude to his girl came, but embarrassed, his breath caught. "She shouldn't have asked you that, Lynn. You're busy."

"It's already arranged. I spoke with my boss last night and he's fine with my taking the rest of the week. I've got vacation time anyway. And Rachel's good with it, too."

Ed struggled—Rachel? Embarrassed, he murmured, "Uh, I'm sorry, Lynn. Can't place Rachel." Just then he got it. "Ah, your wife."

Lynn chuckled. "I still love it when she's called that. Anyway, I just wanted to give you a heads-up that I'll leave tonight—tomorrow's my regular morning at the high school—so how about I meet you at your office at eight, before I'm due at school? I just need you to call your clients for the rest of the week and alert them to my stepping in."

"No, Lynn, I can't let you do this. I, uh, . . ." He ran out of words.

"Ed, you're in no shape to see people after something like this. Let me help."

He blushed. It was one thing for him to know that, but . . . He sighed. *Knock off the false pride.* "You're absolutely right, Lynn, I'm a mess. I'll get on the phone tonight, and I'll meet you at the office. Eight tomorrow morning." He closed his eyes. "And thank you."

"Good," she said. "In the morning, then."

He tapped *End.* He opened his appointment book. Listed tomorrow afternoon's patients—he'd already rescheduled the morning's—and began the calls. He told them the truth, simple and unvarnished. A patient had died, he felt too much grief to be objective, and his colleague was taking over for him for a few days. Two of the five he called said they'd rather just wait to see him, but the other three were grateful. The last woman he called said, "I'm very sad to hear of it, Ed. Please take good care of yourself, like you keep telling me to."

As he hung up, the tears returned, and this time, they fell.

3

No more than ten minutes later, his landline rang. Ed sighed and climbed up from the couch. *Another call. More sympathy?*

"Ed? Ben Stewart here." His voice sounded choked.

"Ben? What's wrong?"

"What makes you think somethin's wrong? I'm just finishin' a bite of—" Offline, he shouted, "What's the name of this food?" A muffled answer. Ben came back. "*Omelet poivre vert,* whatever the hell that means." He pronounced it *ohm-lay pwa fert.*

Ed tried to translate, gave up. Sighed.

Ben apparently had swallowed the last of his mouthful, because his voice was clear. "Somethin' gnawin' on you, pal?"

Ed told him about the death of Protector; he named her Beatrice John.

"Hmm. That's your multiple brains person, right?"

Ed sighed. "Right."

"Hell's bells, Ed, you know this. A person who offs herself, she's carryin' more baggage than you shrinks can lift. Don't blame yourself."

Ed had nodded. "I know. But I pushed her too fast."

"How long you been seein' her?"

"A year. She was that woman involved in the Warriors of Yahweh cult."

"Hell's bells, Ed, give 'er a rest. Ain't nobody caught up in that kinda shit you can fix in a year of Sundays."

"I suppose."

"Don't suppose. You know this better'n I do. Maybe you oughta call that beachball friend of yours in Minneapolis, have a heart-to-heart."

"Charlie Merwin. I might do that." Merwin, Ed's friend since grad school, had been a staunch support through all the years. And yeah, he looked like a beachball.

"Anyway, Andi in?"

"No. Campaigning."

"Good for her. Have her give me a call when she gets in."

"Will do. Talk to you." Ed hung up. He thought about calling Merwin.

No. Not tonight.

4

Andi came in as Ben's call ended. She saw Ed's reddened eyes and worn look, felt a pang of sorrow for him. "Wow, you look rocky."

He nodded "This damn phone's been ringing off the hook. And you look tired too."

"I am. Who's been calling?"

"Lynn Monroe and Ben. He wants you to call."

She wanted only to sit down, have a glass of wine, veg out. "I can't, not tonight."

As she said it, though, her cell phone rang. Ed muttered, "God."

The phone's screen read, *Xavier Contrerez.* "Xav? What's up?" *Oh, oh. Something wrong with the case?*

"Hey, Andi. I just got off the phone with our friend, Bradley. He tried to bribe me to vote for him."

"No." She took a quick breath, straightened her back. *How do I use this?* "Mind if I put this on speaker so Ed can join us?" To Ed, she mouthed, *Okay?* He nodded, despite his sad eyes.

"Go for it."

She did. "Okay, tell me about this bribe."

"Well, he starts out, 'Got a question, my friend.' Asks me if anybody in the department will vote for him. I go, 'Well, you'll get one vote.' He's pissed, but he kind of does a double-take. If you can believe it, he goes, 'Why are you guys so gung-ho for Pelton? You want a woman running the department?' Then he says he heard you botched that entry—just like that mailer said. I told him what went down, that it was by the book, just the way he likes things. I asked him where he gets his attitude about you. Guess what he said?"

"No idea. His father spanked him too hard?"

Ed almost smiled and Xavier laughed. "So, he gets this look, kind of half-mad and half-sad, you know. 'Back in LA,' he says, 'I had a woman partner, a rookie. One afternoon we went in on a motel domestic, side-by-side rooms, two guys start shooting.'"

Andi said, "Yeah, he told me the same story. The rookie jaked out on him, and he hasn't trusted women since."

"Yeah, that's it. I told him you're not like that, you're tough as they come. Get this, though. He killed one of the shooters, just like you. Anyway, when I said you're tough, that's when he offered me the bribe."

"What was it?"

"He says, okay, maybe you were a good cop, but he was going to win the election and he wanted me on his side. He said if I bring the Latino votes, he'd make it worth my while when he takes office. Said there'll be a senior deputy position open."

Andi gasped. "So, he's going to fire Pete too?" Ed jerked up straighter, his face now alarmed.

"Or knock him down a grade. I don't know. Anyway, I told him to go to hell."

Andi slowly shook her head. "Thanks for letting me know, Xav. I don't know how I'll use this, but we'll find a way."

5

Brad Ordrew laid the salad he'd made for supper on the table, but didn't touch it. He mulled over what Xavier Contrerez had told him about Andi, how she'd handled the motel entry by the book and gotten shot doing it. He stared at the salad, lifted a forkful of lettuce to his lips, then set it back down. *Not hungry.* He didn't know what to make of what he was observing about Andi and hearing from the other guys about her. What Xavier had told him about the motel entry had staggered him. His stomach cramped at the memory of his own motel entry, getting shot, his time in the hospital. The old familiar fury started to boil. *Fuck this.*

He roughly scraped the uneaten salad into a bowl and tossed it into the refrigerator. *Admit it: I'm confused.* That females don't make reliable cops had been his lode star, drilled into him by his father, locked in when he got shot. *I can't let Pelton shake that.* As he was rinsing his plate, his cell phone rang. While he dried his hands, he looked at the screen: *Rev. Loyd Crane.*

"Deputy, I read your statement in your paper. I'm baffled. What led you to make such an admission in public? Haven't I—"

"Look, Crane, there are some things people here don't tolerate, and anonymous character assassination is one of them. After she made that radio statement, people were starting to ask me if I'd heard it and what did I think about it. I had to say something or people would start wondering about me."

"You've touched on an important point, Deputy. What *do* you think of her story?"

There it was. The question he didn't know how to answer. "Your Greater Truth would say the facts of what happened don't matter as much as how I can manipulate those facts in favor of my campaign. Right?"

"As far as it goes. But you didn't answer my question. What's your opinion about her story?"

He took another breath. "I don't know. At first, I believed what your mailing said. But I've asked some of the other deputies, and they all deny it. They say she operated professionally, did things by the book."

"Nonsense. Deputy, I was in that room. I saw it all. We were having a quiet meeting to discuss tax reform. Unprovoked and unannounced, she burst into the room and started shooting. I thank God every day that only one of my associates was killed. Another fired back and wounded her. We were all arrested based on her scurrilous lies about me."

So, this is why he hates her. "Sir, with all due respect, that's not at all what the deputies tell me, including our Acting Sheriff, who was also there."

Crane's silence stretched out. Ordrew waited. "Deputy, you do recall, don't you, that I am funding your campaign out of the grace I bear toward you? Where does your loyalty lie?"

Ordrew recoiled. *Grace? What kind of bullshit is this?* He swallowed. "Reverend, I am grateful for your support. But my loyalty is first and always with the law and the rigorous enforcement of the law. I'm a policeman, not a disciple." When he finished, he was trembling. Would this cost him Crane's support? He panicked. Everything rode on winning this election.

He scrambled. "Sir, I'm sorry. I haven't a reason to distrust your description. If it were just the other deputies' word against yours, I'd have no trouble saying my loyalty is to you. It's just that I've been watching Pelton closely and what I see suggests she's competent."

"Oh, she's competent. A competent *killer*."

Ordrew waited a moment, unable to swallow, then said, his voice soft, "I don't doubt you, sir. And thank you for your help clearing it up." He felt sick, revolted by his words.

"I expect your behavior to reflect your loyalty, then, Deputy. As I told you before, at every opportunity, you are to attack Pelton with the same vigor you seem to feel for the law. Am I clear?"

"Perfectly clear."

The line went dead and Ordrew dropped the phone, went to his bathroom, and threw up.

TUESDAY, OCTOBER 2

1

Seven a.m. On the porch, Ed waited, stunned with apprehension. Coffee steamed in the mug he'd set on the railing. The first sun in over a week reddened the mountain snow; above, the sky shone, startlingly blue. He didn't see it. He didn't feel the soft breeze on his face, a breeze promising the return of warmth. Though he looked pensive, he was not thinking. He couldn't bear thinking, because all he thought about was Protector lying in her small bed, dying alone.

His watch showed seven a.m. Ten o'clock was three hours away, the hour that had been Protector's appointment every Tuesday for the past year. He shrugged on his jacket, found the keys in its pocket, and climbed into his pickup. Steam rose from the coffee cup forgotten on the railing.

Where to? He didn't care. To himself he whispered, "Just drive." Maybe south to the riverside grotto where he'd always found peace in the dim light and soft eddying flow of the river? But before he reached even the edge of town, he knew where he was heading: up Mount Adams to the base of the Coliseum. To St. Brendan's Monastery. He pulled over, took out his cell, pulled up the Abbot's number, and called. Abbot Timothy said he was free all morning and agreed to see him.

His tears welled again and he laid his head on the steering wheel. He could not pull back on the highway for many minutes.

2

Abbot Timothy met him at the monastery door. "Ed. How are you doing, my friend?"

"Not well, Tim." He described Protector's death.

Timothy shook his head. "Tragic." He took Ed's arm. "Come back to my office."

"No, Tim, I have a favor to ask."

"Anything."

"You folks still building those beautiful caskets?"

The abbot smiled. "Indeed. It's our livelihood."

"Could we go out to the workshop? I'd like to buy one."

Ed remembered the workshop from four years ago, when Grace's mother had died, leaving her in Ed's care. Grace had asked to have her mom buried in Jefferson, and he and she had visited St. Brendan's to choose one of the monastery's beautiful caskets. The shop was behind the monastic enclosure itself, and Timothy led the way down a stairway to a back door.

This high on the mountain, ten inches of autumn snow had accumulated, but the monks had opened a broad path from the monastery to the workshop. The intense sunlight filtering through the dark green trees cast blue shadows on the drifts. Stepping through the door, Ed smelled the sweet scent of pine being cured and cut and carved. Between two wide windows that lit the shop, a small altar bore a statue of a carpenter working wood. Ranks of broad workbenches faced the door, and half a dozen monks in jeans and denim shirts worked at various stations; all the sounds were the music of peaceful work. The monks looked up when Timothy and Ed stepped in through the door.

"Brothers," the Abbot said. "Take a break. Ed's come to see our caskets."

One of the younger monks stepped up, extending his hand. Ed remembered him. "Brother Anselm." he said.

The young man nodded. "Except now I'm Father Anselm. Ordained last year. I've been filling in down at St. Bernie's."

Ed, through the fog of his grief, remembered enough of his Catholic upbringing to recognize the promotion. "Congratulations, Father."

Timothy said, "Let me show you our finished products. You can take one, or you can order one custom made."

Ed shook his head, as much to push back his sadness as to rule out the custom-made option. "No, I need the casket today."

"Ah," Timothy nodded. "For your patient."

Ed nodded, unsure of his voice.

The abbot took his arm. "Let me show you what we have," and guided him toward a large room off the main workshop.

He saw it immediately, the second one Timothy showed him, blue pine with a lovely burgundy glow, shining like a lover's eyes. Ed said, "What's the finish on that?"

"We finish these with unrefined lacquer, which gives the orange-red cast. Stradivarius used it on his violins."

"God, it's beautiful."

Timothy nodded, looking pleased.

"I'll take it. How much?"

Timothy shook his head. "You've done St. Brendan's many favors, Ed."

True enough, Ed thought. Several times, he'd helped one monk or another weather a storm of depression or anxiety, or a crisis in his vocation, *pro bono*.

Abbot Timothy patted the Stradivarius. "This one's priceless. It's yours."

3

While the monks wrapped the casket in plastic and loaded it in his pickup, Ed asked to use the abbot's phone.

"Of course." The abbot showed him into his office, then stepped out and closed the door.

Ed dialed Doc Runge. The old man answered on the second ring. "Runge, here. What can I do?"

"Doc, it's Ed Northrup. I'm calling about Protect—, uh, Beatrice John. Do you still have her?"

"Your timing's perfect. Pat Bayless from the funeral home is picking her up in an hour. Andi Pelton—oh, you know Andi, sorry, brain fog—has been searching the databases for next of kin, without success. So, Pat's going to cremate her tomorrow."

Ed shuddered. "No, not cremation." Ed remembered Andi's story of Beatrice lying naked on the crematory table, about to be burned alive by the "bishop," the leader of the sex trafficking gang they'd investigated last fall. "I'm going to bury her. I'll head right over to the funeral home and make the arrangements."

Doc said, "Good for you, son. Nobody should end their time in the world alone."

He opened the door. The abbot waited in the hall. "Join us for midday prayers and lunch, Ed."

"I'd like that, Tim, but I want to get back down to Jeff with the casket before it's too late."

"Too late?"

"She's been in the hospital morgue, and they're planning to cremate her. I've been too wrapped up in my own grief, so I need to get back and make sure she's properly buried."

"Understood," the abbot said. "Come with me, though. This'll only take a minute."

They walked into the monastery church and Timothy led Ed up to the altar. He opened the big red Gospel book that rested on the bare stone table. "You said that this patient of yours had multiple personalities, and harbored a young child as one of the . . . What do they call the parts of the mind?"

"Alters." Ed felt his throat closing with emotion. "The child alter's name was Connie."

"Today we're celebrating a feast devoted to the guardian angels, who we believe watch over children. Read this from the Gospel that we heard this morning." Timothy pointed to a paragraph.

Ed leaned closer to the book and started reading aloud.

> *The disciples approached Jesus and asked, "Who is the greatest in*
> *the Kingdom of heaven?"*
> *He called a child over . . .*

Ed couldn't finish aloud. His throat closing and his eyes swimming, he made his way through the text silently.

> *He placed the child in their midst, and said, "Amen, I say to you,*
> *. . . whoever humbles himself like this child is the greatest in the*
> *Kingdom of heaven. And whoever receives one child such as this in*
> *my name receives me."*

Ed braced his arms on the altar, tears falling freely. Abbot Timothy rested his hand on Ed's shoulder. When Ed reached for his handkerchief and wiped his eyes, Timothy spoke kindly. "You received her, Ed."

4

That evening, Andi sat in her SUV, Grace in the passenger seat, watching the setting sun light up the mountain ridges, their snows glowing rose. They'd picked up yet another meal of burgers and fries at Alice's Village Inn and parked outside the Legion club to eat before the next speech. Andi, a bit queasy, doubted it qualified as dinner. She also doubted she was doing well in the campaign.

Grace stuffed fries in her mouth, then said, "Ufeeenba?"

Andi had aimed a couple fries toward her mouth, but stopped in mid-air. "What'd you say?"

Grace sipped a swallow of her Diet Coke and gulped the fries down. "Sorry. You feeling bad?"

"I can't quit thinking I'm screwing up this campaign. And I feel terrible for Ed's patient." She wedged the fries into her mouth. talking through them. "Ashuallyfred."

Grace grinned. "What'd *you* say?"

"Sorr—" She chewed, swallowed. "I said, 'Actually, for Ed.'"

Grace grew serious. "Yeah, he's taking it hard." She reached for her drink cup. "Maybe you're just tired, Andi."

"The weekend took more than it gave," Andi agreed. "Nobody was interested in anything else than did I shoot the asshole in cold blood." She sighed. "I'm losing this thing."

Grace sucked Diet Coke through the straw. "Naw. Way more than half the kids in civics class are mad about the ads and the mail thing. They're starting to come over to your side."

Andi, burned by the hard weekend, grunted, tried to stifle her reaction, but it snapped out anyway. "Kids don't vote."

"Lisa McCarthy says they reflect their parents' votes, though. I think it's a good sign."

Andi looked over at her. "I'm sorry, Grace. I'm on edge." She wrapped up her burger and put it back in the bag. "No appetite."

Grace said, "I have your fries?" When Andi nodded, she pulled them out of the bag. "Who's this meeting with?"

"Adams County Elk Association," Andi said, then yawned. "Sorry. Not sleepy, nervous. Elk hunters, mostly. They'll probably all ask why I want to confiscate their rifles."

"Tell them a joke."

"I'm sick of that sheriff and the politician joke."

"No, tell them an elk hunting joke."

Andi tried to keep the irritation out of her voice. Grace was just trying to help. "I don't know any damn elk hunting jokes."

Grace pulled her phone out of her pocket and tapped in some text. After a minute, she chuckled. "Try this: Two hunters were dragging their dead elk back to their truck. Another hunter approached pulling his along too. 'Hey, don't let me tell you boys how to do something, but I can say it's easier if you drag the animal by the hind legs. Then the antlers won't dig into the ground.' After the third hunter left, they decided to try it. A little while later one hunter said to the other, 'You know, that guy was right. This is a *lot* easier.' 'Yeah,' the second guy says, 'but we're getting farther from the truck.'"

Andi smiled. "Got another? Don't want to call elk hunters stupid."

Grace scrolled a moment, then chuckled. "Here's a good one. A man kills a deer and takes it home to cook for dinner. Both he and his wife decide that they won't tell the kids what kind of meat it is, but will give them a clue and let them guess. The kids are eager to know what the meat is on their plates, so they beg their dad for a clue. 'Well,' he says, 'it's what mummy calls me sometimes.' The little girl screams to her brother, 'Don't eat it, it's an asshole.'"

Andi laughed out loud. "Think I should?"

"Tell it? Absolutely."

Andi smiled. "Maybe it'll distract them from the Second Amendment."

WEDNESDAY, OCTOBER 3

1

Andi arrived at work blurry with fatigue. When she came through Reception, Callie was arranging herself at the desk. Andi yawned. "Can't do the Ladies' Fishing Society tonight, Callie," she said. "Two speeches, back to back."

"When's your first?"

"Seven, at the Legion Club, then eight o'clock at the Women's Sodality at St. Bernard's."

"What's a sodality?"

"Beats me. Some kind of club, I suppose. Anyway . . ." She yawned again. "Man, I didn't get enough rest last night."

"You up for *hors d'oeuvres* at the Angler instead of our regular meeting? I'll call the Ladies' and set it up for, what? Five? Five-thirty?"

Andi sighed. "How about five-thirty? That way, I can run home for a nap after shift change."

"You're on."

•   •   •

A little after ten-thirty that morning, Andi was on patrol, driving leisurely around the network of roads and farm lanes in the northern half of the valley. Jefferson was small, roughly sixteen blocks square, about 900 people, so if there was trouble, from the station a deputy could reach any place in town within a couple minutes. During the day shift, Ben assigned another deputy to drive the rural county roads to cut response time to an incident out there.

Her radio crackled with static. "Andi, Base here. Come in."

Crap. Ben have another heart attack? She grabbed the mic. "I'm here, Callie. What's wrong?"

"Irv Jackson just called to remind you to be in court in thirty minutes. Essex's lawyer's coming over to ask Dickie Flure to revisit the bail."

Andi frowned. "Did I miss something? I don't remember being informed there was a court date."

"You weren't. Norton's jerking you around. She arranged it with Irv Jackson and the judge's clerk, then told them she'd notify you."

"Damn," she said. "What time's the hearing?"

"Eleven-thirty."

"Crap." She wasn't prepared for a hearing. "All right, on my way."

2

At five-thirty, when Andi walked past Ted's bar on her way back to the River Room, Ted waved. "Your group's in back already. A glass of my best Pinot Noir, Andrea?"

"I'd love it, but no, Ted. Speeches to give."

"I'm hearing good things." He pointed to the big jar on the end of the bar. Its sign read, *Support Andi Pelton for Sheriff.* "Half full already," he said.

"That's great, Ted. I hope those dollars have votes behind them."

"All will be well," he said. "All will be well."

I hope so, she thought as she walked through the dining room. As Ted had said, the Ladies' Fishing Society had already convened in the River Room. The towering cottonwoods in the Angler's back yard, lining the river, had begun their turn to yellow, and the late afternoon sunlight shining through the room's tall windows splashed gold on the pine furniture. Stepping into the light, Andi was dazzled.

The others were gathered around the table. "Beautiful, isn't it?" Lane said, seeing her smile.

"Sure is. Makes my otherwise lousy day worth it."

"Come, take a load off, girl," Bernie said, patting the chair beside her. "Callie here was filling us in on your bail hearing. Didn't go so well, eh?"

"Worse. Judge Flure agreed to $200,000, his original number, and then Norton whittled even that in half. Essex made bail a half-hour after the hearing." As she was speaking, Andi realized she hadn't called Brenda Cantor with the news. She said, "You guys excuse me a minute?

I have a call I forgot to make." She stood to go, said, "Save me some of those," pointing at the platter of something that looked delicious.

•   •   •

Brenda didn't take the news calmly. "My god, he's already *home*? You didn't *call* me?"

"I'm sorry, Brenda. He doesn't know I talked to you more than any of the neighbors. I deliberately kept my testimony vague on that. I always said things like, 'We were told by a neighbor.' And none of the serious things come out in a bail hearing, just things related to his likelihood of fleeing." Andi could hear rapid, heavy breathing on the other end. "Do you want me to come over?"

"God, no. He'll know for sure I've been helping you if he sees your car here."

Andi looked down, thinking fast. Mishandle this, and Brenda might refuse to testify. "I get that. Look, you still have my card?"

"Somewhere."

"Let me give you all my phone numbers, not just the station number. Have a pen?"

"Yeah, go ahead."

She dictated the numbers, both the cell phone and the landline at home. She added the station desk, in case Brenda had lost her card. "If you call me at home, my husb-, ah, boyfriend might be the one to answer, but he'll get your message to me right away. Call me if anything changes with Essex—any time, day or night. I'll come over as fast as I can—you know I'm campaigning, so if I'm in the middle of a speech I'll call as soon as I'm done. And if he tries anything, we'll get an injunction to keep him away from you." *Or charge the bastard with intimidating a witness.*

"I hate this, Andi."

"I know. But if he does anything scary, anything at all, we'll handle him. It'll work out. I'm serious."

"Okay, I guess. Just stay close to your phones."

Andi ended the call after a few more assurances, then went into the River Room. The sunlight through the cottonwoods had softened as sunset approached, but the food looked wonderful in its glow.

"Take care of business?" Callie asked.

"Hope so." She glanced at her watch. "I have forty-five minutes. What's on the menu?"

Lane pointed to small triangles. "These are brie and mushroom phyllo puffs."

Bernie, her mouth full of one, said, "Sweetness, one bite, you ascend to heaven."

Lane pointed to skewers of meat. "Indonesian pork satay—skewers of pork marinated in peanut sauce."

Andi picked one up. "A little more sophisticated than my weiners in BBQ sauce."

Lane smiled. "I unfairly disparage Li'l Smokies. Your barbecue sauce reminded me to be humble."

Maggie said, "I heard a rumor that one of Ed's patients died. Committed suicide, I heard. That right?"

Andi nodded, swallowed the last bit of pork. "Yeah. He's taking it hard. I think he blames himself, though he hasn't said that in so many words." She took another bite. "He bought one of the monastery's caskets and is having her buried. But I'd appreciate you guys not talking about that until it happens, okay?"

Lane nodded, but Bernie shook her head. "Hell, girl, there's not a damn thing wrong with Ed burying that poor woman, and I'll bet nobody thinks so. And anybody who does will burn in hell."

Andi was surprised. *Why am I being so cautious?* And answered herself immediately: *To protect my campaign.* And then realized further, *From what? Rumors that Ed's a decent man?* She almost laughed at herself. "You know, you're right. I'm starting to think like a politician."

Lane looked horrified. "God help us one and all."

FRIDAY, OCTOBER 5

1

Ed slipped out of bed, trying not to disturb Andi. Outside the window, the morning twilight made ghosts of the trees stretching down toward Jefferson and the river. The air was warm; he didn't need a jacket for his morning run. By the first mile he was already sweating. A perfect fall morning in the mountains.

As he reached the bridge and his first break, rising light graced the black-traced edge of the Washington Mountains to the east. He listened for a moment to the burbling of Milk Creek, running high over its rocks after last week's rains. The riffles made the sound of quiet weeping.

His mind ran full of unknowns. Could he have handled the week's patients had Lynn not stepped in? Had he pushed Protector and Connie too fast, too far? Should he have backed off when Protector protested that Connie's life was at risk? He wanted to answer no to each one, but couldn't. Not yet.

He turned from the bridge rail and resumed his run. As he ran, he thought about Elizabeth Murphy, thirty-three years ago. Just turned fourteen, already desperate, she'd hanged herself after her mother abused her one time too often. He'd failed to save her, as he'd failed to save Protector and Connie and the One, and all the others, whoever they were. Elizabeth, cut off before her life began—like the boy shot in Daniel Essex's garage. Beatrice, released from an all-too-lengthy life that had held relentless suffering.

After ten minutes, breathing heavily, he reached his turnaround point, the abandoned railroad that once had linked Jefferson to the copper mines on the *Double-A* ranch. When the copper ran out, so did the railroad; the old right-of-way was overgrown with weedy aspen and dense stands of thimbleberry. Ed made his turn toward home, two miles back.

At Milk Creek, where he routinely paused, he kept running, kept running up the long curve of his drive and past the cabin and into the woods behind it, along a trail he'd maintained since he built the place. A few hundred yards into the trees was a clearing, a natural meadow there for no reason he had ever been able to figure out. He stopped in the center of the meadow and watched the first sun lift above the ridgeline. Soft light filtered through the pines. He waited, listening to the breeze breathing in the trees, hoping for answers to his questions. For the courage to forgive himself. He watched until the sun hung a hand's breadth above the mountains, but the sky was silent, and no answers came.

2

Vehicles filtered into the cemetery, parking along the single loop road. An open grave, its mound of fresh brown dirt beside it, gaped ten feet west of the grave of Grace's mother, Mara Ellenson. While Ed's friends made their way to the open grave, Grace visited Mara's, plucking some weeds that had sprouted in the grass, whispering to her mother. Andi, just arrived from work, chatted with Pete Peterson and Lynn Monroe.

After a while, Grace joined them, giving Andi a hug. Bernie O'Reilly climbed down from her Chevy pickup, and Ben Stewart came around from the passenger side. Lane pulled up in his Rav4, Ted riding beside him. They all turned to watch Ed drive up and get out of his pickup. His face registered surprise.

"I wasn't expecting anyone. This is so kind of you all. Andi's the only one knew Protect—, uh, Beatrice."

Ted said, "True, Edward, but we know you."

"How'd you hear about—" He was interrupted by the crunch of another vehicle entering the cemetery. They all turned to look. The hearse from Bayless Funeral Home pulled slowly up beside the grave. Pat Bayless got out. "Everybody here?"

Ed said, "We are." He glanced at his watch. "Right on time, Pat."

Pat grinned. "You specified ten a.m., on the button." He opened the rear door of the hearse. "Can I get six strong people here?"

When Ben stepped toward the casket, Bernie grabbed his elbow. "Benji, no heavy lifting, remember?" She moved around him and joined

Ed, Pete, Andi, Ted, and Lane. Eyebrows lifted. "Keep your eyes in your heads, boys. I'm representing 77 Russell Fork Road."

Lane said, "So, it's public now?"

Ed asked, "What's public?"

Ben broke in. "Crap on toast, let's get this buryin' done, shall we? We can gab later."

Pat Bayless drew the gleaming casket slowly from the hearse. The morning sunlight graced its violin beauty, and the blue-green veins in the amber wood echoed the serenity of the morning sky. After a life of suffering and degradation, Beatrice John's vehicle for her journey out of time glowed with unsullied serenity. One by one, each took a handle and bore it to graveside.

"Anybody have anything they want to say?" Bayless asked mildly.

They all looked at Ed. His throat was working. He squinted at the casket. After a long moment, he nodded, cleared his throat. "Beatrice John was a woman who lived a terrible life, abused, tormented, reduced to hiding herself. No one loved her. No one came to her defense, ever." His closed his eyes a moment. Opened them and looked at his friends. "I want to thank you all for being here. Thanks to you, for the first time perhaps in her life, Beatrice John has good men and women standing with her." He held in a breath, then slowly let it out. "Let's let her rest."

Lunch would be served at the Angler. As they walked toward their vehicles to drive there, Ben asked, "Why ten o'clock 'on the button'?"

"Every Tuesday and Friday for almost a year, ten a.m. was her appointment." His voice roughened. "I wanted to spend the last one with her."

TUESDAY, OCTOBER 9

1

After four evenings and two weekend days spent door-knocking, Andi lay stretched out on the couch, exhausted, watching TV news before bed. Grace paced, restless, between Andi and the TV.

"Come sit by me," Andi said, pivoting to a seated position and patting the cushion.

"Can't. I'm scared we'll see another ad, and I'm nervous about the town hall on Friday." She paced some more.

Andi said, "Girl, you're wearing me out, and I'm already worn out more than I've been in years. Go pour yourself a glass of wine—and bring me one too."

From the kitchen, Grace called, "Where's the corkscrew?"

Andi chuckled. "I believe it's in Missoula. In your dorm room."

"Oh, geez, you're right."

"Use the Swiss Army knife in the drawer. It's got a corkscrew on it."

After she got the wine, Andi sat up and Grace slid onto the couch beside her, and they clinked glasses. "Here's to your town hall Friday," Andi said. She started to say something, when on the television, an ad started.

> ESTABLISHING SHOT: GRAINY, POORLY LIT, TWO
> PEOPLE, FILMED THROUGH A WINDOW, KISSING
> ON A COUCH.

Grace spluttered her wine. "Omigod, Andi, that's you and Northrup."

> VOICEOVER: *She wants your vote for sheriff . . .*

CUT TO: QUICK SHOT OF COUPLE KISSING AGAIN.

VOICEOVER: . . . *but she sleeps with a man she's not married to.*

CUT TO: THIRD SHOT OF THEM KISSING ON THE COUCH. GIRL APPEARS IN THE BACKGROUND.

VOICEOVER: *She satisfies her lust in front of her lover's daughter.*

CUT TO: FOURTH SHOT OF THEM KISSING ON THE COUCH.

VOICEOVER: *Is this the kind of person you want for sheriff of Adams County? A vote for Pelton is a vote for a slut and a whore.*

CUT TO: AMERICAN FLAG RIPPLING IN THE BREEZE AND THE UNFURLING WORDS, *BRAD ORDREW FOR SHERIFF.*

VOICEOVER: *Paid for by Friends of Ordrew for Sheriff.*

Grace sat stunned, one hand over her mouth. Andi was enraged. The bumping noise, the footfalls of a runner, a car crunching gravel that she and Ed had heard in the night three weeks ago—now she knew: Someone had filmed them through the window. She wanted to act, but Grace looked shell-shocked. Andi reached for her, pulled her close, rocked the girl in her arms. Being tender helped contain her fury.

The sound of tires on the gravel outside alerted her. She put a finger to Grace's lips, and whispered, "Let's see who this is."

Grace, looking a little less shocked, nodded. Andi went to the coat rack and unclipped her weapon, then looked cautiously out the window. A door slammed. She straightened, relieved. "It's your dad."

In a moment, they heard footsteps on the porch and Ed stepped through the door. Seeing Grace on the couch, still looking wobbly, and Andi at the window, gun in hand, he said, "What the hell?"

Just then, Andi's cell phone buzzed.

2

As soon as the ad finished, Ordrew jumped up and grabbed his phone, punching in Crane's number. He hardly waited for the Reverend to say hello. "Take that ad down," he almost shouted. "It's obscene and I won't tolerate it."

Crane said nothing.

"I mean it, goddamn it. Take it *down*."

"I needn't remind you, Deputy, that you are not responsible for the ads. Nor do you decide what I do with them."

Ordrew felt his fury rise. "Crane, if you don't take the ad down, I will publish your name and disown your support publicly."

"Oh, my. Shall I tremble? You already gave that weak-assed statement saying the Friends don't speak for you. What will you say this time? And you seem to forget that doing so will harm only yourself."

Ordrew snorted. "Putting distance between my campaign and your lies can't hurt me."

"No? My releasing the details of your dismissal from the LAPD most assuredly can. Shall we trade revelations?"

Ordrew choked. He took a moment to calm himself. "I was fired for demanding that we live up to our oaths as police officers. I have nothing—"

"Shut up, Deputy. You were fired for insubordination, as the confidential Internal Affairs file on you says, copies of which I have and will be pleased to pass along to the media."

Ordrew shouted into the phone. "How the shit did you get that file?"

"Deputy, I can do things you cannot imagine. And don't mistake me: If you play games with me, I can just as well put out ads that attack you with the same vigor with which I'm attacking Pelton. Are we clear?"

Ordrew almost hung up, his words sticking in his throat. Instead, he waited, pondering whether winning the election outweighed letting this obscenity stand. The *Greater Truth* warred with his integrity. After a long silence, he managed, "We're clear. But no more ads."

"Again, Deputy, you do not call that shot."

Ordrew swallowed. Hard. And hung up. But his shame rang in his ears. Here he stood, worrying about winning, when Andi Pelton, no doubt, was feeling devastated. He should call her. *No. I can't face her.*

3

Andi grabbed the buzzing phone and scanned the display. Hit *Talk.* "Pete? Did you see it?"

"Just now. I'm so damn angry I could shoot. Lucy's crying. It's Ordrew."

Ed was standing motionless, the door still open. Andi beckoned him in and pointed at Grace. Ed sat beside her. "What happened?" he asked her as he held out his arm. Grace leaned against him, whispered, "It's another horrible ad."

Andi forced herself to focus on Pete's call. "It's Crane's doing. But why would he want me hurt so badly? And Grace?"

Ed looked up at her, bewildered. He tilted his head, mouthed, "What's going on?"

Andi held up a hand, mouthed back, "A minute."

Pete was saying, "You killed his henchman and ruined his scam here in the valley. My guess is, revenge. You need to issue a statement tomorrow, tomorrow morning, first thing."

"Saying what? They caught me on videotape kissing Ed." She caught Ed's look. "It's a fact. If I say anything, it'll sound like I'm defensive." But she thought of Ben's advice—turn a scandal to her favor. *How, for God's sake?*

Just then, the landline rang. Ed jumped up and took it, then sat back down, putting his arm back around Grace's shoulders. She snuggled close. "Hey, Ben. . . . No, something about Andi and me kissing on videotape. What the hell's going on?" He listened carefully, his look pivoting from confusion to fury.

Covering her own phone, Andi called to him, "Is that Ben?" He nodded. "Tell him to wait, I want to talk to him." She went back to Pete.

Ed told Ben to hold the line, then said, "Oh, okay," and ended the call. Andi glared at him.

When she got off the call with Pete, she said, "Damn it, I asked you to keep Ben on the line."

"He'll call back. He's calling KEMT to find out who bought the airtime." He stood and went over to Andi and embraced her. "It sounds ugly."

"Worse than ugly," she muttered as she broke out of the embrace and went to Grace. "Give me a hug?"

Grace stood up into her arms. "Oh, man, Andi, I feel terrible, and scared. How'd they get me in those pictures?" She straightened her shoulders. "Screw that. I feel worse for you. And mad."

"Kiddo, you've got no idea how mad I am." As they stepped out of their hug, Grace bumped the couch and the wine glass she'd placed on the arm of the couch fell to the floor, the dark red wine spreading across the wooden floor. "Shoot." Grace ran to the kitchen for a rag and began sopping the spill.

Andi said to Ed, "Pete thinks I should react publicly, but I'm damned if I can figure out how."

Northrup narrowed his eyes, thinking. "That'd be a risky move, I think."

Andi started to say something when the landline rang again. It was Ben. "Hey, Ben, let me put you on speaker so Ed can hear." She did it.

"Goddamn TV station gave me nothin' but a company name."

"George String, Incorporated, by any chance?"

"Jesus in a sidecar, yes. How'd you know?"

"It's Crane, Ben. Anyway, Pete wants me to make a statement tomorrow. Do you think I should?"

"No damn way. Defendin' yourself about doing your job, that's one thing. This, goin' public just gives the little jerk the advantage—the girl can't take the heat, that sort of crap. No, there's plenty of folks in the valley who'll say everything that needs sayin'. Me and Mack'll see to it. You just work up a damn strong answer for the Q & A you're goin' to get. And take it to Ordrew every chance."

"I don't think Ordrew is behind this. It's Loyd Crane."

Ben said nothing for a moment. "Ordrew is Crane's damn beneficiary. He's the one you gotta hang this on."

Grace, still on her knees mopping, spoke up. "You're right, Sheriff Ben." Andi and Ed looked at her.

"Thanks, Gracie girl." A pause. "But what the hell you doin' here? Ain't you supposed to be in college?"

"Independent study. I'm working on Andi's campaign."

"Well, ain't that good news," Ben said, delight shouldering aside the anger in his voice.

Andi said, "So, I need to find out if Crane's behind George String, Inc."

"Crap on toast. Of all the bastards we've run into on this job, Crane was the worst. Except that sex trafficker bishop, Scopus. Damn it all to hell."

He was huffing.

"Easy, Ben," Ed said. "Don't have another attack over this."

Andi jumped in. "Ben, how can we dig into the ownership of George String, Inc.?"

"Easiest way's a court order, but Dickie Flure'll want evidence of probable cause."

"If Ordrew tells the judge what he told me?"

Ed shook his head. "What're the chances he'll jeopardize his election to help you expose his honeypot?"

Ben's voice growled. "My thinkin' exactly."

Andi's anger, a burn deep in her chest, throbbed. "Damn!"

Ed's cell phone rang. It was Magnus. He said, "Hold on, Mack," and handed the phone to Andi. "For you," he said.

With her other hand, she grabbed it. "Ben, Magnus Anderssen's on the other line. I'll talk to you in the morning."

"Do that," Ben said, and hung up.

"Magnus? Thanks for calling."

"This helps your opponent, but I don't believe it comes from anyone in the valley, Andi. Some outsider is behind it," the rancher said, his commanding voice projecting his anger.

"I know who it is, Magnus. It's Loyd Crane."

"Crane? My Lord, there's no end to the damage that man inflicts." Magnus and Loyd Crane had been novices at St. Brendan's Monastery, back in the '70s. Crane had somehow ferreted out that their novice master, Father Jerome, had fallen in love with Magnus, who in turn felt affection for the monk. Crane had told Jerome that Magnus wanted to "service" him, when all that Magnus had said was that he loved the novice master as a second father. The result was that Jerome had raped Magnus, thinking his attraction was reciprocated. On the phone, Magnus's voice took on an edge of steel. "I will deal with that bastard."

The big man's anger was like a sun, and she felt warmed. "Thanks, Magnus, but I need your support here in the valley just now."

"Luisa and I are prepared to support you, and in more ways than money. We'll discuss that later. For now, let me make inquiries that your department can't make, and when I confirm Crane's behind this, I will let you know." He paused. "Or I'll take care of it privately."

Andi wondered, *Should I be alarmed?* Decided no. Magnus was too moral to resort to crime. "Thanks, Magnus. I appreciate the support. Can you speak with some of your friends and ask them to voice their support—if they feel it?"

"Of course, and you're welcome." She heard the big man clear his throat. "My friends call me Mack. Please do."

Andi had been standing, holding the phone. "Thank you, Mag—, uh, Mack." She hung up, joining Ed on the couch. Ed put his arm around her shoulders. Grace finished her rag work and joined them.

She said, "While I was mopping, I had an idea. I want to avoid giving Ordrew publicity. What if instead of having the two candidates at my Town Hall, I let the kids discuss amongst themselves whether free speech permits lies or character assassination, like these ads do?"

Andi said, "I think it's a good idea, but I've already scheduled it and I'm sure Ordrew has too."

Grace shook her head. "He hasn't responded at all. And we're less than three days out."

"Well, give him a chance to agree either to come on Friday or to the change of plans, and I'll go either way."

"You got it, Andi. You have his number?"

Andi pulled it up on her phone and Grace took it and dialed. She left her message, adding at the end, "I need your answer by noon tomorrow, thanks. If I don't hear by then, I'll assume you're not coming and we will change the program. Noon tomorrow."

"Nice job," said Ed.

Andi put a hand on her arm. "Thanks, Grace. For being here." Suddenly, all three were in an embrace, and Grace was breathing heavily. After they all settled back, Ed said to Grace, "Kiddo, how about it? Hit the sack and get some rest?"

His daughter smiled sweetly and lifted her now-empty wine glass. "I believe I need to finish a glass of wine first."

PART FOUR

The criminal investigation and trial is a sibling of the political campaign. They share genes—a long period of tensions, arguments, attacks, theorizing, dead ends, probes gone awry, guesses gone wrong, attacks and their defenses, and debates, all rising to the crescendo of a trial—either in a courtroom or on Election Day. No climax is as final and resounding as the verdicts of the jury or of the electorate—and few climaxes leave the victors so undeservedly proud and the vanquished so sure that justice has miscarried.

Anonymous

FRIDAY, OCTOBER 12

1

After four days of high blue skies and air as sweet and warm as a Caribbean cove, autumn fell apart. Dark clouds appeared in the north, sailing on cold gusts that steadied into a piercing, relentless wind. In town, people kept their heads down, occasionally looking up at the darkness approaching in the sky. In the shops, the talk rated the kind of winter coming; *brutal* got more votes than *bad as usual*. By noon, Jefferson lay beneath the frontal edge of a steely plate of cloud; by mid-afternoon, the clouds had pushed another twenty miles south. In that time, the temperature had dropped fifteen degrees. The wind grew, stronger gusts rattling windows the length of the valley.

After dropping in on a busy Grace, who was setting up chairs in the high school auditorium for her Town Hall Forum, Andi wished her good luck and left for *her* newly scheduled meeting with the Adams County Conference, the Tea Party group. Ordrew had contacted no one about his plans for this evening, so Grace had changed the program.

The atmosphere greeting Andi was tense. The usual smiles at Andi's jokes or head nods for her Big Idea weren't in evidence. She wrapped up her speech and asked for questions, tensing for the first one about the "slut" ad. It had been the first question the last two days. But the questions were supportive, which surprised her. *Ben and Magnus have been talking to folks.*

Then, a guy in back stood up and yelled. "You'd leave us vulnerable to civil unrest, you'd take away our guns and revoke the Second Amendment, you'd let all kinds of immigrant trash into the valley to steal our jobs." He grabbed a breath, forged on. "You live in sin with a man you're not married to. Beside dismantling the Constitution, what's your business here? Go back to Chicago and leave us in peace."

Despite the gall in her throat, Andi nodded. "And your question, sir?" That, at least, roused a couple of chuckles.

"I stated my question. What's your business in the valley? You don't belong here, you're not one of us."

The few people who'd smiled at her jokes and seemed sympathetic were craning their necks to see the man. Others stared stonily at her. Andi took a moment to gather her thoughts. "My business in the valley? My business is much the same as yours and almost everybody's who lives here: It's to make life safer and better for us all and to take care of one another. To help the community remain the fine place to raise kids that it's been for generations." She refocused on the crowd. "I'm working in the sheriff's department, but all of you folks work in jobs that have the same basic purpose: To earn a living and to work together to make and keep Adams County and the Monastery Valley a place we want to live in. If you elect me, I intend to—"

The man shouted her down. "Liberals from Illinois know shit-all about Montanans and our traditions. We're people who love our guns and our freedoms and don't intend to allow you to steal either one from us."

Andi felt herself getting hot. "Hold on, sir," she shot back, lifting her hand. "When I came to Adams County, I took the oath of office all public servants take. I swore then, and I'll repeat it now, 'I do solemnly swear that I will support, protect, and defend the constitution of the United States, and the constitution of the state of Montana, and that I will discharge the duties of my office with fidelity, so help me God.' You may not approve my way of doing so, but I have lived and worked by that oath and by the Constitution, and my conscience about that is clear. If you have specific allegations of my having failed in my duty and my oath, please state them. If not—" She let her eyes move over the audience. "May I have another question?" She wondered who the man was; she knew most everyone at her speeches, some better than others, but not this fellow.

The man angrily pushed his way out to the aisle and toward the back door. There, he turned and reached under his jacket. His hand came out holding a gun, which he pointed up. Someone cried out, "Gun!" People ducked under chairs. "You'll be elected over my dead body," he yelled.

Andi went taut. *Down behind the podium.* But then, *No.* If she gave herself as the target, others might not be shot. She stood taller, stepped away from the podium and into the aisle, toward him. She stood, arms at her side, visible to him. "Sir," she said, firming her voice. "It's your right to carry that weapon, but it is not your right to threaten these folks with it. I'm going to ask you to put it away or I will arrest you." She watched his hand, which did not level at her, but stayed aloft.

"So, you can steal my weapon, bitch?"

"No, sir. So, I can protect these good folks."

In the front row, a woman who'd been peering back at the man, turned, looked at Andi. She stood. She moved into the aisle and approached Andi, who tried not to flinch. The woman turned again, put herself between Andi and the man with the gun. After a shocked moment, two men joined her, then more women, until Andi stood behind a sizable crowd, a crowd larger than the group of those left crouching on the floor.

After an almost unbearable moment, the man lowered his gun and put it under his jacket. He said, "I'm not finished." But he turned and banged out the door.

She felt her body relax, her shoulders softening. As the group that had shielded her turned to face her, some returning to their seats, Andi began to thank them.

The first woman raised her hand. "Andi, there's some in this room who disagree with you, but we saw you stand your ground for us. It was the least we could do." She started to clap. The rest of the crowd joined her in a rippling rhythmic applause.

2

Coming into the high school's auditorium, Ed saw Lynn Monroe talking to Lisa McIntyre. He joined them. Lynn smiled. "How you doing, Ed?"

"Getting through it, thanks to you," he said. "Hi, Lisa."

Lisa, the civics teacher, looked over his shoulder. "Trouble."

He turned. Brad Ordrew had pushed his way through a group of kids and was striding toward them, frowning.

Lisa whispered, "He never replied to Grace's message, so we've changed the format. No candidates allowed."

Ed felt his stomach tighten; this could throw a real wrench in Grace's Town Hall. Ordrew brushed past Ed without even a nod, and confronted Lisa. "I'm going to give a short speech at your meeting." His tone was peremptory, loud. Heads turned.

Lisa shook her head. "I'm sorry, Deputy, but when you didn't respond to Grace's message, we changed the agenda. This event's for the students, now. We're having a general discussion about free speech. You're welcome to listen in the audience, but I can't allow any politicking."

Ordrew's eyes went dark. "You'll allow it if your principal orders you to."

Lisa smiled. "Jack won't be ordering me to do anything. He allows us to run our own shop until and unless we run into trouble." She waited a heartbeat. "And then he has our backs."

Ordrew turned away. "He's a fool, then." He brushed past Ed, again unspeaking.

Grace came over as Ordrew moved toward the doors. "What'd he want?"

Ed said, "He wanted to give a speech. Ms. McIntyre told him to get lost."

"Way to go, Lisa," Grace said, lifting her hand, which the teacher high-fived.

Lisa? Ed thought. *I am getting old.*

"Northrup," said Grace. "This is going to be awesome."

•   •   •

Thirty minutes later, Ed was thinking, *It* is *awesome.* He watched yet another student approach the microphone. "I think free speech is one of the most important rights we have," she said, "and that includes opinions. So, any opinion has a right to be said."

Another kid cried out: "Even if it's a lie?"

"You can't know," the first student fired back, "if somebody's opinion is a lie or just wrong. They have a right to say it."

A small whirlwind of arguments, none with benefit of a microphone, ensued, until Grace roped the students in and restored order.

In the back, Lisa McIntyre stood against the wall, her arms folded, watching with a half-smile on her face.

After forty minutes or so, an unhappy-looking girl a few rows in front of Ed reached for the microphone, looked hard at Grace, and asked, "How much are you being paid to distract us from the real issue?" Her voice wavered.

Ed sat up taller.

Grace shook her head. "I'm not. I'm doing this as a civics project, Mona. We all are." She gestured to the three seniors, her co-moderators, who were carrying microphones when speakers stood. The seniors all nodded.

"That's a lie," the girl said, her voice the smallest beat shaky. Northrup decided she sounded more nervous than malevolent. "We should be telling the truth about Deputy Pelton. The facts are there for everyone to see. She's a whore and a slut, but her and you won't let anyone talk about it."

Ed, breathless, stood, but Grace signaled with her eyes to sit down. He did, then he glanced back at Lisa McIntyre. Her arms had unfolded, and she watched the girl, Mona. He made his way to the aisle and back to her side. She whispered, "New girl in school. I don't know her. Grace'll handle it."

Grace spoke calmly, slowly. "Mona, it's your privilege to believe anything you want to believe. But the topic of our town hall forum is free speech and what it means. Most of us here, and I'd say most people in the valley, are all for free speech, but we're not for character assassination masquerading as 'free speech.' Did you have something to add on our topic?"

"I do. You say this is all about free speech, but when I bring up an important point, which is my free speech right, you're trying to shut me down."

Grace nodded. "All right, Mona, have your say. Just avoid using derogatory words about anybody, okay? Then we'll see what others think."

"If one of us girls was openly sleeping with her boyfriend, everybody'd call her a slut. Well, Deputy Pelton sleeps with your father night after night without being married, and nobody peeps." A few students swiveled their heads to look at Ed. He kept his face neutral. Mona went on, "I say that's a double standard and I say the question everybody has to face is, do you want somebody like that for your sheriff?"

Grace reddened, but Ed saw her pull in a long breath, and then she half-smiled. "Thank you, Mona. Anyone else care to comment?"

At first, no one called for a microphone, until a young girl stood. It was Pete Peterson's youngest, Emily. She turned and found Mona in the audience. "I don't know what's bothering you," she said, "but my dad told me he would trust Deputy Pelton with his life. She got shot protecting us here in the valley. That's good enough for me." She sat down, and a smattering of applause followed. Mona looked stonily at the ground. Ed watched her back; her breathing was fast. *Scared*, he thought. *And alone.*

Another girl stood up. "Okay. Well, I agree with Mona about the double standard." The audience stirred. "But I don't agree that Miz Pelton's a slut. I think if a girl wants to sleep with somebody she loves, it's her business, well, okay, it's his too—" The audience laughed. "Let's not call people sluts because they love somebody." More applause.

Ed caught Lisa's quick smile, then looked across the room at Mona. Her head remained down.

Grace said, "Thank you, Alison. So, to get back to our topic, free speech and respectful discourse, anyone else have anything to say?" Grace looked at Mona, who hadn't yet looked up and did not see it.

When no one called for a microphone, Grace thanked the audience and all the speakers and declared the town hall forum adjourned. She clicked off the microphone and looked hard at Mona. Then she smiled, and turned toward Northrup. She was pleased about something.

•　　•　　•

Later, outside, Grace was surrounded by a crowd of kids clustered together, buzzing. Grace broke free and came over to him, giving him a huge hug. "Thanks for coming, Northrup. That was quite an ending, wasn't it?"

"Sure was." She moved closer and lowered her voice. "I know who's behind the ad."

"You do? Who?"

She said, "I want to make sure first, before I accuse anyone. But I think she gave it away. She used almost the exact words."

"You're thinking Mona filmed us kissing?"

"God, no, Northrup. But she's new to the valley, and her dad's apparently creepy. I'll bet it's him—but don't tell anybody till I'm sure, okay?"

"How are you going to find out?"

She looked serious. "I'm going to make her my friend. She's new, she's lonely, and I don't believe she means those things she said. So, I'm going to get her on my side."

It took his breath away. "You're turning into a fine young woman, Grace."

"Don't be a mushy-head, Northrup. If I get her on my side, that's one more vote for Andi in our straw poll."

He chuckled. "She's new, eh? Where does she come from?"

Grace screwed up her forehead. "Somewhere, like, . . . I don't remember." She beckoned to her boyfriend Zach, who'd driven over from college for the forum. In the biting wind, Northrup was freezing— he'd left his jacket at the office and walked over in a light sweater. Zach wore a T-shirt and basketball shorts.

"Aren't you freezing?" Ed asked him.

"Naw, Doc N. It's not winter yet."

Grace said, "Zach, where's Mona from?"

The big barrel-chested kid shrugged. "How would I know?"

One of the girls standing nearby said, "Carlton," she said. "They just moved here."

3

Brad Ordrew had lurked in the doorway of the auditorium, listening to the town hall. He cringed when Mona had attacked Pelton for sleeping with Northrup.

"Sex," he muttered to himself, "is off limits. People have a right to . . ." He stopped. "Not according to Crane," he said aloud. A few kids heard him, turned, looked at him. Hard. Like *Shut up*. He could feel his face redden.

He stalked out of the school.

TUESDAY, OCTOBER 16

1

After morning report, Andi stopped Ordrew in the deputies' room. He felt a momentary flurry of anxiety, standing this close to her. Since the "slut" ad, he'd avoided her.

She said, "I haven't heard your answer about a debate."

He swallowed. "I don't need to debate you, Andi. I'm ahead in this thing and I'm staying ahead."

"You don't know that," she snapped, but he relaxed at the flash of uncertainty in her eyes. "I *do* know it. Come over to my desk, I'll let you see."

He handed her a one-page printout. "It's down at the bottom." He pointed to the three lines that mattered:

Bradley Ordrew: 49%

Andrea Pelton: 46%

Undecided: 5%

He watched her face, her eyes narrowing. "Was this poll taken after the 'slut' ad?" she asked.

When she mentioned the ad, he felt his face redden. "No. The poll was taken two days before the ad came out." He started to say that the numbers no doubt were even better for him now, but stopped. "Andi, you know I'm not in control of the ads. I imagine they're, uh, painful for you."

She seemed to shrink. All she said was, "Damn right," before she walked away.

Ordrew wondered how it would feel, facing people who'd seen you shamed like that?

If I care so much, why do I keep trying to hurt her?

He wished he knew.

2

Ed wasn't ready yet to fill Protector's appointment time, so during his empty ten a.m. hour, Ed dialed his old friend, Charlie Merwin. Burying Protector had helped. Since then, he'd been sleeping better, if getting five hours instead of three before tossing awake and staring at the yard light outside the window was better. His focus on Andi's campaign problems had been distracting him from his preoccupation with the suicide. In the office, Lynn had been wonderful—after returning to Missoula on Friday afternoon last week, she'd called each day to chat and, he knew, check his mood.

But he needed Charlie Merwin.

"Eddie, lad. How's your home-spun life in that valley of yours?"

"Charlie, I need your help."

"Ah, dispensing with the customary pleasantries, I note. Thus, something serious. What's disturbing your peace?"

Ed grimaced at his brusque opening. "I'm sorry, man. How's your health?"

"Ironic you should ask. My doctor of forty-three years retired *sans* my permission, and I was handed over to a young thing fresh out of residency. She went over me stem to stern, inspecting what she'd inherited, and aside from a few small inconveniences of age, I take the position that until she informs me differently, I am still alive and kicking."

"Good, good."

"So. You need my help. And the problem is . . .?"

"I lost a patient eighteen days ago, and it's got me . . . I'm not sure how to put it."

"Lost a patient? Another suicide?" Merwin knew all about Ed's losing Elizabeth Murphy so long ago, had supported him through the lawsuit filed by the girl's parents and their subsequent complaint to the Psychology Board that had ultimately driven him to Montana to start anew.

"Yeah. That multiple I called you about. It's got me pretty messed up."

"As is to be expected." Merwin's voice was soft, almost intimate. "It's a wrecking ball to the heart."

"The worst part is, I think I may have caused it."

"Oh. Listen, dear, which do you prefer: My lecture on how we don't cause suicides, or the opportunity to explain yourself?"

"Let me talk."

"Splendid. I've always disliked that lecture. Speak."

Ed did, recounting his fear that he had pushed Connie too soon, or somehow had weakened Protector's hold over Connie. As he finished the tale, he knew what Merwin would say.

But his friend surprised him. "You may be right."

"*What*? If you thought that, why the hell didn't you say so when I first consulted with you?"

"Because I didn't think it then, old son. To be candid, I don't think it now. But what *you* think is the issue here, and I said you *may* be right. Not, God forfend, you *are* right."

"What you think matters to me."

"Or you wouldn't have called. A few questions, then. I believe you told me she has little social support?"

"None whatsoever."

"Other than yourself, of course. How malignantly had she been treated, and for how long?"

"Horribly, and all her life. I suspect an incestuous childhood and we know her adulthood was trapped among sex traffickers. Could be she was raised in the trafficking cult."

"And if you had backed away from her, estimate the likelihood of her killing herself at some point?"

Gut-punched, he struggled to breathe, searching for an answer. A true answer. "The odds? Very high. Inevitable, unless someone broke through with care for her."

"Precisely, old chum. Lifelong suffering, altogether unloved, completely lacking in social support—such persons seldom fulfill their appointed three-score and ten. None of us survives long alone and bereft."

"She had no one."

"Ah, in that regard, Eddie, you are *so* sadly mistaken. *You* cared for her. Granted, you cared in the woefully inadequate manner of our profession, but nonetheless, you cared."

"But . . ." Ed couldn't finish.

"But you couldn't save her." Merwin sighed, a deep, soothing sound over the phone. "Alas, old son, there is no saving in this wide world." Merwin's voice was vibrant with sorrow. "There's only what love we can muster against the cold."

THURSDAY, OCTOBER 18

1

After another exhausting door-knocking evening, Andi sank onto the couch beside Ed and stared at the fire. The glass of wine he'd poured rested in her hand, unsipped. "I can't believe how many church women there are in this town," she muttered.

"The backbone of society," Ed said.

"A spineless backbone," she said, her voice gravelly with fatigue. "One of the ladies tonight asked if I knew I'd be going to hell for sleeping with you." She screwed up her nose, made her voice whiney. "'For the sake of that sweet girl? Can't you get your own apartment?' I didn't know whether to burst into tears or slap her."

He laid his hand on the back of her neck, as soft as a whisper. "You need some time away from this thing. Let me cancel the weekend meetings."

"I can't." She told him about Ordrew's poll.

He pulled back his hand. "For real?"

"He could've just typed up the numbers himself, but they were on letterhead from someplace called Montana Polls, and it looked pretty professional." Ed picked up his laptop and started typing. She took a sip of wine. "Callie told me more people are showing up at his meetings than are coming to mine."

"How does Callie know?" He stared at the computer screen.

Andi chuckled. "The Ladies' Fishing Society. Callie or Bernie have been going to his speeches, and they report the numbers."

"Doesn't he recognize them?" He leaned toward the computer, peering at its screen.

"Sure. Callie, at least. Callie says it'll make him think she's a supporter—or make him crazy." She sighed.

After a moment, he said, "Yep, they're for real." He turned the screen to her, so she could read the site's name: *Montana Polls.com*.

"Jesus F. Christ." She took another sip of wine, reminded of her dad, who swore like that whenever he was exasperated. "Ed, I'm fried, plain and simple. And something's bothering me about Ordrew."

"Your opponent."

"My opponent. I'm getting strange vibes from him—now and then, it almost seems like he's softening toward me. But Callie says he's attacking me hard in his speeches. I don't get it."

"Softening? What do you mean?"

"A couple days ago, when he showed me the poll, he almost apologized for the 'slut' ad. I got the feeling he felt sympathetic. He's been a bit more respectful at work—he helped me think through some details of the Essex case. So, why's he still attacking me publicly?"

Ed sipped his wine. After a moment, he said, "Care for a shrink theory?"

"I remind him of his beloved mother?"

Ed for a moment looked amused. "Wouldn't be the first time. No, from what you said about his reactions to a couple of the ads, I'm guessing he feels guilty about them. We know Ordrew's a stickler for procedures, rules, that sort of thing. So, the way he's running his campaign could be aversive for him."

"Aversive?"

"Morally repugnant. It could be he needs to suppress that reaction—how could he attack you if he feels sympathy and guilt toward you?"

"So, why attack me? I don't see this theory answering that question."

"Think about it. He represses his sympathy and guilt. Repressed emotions tend to be projected onto someone else. If you weren't in the race, he wouldn't need Crane's help, which he feels guilty about accepting. So, unconsciously, to him *you* cause his guilt. So, he attacks the cause."

Andi didn't say anything.

Ed shrugged. "It's kind of Psych 101."

"You know what I thought of Psych 101?"

"Nope."

"Bullshit with big words."

2

Outside, the PV drove into the yard. Andi watched the fire darting and crackling in the stove, wondering when it would soothe her. Or *if* it would. Except for firelight and Ed's computer's blue screen light, the room was dark. She'd seen the hurt in his eyes when she'd called his theory bullshit. He'd been very quiet for the last ten minutes. She moved a little closer. "I'm sorry I said that, Ed."

Before he answered, Grace came in, taking in the scene. "Are you two fooling around again?" Apparently answering her own question, she plopped down on the couch, in the narrow place between them. Andi's wine almost spilled as she jerked sideways, making room. "Damn, Grace, be careful."

"I'm sorry, Andi. My fault."

Andi regretted it as soon as it came out her mouth. "Me too, kiddo. I'm frazzled and cranky."

Grace patted her arm. "No problem." She turned toward Ed. "Northrup, Mona invited me for dinner tomorrow. You okay with that?"

"Sounds like your befriending campaign is working."

"Yeah. She's all right. She wants me to meet her father, who's a true asshole."

Andi stiffened. "What do you mean by *asshole*?"

Grace shrugged. "Well, he won't let her join any clubs or go out for any sports, he won't take her home to see her friends, that kind."

Ed glanced at Andi, then back at Grace. "You still think he's behind the ad?"

"I'm not so sure now. Whenever I ask her about what she said at the town hall, she, like, changes the subject. She was maybe repeating things some of the kids were saying, just to be popular, but now she's embarrassed."

Ed thought for a moment. "If the father's involved with the ad, going there may not be such a good idea. Why don't you invite the two of them over here for dinner?"

Andi tensed. "I'll be camping out at the Jeff House during *that*."

Grace said, "Northrup, please. He won't let Mona go anywhere. She's real lonely."

Ed looked again at Andi, who said, "Your call, Dad."

He turned back to Grace. "Okay, that's fine by me." He thought a moment. "No, wait. You're in college now, and I said how you spend your time is up to you. It's *your* call, Grace."

Grace looked at him for a few seconds. "Cool. So, I'm going. Thanks, Northrup."

Ed started to answer, but Grace was already up and on her way to her room. He shrugged, said to Andi, "So, the weekend off? You need some down time."

"Don't push it, Ed. I need to win this election or I'll have all the down time in the world."

"I get that, but it won't help if you get sick mid-campaign."

Andi felt her face flush hot. "Ed, stop, damn it. It's hard enough without you nagging me."

His face darkened, and Andi could see the struggle in his eyes. After a moment, he said, "Sorry for that. I, uh, I guess I'm maybe wanting some time with you. This business with Beatrice John is hard." His words ended in a kind of choke.

Her eyes misted, her annoyance melting into sympathy. *I'm a damn machine.* "I'm sorry too. I haven't even thought about you in all this. This campaign's eating me alive. I should—"

He gripped her arm, stopping her. "It's okay, Andi. I'm a little needy, is all. You've got more important stuff to deal with. What were you saying?"

She took a moment to sip her wine and to weather the sudden gust of guilt. "I'm nervous about my testimony against Essex, I'm stumbling in the speeches, I'm two lousy weeks behind on my paperwork, and I'm behind in the polls." As she spoke, her chest tightened: She was going to lose the election, and then she feared losing Ed and Grace and the life she'd been building here in Monastery Valley. She squeezed her eyes shut, trying to get a grip.

Ed moved closer and put his arm around her, but she pulled away. "What?" he whispered.

"Time for me to cowgirl up."

FRIDAY, OCTOBER 19

1

Ed came into Alice's Village Inn after Andi got there, and kissed her before sitting down. He noticed a few people staring. *Thinking about the 'slut' ad*, he wondered. *Let 'em*, he decided. After ordering, he said, "Grace's over at Mona's for dinner." He squinted. "Look, I was out of line last night. I worry about the pace you're keeping, but I was pushing you to take time off for my sake, not yours."

"No apology needed. Pete told me I made a big mistake on an arrest report. Ordered me to take the weekend off."

"Ordered you?" He tried to picture Pete doing that. Or Andi allowing it. "You going to?"

"I am. I'm sleeping as long as I want, and after that, I want not to have to say two words in a row to anybody."

He wasn't quick enough to hide his disappointment. "I thought maybe we'd drive over to Missoula, spend the night, have a nice dinner."

"I need to recharge, get some private time."

Disappointed or not, he knew she had to manage herself. "Got it. If you change your mind, we'll do whatever you like."

Andi softened. "I appreciate it, Ed."

"Sure. You've got the world on your shoulders, so whatever you need . . . You still giving your speech tonight?"

"Yeah. It's too late to cancel. But none this weekend. I'm out of commission till Monday."

Their orders arrived and they focused on the burgers and fries. After they'd finished, he drove her to the community center for the Montana Democrats meeting, and waited for her in his truck, writing notes on the day's patients. As the women began straggling out of the meeting, his cell phone buzzed.

It was Grace. "Hey, Northrup, the PV's dead. I tried to start it but all I heard was a bunch of clicks."

"Real fast clicks? Or just one each time you turn the key?"

"Real fast clicks."

"Battery could be dead. Where are you?"

"At Mona's. You gotta get over here." He heard the subtle tension in her voice, as if she were trying not to let someone hear it.

"What's happening?"

"Uh, nothing. We, uh, need a ride."

"Got it," he said. *We?* "Where does Mona live?"

Grace gave him the address. He said, "I have to wait till Andi's done, then we'll come and get you."

"Don't wait too long, Okay?"

Ed started to insist she tell him what was going on, but saw Andi coming out. "We're on our way. One minute."

2

Mona Frantz and her father lived in a peeling shack three blocks west of where the Monastery River flowed behind the Division Street businesses. The hard-packed dirt of the weedy gray yard bled into the gravel street, patched with yellowed dead leaves.

As he parked behind Grace's PV on the packed dirt, Andi said to Ed, "Reminds me of a dead railroad yard." *Or worse.*

"Or skid row. There are the girls."

Grace and Mona sat on the upper step of a two-step porch of splintery boards. Grace waved and stood up. Ed and Andi got out and walked toward the girls. Getting closer, Andi saw that Mona had a serious black eye—and bruises on her arms.

"Hi, Mona, I'm Ed Northrup." He pointed to her eye. "How'd that happen?"

The girl turned partially away. "I, uh, . . ." She didn't finish.

"Northrup," said Grace, "we gotta move along. Please." That was when Andi saw that Grace too had blood on the shoulder of her shirt. She looked more closely; Grace's hair on that side of her head, just above her ear, was matted. In the dim light, it looked like blood. Ed saw Andi looking, peered at Grace too, and whispered, "What the hell, Grace? What's—"

"Later, Northrup. Mona's coming home with us. We can talk when we get home."

Ed looked at Mona. "Is that all right with your father?"

"He's drunk, Northrup, passed out. We need to get out of here. Now."

He made the decision. "Okay. Let's go. We'll all squeeze in."

3

Andi couldn't wait. While Ed tended to Grace's head—a small laceration under her hair, just above her ear, was still oozing blood—Andi, seeing how terrified Mona looked, turned to Grace. "Grace, what happened?"

Grace winced as Ed gingerly cleaned her wound. "Can we talk about this in the morning?"

Ed said, "Nope. Now." He applied some antibiotic cream to Grace's scalp.

Mona gasped. "My dad knows where you live. When he comes to, he'll know where I am."

Andi said, "I'll lock the doors, then we'll talk."

When she came back, she asked Mona, "You're new to Jefferson. How does your dad know where we live?"

Mona looked, if possible, even more upset, but she said nothing.

Grace said, "Can I tell?"

Mona nodded, hesitant.

"Her father took the video of you guys kissing. Then he photo-shopped me in. He bragged about it after he got drunk. Somebody named Crane paid him."

Andi grew still, glancing at Ed, who'd frozen. To Mona, she said, "What's your father's name, honey?"

Mona took in a long breath. "Charles Frantz. That's 'tz' at the end."

"Did he give you the black eye and those bruises on your arms?"

Mona nodded weakly.

"Did he hit Grace?"

"Andi." Grace jumped in. "Can't you see she's scared?"

"Yes, I can, and I need to know what we have to do to keep her safe. If I don't have a good reason for her to stay here, her father could accuse us of kidnapping."

"Oh." Mona's eyes widened. "Can I say something?"

"Of course," Andi said, smiling.

"I feel real bad about those things I said about you in the Town Hall meeting. I didn't mean them—my dad told me to say them or he'd beat me worse."

"He beats you other times than this?" She nodded toward Mona's eye.

The look on the girl's face was pure pain. "All the time. That's one of the reasons he was in prison—he almost killed my mom because she tried to stop him beating me."

"When did he get out of prison?"

"July, this year."

"Why are you with him? If he served time for beating your mom, and he beats you, I'm surprised he has custody of you."

"He doesn't."

Andi angled her head, disliking where this seemed headed. "He doesn't have custody, but you're here with him?"

"He got a judge or somebody to let him visit me in Billings—my mom was at work. After he picked me up—I was scared of him—he brought me over here." She began to cry. "My mom doesn't know where I am."

Andi gentled her voice. "Do you think your mom would have agreed to have you go with him? She has custody, right?"

"Uh huh. I don't know . . ." Mona's voice faded, her eyes welling.

Andi wanted more information, but the girl's tears slowed her. After a moment, she asked, "Have you tried to call your mom?"

Mona shook her head, her eyes gray with fear. "He told me if I called her and he found out, he'd kill me and then he'd go to Billings and kill her." She wiped her eyes with a finger. "I believed him. He'd almost killed her before."

Ed said to Mona, "Want me to call her?"

Mona nodded.

"What's her phone number?"

Ed wrote it as Mona recited it, then said, "Will your mom be at work or at home?"

"She's always at work—she's got two jobs. That number I gave you is her night job."

Ed looked briefly at Andi, whose eyes were sad. Ed went to the bedroom extension to call.

Andi called after him, "Get the name of the judge who okayed the visit." She turned to Grace. "How'd you get hurt?"

"Her dad."

"Tell me what happened."

"It was after dinner. He was drinking a lot of beer, what he called his 'home brew.' After we ate, he had an empty beer bottle in his hand, and when Mona asked if she and I could go for a walk, he hit her near her eye with the bottle and then on her arm. He was going to slap her with his other hand, so I grabbed his arm, and he swung the bottle at my head. I guess he hit me, but I didn't feel anything. I was too mad."

Andi glanced at her gun belt hanging on the hook by the front door. "What happened after that?"

"He grabbed another beer and went into the living room. We went out on the front porch and when I went back inside to get my things, he was snoring on the couch. That's when I tried to start the PV and called Northrup."

Ed came back into the kitchen. To Mona, he said, "You want to speak with your mom?"

Mona looked terrified. Ed said, "She's not mad at you, honey. She's crying too."

Mona took the phone into the bedroom and closed the door.

Ed said, "Her mom's going to come and get her, but she can't leave till Sunday evening after work, so she won't get here till late that night or Monday morning. So, we need a plan to keep Mona safe."

Andi nodded, then added, "Not just Mona. Frantz hit Grace with a beer bottle. And the PV is still over there."

"He hit you with a bottle?" Ed's face flared red, and he started toward the door. "I'm going over there."

Grace stood in his way. "Northrup, please. Don't. He'll kill you."

Andi said, "Hold on, Ed. I'll get Pete or whoever's on duty to go over there." She put her hand on his arm. "They'll handle it."

For a moment, Ed was silent. Then, "Okay. But call them now."

"Before I do, did you get the name of that judge?"

"There's no judge. Mona's mom—her name's Margie—didn't know a thing about it. She called the Billings police to report Mona missing. I guess she's been terrified."

"Okay. Let me call Pete. We'll add kidnapping to the charges." As she grabbed her cell phone and went out to the porch, Mona emerged from the bedroom, her face streaked.

Ed said to her, "Are you okay staying here tonight? And maybe till your mom gets here, if we can work that out?"

Mona looked scared. "Why couldn't you?"

"Your father's been abusive of both you girls, and it sounds like he kidnapped you, which is two crimes. The sheriff's going to arrest him, but we might be required to take you to a family shelter till your mom gets here."

Andi, her call done, came back in, holding up her phone. "Girls, I'm going to take some pictures to document your injuries."

"Why?" Mona asked.

Grace answered. "To use in court to send your dad back to prison."

Mona whispered, "He told me he'd kill himself before he'd go back there."

Grace snorted. "Maybe we should just let him do it."

4

"Pete?"

"Andi, hi. What's going on?"

"Trouble. I'll keep it short. We got a guy who just assaulted Grace and her friend, Mona Frantz. The guy's Mona's father, name's Charles. The girls are safe with Ed and me, and the last they knew, Frantz was passed out on his couch."

"Drunk or medical?"

"Drunk. You think you could get whoever's on duty to get a warrant and go over there and pick him up? Child abuse and possible kidnapping. It turns out he knows where I live, so I'd as soon stay here with the girls and Ed in case I'm wrong and he comes by."

"Any evidence of the assault? We'll need probable cause."

"Yeah. Grace has contusions on her left temple under the hair, and Mona has a shiner and a couple of bruises on her right arm. I've taken pictures."

"Okay, I'm on it. I'll go see Dickie Flure myself. Might not happen till morning though. Hang in there."

"Get the warrant and go tonight, and be careful, he's an angry drunk."

"We'll handle him just fine. I've got a special way with drunken child abusers."

SATURDAY, OCTOBER 20

1

Late as it was, after one in the morning, Ed went to the kitchen and returned with a tray carrying two glasses of wine and two Cokes. "Didn't you say your dad was just released from prison?"

Mona nodded. "Yeah, in July."

Ed turned to Andi. "Wouldn't all this be a violation of his parole?"

She jumped up and headed for the phone. "Sure as hell would." She called the station. They listened. "Kris, who's on tonight?" She listened. "Great. Is he out getting Frantz? . . . Uh- huh. Have him . . . oh, good, I'll wait."

To Mona, on the couch, she said, "Two deputies are going to arrest your dad. They'll call me when it's done. He'll be buttoned up tight, you're fine with us till your mom gets here."

"Do you think, since he's in jail, I could go to his house and get my things?"

Ed answered. "You bet. First thing in the morning. We'll see what's going on with the PV too."

Mona looked confused. "What's a PV?" She hadn't been around when Grace named her car.

Grace grinned, and explained the name.

Mona turned as red as a rose.

2

In the morning, Ed drove the girls back to the Frantz shack. While Mona and Grace went inside to get her things, Ed climbed into the PV, inserted the key, and turned the ignition. It started just fine. *Hmm.* He shut it down and climbed back into his pickup.

In ten minutes, the girls came out of the house. Grace carried two suitcases and Mona two more. She had a stuffed backpack hanging from one shoulder. The way they drooped told him the bags were heavy. He hopped out and helped them load the bags into the PV. They *were* heavy.

"Your car started right up, Grace."

"How could it?"

"No idea."

Grace shook her head. "I worried about my poor car all night."

Ed tried not to smile. Grace got in, turned the ignition, and nothing happened. "Northrup, see?"

This time he did smile. "Let me check the battery cable. Open the hood, please."

Sure enough, the positive cable was loose. He grabbed the ratchet set from his truck's toolbox, tightened the cable connection, and said, "Try it again." It started.

"Okay, shut it down, then try it again." Again, it started. "Problem solved."

All problems should be this simple.

3

Ordrew's phone rang. He picked up, feeling vaguely guilty for being home. He ought to be out door-knocking.

"Brad? It's Andi. Look, I wanted to let you know that we've arrested the man who filmed the 'slut' ad. Last night, he assaulted Grace and his own daughter, whom we think he kidnapped and brought to Jefferson."

He felt rage flare in his chest, choking him. He tried to breathe through it.

"Brad, you there?"

"I'm here, Andi, but I'm almost too angry to speak." He took a long breath. "This is outrageous." A new thought stopped him. "We thought Crane did the ad."

Andi said, "He did. This guy works for Crane."

His breathed hard through his nose. "I, uh, appreciate you telling me, Andi."

"There's another thing. The guy—his name's Charles Frantz—just got released from Deer Lodge after doing a ten-year ticket for assault on his ex-wife. It appears he kidnapped his daughter in Billings and brought her to Jeff."

"Kidnapped? Damn." His chest hurt. "You're saying he works for Crane? How do you know?"

"He bragged about it to Grace. Before he hit her with a beer bottle." Ordrew heard the contempt in her voice.

His anger welled again.

Andi was going on. "I informed Pete and I wanted you to know in case this situation comes up in your Q & A."

Ordrew felt the boil in his chest. But beneath it, another feeling. *She's wanting me to be prepared, even though I could use it against her*, he thought. The thought of attacking her in his next speech sickened him. He managed some words of thanks and hung up.

Am I being unfair to her? Of course he was. He knew it. But you don't get elected by being fair. He knew that too. Still. It galled him. Shamed him. *Not who I am.*

Began tapping another number into the phone, hard.

4

The call rolled over to voicemail, which might have relieved Ordrew in the past, but inflamed his anger now. He waited for the beep, then barked, "Crane, this is Ordrew. Your stooge was just arrested for assaulting Grace Northrup and his own daughter. I'm done with you. Your TV ads and mailings are scandalous, not to mention libelous, but your guy attacking the girls is child abuse, damn it. Any agreement you think we have is off. Entirely. And if I win this election, don't show your wretched face in my county or I'll haul your ass to jail for this."

He wasn't sure, as he hit *End*, whether his message had been clear enough, but he no longer gave a rat's ass.

MONDAY, OCTOBER 22

1

Everybody got up at six in the morning. Grace and Mona moved like zombies until they downed their first coffee. Mona's mom, Margie Cook, had arrived from Billings around eleven last evening, and her reunion with her daughter had been emotional—tears, anger, relief. Afterward, they'd sat around, getting acquainted, sipping glasses of wine. Under the circumstances, Margie had decided Mona could have one glass to celebrate.

During their conversation, Andi had asked Margie, "By the way, can you stay until maybe ten o'clock tomorrow morning? Frantz's probable cause hearing is at nine, and we need Mona to testify."

"Oh, God, Andi, I can't. It's almost five hours back to Billings and I start my evening job at the nursing home at three. I can't afford to be late."

Ed had said, "How about using your pictures instead of Mona appearing in person?"

Edgy, Andi had thought. "Maybe. I'll call Irv Jackson first thing and see what he says."

This morning, she called Irv just after seven a.m. and told him the problem.

"Sorry, but no. For the kidnapping charge, I'll need the mother's testimony that Frantz doesn't have custody or permission. We can use the pictures for the abuse charge."

Damn. "Okay, I'll talk with Margie."

Margie heard her out. "Is the kidnapping charge important?"

"Very important. We have the other charges, but this will be the strongest one and, with your testimony, the one with the best chance to put him away. For a long time."

Margie took a deep breath. "Okay, we'll stay. I'll find another evening job."

•   •   •

The hearing was successful, resulting in kidnapping, child abuse, and parole violation charges against Frantz. After an early lunch, Andi and Ed stood outside the Angler and waved as Margie backed her car around and drove north with Mona beside her. Andi said, "I hope she doesn't lose her job."

He nodded. "How'd her boss sound when you called?"

"All he said was, 'Tell her to get her buns in on time tomorrow.'"

"Ouch."

2

Back at the station, Andi pulled up the Essex file. She'd just waded in when Callie buzzed her. "Andi, line two for you. Irv Jackson."

She pressed the flashing button. "Hey, Irv. I'm staring at the Essex file."

"Stare hard. You're up Thursday morning for evidence authentication. Jury selection'll take most of the afternoon, so your testimony's first thing Friday morning."

"What time?"

"Knowing Dickie, he'll be in rocket-docket mode. So, plan on nine o'clock sharp. After you, I'll call Brenda, and then Oxendine and Xavier. I've got an expert on obsessive-compulsive disorder, but Norton does too, so they'll cancel out, although my guy thinks her guy is weak. I'll call neighbors to corroborate what you got from them."

"Why put Brenda second? Wouldn't Xav and Phil Oxendine logically follow me?"

"Brenda's important, but she's my weakest link. If she doesn't do well, Oxendine, Xavier, and my expert will leave a stronger impression on the jury." He rustled some papers. "So, bottom line, can I get with you for a couple of hours today to prep?"

She rubbed her eyes. "What time?"

"Now."

3

As she was packing her paperwork, her phone buzzed again. "Andi, line one. Ben."

She stretched her back and shoulders and picked up. "Hey, Ben. What's up?"

"What're you doin'?"

"Prepping with Irv Jackson for my testimony on Friday."

"Wrong answer. You talk to Mack Anderssen about money yet?"

She grimaced. "Uh, no. I, uh, needed to rest." *Lame.*

"Naw. Ain't no rest for the campaigner. How about your boyfriend?"

"Guilty again."

Ben was silent, which Andi took as a signal to duck. "I'll do it tonight, Ben."

"Do it. Mack too. And hit up Jerry Francis and Marty Bailey at the bank. Marty's always good for Democrats. Money's gas for a campaign's stove. Don't turn that burner off."

Before she could answer, he was gone.

She finished packing her Essex file, tried to reconstruct the evidence as they had found it, but her mind drifted like an unmoored boat. *Money.* She'd avoided the whole issue, but there was no avoiding it now. Ben was right. The cupboard was bare. *Either I use my 401(k) or I talk to Ed and Mack. Damn.*

Why not *borrow* from Magnus and Ed, and buy the chance to win? She could pay them back eventually. Screw Ordrew's threat. If she lost the election, she'd fight any attempt he'd make to fire her. And winning the election didn't just mean staying in the valley. It meant being able to stop men like Essex from getting away with murder, and people like Frantz from abusing girls, and guys like Loyd Crane from lying and manipulating. Surprised at herself, she felt a burst of resolve, and left for Irv Jackson's office.

4

When she got home, Ed had dinner waiting. Money-talk could wait.

After dinner, she sighed, unable to find a way around it. "Gotta talk campaign money."

He smiled, carrying their dishes to the sink. "Now you're singing my tune." He wiped his hands and grabbed his briefcase from below the coats. "I've got a check written out for ten thousand dollars, and there's more if we need it."

She caught her breath. "My God, Ed, that's too much."

He laughed, cutting her off. "Quiet. Grace and I talked it over and that's what we agreed. And I called Mack and he's in for ten grand on top of that. So, you've got a little over thirteen hundred a day for the last fifteen days of the campaign."

"Jesus, twenty thousand dollars . . ." she whispered, fighting hard not to give way to guilt. *Knock it off,* she told herself. *You're a candidate for sheriff, damn it.* "Okay. Uh, thanks. Thanks a lot."

"You're welcome. Let's talk about how to spend it." He drew a manila folder out of his briefcase. "I did a little homework while I was waiting for you to ask."

She was curious. "Why didn't *you* bring it up again?"

"Somebody pretty influential around here told me not to." He grinned. "I'm getting pretty good at waiting for you to be ready for things." His eyes twinkled. He was teasing her, she knew, about her making him wait years to talk marriage.

"Ah, *touché*. And you're enjoying yourself, I can tell." She was too, all at once.

He chuckled. "I am. So, business. We're down to the wire, and I was getting nervous. I decided if you didn't ask, I was going ahead anyway." He pulled out a sheet of paper and looked at it, then handed it to her. "Bud Groh charges forty dollars for a thirty-second ad. I talked to some marketing guys in Missoula, who told me it takes a minimum of three hits for a person to remember an ad, so I'd say we want to air an ad in the morning at milking time, again around lunch, and then in the evening drive slot. Every day between now and the election. That's forty-five spots, eighteen hundred dollars."

"Around *milking* time?"

"An expression from Minnesota. Bud broadcasts milk, beef, and pork futures prices every morning between six and seven. That's milking time for the dairy farmers and breakfast time on most of the other ranches. I checked around."

A new tingling formed in her chest. Maybe this would work. Twenty thousand dollars would go a long way. Then, a flash of reality hit and she felt the tingling fade. "Oh man, I've got to write some ads. Did you say forty-five? I don't know if I—"

"You won't be doing that. I've already hired a scriptwriter and an actor, and they've been working on the spots. They'll be ready to go with the first two days' ads within ten hours after I give them the signal. They've agreed to do this for three thousand each, which is a steal, plus fifteen hundred for the recording studio. Shall I call?"

"Wow. You've been busy. I like it. Shouldn't I review the ads, make sure I approve?"

"Do you trust me?"

"Of course."

"You already approved them."

She couldn't help grinning. "All right, big operator. Make your call." The tingling had returned, in the vicinity of her heart.

He was away for ten minutes, then returned, carrying two glasses of wine. "Okay. The first ad's ready, so it'll air in all three slots tomorrow. Bud's already got the slots reserved every day till the election. We'll run the first one both tomorrow and Tuesday as well, then the second one Wednesday, and so on." He pulled another sheet from his folder. "Next, polling."

Andi sank back into the couch pillows. "Something tells me you've already talked polling with somebody." The excitement in her body felt wonderful.

"Very perceptive—you must be a detective. Here's the deal. We, or I should say the polling firm, will leave a phone message on every phone number in Adams County, asking them to vote for you. That's twelve hundred dollars. After that, they'll do three random sample surveys of the valley's population. Each one will cost twenty-five hundred dollars. I already designed five questions they'll ask, and the company is all set to start tomorrow." He hesitated. "If you give the go-ahead."

"Go-ahead given," she said. A laugh bubbled up from that tingling spot.

He grinned. "Actually, I already signed the contract. They'll start tomorrow. The vote-for-Andi calls will take place tomorrow, Wednesday, and Thursday. Then they'll do three more randomly selected lists, one this coming Friday, one the following Friday, and one the day before the election. All told, polling will cost eighty-seven hundred. Now, exit polling."

"Whoa. What's the total so far?"

He scanned the three sheets he'd been looking at. "Eighteen thousand. Leaves us two in reserve, and Mack said to call if we need more." He smiled. "And Grace said, 'It's my money, Northrup. From my mom. Spend it for Andi.'"

Her throat thickened. *Gratitude*, she thought. "I interrupted you when you said exit polling. How much will that cost?"

He grinned. "I've taken the liberty of contracting a group that solely does exit polls. They're surprisingly cheap."

"How cheap?"

"Well, it turns out, they're volunteering their time for you."

Andi was stunned. "What pollsters would do that?"

"You'll be amazed."

She squinted at him, thought about pushing him, decided to let it ride. They sipped their wine in silence. For the first time, Andi sensed the campaign had morphed into a team effort, no longer just her problem. She felt relaxation seeping into her muscles, and realized how tense she'd been. *What happens, happens*, she thought. Leaning over, she kissed Ed. "What if I hadn't brought it up?"

Ed shrugged. "I was all set to declare myself a SuperPac."

5

Later, after they'd talked more about Ed's plans, they relaxed on the couch, watching the fire. Ed said, "Want to hear your first ad?"

"Absolutely."

Ed opened his email and played the recorded ad.

> VOICE: *When you love a place, you protect it, you serve it. You do all you can to preserve what's great about it, and all you can to improve anything that needs improving.*
>
> *Deputy Andi Pelton has made the Monastery Valley her home, and she loves it as you do. Her commitment is to protect, to serve, and, in Ben Stewart's tradition, to be the best sheriff she can be. She'll make the valley safer and better.*
>
> *On November 6, vote for Andi Pelton for Sheriff of Adams County.*
>
> *Paid for by the Friends of Andi Pelton Committee*

After it finished, she said, "I like it. A lot." She started to detail her reaction when her cell phone buzzed. "Huh," she sighed. "Do all politicians work late?" She hit *Talk*.

"Andi, Callie here. Look, I jus' got back from listenin' to that jerk's speech to the Elks. Bill's a member, so we went. I'm so pissed I could spit."

"His usual three lies?"

"Worse. On top of the riots we're going to have, the gun confiscation you're planning, and the immigrants-coming-for-your-jobs part, he tacked on this stinker: 'My opponent is challenging Montana's stand-your-ground defense.' Oh, and the usual 'the valley's not ready for a woman sheriff' crap. Came right out and said it. My blood's boiling."

Andi sighed. "Nothing new there; we know he feels that way." She thought for a moment. "Brad's been a little nicer lately, at least when he talks to me. Ed thinks he feels unconsciously guilty for the ads and blames me for them, so he attacks."

"Blames *you*? Please. Look, I got a suggestion."

Ed was watching, curious. Andi said, "Can I put you on speaker for Ed?"

"Can Clint Eastwood talk to chairs?"

Chuckling, Andi pressed the speaker button. "Okay. What's your idea?"

"First, we get you and the little dink in the same room together."

Andi shook her head. "Won't work. He refuses to debate me. Says he doesn't need to."

"Already figured that one out. Mack and Luisa Anderssen were there tonight and we talked. They're mad as me. You're making a speech at their place next week, right?"

Andi thought about her schedule. "Yeah, a week from Friday, I think."

"Right. Luisa and Magnus are going to buy time on the radio and make an announcement in the *Bee* inviting the bozo to debate you. So, either he doesn't show and we spread the word he's afraid, or he shows and we nail him."

"How?" Andi couldn't pin down how she felt about this—department employees were supposed to be neutral.

"Bernie's got a couple of zingers to ask him that he won't be able to answer without showing what a Neanderthal he is, and Lane's going to confront him about that mailer that said you were a murderer."

No conflict there. Relieved, Andi remembered what Xavier had told her. "Callie, I can give you something else Lane can use. Back in Los Angeles, Brad went on a motel call just like our entry with Crane. There was shooting, and apparently Brad killed one of the bad guys. I doubt anybody accused him of murder for that."

Callie was quiet. "Hypocrite. All right, I'll pass that along to Lane. He'll make good use of it."

After the call, Andi stood up.

Ed asked, "That should be a wild debate. Where're you off to?"

"I've got to rewrite my speech. I'm going after Ordrew now."

FRIDAY, OCTOBER 26

1

At nine o'clock, Judge Richard Flure gaveled Daniel Essex's murder trial to order. Pre-trial motions had been argued and decided on Monday. All evidence exhibits had been authenticated, marked, and admitted into evidence yesterday, and the jury selected. The judge nodded to Irv Jackson. "Prosecutor, your opening statement, please."

Jackson stood. "Thank you, Your Honor." He approached the jury. "Good morning," he said, pausing long enough that a few of the jurors, nervously, said "good morning" back. He smiled. "I'm Irving Jackson, district attorney for Adams County. As you know, we're here to answer a very simple question: Is Mr. Daniel Essex—" He turned and gestured toward Essex at the defense table. "—guilty of murder in the death of Bernardo Cirilo on August 25. We're going to show you evidence to support our case that he is. We'll describe how he put beer in his garage refrigerator—even though he doesn't drink beer himself—and left a twelve-pack on the workbench and the garage door open. We'll prove that he rigged the refrigerator so he could hear if anyone opened it and took beer out. We'll establish that when he heard this, he went outside, braced his gun on the hood of his car, and shot young Mr. Cirilo in the back."

He paused a moment. "We'll provide evidence that Mr. Essex lied at least five times to the sheriff's deputies. First, he let them believe that the gun he was carrying was the one he shot, when in fact he had hidden the real murder weapon. Second, he claimed his garage door was closed when in fact it was open, allowing anyone passing by to see the beer left out on his workbench. Third, he stated that he simply 'forgot' to park his car inside the garage, when in fact he did so deliberately. Fourth, he told the deputies that Mr. Cirilo attacked him and that he shot the boy as Bernardo rushed toward him, which we'll show was a lie. We'll demonstrate that the young man was shot *in . . . the . . . back* outside the refrigerator with a can of beer in his hand."

Jackson gave the slightest shake of his head, appalled at the outrage. "We will show you evidence that Mr. Essex's statement that his garage had been burglarized and his beer stolen a couple of weeks earlier is false. We will present testimony that he expected a home intrusion, to the extent that he wore his gun-belt around the house and placed a baby monitor in his garage refrigerator to alert him to an attempt to steal his beer—beer he never intended to drink."

After turning sorrowfully toward his table, he paused, then turned back toward the jury. "In short, ladies and gentlemen, we will show that Mr. Essex baited his garage with beer, attracted a fourteen-year-old high school freshman with that bait, and shot this poor young man—who wasn't acting lawfully, of course, but plainly was acting like many teenagers—shot him in the back. The people of Adams County are going to ask you to deliver a verdict of murder in the shooting of young Bernardo Cirilo. Thank you."

2

As Jackson took his seat, Angela Norton stood. She nodded to the judge. "Your Honor." She came around the defense table and stood before jury. Andi, in the back row of the gallery seats, watched the back of Essex's head. He was looking straight ahead, unmoving. No doubt Norton had coached him to look friendly. No doubt he had refused to listen.

Norton began. "Ladies and gentlemen, thank you for serving on this case. The jury is always the final decider, the best defense of the rule of law, and I for one appreciate the sacrifice you are making, of your time, of your incomes, and of your freedom to come and go as you wish. My client—" She turned and nodded toward Essex, who grudgingly turned toward the jury box. "—is Daniel Essex, an independent software consultant. Daniel has personal issues, which you will hear about, but none of them accounts for the events of August 25. We will show that many of the points the prosecution intends to make are based on inferences that may or may not be based on the facts of the case, at least not firmly enough to draw conclusions that are beyond a reasonable doubt. Montana law is clear: A person can use force, even lethal force, if he believes that either his person or his property is under attack. We will show that this is precisely what Mr. Essex believed on that tragic night: That unless he stood his ground, he or his property were in jeopardy."

She lowered her voice. "The question you will be asked to answer in this trial isn't whether Daniel's home was burglarized earlier. It isn't whether Daniel lied or told the truth to the deputies. It isn't whether Daniel is mentally troubled. The only question you must answer in this trial is whether he was standing his ground in accord with Montana law, protecting his home as you or any ordinary citizen would do. And the standard you must apply as you answer that question is whether the state has proven their contention *beyond a reasonable doubt*.

"Again, ladies and gentlemen, I want to thank you in advance for your service in this matter, which is nothing less than the cause of justice. You have a noble burden, and Mr. Essex and I deeply appreciate your shouldering it."

3

At precisely nine-twenty, Andi stood and was sworn in, then took her seat. Looking out to the crowded gallery—almost every chair was filled—she saw the Cirilo family in the front row. She gave a confident smile, though she felt anything but confidence. None of the Cirilos managed a return smile, but the mother nodded, her eyes dry and red.

Irv Jackson came toward the witness stand and, after establishing Andi's credentials for the jury, led her through the chilling facts of Bernardo Cirilo's murder. Andi kept expecting objections from Angela Norton, but she was as careful in her answers as Jackson was careful in his questions, and none came. She studiously avoided looking at Norton and Essex at the defense table, focusing instead on Irv when he asked a question, then directing her answer to the jury.

Once the basic facts were established—the boy lying with his face against the shelf, two bullet holes and blood on the back of his sweater, none beneath him, the unusual placement of the car, the garage left open, the beer visible on the workbench, the baby monitor in the fridge—Irv's questioning next shaped her chronicle of Essex's lies: the wrong gun, the car and the noise of the garage door, the non-existent burglary that justified his stand-your-ground defense, the claim that

Bernardo had charged him and crawled back to the refrigerator after Essex shot him in the front. At that point, Irv had switched on his laptop and showed a slide of the two bullet holes in Bernardo's sweater soaked with blood. Mrs. Cirilo gasped.

"Is this photo of the back of Mr. Cirilo's sweater?"

"Yes. You can see the two holes and the blood stain," Andi said.

"So, is it your testimony that Mr. Essex lied to you about the gun, about the sound he heard, the burglary, and most importantly, about how he shot Bernardo?"

"Yes."

Jackson left the image of Bernardo's sweater on the screen and picked up a page. Tension crackled in the gallery. The jury peered at the screen. Norton stood. "Your Honor, may I request that the prosecutor turn off the slide? It is prejudicial to my client."

"Mr. Jackson, do you have a reason to leave the picture on?" Flure asked.

"I'm sorry, Your Honor, I'll bring up the next slide." He touched a key and a photo of the refrigerator came up. Out of the corner of her eye, Andi looked at the Cirilos. Mrs. Cirilo's face was wet with tears, her eyes closed. Andi focused on the facts she needed to present.

First, they worked through the details of the alleged burglary: Essex's refusal to file a police report, the ten stolen beers, and Andi's failed efforts to track down any replacement beers through Essex's VISA statements and sales receipts.

"You're saying that no replacements were bought with his credit cards?"

"I am."

Irv pulled up another slide, this time showing two sales receipts, side by side. One was clean, the other soiled and wrinkled.

Andi was startled to see Brad Ordrew slip into the back row of the courtroom. *What's he doing here?* She refocused on the slide.

"Please describe what we're seeing."

She focused her attention on the screen. "These are two copies of the same sales receipt—the one on the right I obtained from the manager of Art's Fine Foods on September fourth. The one on the left, which is soiled and wrinkled, I found in Mr. Essex's garbage can on August twenty-eighth. Except for their condition, they are identical, and they show the purchase of the sixty beers we found in the refrigerator. The defendant bought them on July sixteenth. You can see the circles around that information."

Irv shut off the slide. "Why were you so interested in beer purchases?"

"Mr. Essex's previous misleading responses made us suspicious about whether a burglary had in fact happened. Finding that he purchased replacement cans would rule out our suspicions."

"I see." Irv turned to Judge Flure. "Your Honor, as you know, we have two dozen sales receipts from Art's Fine Foods alone, and another seventeen from the other three stores where beer could have been purchased. As we discussed yesterday, Ms. Norton and I would like to stipulate that they contain no evidence that beer has been purchased with credit in these stores between June fourth and the night of the shooting. Except, of course, the original sixty found in the garage."

Flure said, "Ms. Norton?"

"I agree, Judge. I've studied all the receipts."

"Very well, then, so stipulated."

"Thank you, Judge." He turned back to Andi. "So, it's your testimony that aside from the original sixty beers from July sixteenth, you found no evidence in his credit card statements or the sales receipts linked to them that Mr. Essex replaced the ten stolen beers."

"Yes, it is."

Murmuring swept through the crowd. While the judge banged his gavel, Andi looked at Ordrew in the back row. He was bent forward, his elbows on his knees and his fingers hard against his lips.

Jackson asked, "Have you found any evidence that Mr. Essex paid cash for beer?"

Andi described three sources of information about that. First, none of the clerks in the four stores saw Essex use cash for beer—or for anything. Second, the statements of Brenda, Xavier, and Ella Parks that Essex considered cash to be infested with microbes and that he refused to touch it.

Norton was on her feet instantly. "I object. This statement is hearsay not covered by any hearsay exception." Essex looked furious.

Judge Flure addressed Irv. "Mr. Jackson, do you intend to call these persons who are the source of the witness's information?"

"I do, Your Honor. One of them, Ms. Cantor, is my next witness."

"And the others?"

"Deputy Xavier Contrerez and Ms. Ella Parks, a clerk at Art's Fine Foods. Both will be called."

Flure took some time thinking about the objection. Then, he looked down to Norton. "Counselor, if the source of the information testifies to it, it won't be hearsay. I will defer my decision on your objection until after we hear whether their testimony confirms the statement."

Plainly annoyed, Norton said, "Thank you, Your Honor." She sat down and whispered something to Essex, who shook his head vigorously. Andi thought he looked disgusted.

Irv's next line of questions focused on the third finding that supported the argument that Essex hadn't paid cash for beer: The fact that Kokanee Lager and Bud Light were only sold in multiples that could not add up to ten. Four packs, six packs, eight packs, twelve-packs and so on, but no combination that allowed him to buy ten.

"What if he bought an eight-pack and two singles?"

She explained how Laurie Swanson had learned from her distributor that no stores sold singles in southwest Montana.

Andi saw Norton whisper something to Essex. His face reddened. Norton jotted a note.

"So, what conclusion did you draw from these facts?"

"We concluded that if he replaced fewer than ten, we should've found fewer than sixty, or if he replaced more than ten, we should have found more than sixty. Instead, we found exactly sixty."

Norton stood. "Your Honor, may I ask where this is going?"

"Mr. Jackson, do you have a goal here?"

"Yes, sir, I do, a very important goal. As I said in my opening statement, the state intends to show that the defendant was never burglarized, and instead was using beer as bait for garage-hopping teenagers, whom he intended to shoot and then use stand-your-ground as his defense."

"Very well, get on with it. We're getting perilously close to lunch."

Irv turned back to Andi and raised the issue of alternative explanations for finding sixty beers, no more, no fewer. Perhaps he bought a twelve pack or more and drank the extras? Andi described Brenda's assertion that Essex never drank beer, always expensive Scotch. Perhaps a friend came over and drank the extra beers? No, Brenda said that during their affair no one had visited Essex, that he and she had been alone every night.

At that, audible gasps came from a few people, and Norton stood. "Your Honor, I object. The witness's statements, still hearsay in my opinion, are prejudicial to my client and may damage our ability to provide an adequate defense. I ask that the witness's last statement be stricken from the record and the jury instructed to ignore it."

Flure nodded. "Sustained." He turned to the jury and told them to ignore the statement.

Andi smiled inside. *Damage done. Juries don't ignore bombshells.*

Irv Jackson said, "So, Deputy, how do you explain what happened?"

Norton again got to her feet. "Objection, Your Honor. The witness is not qualified to testify as an expert forensic investigator."

Judge Flure, eyebrows arched, looked at Irv.

"Your Honor, Rule 701 makes it quite clear that a lay witness can offer an opinion provided three conditions are met, which I'd be happy to recite for the court."

Flure frowned. "I'm quite familiar with Rule 701, prosecutor. The objection is overruled. You may proceed."

"Thank you, Your Honor." To Andi, he repeated, "How do you explain what happened?"

"My conclusion is that there never were any missing beers. The beers purchased on July sixteenth were the same ones we found on the night of August twenty-fifth. Either the first intruder didn't take any beer, which would mean Mr. Essex's claim that ten beers were stolen is a lie."

Irv smiled. "You used the word 'either' in that last sentence. Is there an 'or'?"

"I'm sorry, yes, there is. *Or* there was no burglary in the first place."

Again, rustling murmurs spread across the courtroom. Andi glanced at Ordrew, whose eyes registered surprise. His mouth had opened a bit. She'd never mentioned this conclusion to him when they discussed the case. Irv waited a moment, then asked, "And what does that imply to you?"

"Given the facts that he left his car outside the garage and the garage door open and lied to us about it, that he lied about the weapon used, that he lied about the burglary, and that he'd put a baby monitor in the refrigerator and beside his chair, and lastly, given that he shot Mr. Cirilo in the back and lied about it—" She saw the Cirilos take each other's hands. "—we concluded that Mr. Essex had baited his garage with beer to attract an intruder, whom he could shoot."

This time, the buzz in the gallery drew Judge Flure's gavel.

Irv waited a moment before asking, "And what was the defendant's motive for shooting the victim?" He turned and walked to his table as Andi began her answer. She told the jury about Detective Rick James in Brookline, Massachusetts and the story of the alleged rape by an older boy when Essex was eleven.

Norton jumped up. "Objection. The detective's statements are hearsay."

Irv shook his head. "Your Honor, Exhibits T and U were admitted into evidence yesterday and Ms. Norton accepted them at that time." Flure rummaged a bit, found his copies. Irv went on, "Exhibit T is the police report of the alleged rape, including the evidence sheet describing what evidence they found. Exhibit U is a sworn affidavit filed by Detective Rick James, who has known the defendant since Mr. Essex was twenty."

Judge Flure nodded. "Objection overruled."

Irv turned to Andi. "So, your conclusion as to motive?"

"That Mr. Essex planned to attract a high-school age male into his garage and shoot him to act out his long-harbored anger toward that age group and gender." Andi expected Norton to be on her feet again, but was surprised. *Ah. The psychiatric interview.* Essex had told Irv's psychiatrist the same story of being raped that she'd obtained from Brookline, and had gotten agitated during the telling.

"Thank you, Deputy." Irv looked to the bench. "Your Honor, I'm finished with Deputy Pelton, although I reserve the right to re-direct."

The judge glanced at the clock on the wall. "Excellent. I believe this is a good point to adjourn for lunch."

Andi, stepping down from the witness stand, saw Ordrew slip out the courtroom door.

4

After lunch, before resuming her seat on the stand, Andi stopped by the front row. Mr. Cirilo stood. "*¿Como vamos?*" he asked.

Andi's heart went out to him. So traumatized, he was reverting to Spanish. She said, "'How are we doing?'" He nodded. "We're doing well, Mr. Cirilo. We're fighting hard for your son."

He nodded and sat down. She went through the gate and took her seat on the witness stand, reached for the bottle of water in the cup holder on the witness chair, took a sip, then sat up straight, startled. Brad Ordrew had come in and taken the same back-row chair. She tried to catch his eye, but he looked away. *What the hell's he up to? How will he use this against me?*

The judge's voice broke into her thoughts. "Deputy, remember you're still under oath."

Andi looked up at him and nodded.

Angela Norton stared a moment at Andi from behind her table, as if taking her measure. Then she stood and approached the stand. "Deputy, you just testified to a very complicated theory." Her subtle emphasis on *theory* was for the jury.

Andi waited.

"I have a few questions for you."

Andi said nothing.

"Let me start with your testimony that you showed pictures of my client to all the clerks in the stores where he might have bought beer with cash, and none could remember his doing so. Is that correct?"

"Almost," Andi smiled. "They didn't say they couldn't *remember* his paying cash. They all said they hadn't seen him do so."

"But that implies that the clerks could not remember his doing so. I suppose we could bring all those clerks in and put them under oath and ask them which it is. Otherwise, we'll never know the truth beyond a reasonable doubt, will we?"

Andi didn't reply.

"Will we, Deputy?"

Irv got to his feet. "Objection, your Honor. Asking for speculation."

"Sustained."

Norton nodded. "You looked into the sales slips of four stores. How many towns and cities are there within, say, six hours' drive time from Jefferson?"

Irv was on his feet. "Objection, Your Honor. Calls for either specialized knowledge the witness should not be expected to have, or pure guesswork."

Flure asked, "Where are you going with this, Counselor?"

"Reasonable doubt, Your Honor. Weaknesses both in this witness's logic and in her evidence."

"Very well, let's go straight at it. Objection overruled."

"Thank you, Your Honor. Deputy, would you agree that there are arguably many stores where someone can buy beer within a few hours of Jefferson?"

"We considered that, of course. But we couldn't come up with any reason for him to do so. There's no crime in replacing stolen beers."

"Perhaps he wanted to conceal the purchase."

"Again, he had no reason to do so. Buying beer isn't a crime."

"Perhaps he was traveling for work and it occurred to him to replace the beer."

"Mr. Essex works from home, and—"

"A pleasure trip, a small vacation."

"His VISA statements don't include charges for meals or lodging in any other communities between July sixteenth and the night of the shooting."

"So, you're stating that it is impossible that Mr. Essex paid cash for the replacement beers, even somewhere else?"

"No, ma'am, I'm not saying it's *impossible*. This is a wide world and I'd never say it was *impossible*. What I am saying is that there's no reason for him to have done so. As I said—"

"We don't need either your repetition or your lectures on philosophy." She turned toward the jury. Andi waited.

"Deputy, you have asserted a number of times that my client is germ-averse and therefore refuses to use cash. Would it surprise you to learn that he denies that vigorously?"

Irv jumped up. "Objection, Your Honor. There is nothing in evidence or testimony to support that statement. Further, may we approach?"

"I'll sustain you, Mr. Jackson."

"Thank you, but there's another issue as well."

"Approach," Flure said, irritated. The lawyers stood together in front of him; Judge Flure turned off his microphone. "Keep your voices down," he growled.

"Your Honor, Ms. Norton may have violated attorney-client privilege in this matter, which constitutes either a voluntary waiver by Mr. Essex or an involuntary waiver by her disclosure."

"Ms. Norton?"

"Mr. Essex permitted me to disclose that he denies being averse to germs."

Jackson pounced. "In that case, the common law exception says the prosecution is now able to hear all communications between Ms. Norton and Mr. Essex on this particular matter."

"Your Honor, I've already said out loud everything Mr. Essex communicated to me about germs: He denies being germophobic."

"Your Honor, that is only one element of the issue at hand. Other elements include the larger question of whether he bought replacement beers with cash, and where, and when, and how many. Another is why he may have left Jefferson to do so. Another is—"

"Enough already, Mr. Jackson. Ms. Norton?"

"Mr. Jackson uses two similar phrases: 'this particular matter' and 'the issue at hand.' I would argue that either phrase refers solely to Mr. Essex's denial of an aversion to microbes, not to those other issues, which have nothing to do with germs."

"Your Honor, really. The defendant's feelings about germs are central to whether there is an arguable case that he never replaced any stolen beers, and that no beer was stolen in the first place. In other words, that he lied to the sheriff. Ms. Norton prefers to allege that it has no larger meaning. My argument is that we deserve to hear more on the subject of buying replacement beer—under oath—and that on this subject, the privilege has been waived."

"Very well," Flure said, leaning his chin in his hand. "Back to your tables. I'll rule in a moment."

Andi had been watching the jury, who strained to hear the *sotto voce* conversation at the bench. She also glanced a couple times at Ordrew, who looked distressed. He seemed far more interested in her performance than she could find a reason for. Maybe the campaign? For a moment, she felt a flurry of anxiety.

Flure cleared his throat. "On the matter of Ms. Norton's question, the objection that it is not based on previous evidence or testimony is sustained. On the second matter, I'll consider the arguments and rule later. Ms. Norton, take another line of questioning."

"I will, Your Honor." She approached Andi. "Let's assume, for the moment, that your notion that there was no earlier burglary were true. What on earth has that to do with the shooting on the night of August twenty-fifth?"

"In his statement, Mr. Essex said the trauma of the first burglary justified his shooting Bernardo Cirilo to protect himself. But when the evidence strongly suggested there was no burglary in the first place, and therefore no previous trauma, we concluded your client had a different motive for the shooting. Instead of protecting his property, standing his ground against an unexpected threat he couldn't avoid, he was using beer as bait to draw a kid into his garage so he could shoot him."

Norton turned toward the jury. "An extraordinary string of fantastical ideas, which I'm sure the jury sees through." She faced Andi. "Isn't it true that you got this amazing idea from my client's ex-girlfriend?"

Andi now saw where this was headed: Discrediting Brenda's testimony. "Absolutely not, ma'am. Ms. Canter never mentioned that idea, and we never discussed it with her."

Norton, obviously displeased, moved back toward her table. As she went, she said, looking at the jury, "So, just to be clear, Deputy, are you claiming you drew your absurd conclusion from something other than third-hand reports of a disgruntled ex-girlfriend?" She reached the defense table, but kept her back to Andi, waiting. Essex had narrowed his eyes and was glaring at her.

Andi didn't let her smile show. Why had Norton opened this door, giving her another chance to list Essex's lies? She walked through that door. "Yes, ma'am. Ms. Cantor's statements fit the other evidence we'd found of Mr. Essex's lies. He told her—"

Norton, perhaps recognizing the danger, interrupted her. "Thank you, Deputy, that's enough."

Irv jumped up. "Your Honor, Ms. Norton asked the question. Please instruct the witness to finish her answer."

"Sustained. Go ahead, Deputy."

Norton glared at the judge, but then faced Andi, who said, "Mr. Essex repeatedly behaved and spoke in ways that confirm his belief that cash carries germs. Once she paid cash for a meal and he insisted she wash her hands before getting in his car. He told a clerk at Art's that cash is 'infested' and that he never touches it. He acknowledged that belief to Deputy Contrerez. He lied about his car being left out. He lied about the garage door being up. He lied about the gun he used in the shooting. He planted a baby monitor in the garage refrigerator. He collects and drinks expensive Scotch and subscribes to *Whiskey Magazine* and he doesn't drink beer. He lied about the burglary of ten beers, for which there is no evidence at all." *Hammer it home.* "And he lied about shooting young Bernardo Cirilo in the back."

Out of the corner of her eye, Andi saw Mrs. Cirilo flinch in pain. In the gallery, Ordrew, who'd been leaning forward tensely, fell back in his chair.

Andi braced herself for whatever Norton hit her with next.

But, utterly surprising her, Norton said, "No further questions, Your Honor."

"Reserve re-cross, Ms. Norton?"

"I'll reserve the right, Your Honor, although I think we've heard enough from this witness." Norton injected contempt into the word, *witness*: Andi knew she'd won the round.

5

Walking toward the gate in the bar, Andi looked at Ordrew. *Why are you here?* Their eyes locked again. In his, Andi saw something with no name she could muster, something new she'd never seen. He gave a small nod, and stood. As she passed through the gate into the gallery and walked toward the back, he moved to the aisle and they stopped within a foot of one another. He whispered, "Impressive job."

That so surprised and confused her, she couldn't reply before he left the courtroom. She sat down on the prosecution side of the gallery, in a swirl of emotion. Glad she was done with her testimony. Pleased with how it had turned out. Bewildered by Ordrew's behavior and words. Apprehensive about what they might mean for the campaign.

She'd just gotten seated when Brenda came through the courtroom doors, looking pale, her left hand gripping and re-gripping her purse strap. Her eyes looked haunted when she spotted the back of Essex's head at the defense table. Andi forgot all her other feelings in a rush of sympathy. *This is going to be brutal.*

Inside the bar, Essex and Norton were whispering intensely, their heads close together. He was shaking his head, no, no, no. After a moment, Norton stood. "Your Honor, may I request a brief recess so my client can use the restroom?"

Judge Flure sighed. "Very well. Bailiff, please accompany Mr. Essex to the men's room. We'll recess for ten minutes."

After ten minutes, Essex and the bailiff hadn't returned. The judge said to the clerk, "Go knock on the men's room door and find out what's taking so long." When the clerk left, the judge instructed the jury to return to the jury room and wait for his summons.

After a time, the clerk returned, and Judge Flure asked. "What's going on?"

"Glen says Mr. Essex is sick. Vomiting. He says Mr. Essex thinks it's food poisoning."

Flure frowned. "Okay. Go to my chambers and call 9-1-1, then tell Glen to go with Essex to the emergency room and stay with him until he can return." To the court reporter, he said, "Would you please call the jury back in?"

When they were settled, Flure told the court, "It appears that Mr. Essex has become ill. I'm going to take a longer recess of one hour, then we'll gather back here and hear the next witness's testimony, or adjourn for the weekend." To the jury, he said, "While you wait in the jury room, please do not discuss the testimony you've heard so far today. My clerk will help you get coffee or water or soft drinks. We'll reconvene at three p.m."

•   •   •

An hour later, everyone gathered. Andi had spent the time with Brenda, trying to help her stay calm, without much success. Judge Flure said, "I'm sorry for the inconvenience. Mr. Essex has been admitted to the hospital with food poisoning. The doctors expect him to be fine tomorrow, two days maximum, so we'll adjourn until Monday morning at nine o'clock." To the jury, he repeated his admonition. "Over the weekend, please don't discuss this case with each other or with anyone else. I doubt that there will be any media coverage, but if you run into any, please ignore it. Thank you for your service today, and we'll see you on Monday morning."

<h1 align="center">6</h1>

When Brad Ordrew left the courtroom, his mind seethed with contradictions. He climbed into his car and started driving, conflicted. He turned north onto the highway. This clash was as familiar to him as his name. He'd wrestled with it all his life, ever since his father had beaten into him a profound, almost terrifying, respect for the hard edges of rules, of procedures and protocols.

But his father's cruelties forged another, deeper effect—an arrogance born of surviving, an interior hardness his father could not reach or break. And when he had joined the police, his arrogance seduced him into the conviction that he could run a police unit up to the necessary standards of rigor and righteousness, which none of the leadership seemed able to do or even to care about. And so, Brad Ordrew's abiding tension took root: His passion for correct procedures, unaltered protocols, and unblinking respect for authority—at war with his ambition to overthrow those authorities, to be the man who led and who could instill his own passion for the rules in his men. Now, driving north, this conflict made him sick to his stomach.

At Highway 36, he turned east and followed it up into the mountains. Soon after he'd come to the valley, he'd found a side road that petered out in a deep grove of cedar and fir, where he'd often retreated to sort out his many sorrows. He drove to it, left his car at the end of the dirt road, and walked deeper into the woods. He'd accepted the fact, long ago, that his rigidity and adherence to high standards of policing made him hated. It was why LAPD had fired him, though they'd written it up as insubordination. Sure, no cop was perfect. But you could try for the best, aim for it, work for it until it drew close. If the slackers didn't like it, screw them.

In this cedar grove on the mountainside, the air was pure, clean, clear. This air always put him in mind of the rigor of the law. Sure, politicians could write bad or imprecise laws. But the laws that survived judicial review—they were clean and hard, their edges sharp, honest.

His turmoil, now, muddied this rigor.

To his chagrin, Pelton's testimony had rested on good police work, careful analysis, the strict assembling of facts, and logical inference from them. Her procedures had been tight. She'd followed protocol. Despite his ridicule and early contempt, she'd pursued her "discrepancies" thoroughly, tenaciously, and she'd followed them to the conclusion they demanded. All along, she'd been, he'd realized in the courtroom, right. He had to admit, he'd been pleased when she'd asked him to help her think through how to use Essex's credit cards against him. And what he'd learned from Xavier—that Andi had been shot during an entry that she'd led *by the book*—had forced him to rethink his opposition to her.

His faith that women shouldn't be police officers had been weakening for months. And then this damn campaign happened. His stomach turned. He steadied himself by placing his hand against the bole of an old cedar. The facts felt unendurable: Pelton's campaign had been upright—while his own had fallen into corruption. *Corrupt*: The word he'd always applied to others—to his father—whom he could then despise. To name himself corrupt rocked him. He focused his mind on the press of the rough bark against his palm, on the roil in his belly, the cold sheen of sweat on the back of his neck. He'd believed he wouldn't let it happen after he'd accepted Crane's support, but honesty required acknowledgment: He'd fallen.

Momentarily faint, he leaned against the tree, his stomach surging.

After the urge to vomit passed, he wandered for a time in the trackless wood. Every star guiding him during his career in law enforcement led him to a single, inarguable conclusion, one that mocked his unbearable desire to be the sheriff. Could he even consider it? But when, after an hour, he glimpsed through the trees the black flash of sunlight off his car's windshield, he knew what the tectonic pressure of his faith in the rules demanded of him.

MONDAY, OCTOBER 29

1

A few minutes before nine, Irv Jackson held open the gate to the bar and gestured Brenda Cantor politely in. She and Andi had had an early breakfast at Alice's Village Inn, and Andi thought Brenda was ready. The weekend had allowed her to settle herself, and she seemed more confident than she'd looked Friday. Still, when she went through the gate, Andi could tell she avoided glancing at Essex, who looked recovered.

After Brenda was sworn in, Irv Jackson began with a series of gentle questions, trying to put her at ease. When she seemed ready, he led her through the story of her relationship with Essex, and as she told it, he inserted the crucial questions: Did he wear his weapon around the house? What did he say about the stand-your-ground laws? What did he say about home intrusions and intruders? What was his relationship with guns? How often did he bring up these topics? What were his habits regarding the car and the garage? Did he drink beer? Did his friends drink beer? What, you say he didn't have friends in during the whole time of your affair? Okay if he didn't drink beer, what *did* he drink? Did he use cash? Why not? How can you be sure? Finally, he asked how the relationship had ended.

As he did so, Andi cursed herself: In her summary of her interviews with Brenda that she'd written for Irv Jackson, she'd forgotten to include the fact that Essex had waved his gun at Brenda when she tried to leave. Worse, she'd failed to get that into her testimony. She hoped Brenda would say it on her own.

But after she'd given the facts of Essex's anti-Semitic outburst the night she left, Irv, not knowing about the gun-waving, asked, "And did he do anything to harm you?"

Brenda concentrated, looked deep in thought. At last, she said, "No, sir."

Irv thanked her. "I have no further questions at this time, Your Honor."

Andi bowed her head, annoyed with herself. It would have been a valuable detail, showing Essex's temperament and his recklessness with guns. And his disregard of Brenda. *How'd I leave that out?* After a moment, though, she sighed and put it out of her mind.

She watched Angela Norton again shuffling through papers on her table. *Letting Brenda's anxiety grow*, she thought. After waiting a minute or so, the judge said, "Ms. Norton? Your witness."

Norton looked up. "Thank you, Your Honor." She stood slowly and walked to the witness stand and leaned in, getting as close to Brenda as she could. "Ms. Cantor, may I call you Brenda?"

Andi felt alarm. *Say no.*

But Brenda said, "I suppose so."

"Fine, then, Brenda. Please remind us, how long did your affair with Mr. Essex last?"

Brenda closed her eyes momentarily. *Ashamed*, Andi thought.

Brenda opened her eyes, told Norton, "Uh, three months and about a week, I think."

"You *think*?" She glanced toward the jury. "I believe you testified that Mr. Essex expected you to spend every night with him, so you were with him most of the time except when you went to work, am I correct?"

"Well, mostly, I guess." She looked anxiously over the crowd, found Andi. Her eyes looked afraid. Andi tried as kind a smile as she could. Brenda said, "He wanted me to do the shopping for us, so I'd be alone then. Well, there were other people were in the grocery."

There was tittering in the audience. The judge banged his gavel. "Enough of that," he said.

Norton waited a moment. "But for three months and a week, you ate Mr. Essex's food every day, you drank his liquor every evening, you—"

Brenda interrupted. "No, ma'am, I have a job. I didn't drink every night. Maybe one evening during the week, and Saturdays, most weeks."

"Fine, but you did drink *his* liquor, slept in *his* bed every night, you gave *him* sex—and then, after three months and a week, you ended the relationship. All of a sudden, he became *unsatisfactory*, Brenda?"

"There were good things at first. I said that."

"So, when these good things weren't forthcoming, you walked out."

"No, that's not right."

Norton looked at the jury. She looked back at Brenda, and Andi caught a look of contempt on her face. "'*No, that's not right*'? Perhaps, then, you'd be so kind as to share with the jury what happened that caused you to dump Mr. Essex, despite his generosity."

Here's the chance. Andi hoped Brenda would include the gun-waving.

For a moment, Brenda's eyes stayed wide. Was she still frightened? Andi watched her, hoping to convey support in her gaze. Then Brenda closed her eyes and Andi could see her take in long breaths, once, twice three times. She opened her eyes. "Yes, ma'am. I'd be glad to. It was the last night we were together. We'd been drinking, me a vodka sour—" She turned slightly, faced the jury. "*Daniel's* vodka." She looked back at Norton. "He was drinking his Scotch, Macallan's eighteen-years-old, I recall him bragging."

"Bragging?"

"He was proud of his Scotch. He said 'educated drinkers' drink single malt Scotch. Not 'crappy beer'. . ." She made finger quotes. "'like high school kids like to steal from garages.'"

Andi wanted to applaud. A great line, linking the garage and the Scotch.

As Brenda went on, Andi watched something changing in her face, something firming up. Her eyes had lost the wide nervous look. "Anyway, he announced we were going to Boston together the third week of September, and I said I couldn't. He asked me why not. I told him the date he'd mentioned was Yom Kippur, and I wanted to spend it with my parents at their temple. He got all red in the face. 'You're eff-ing Jewish?' he said. I said I was."

Irv rose, said, "Objection, Your Honor. Please instruct the witness to give complete quotes."

Andi stifled her grin. Brenda looked embarrassed. The judge repeated Irv's request. "Yes, sir," she said. "Daniel said, 'You're fucking Jewish? You're fucking with me.' I said, 'No, it's true.'"

Andi glanced toward Essex, who was staring straight ahead, unmoving.

"He started yelling terrible things about the Jews, how they killed Christ, how they control the world through banks and Hollywood, things like that. I hadn't challenged him on all the other things that bothered me, the gun and the stand-your-ground talk and his hate for black people, but I told him the anti-Semitic stuff was wrong and I wouldn't tolerate it. He said he oughta kick me out on my, uh, 'fat Jewish ass—'" She blushed. "I was mad, so I said, 'We're done here,' and got up to leave. That's when he went crazy with his gun."

Andi expelled her breath. *Ah.*

Norton retreated swiftly toward the defense table, and Andi saw her face had gone pale. She didn't dare ask what that meant, *he went crazy with his gun,* but how could she leave that hanging for the jury to chew on? After a moment, she said, "A provocative story, Brenda. You'd like us to believe that you broke it off with Mr. Essex because he was anti-Semitic."

Brenda looked expectant, but kept her mouth closed. Irv and Andi had both coached her not to answer anything that hadn't been asked.

Norton went back to her table, picked up another sheet of paper, read it. Andi thought, *trying to get out of this fix.* After a moment, the lawyer said, "You didn't like his gun-talk, his attitude toward African Americans, his preoccupation with neatness, his wanting you to be near him—but it was all acceptable until he sounded anti-Semitic."

Irv stood. "Objection, Your Honor. Is there a question?"

The judge said, "Let's move along, counselor."

Norton looked thoughtful. "Yes, Your Honor. I'm sure the jury will know what sounds truthful and what smacks of victim-thinking."

"Objection." Irv, still on his feet, sounded weary of repeating it.

"Sustained," the judge said. "Please, counselor. Questions."

Brenda looked up at the judge. "May I say something, sir?"

Norton swiftly interrupted: "I have no further questions."

The judge said, "I have a question, Ms. Cantor. You said—" He looked down at his notes. "—Mr. Essex 'went crazy with his gun.' Please tell us what you observed."

Norton hadn't even gotten seated, and objected swiftly. "Your Honor, the witness is not qualified to judge someone's mental health, to evaluate him as 'crazy,' and research shows that eyewitness testimony in high-anxiety situations is notoriously unreliable. This could potentially prejudice the jury against my client."

The judge narrowed his eyes and stared at her for a moment. Then, he said, "Ordinarily, I'd trust the jury on something like this, but your two points, taken together, could set up an appeal no matter how this trial turns out. Objection sustained."

Andi smiled to herself. The damage was done. Brenda's "he went crazy with the gun" not only hung in the air like a foul fog, but the judge had spotlighted it. The lady in the back row of the jury box was smiling.

2

Back at the department, Andi finished her shift and walked across the hall to Ed's office. Time to get back to campaigning. Tonight, she'd try a new speech out at the Knights of Columbus meeting at St. Bernie's. She felt something unfamiliar: Confidence.

Inside, Ed and Grace were stuffing envelopes, their home-grown direct mail campaign.

"I appreciate you guys doing so much."

Grace looked up. "We're going to win, Andi. I can feel it."

She smiled and patted Grace on the back, then turned to Ed. "We hear from the pollsters yet?"

He glanced at his clock. "They promised the first report at five. Should be any minute now."

Andi saw Grace give Ed a quick, full-of-something glance, then caught his return nod. She tilted her head. "What's going on, you two?"

Grace bubbled. "Andi, your exit pollsters? It's Jen, Dana, and me."

Andi needed a moment to catch her breath. "How can . . . uh . . . no . . . I mean . . ." She quit sputtering and laughed.

"One day Northrup and I were tongue-wagging about it and I Googled 'how to do exit polling,' and there it was, on the very first page, 'How to conduct a local election exit poll.' Fourteen easy steps. After Northrup and I studied it a while, I knew we could do it." Her eyes were shiny. "So, Northrup's writing the poll questions and Jen and Dana are making up the data sheets and Northrup's teaching us how to run the statistics." She was beaming.

Andi caught her enthusiasm, and felt her own. "I'm completely blown away, Grace. Thank you so much, and thank your girls too."

Ed's eyes were smiling and he almost spoke, but his phone rang. He answered, jotting notes as he listened. When he hung up, he held up the page. "Poll numbers."

Andi jumped up. "*Go.*"

Ed smiled. "They randomly selected thirty-three percent of the phone numbers in the county and spoke with someone at sixty-three percent of those, which is a fantastic sample, a bit over twenty-one percent—"

"Hey, just give me the numbers." Andi felt a thrill of anticipation.

"You're down forty-eight-point-six to forty-six-point-four, with five percent undecided. The margin of error with that size sample is three point four percent, so it's very good news."

She crashed. "Hell, not if I'm losing."

"No, the margin of error means you could be leading by two."

She knew he was trying to bolster her confidence, but the steam of her excitement evaporated. "Or down by five."

Ed said, "Whoa, don't go there. It's a good result, considering we only started the ads and the calls Tuesday. I doubt we'll see a real polling effect till next week, when the ads start taking hold."

"Damn. I was hoping I had pulled ahead. Why am I losing?" She clamped her hand over her mouth. From behind fingers, she mumbled, "All right, I'll quit whining."

"That's the spirit," Ed said. "Turn lemons into lemonade."

Grace jumped in, "No, turn chicken shit into chicken salad."

WEDNESDAY, OCTOBER 31

1

In Irv Jackson's closing argument, he walked the jury through a simple but thorough recounting of the evidence and logic that, he told them, forced the conclusion that Daniel Essex not only lied repeatedly about shooting Bernardo Cirilo, but that he planned it beforehand and did it out of long-held rage against teenagers based on his own suffering at one older boy's hands. "But tragedy in one's childhood, while it may stir our hearts with compassion, is no justification for the murder of another. Ladies and gentlemen, I'm asking you and trusting that you will deliver a verdict of guilty of mitigated deliberate homicide. Thank you."

2

Where Irv had been calm, Angela Norton came out swinging. She walked to the jury box, placed both hands on it, and leaned in closer to the members. "The prosecution's argument is preposterous. 'Beer as bait.' They expect you to accept a string of absurdities, none of which can be proved beyond a reasonable doubt.

"They say Daniel lied about the garage door being down and the car being out in the driveway, and for proof they cite some neighbors' opinions that this was unusual." Norton made a disgusted look. "How many of you could testify, under oath, about whether your neighbor's garage door is up or where he parks his car on any given evening? They expect you to believe that the intruder in his garage never threatened Daniel. The intruder may have been shot in the back, but there is no conclusive proof that my client lied about what happened before the shooting. Is it impossible that the young man started to charge, saw the gun, and turned back in hopes of escaping just before my client fired? Of course it isn't.

"They'd like you to believe Daniel's angry ex-girlfriend's claim that he doesn't drink beer. Of course, no one can prove that, because again, it's 'she said, he said.'

"And on the basis of that same disgruntled ex-girlfriend's testimony, who disapproves of Mr. Essex's political views, you should believe that the presence of beer in the garage refrigerator amounts to proof that he lured a teenage boy into his garage.

"They want you to accept the silly notion that my client cannot touch money for fear that it is infested with germs, despite his denying it."

Irv stood. "Objection. That denial is not in evidence." Norton had decided not to call her client to the stand.

"Sustained."

Norton took a breath. "Sure, Deputy Contrerez asserts that Mr. Essex confirmed that aversion on the night he was arrested, but isn't it reasonable to think my client was beside himself with anxiety? He was being charged with murder, for God's sake."

Judge Flure cleared his throat. "Perhaps a bit less drama, Counselor?"

She cast her eyes to the ceiling, broadcasting exasperation with the judge's inability to perceive the enormity of the injustice being perpetrated by the prosecutor. She came back to the jury. "Most disturbing, you are asked to believe the absurd idea that my client was raped when he was eleven—which the local police could not verify. But more importantly, you should believe that this alleged rape is his motive for shooting an intruder in his garage thirty years later. Mr. Essex is forty-one years old. Why would he wait thirty years to take his revenge? Whatever may have happened to him thirty years ago is wholly irrelevant to the present day. Don't be fooled by this blatant blaming the victim. The notion that anyone abused in earlier years is inevitably violent and vengeful thirty years later has been disproved countless times. As you heard from Dr. Penguard, the psychologist, the vast majority of abused children do not grow up to be abusers."

Irv jumped up, but then shook his head and sat down. Norton stepped back and gave a slight bow to the jury. "Ladies and gentlemen, I am profoundly grateful for your service, and I respectfully ask you to return a verdict of not-guilty by reason of Montana's stand-your-ground law, because the prosecution has not proven its case beyond a reasonable doubt."

She returned to her table and before sitting down, she touched Daniel Essex softly on the shoulder, as if she were his mother or a kindly aunt.

•   •   •

After a brief recess, Judge Flure gave his instructions to the jury and asked the bailiff to show them to the Jury Room. They filed out somberly, and the woman in the back row of the jury box turned before leaving the courtroom and looked a moment at Daniel Essex. She'd been the one who smiled after Andi's testimony. Essex glared at her, then angrily turned away.

FRIDAY, NOVEMBER 2

1

Andi woke into a dark world. For a few minutes, she lay still, hoping she'd fall back asleep, knowing she wouldn't. She got up soundlessly so she wouldn't wake Ed.

After dressing, surprised at how early it was, a bit after four, she took a cup of coffee to the porch; the caffeine sharpened her expectancy. Tonight was the debate with Ordrew out at the Anderhold, and as of last evening, Ordrew hadn't notified anyone, not her, nor Mack or Luisa, that he'd be there. *No use sitting around here feeling nervous*, she decided.

Inside, she poured another cup of coffee, then looked in on Ed, who still slept. She gathered her gear and drove into town, mentally tweaking her speech yet another time. And trying not to worry about how Reverend Loyd Crane could ruin tonight's work with yet another ugly ad.

•   •   •

Andi had been assigned morning patrol, so after report, she drove north. Powdery snow dusted the roads and swirled up in clouds behind her car. Little traffic disturbed the morning, and the quiet in her squad had not helped her nerves about tonight's debate with Ordrew, so she used the time to rehearse her speech. Again. And again.

While she was parking the squad behind the station at noon, Callie called on the radio. "Irv Jackson just called. He said they've reached a verdict. I told him you'll call him right back."

"Will do. I've got his number."

When she reached him, Irv said, "Good news. Guilty as charged."

Her eyes closed and her head went back. A fullness entered her chest. "Fantastic. Thanks so much, Irv. You did a great job. What's your guess about the sentence?"

"I'm going to ask for twenty-five years. Norton'll argue for ten, the minimum, and I assume Dickie'll go for fifteen to twenty, split the difference. We'll see."

"Think Norton will appeal?"

"I can't see it. The beer-as-bait conclusion was just too strong. Norton tried hard with the stand-your-ground defense but her client had too many strikes against him. The fact that Bernardo was shot from behind was probably what sank her ship."

Andi laughed. Irv said, "And Dickie didn't make any serious mistakes to support an appeal. No, I think our boy's going away for a long time."

"Good work, Irv."

"Hell, you did the work. I just asked the questions."

Andi rubbed her eyes. Time to call the Cirilos.

2

"We know," Mrs. Cirilo said on the phone. "*Señor* Jackson called us to come and hear it. Thank you for your help."

"You're welcome, Mrs. Cirilo. At least Essex will be in prison a long time."

"Which will not bring *mi hijo* back, will it?"

3

That evening, parked pickup trucks and cars lined the long driveway up to the Anderhold, Anderssen's massive log home, and more vehicles filled the wide gravel yard below the great porch. In the spacious yard, Magnus had put up two signs, "Reserved for Deputy Pelton," and beside it the other, "Reserved for Deputy Ordrew." Ed pulled into Andi's spot. Ordrew's was empty. "Think he'll show up?" she asked as she and Ed mounted the steps to the deep porch.

"He loses if he doesn't."

327

She held the big wooden door open for a couple who'd come up behind them. The man greeted her. "You're Deputy Pelton."

"I am. You're Dale Enright." She extended her hand.

He shook it. "Good memory, Andi. I'm supporting Brad Ordrew."

"Give me a chance to change your mind?"

His wife said, "You bet he will. I'm on your side, and I told Dale, no fooling around until he swings our way."

Everyone chuckled.

Luisa Anderssen stood in the foyer, graciously directing people toward the enormous great hall. Immense dark beams supported the huge room's twenty-foot ceiling, and a fireplace large enough for a tall man to walk into filled much of one long wall. Before the fireplace stood two stools and a podium, and facing them in an arc, chairs for more than a hundred. An American flag hung gracefully from its staff to the left of the hearth. Large arched windows allowed the yellowing evening light to flood the room. The usual furniture had been moved out, replaced with curved rows of folding chairs.

Grace, who'd arrived ahead of them, was waiting at the archway leading into the great hall. She whispered, "This room's like a church."

Magnus saw them and waved them over. Grace said, "I'll wait here for my girls."

The men gathered around Magnus widened their circle to include Andi and Ed, shaking hands, introducing themselves. Mack said, "Congratulations on your verdict this morning. Justice done."

One of the men shook his head; Andi went on alert. The man, dressed like a rancher but one Andi didn't recognize, said, "Not so fast, Mack. That boy was protecting his home and himself."

Magnus shrugged. "So he said, but it seems he didn't impress the jury, did he?"

Andi offered her hand to the man. "I'm sorry I don't know you, sir. I'm Andi Pelton."

He took her hand and squeezed it too hard. "Carl Jensen. Run a spread a couple hours from here, northeast corner of the valley."

"I appreciate your coming out, then. That's a drive."

He nodded. "Hope it'll be worth my while." Andi kept her smile, noticed Ed watching Jensen.

Danny Fillmore, another rancher in the north end of the valley whom she did know, extended his hand. "I been hearin' those radio ads of yours."

Buoyed at that, she shook his hand. "Have you, Danny? What do you think?"

"You're bringin' me round, I gotta tell you. What's your thinkin' on terrorists here in the valley, though. Ordrew's got himself a point there, don't he?"

She smiled. "It's never smart to say 'never' about terrorism, but we already *have* a strong plan to protect the valley from all kinds of disasters, including a terrorist act. My opponent's still thinking like a big city cop." Most of the men in the circle chuckled, but Carl Jensen looked like she'd just rustled one of his cows.

Ordrew hadn't arrived. Andi excused herself and moved around, working the room while they waited. After a few handshakes and chats, she started to relax. This crowd seemed sympathetic. The smiles and encouraging words heartened her.

Then, just as Magnus told her he was about to start the show, Ordrew strode in. Andi shot a glance at Ed, who looked at the entry and saw him. "He looks nervous," Ed said, just loud enough for her to hear above the noise of fifty conversations. She agreed with him.

Then, without notice, her own nerves were acting up. As Magnus approached the front of the room, she said to Ed, "Give me a kiss."

He leaned in and kissed her, then she turned and went up front, ignoring the few dark looks. *This is going to be big,* she thought.

4

Andi took the stool closer to the flag. For a moment, she watched Bud Groh fiddling with a sound mixer in a corner. The plan was to broadcast the debate live over the radio. She liked the idea: It would get her message out to folks not here. She felt ready.

Ordrew approached the front and moved toward the other stool. Andi stood and reached out to him. "Good luck, Brad."

His face registered surprise, and he hesitated, then shook her hand. "Andi, I . . ." He stopped. "Never mind." He moved to the other stool, so Andi sat. She saw what looked like curiosity on many faces.

Bud Groh sat at the console and gave a nod to Magnus, who stepped to the microphone and led the crowd in the Pledge of Allegiance. Then he offered a brief and friendly introduction to the evening and to the candidates. "It's not a debate," he said. "Each of our candidates will have fifteen minutes for their remarks, and then we'll have questions." He turned and faced Andi and Ordrew. "Will you both join me for a moment?"

When they stood, Magnus showed them the silver dollar he'd taken from his pocket, and said, "Deputy Ordrew, heads or tails?"

Ordrew's smile looked frozen. He said, "Heads."

He won, and chose to speak second. He returned to his stool.

Andi's speech took a mere ten minutes. After the warm-up, she fired her opening rounds. "My opponent is telling you that our department is poorly run, that we're behind the times, that we're not prepared for a terrorist attack or a race riot, that we want to take away your guns. I'm here to tell you that's a pile of bull . . . manure." Heads lifted. She ticked off her rebuttals to each of the negatives, then pivoted. "How many government agencies or even businesses do you folks know that deliver their services on time, every time? For instance, have any of you ever called 9-1-1 on a police matter?" Hands raised across the room. "Did the deputies respond in a timely manner?" She waited while a few heads nodded. "Come on, tell me if we haven't. Were we on time or were we late?"

Al Harken, a rancher Andi recognized, stood. "Well, ma'am, once one of my cows broke through the fence and was eating my neighbor's flowers, so she calls 9-1-1. Took the deputy thirteen minutes to get there. Thirteen minutes for a cow means a lot of pansies."

After the laugh, Andi smiled. "Al, you live out on Highway Thirty-six, right? About thirty miles from town?"

"I do."

"So, is thirteen minutes fast or slow?" Laughter rippled across the room, and Al grinned. "Near as fast as my boy drove it when he was sixteen." Another round of laughter rolled through the crowd.

Andi pushed on. "My opponent complains that our equipment is out of date. I'll admit, our riot shields and tear gas guns aren't the latest models, but when my weapon, a Glock 19, got to be twenty years old, Sheriff Stewart insisted the department buy me a new one. State of the art. I don't know about *all* the deputies, but I'm aware that he's done so with at least five of my colleagues. Our vehicles are up to date. Our communications are up to date. And Sheriff Stewart has balanced his budget every year since he was first elected in 1984. Poorly run? The Adams County Sheriff's Department is as poorly run as Magnus Anderssen's Double-A ranch."

Magnus laughed, and many in the audience followed suit. Andi smiled at a few who didn't.

"And I intend to run it just as well." There were a few nods, and a couple of people clapped. "Thanks," she said. "My opponent is worried about a terrorist attack. I'm worried about that too. But I'd like to hear him answer a question." She turned and nodded at Ordrew, sitting to her right. She faced the audience again. "How do you prepare for an event that you can't predict? Here's my answer: *training* and *intelligence*, not just weaponry. You folks know this: If you have all the tools you need to repair your barn roof, but you don't get a weather forecast in time, and a freak blizzard collapses the roof before you fix it, the tools aren't much help. What you needed was a good weather forecast. Good *intelligence*. Thanks to Homeland Security, Adams County has all the weaponry we need to deal with an event that requires it, and what we don't have we can helicopter over in an hour from Missoula County. What we don't have enough of and can't ever get is enough advance warning. Good *intelligence*. On that score, we're linked to Montana Emergency Management, and through Montana, to all the federal intelligence agencies—the NSA, the CIA, FBI, Homeland Security, and FEMA. If any of them gets wind of something about to go down here in Adams County, we'll know. And we'll act with all necessary force."

She let that sink in a moment. "And we train. Let me tell you what we do to prepare. Once every quarter, we train with either the Bureau of Criminal Apprehension, FEMA, Homeland Security, or the FBI on preparedness for a major incident. One morning a month, our deputies train for such an event, like a school shooting or a hostage situation. Every two months, the entire department trains with the volunteer fire department and with the Adams County Search and Rescue on coordinated responses to incidents such as a wildfire or major storm damage. My opponent has been part of all this training, and he knows that claiming we are not prepared is nonsense." She paused. "Or just plain false."

She looked around the audience. "Sheriff Stewart is behind the times? What times does my opponent think Ben is behind?" She again swept her eyes over the audience. "How many of you have had an evening on the corner with Ben?" A few hands raised, tentatively, then more, and more, until almost every man in the room had his hand up. She thanked them. "You may lower your hands, class." Everyone laughed. "We all know Ben didn't sit on the corner in the bar with us ladies for an obvious reason, but when you elect me sheriff, I'll be on that corner every evening just like Ben has been for thirty years—only this time, I'll have the ladies with me too." What began as scattered applause continued and spread through the audience. Andi saw wives nudging their husbands, and many folks turning to find Ben, sitting in the back with Bernie beside him, beaming.

"So, all you guys out there: Was Ben Stewart behind *your* times? Or did he understand your needs and the needs of your families and your ranches and businesses? Maybe Sheriff Stewart wasn't as up to the same kind of times—" She decided to use her line. "—as police in the big city." Chuckles rippled across the crowd. "But Ben was plenty up to date here in Monastery Valley."

She got applause on that line, and she finished. "I'm asking for your votes, but not because I desperately want to be sheriff. I'm asking for your votes because I love this valley and its people and I want to protect the way of life you and your families for generations have built with your sweat and hard work. I intend to make our valley safer and better than ever. I'll appreciate your support and your vote on November sixth."

Grace and her girls leaped to their feet, clapping. Andi was surprised that many of the ranchers and their wives rose too, smiling and clapping, more, maybe much more, than half the crowd. She felt a thrill.

5

Brad Ordrew forced his smile as she handed him the microphone, but his heart beat in a tight chest. Since Andi's testimony at trial and his walk in the woods, he'd felt diminished, sure of what he had to do, but unsure whether he could manage it. Doing it would mean the end of the campaign, would mean he would lose and go to work for a woman. It would mean he would have to leave.

He slumped a bit. "Thanks, everyone, for coming out. I know you're expecting fireworks, and my opponent lit the match with her speech. Until a few days ago, I'd have taken that match and put it to the fuse." Then, he straightened his back. "But I have a confession to make."

A murmur went through the crowd. As Ordrew waited out the mutterings, he wondered what Andi was thinking. "You all know about the ads that have been run on my behalf. My confession is not simply that they are untrue and disgusting, but more importantly, that I never spoke out strongly against them . . ." His mouth was dry. He turned and took a swallow of water from the bottle beside his stool. As he did so, he stole a glance at Andi. *She's surprised.* "I didn't speak out because I wanted to win so badly." He let that sink in. "Let me tell you something about myself." He smiled. "If I'm going to be your sheriff, you should know this."

The crowd sat silent, entranced.

"I was raised by an abusive father, himself a cop. Not an excuse for anything, just a fact. He beat a love of rules and regulations into me that I've never lost. Not too many cops are as fanatical about that as I am, and not too many cops end up liking me. One of the results of that is that I've never much liked many cops either, for the opposite reason. I was chiefly prejudiced against women in the police force, and I've been particularly hostile to Deputy Pelton since I came here. I have no honest excuse for that.

"But during this campaign, I've been supported by an evil man who stooped to any low to ensure that I win. Many of you will know or remember him, I'm told. His name is the Reverend Loyd Crane." Recognition rippled through the audience, people nodding, looking at their neighbors. "At first, I was thrilled to have his money and the support of his ads. I thought I could rise above his reprehensible attacks and not be sullied. But I failed.

"I'm not turning my back on the core issues of my campaign. I still believe that we need to be vigilant in protecting all our citizens and all our rights—most importantly, the right to keep and bear arms. We need to stand our ground against threats to any of our liberties." The applause stunned him. He'd expected to lose all his support tonight. "I'm still committed to the idea that police work is not women's work. But the extreme and dishonest ads that supported my candidacy, I want you to know that I hated them. They are evil, and by tolerating them, I participated in that evil. Being an officer of the law is a high calling, and

I debased it. It is my shame to have accepted that kind of support. Please know that if you can see your way to voting for me, I appreciate your support and I will try to serve the valley with the same integrity as Sheriff Stewart and my opponent have demonstrated."

He turned around, handed the microphone back to Magnus, and walked out the big front door of the Anderhold, as more applause broke out and the room erupted in a hundred conversations.

6

Brad Ordrew's phone rang a little before eleven p.m. He knew who it was, despite the "Unknown Caller" display.

He considered not answering. *The hell with him.* He hit *Talk.* "I figured you'd be calling."

Reverend Crane's growl was savage. "One of my people was at your so-called debate. I'm informed you've named me publicly and have apologized for the help I gave you."

"Yes, Crane, I have."

"I have lost patience with you, Ordrew."

Disgust soured his mouth. "Frankly, I don't give a crap about your patience."

Listening to the vast silence at the other end, Ordrew pondered hitting *End,* but Crane spoke before he could. "Deputy, I've invested a lot of money in you, and I expect return on my investment."

"Or what?"

"Or I will destroy you and your career in law enforcement."

"Huh." For a moment, his chest went tight. But immediately, anger loosened it. "Crane, if I win this election, you can take your return on investment and shove it. If I lose, I suspect it is precisely your ads that sank me. What you've done on my so-called behalf and your dishonest attacks on Andi Pelton sicken me." He took a breath. "Send me the fucking bill for your obscene ads and your slimy mailer."

When Crane spoke, his voice was cold as sharp steel. "Whether you win or lose, I will see to it that your career is ended. It will happen on my timeline, and you will never see it coming."

Ordrew almost laughed. "You can go to hell, Crane. I worked eleven years in undercover vice, so your cheap threats don't scare me. There's a lot worse than you where I come from."

And then, finally, he hung up.

MONDAY, NOVEMBER 5

1

Lunch time. Andi and Ordrew were alone in the squad room for the first time since Friday's shocking "debate." He'd avoided her eyes during morning report, and later when they'd come back to their cubicles for paperwork, she'd said good morning but he hadn't answered. Andi stood at her desk a moment, then walked over to his cube. "I think we should talk."

His shoulders sagged, but he swiveled his chair around. "Probably should, I guess."

"What changed?"

"Good question." His forehead wrinkled. "I've been wondering about it. The start, I think, was shame about the ads. I was in love with that first one, and Crane promised more of the same. But it was a lie, all of it. The point is, though, I bought it, because I wanted to win so badly. I shamed myself, and I couldn't stand it that your campaign was clean." He looked down.

Andi waited. She remembered Ed's psychology 101 theory.

"That day you asked me to help you with the Essex case? I know how you felt about me then. So, setting aside your feelings about me for the good of your case impressed me. On top of that, you impressed me with your analysis."

"That's what you said in court. 'Impressive job.'"

He met her gaze, then looked away again. "It was, Andi. Your testimony made me realize a couple of things. You didn't let the stand-your-ground defense intimidate you or stop you from doing good police work. Between feeling like I corrupted myself and watching you testify, I felt so rotten I left court and went into the woods and almost vomited. Later, I did."

Andi felt a sting of sympathy. "That bad?"

He nodded. When he looked up, his eyes looked sad. "That bad. It was like I was puking up a lifetime of being pissed off." He sighed. "No huge miracle, though. I'm still going to win."

"Which remains to be seen." She considered whether to ask it. Decided. "If you do win, are you still planning to fire me?"

Ordrew once again looked away. "I respect you now, but police work isn't for women."

She just looked at him a long moment, then shook her head. As she turned to go back to her cubicle, she said, "You've got a hell of way of showing respect."

TUESDAY, NOVEMBER 6, ELECTION DAY

1

Election day dawned cold, the dim sky steel gray, gusts of wind blowing sheets of powdery snow across the roads. Shortly after the polls opened at seven, Andi and Ed walked into the high school gym to vote. Grace and her girls were already stationed at their exit poll table down the hall, the required distance from the polling place in the gym. As they passed their table, Grace had whispered, formally, "Good luck, Andi."

Andi looked around. "Where's Brad's exit poll team?"

Ed shrugged. "Maybe he knows he lost."

She felt like that might jinx the outcome. "Or won."

Inside the gym, Loretta Tweedy and Ardyss Conley were two of the election judges. "Morning, ladies," Ed tipped his cap. He looked around the high school gym fitted out with three voting machines. "Not too busy yet."

Loretta smiled. "Just opened, and the snow keeps people in for the early hours, but they'll come. I've been a judge for sixty-six years, and we've never had lower than fifty-eight percent turnout in Adams County. In '78, the snow was already a foot deep when polls opened, but we still had sixty percent."

Ardyss Conley chuckled. "Loretta thinks the valley's turnout is her doing. The one thing she's prouder of are her prize-winning daylilies."

Loretta clucked. Andi and Ed laughed, presented their IDs, and went in to vote.

Grace, Jen, and Dana were waiting when Andi and Ed came out. Brad Ordrew was coming in from the parking lot. Without a word, he skirted around them and walked into the gym.

Andi turned and watched him go in to vote, then she and Ed turned back to leave.

In her hand, Dana held a counter, one of those little clicker devices. She peered at it and jotted a mark on her clipboard.

"Excuse me," Grace said to Ed, "would you mind answering a few questions for our exit poll?"

He smiled. "Forgot to tell you this," he said. "You don't interview the candidates or their families."

Grace frowned. "Why not?" But she brightened immediately. "Bias, right?"

"That's it." To Jen, he said, "My girl's one quick study."

Grace beamed.

Andi took his arm. Grace nodded toward the gym doors.

Ordrew emerged. Andi blocked his way. "Brad, however the day turns out, I want us to put this behind us and cooperate. For the good of the department."

Ordrew's lips drew into a tight line, and he looked away from her. Without a word, he nodded and walked away.

2

The department was quiet as a morgue. Apparently, the snow and Election Day were enough excitement for the valley. Not a single call came in all morning. Andi stacked the piled paperwork burying her desk; she re-stacked it alphabetically, then re-stacked it chronologically. She made a stab at prioritizing the folders, but gave up and took the top one. Opened it. Closed it. Opened the second one, stared at the face sheet.

Around noon, she'd made very little dent in the logjam. Ben stopped by the deputies' room and said, "Lunch, anybody?" Andi said, "Sure. I'm getting nowhere with this pile."

• • •

When they returned, Callie said, "Your exit poll called for you, Andi. Sounded a lot like Gracie Northrup to me."

When Andi returned the call, Grace was all business. "Andi, here's our first report. As of one p.m., there have been two hundred ninety-one people who entered and left the polling place. Northrup said we don't know, scientifically, if they voted, but it's a reasonable assumption, and we are using that number as a baseline. At this point, our exit polling suggests that Brad Ordrew is leading with fifty-two point nine percent of the vote to your forty-seven point one. However, the margin of error with such a small sample is far too high to make any predictions."

Andi, thanks to Ed's briefing, knew better than to react to these early numbers, but she couldn't help a gulp of apprehension. "The percentages are tentative, right?"

"At this point, yes. All we know is two hundred ninety-one people have come and gone from the gym, and sixty-five percent of them answered our poll." Andi smiled at Grace's professional tone.

"Well, thanks for the report. How often will you be calling?"

"Two-thirty's the next report, and four o'clock after that. Then it's every hour till the polls close at eight."

The numbers barely budged through the long afternoon. Grace said Loretta Tweedy predicted there'd be a rush of voters after chores were done and businesses closed.

About four-thirty, Andi stood up and stretched. "Longest day of my life," she groaned, to the empty squad room. Ordrew hadn't come in all day, and the evening deputies were busy somewhere. She grabbed her things and went out into the blowing snow.

3

When Andi drove up to the yard, her cell phone buzzed in her pocket. *Grace.* She parked and answered. "Five o'clock report, Andi. First, turnout is increasing. There's a line waiting to vote, just like Loretta said. Okay. As of this hour, we have had either one thousand five hundred and ninety people who have entered and left the voting area or one thousand five hundred and seventy-nine. We think eleven got missed during bathroom breaks."

Through her tension, Andi chuckled. Grace was talking. ". . . based on our algorithm, it appears that the situation is getting closer. Bradley Ordrew now leads with fifty point one percent of the vote, with a margin of error of two point seven percent. The polls will remain open for another, ah, two and three-quarter hours, and it is impossible at this point to project a winner." Grace paused. "I think you should plan on a long night. My girls and I, I mean, our team will be here until all the votes are counted."

Ed arrived an hour later, an hour Andi had spent alternately pacing and prepping dinner. She seldom watched the afternoon news, but today she left the TV tuned there and kept leaving the kitchen area to see if a crawler said anything about the election. *I'm acting nuts.* Adams County was one of the smallest counties and nobody in the big TV markets cared about this election. She glanced at her watch: *6:10.* The polls wouldn't close for another hour and fifty minutes.

"How're we doing?" Ed asked, as he took off his coat.

"I'm wearing a track in the floor. Nervous as a kid on her first date." She gave him the latest numbers.

They ate watching TV. Even with a plate on her lap, Andi got up, sat down, got up again, and walked around. Ed laughed. Outside, the snowfall continued, maybe slower.

Grace called with the seven o'clock report: The race was now tied at 50% each. "We're finding that men are voting fifty-eight percent for Ordrew, women almost sixty percent for you." Andi thanked her. To Ed, she said, "I gotta get out. Let's go for a walk."

They bundled up and walked a mile or so in the darkness, crunching on the new snow. On the return leg, the snow resumed, heavy now. By the time they reached the porch, there was another inch. Andi had been willing her cell phone to buzz, but it was silent.

At eight, they turned the TV back on and sat close on the couch, surfing the channels broadcasting the national and local returns. Grace had called a few minutes earlier, reporting that at closing time, the election still appeared dead even. The margin of error was down to one-point-four percent. Grace told them that men were voting fifty-nine percent to forty-one percent for Ordrew, women the reverse. When she repeated that to Ed, he said, "If more women vote, you win."

"That's a big *if.*"

4

Grace's car drove into the yard at about ten-fifteen. She bounded up the steps and through the front door. Breathless, she announced, "Counting's done."

"Did they tell you who won?"

"Nah. I kept begging, but Loretta said they can't announce the results till the canvass paperwork is done. Should be done about an hour from when I left." She slumped onto the couch beside Ed, who put an arm around the girl's shoulders.

Andi faced her. "Thanks for a long day's work, girl," she said.

Grace jumped up and hugged her. "I'm going nuts, Andi. How do you stand it?"

Andi started to answer, but they all heard the television reporter mention "Adams County." But the news was, "Too close to call in the Adams County Sheriff's race between Deputies Bradley Ordrew and Andrea Pelton. With approximately seventy-five percent of the votes counted, it looks like each candidate has fifty percent of the vote."

Grace barked at the set. "Hey, the vote's a hundred percent counted. I can't stand this. I'm going for a run."

Ed, alarmed, said, "Wait a minute. It's ten thirty and there's five inches of new snow out there."

"I don't care, Northrup. I'm going spasmotic here!"

Northrup started to object, but Andi said, "Go for it, Gracie. But take your phone." They all remembered: Four years ago, Grace had barely survived getting lost in a blizzard. Andi had tracked her, finding her collapsed in a drift.

"And my tunes," Grace said. She disappeared into her room, and a few moments later, emerged geared for a run, earbuds tight in her ears.

Andi sat down again and tried to snuggle closer to Northrup. "It's been a while since we've had a quiet moment like this. I wish I could enjoy it." She jumped back up and went to the kitchen sink to wash dishes. She kept turning away from the sink to check the TV.

Just before eleven, Ed said, "I'm worried about Grace. She usually runs thirty minutes."

"She's only been gone twenty. Relax, Dad." But Andi couldn't take her own advice, pacing in and out of the kitchen to check the TV. After a few minutes, she muttered, "Screw this," and opened the front door and stepped out on the porch.

An announcer said, "With eighty-eight percent of the returns in the Adams County Sheriff's race in and counted—" Andi bolted back in. "—KEMT News can announce that it is calling the race for Brad Ordrew, a deputy of long-time Sheriff Ben Stewart, who is retiring. Ordrew is projected to win fifty point one percent of the vote. His opponent, Deputy Andrea Pelton, looks to receive forty-nine point nine percent, one of the closest races in Montana history."

Andi deflated. "Damn," she said. She felt a blur of disappointment and loss, as if her future had gone dark as an empty theater.

Ed had stood beside her while the announcement came, and now he touched her shoulder. "She said the votes are eighty-eight percent counted—but Grace said the counting's done. That projection's based on an old report. We don't know what the last twelve percent did."

At that moment, the door slammed open and Grace burst in, shouting, "You *won*. I heard it on Jefferson radio. It's, like, fifty point one percent for you—you won, Andi."

Ed said, "Well, we just heard on Missoula TV that Ordrew won with the same percentage."

The three of them just stood there, mute, staring at the TV. Andi said, "Oh, man. Who's right?"

Grace said, "This sucks."

The phone rang. Ed picked up, listened, handed it to Andi.

She frowned and took the phone. Her frown deepened, and a weak, sad smile touched her lips. "Thanks, Loretta."

When Andi looked up, her eyes shone with tears. Grace said, "What? What?"

Andi said, "I need a big hug."

The three gathered in a family embrace.

After a moment, Ed said, "I'm sorry, Andi. Really sorry."

5

"Loretta said Bud Groh copied the results wrong when she called them in. Ordrew got the fifty point one percent."

"My God," Ed said. He turned to Grace. "Do you know how many votes were cast?"

Grace, still wiping her eyes, grabbed her notebook. "Three thousand five hundred sixty-three."

Ed picked up a calculator, tapped the keys. "Ordrew got seventeen hundred and eighty-five votes." He did it again. "And you got seventeen seventy-eight. He won by seven votes."

Seven votes. Her cell phone buzzed again. Her screen read *Irv Jackson.* For a disoriented moment, she wondered what was happening—at eleven in the evening—with the Essex case. She answered. "Irv?"

"Look, I heard the results. I'm sorry. How many votes separated you and Ordrew?"

"Okay if I put you on speaker, Irv, so Ed can listen?"

"Sure." She touched *Speaker.*

"Seven, Irv. Seven votes."

"Okay. My advice is, demand a recount." He paused. "Four votes could easily flip."

"How do I do that?"

"You need to file a petition with the county election administrator within five days. Your lawyer can do that for you."

"Thanks, Irv. I'll consider that."

After the call, Ed said, "Good idea. Let's call Jerry tonight, get him working on it."

Andi said, "Hold on. I need to think about this."

Grace said, "What's to think about? Do it, Andi."

"No, wait a minute. I need some air." She put on her jacket and went outside. The snow had stopped, and the clouds that had carried the snow had started breaking up. A few stars twinkled in the bitter sky. Cold air burned her nostrils. New snow crackled under her shoes. Andi stood still, listening to the night. Nothing moved or called.

She'd lost. That was as clear as the frigid air. She knew she should call Ordrew and concede the election, make it official. "He can wait," she whispered to the cold night.

Behind her, she heard the porch door squeak. Ed's voice found her out in the darkness. "You okay?"

She turned back, saw him silhouetted against the inside lights. "Yes and no. It's over anyway. Now I fight for my job."

"Come back inside, we'll talk about it."

"In a minute, Ed. I want to feel this." *This* was tears warming her skin. She wanted no consolation and no distraction. For once, she wanted to experience it full on.

•　　　•　　　•

Later, when Andi came inside, Grace jumped up from the couch. "You've got to get a recount, Andi. We can't let him win like this." She plopped down again, and Ed moved aside on the couch, leaving a space between himself and Grace.

Andi sat down between them, but spoke to Grace. "Or a recount could be a bargaining chip. I've got to fight for my job now."

"Why?"

"Ordrew told me he'll fire me if he wins."

"What? Can he *do* that?"

"I'll fight him, but in the end, when he's the sheriff, he'll find a way."

"So, demand a recount. You've got everything to lose if you don't."

"But look, if I threaten a recount, then offer a deal, I might *save* my job. If I go ahead with the recount and then lose again, I've got nothing to bargain with."

Ed rubbed his face. "I see where you're going. You offer to let him have the job with no recount if he agrees to keep you on."

Grace shook her head. "But what about the people who voted for you?" Her voice was shaky.

"Far as we know, seven more voted for him."

"But don't you want to know for sure?" Now, her voice had tears in it.

Andi pulled her into an embrace. "I'm fighting for my job, kiddo. And for our life together."

In her arms, Grace again began to weep. Andi, holding her tight, was already planning her call.

WEDNESDAY, NOVEMBER 7

1

After midnight, when Grace and Ed were getting ready for bed, Andi dialed Ordrew's home number. The call went to his voicemail. She'd planned with Ed what to say, and rehearsed a few times, and while Ordrew's message unspooled, she took a breath and readied herself.

"Hi, Brad. This is Andi." That her voice was as steady as her resolve pleased her. "It appears you have seven more votes than I do, which I'm advised is within the legal margin for me to require a recount. Before I do that, I want to talk with you. I know we're both off tomorrow morning, but I'd like to meet you in the office at eight, so we can discuss it. Good night."

2

When she came into the squad room the next morning, Ordrew lost no time hustling her into the small conference room. "What's this about a recount?"

"I'm going to decide today whether to file a petition for a recount. But I wanted to offer you a deal before I do that."

"You won't win a recount."

"We don't know that, do we? And I know your guy Loyd Crane very well, and he's not above tampering with an election."

"After what he did to your Grace, I told him to go to hell."

She looked into his eyes. They did not turn away. "Crane doesn't go to hell," she said. "He brings it with him."

Ordrew snorted. "I'm not afraid of him."

"You should be, Brad. I know Crane. He'll be back, but it won't be him you'll be up against. It'll be somebody he hires, somebody you won't know, somebody willing to do his work."

He grimaced. "So, what's your deal?"

"I'll concede the election. No recount. You win fair and square." She took a moment to fashion the next part. "I'll help you against Crane, and I'll make sure the other guys give you a chance."

His eyes narrowed. "How'll you help me?"

"If he threatens you, I'll go public about his interference in this election. I can testify against him. And if anything comes to an intervention, I'll have your back."

"Will you work for me? Honestly? I haven't made you a friend."

"I'll work as hard and as professionally as I've worked for Ben—unless you screw around with me."

"And if I do?"

"I'll confront you in person, privately. And if you don't change, I'll run against you in four years and beat your tail."

His laugh surprised her. "So, you help me with the guys, you help against Crane, and you are my honest opposition. What's in this deal for *you*?"

"You agree not to fire me just because you don't like female cops."

His face flushed. "Ah, that." He sighed. "But suppose you seriously screw up?"

Andi waited, then said, "You really want to fire me, Brad?"

This time Ordrew lifted his eyes, thinking for a moment. "Up until this conversation, I thought I did. But what I want now is to know you've got my back."

"Not like a scared rookie in a shootout." She saw his look of confusion, but it was replaced by an embarrassed smile.

"I told you about that?"

"Some of it. You told Xavier the rest, and he told me."

He nodded. "Huh. Well, yeah, not like a scared rookie."

"And there's one more thing. In return for my support with the guys, you agree to consult, either with me or with Pete, on any disciplinary action with any department employee."

"That can't happen," he said, shaking his head, his smile gone. "If I'm the sheriff, I'm boss, not you or Pete."

"You're sheriff if I don't file for a recount. If I do, we don't know who's sheriff."

"But I *will* be sheriff, and I need to run the department my way."

"I won't interfere with your running the department, but I want your agreement to consult with Pete or me on disciplinary actions. Or I'll have a recount."

"That's BS, Andi. I won the election. Elections have consequences." He ran his fingers through his hair.

"Seven votes, Brad. Almost half the voters wanted me. You want to keep hearing that number on the radio? You want to go four years worrying about how fast seven votes flip if you make a single big mistake? Or do you want me on your side, helping you fix the blunders you're bound to make, you the big-city cop in our small-town world?"

He looked cornered. "Basically, you're asking to be co-sheriff."

"Very good." She smiled. "You caught my drift."

He turned away. "I've got to think about this."

"Take your time. You've got till three this afternoon."

"Or else what?"

"Or else I file the recount petition."

3

Ordrew's call came just before noon. "Okay, let's talk."

She grinned. "How about lunch at the Angler."

"People will talk."

"Let 'em."

"You're on."

After they'd ordered, he said, "So, let me clarify this. You'll help me with Crane?"

"I will."

"And you won't backstab me with the guys?"

"More than that, I'll be honestly supportive, and if I disagree with you, I will come to you privately. No office politics."

"I can't surrender my authority. My consulting with you or Pete about discipline is off the table."

"No, it's not, Brad. Let me be as clear as I can: I'm not wanting to challenge your authority, but I want to be consulted. I want a voice and I expect you to listen. The final call will always be yours."

"I, uh, can't agree to that." He rubbed his eyes. "No. If I have a discipline problem with a deputy or someone on staff, and I talk to you or Pete, I'm violating that person's privacy. I won't do that."

Out of the blue, Andi remembered something. A conversation with her mother, a few weeks before she'd died. Andi had a new boyfriend, who was pressuring her to do more than neck in the back seat of his car. A lot more. Her mother had said, "Do you want to?"

"No. I like him, but not that way." Mostly true—she was curious about intercourse, but not with Jacob.

"So, what's the problem?"

"I don't want him to dump me."

"There'll be other boys," her mother had said. "Don't give up what's right just because you don't want to lose something. What's right is right."

She firmed her voice. "Take this off the table, Brad, and the whole deal goes with it. I'll do the recount."

She waited. Realized her shoulders were stiff. Relaxed them.

He looked at the ceiling. When he lowered his eyes, he said, "If I agree, will you oppose me in four years?"

Thanks, Mom. "You—or I suppose Crane—called your campaign 'a patriot's campaign.'"

He broke in. "That was Crane's bullshit, not mine. I'm not sure any more what the word 'patriot' even means."

Andi went on, "Well, let's wait and see about four years from now. We take an oath to protect and defend the Constitution and the constitution of Montana, and the words 'To Protect and Serve' are written on all our vehicles. I think a *patriot's* administration should include as much *serving* as protecting. Show me that you're not just protecting the county, but serving the people, helping them out, going to bat for them when you can. Let's do Cops and Kids. Let's make the sheriff's department an asset for the community. Show me that and four years from now will take care of itself." She waited, but Ordrew said nothing. "So, do we have a deal?"

Ordrew looked again at the ceiling. Then closed his eyes.

Andi inhaled, then took a second breath, a third.

He spoke quietly, eyes still closed. "Yeah, okay." He opened his eyes. "This stays between us."

"No, it doesn't. I'm going to my lawyer's now. I'll be back at three with a statement, which we'll both sign. It'll specify my concession and our agreement: No recount, no firing, my support, your agreement to consult with Pete or me about disciplinary actions, and finding new ways to serve the valley. Then we'll both go over to the radio station and announce it there."

She heard him chuckling, another surprise. His chuckle became a gentle laugh. "Crap, Andi, you're tougher than an LA drug dealer."

"Yes, I am, Brad." She smiled. "But as long as you keep this deal, my tough has your back with Crane—and everybody else."

FRIDAY, NOVEMBER 9

1

The Cirilo family sat in the front row of the courtroom. The youngest cuddled with her mother, and the oldest daughter had her arm around the middle girl. Emilio Cirilo sat tall, stone-faced. Andi came around through the bar gate and greeted them. Mr. Cirilo stood, extended his hand. "You worked hard for us, and we are . . ." He turned to his wife. "*¿Agradecido?*"

Mrs. Cirilo said, "Grateful."

"*Sí,* grateful to you."

"I'm sorry we couldn't do more. This is very sad."

Mrs. Cirilo said, "How much sentence will judge give?"

"I don't know. Judge Flure can give him anywhere from two to forty years." As she spoke, the bailiff came into the courtroom from the jury side, and Andi said, "We'll know in a few minutes. I'd better get out of the way."

She found a seat beside Ordrew and Pete. As she sat, Essex and Angela Norton came through the jury-side door and took their places at the defense table. In a moment, the door to Judge Flure's chambers opened and Glen Barnes, the bailiff, said, "Please rise. The Court of the Twenty-third Judicial District of Montana is now in session, the Honorable Richard Flure, presiding." Dickie Flure swept into the courtroom and climbed the bench.

"You may be seated," the judge said, as he thumbed through some documents. Finally, he signed one and looked up. "We're here, Mr. Essex, for sentencing in the matter of the mitigated deliberate homicide of Bernardo Cirilo on August twenty-fifth, 2018. You have been found guilty by a jury of your peers, and I've received the probation department's pre-sentencing report and heard testimony from numerous witnesses as to your character and consulted with a variety of experts. Has your lawyer informed you of the sentences available to me under Montana law?"

Essex nodded, but was silent.

Flure looked hard at him. "I need a yes, Mr. Essex."

Essex shook his head. Norton whispered in his ear, and after a moment, he muttered, "Yes."

"That's better. I've prepared a formal sentencing order, a copy of which you and your counsel will receive at the conclusion of this hearing. In determining your sentence, I have considered many factors, both aggravating and mitigating factors. However, in my mind, three aggravating factors and one mitigating factor stand out as most important. First, of course, there is the enormity of your crime. Homicide is a heinous act, and the evidence presented in your trial shows that you prepared knowingly and purposely to commit that act. The horrific nature of such a crime is one reason the state of Montana allows the death penalty for deliberate homicide."

Essex stiffened and looked sharply at Norton. She put her hand on his arm. He opened his mouth to speak. She shook her head almost imperceptibly.

"A second factor of great importance is your history of assault against women. The victim is this case was not a woman, obviously, nor was this an assault, technically speaking. But when I put your deliberate preparation to shoot someone together with three previous assaults, I am moved to believe that you are a man dangerous to our community.

"The third aggravating factor I considered is your pattern of dishonesty with the Sheriff's department throughout this case. Finally, I considered, as a mitigating factor, the matter of the alleged rape when you were eleven. Although your counsel argued at trial that this is irrelevant, I don't agree. The record of your anger and violent behavior from your teen years on is clear, and I have little doubt that your experience at an early age was, to a degree, formative. I consulted several mental health experts during the pre-sentencing investigation and they all agree that the rape incident should be taken into account. They also concur that obsessive-compulsive disorder can produce extreme stress."

Judge Flure looked down at his papers, then looked at the Cirilo family. "Mr. and Mrs. Cirilo, do you want to say anything to the court that might help me determine the final sentence?"

Emilio Cirilo stood and pulled a page from his pocket. Andi had worked with the couple to draft the short statement, and Emilio had practiced it with her. But now, he simply stood, paralyzed, the text in hand, tears running down his cheeks. Mrs. Cirilo took the paper from his hand. "Your Honor," she read, "our family has been broken. Emilio and I have lost our dear son. His sisters have lost their brother. Nothing can give Bernardo back to us. One day, we hope to be able to forgive this man for what he has done, as our religion asks us to do, but we cannot do this now. Please give him the sentence you think is just."

Emilio nodded, and they sat.

Judge Flure thanked them, turned to Essex. "Mr. Essex, have you anything to say that may assist me in determining your sentence?"

Essex sat silent, staring straight ahead. He never acknowledged the question.

After a moment, the judge said, "Very well. Mr. Essex, please stand."

Norton stood. For many seconds, Essex seemed rooted, immobile. Norton again whispered to him, and finally, he stood.

"Mr. Essex, having considered both aggravating and mitigating factors, the evidence and testimony presented at trial, and the opinions of various experts, I hereby sentence you to serve forty years in Montana State Prison, with no parole for the first twenty years, and to pay a fine of fifty thousand dollars, both the maximum under the law. The fine will be deducted from the cash bail you posted. You will receive fifty-one days' credit for time served prior to your posting bail and since the verdict. I am allowing you one week to put your affairs in order. You will report to the Adams County Sheriff's department no later than ten o'clock in the morning on Friday, November sixteenth, for transport to Montana State Prison in Deer Lodge, Montana."

Judge Flure banged his gavel. "We are adjourned."

WEDNESDAY, JANUARY 2

1

The day after New Year's, Brad Ordrew rested his hand on a ragged-edged Bible and took in a long breath. Andi, Ben Stewart beside her, and the deputies arrayed on either side, stood at attention. Behind them grouped all the dispatchers and other department staff. Facing Ordrew were the three county commissioners, Jack Conrad in the center. He held the Bible and raised his right hand. Ordrew laid his left hand on the Bible and raised his right hand stiffly.

As Conrad spoke and Ordrew repeated the oath, Ben squeezed Andi's arm lightly, and she glanced at him. In his eyes, she glimpsed the disappointment he'd expressed to no one since the election. Bernie O'Reilly had told the Ladies' Fishing Society about it, though: Ben had wept, alone, in his study at 77 Russell Fork Road. Bernie had listened from outside the door, saddened at the soft sounds.

Andi took his hand, squeezing back. She hoped he saw in her eyes that it would be all right. Since the election, Brad had held to their agreement. He'd even started joking about her being his co-sheriff.

When the brief ceremony was over, Brad thanked the judge and faced the deputies and the department staff. "Well, I'm not one for speeches—"

Chipper Coleman interrupted him, grinning. "Which we know, Brad. We *heard* your speeches."

Everyone chuckled. Since Election Day, they'd found Brad less abrasive, more open to being teased, even to laughing along with it.

This time, he looked embarrassed. "So, just let me get this out, okay? I've got some fences to mend here, and I intend to earn your respect as sheriff. As Sheriff Stewart knows, a sheriff's only as good as his department, and I want to be a good sheriff, as Ben has been, so I need your help."

Ben nodded, studying him.

"I want to announce here that I've asked Sheriff Stewart and he's agreed to serve as a consultant to the department for one year." Sharp breaths were taken in throughout the room, and in a moment, Callie started clapping, soon joined by everyone. Andi, whom Ordrew had told about this, watched Ordrew's eyes, seeing in them a mix of relief and sadness. He'd won the vote, but not yet won their hearts.

When the applause stopped, Ordrew continued, "Sheriff Stewart and I have agreed that his input will focus on two main things: helping me maintain and enhance the performance of the entire department, as well as building good relationships with the people of the valley, something I've not been known for in the past."

Chip Coleman grinned. "Even new dogs can learn old tricks."

Ordrew waited out the chuckles. "So, let me wrap this up. You all know that Andi, Pete, and I are going to cooperate in leading the department. I want to make a promise to all of you: You support me, and I will support you. If you think I'm making a mistake or doing something wrong, come to me."

He looked directly at the deputies, one by one. "Please. Help me."

2

Andi had the evening shift today, so after the short ceremony, she, Ed, and Grace, who would return to college next weekend, joined the other deputies and their wives for lunch at the Angler. As they all gathered at Callie's reception desk before walking across to the restaurant, Grace gasped. Andi followed her gaze.

Stepping through the door, followed by her mother, was Mona Frantz. Her father had been sentenced to four years for his assaults on Grace and Mona, and his convictions for violating parole and kidnapping Mona added another fifteen years to the sentence. Mona and her mom stood shyly in the doorway. Grace ran to Mona and gave her a hug. "Did you come, uh, for the swearing-in?"

"No. We're getting my stuff from my dad's storage unit. But I wanted to see you, and at school they said you were here."

Andi joined them and hugged Mona's mom, Margie Cook. "You two've come a long way from Billings."

Margie nodded. Mona said, "I was sorry you lost the election, and I wanted to come and say I hope those things I said didn't make you lose."

Andi reached out and gave her a hug. "Nope, that had nothing to do with it." She turned to Mona's mom. "You can be proud of your daughter, Margie."

The woman smiled. "I am proud of her."

"Why don't you and Mona join us for lunch?"

"We'd love to, but we have to get back to Billings tonight. I work in the morning, and there's a snowstorm forecast for later."

Grace gave Mona another hug, and Andi said to Margie, "Tell me, did you lose your job?"

Margie smiled. "No. Your phone call helped a lot. Thanks for that. In fact, I got a raise a few weeks ago."

"That's great."

Grace said, "It's true, then."

"What is?"

"Shit fertilizes."

Everyone, after the laugh, filed out. Mona and her mother went out the backdoor to the parking lot, and the lunch-goers crossed Division Street to the Angler.

Brad Ordrew, now Sheriff Ordrew, had gone into Ben's office—which Ben had cleaned out over the New Year's weekend—and closed the door. Alone.

3

Ben, thirty pounds lighter since his hospitalization, rose as the salads were being served. "I ain't much for sentimental stuff, but I gotta say this. I always figured when it came my time to go, I'd want to leave the department to somebody who'd make me and my dad, the original Sheriff Stewart, real proud. Don't know how that's gonna turn out, but I know our new sheriff's gettin' himself a damn fine department. I'm proud of all of 'em." A tear drifted down his ruddy cheek. "Time I shut up and ate my salad." Bernie O'Reilly tissued his cheek dry.

Grace said, "Andi, it's your turn."

355

Andi felt Ed's hand touch her thigh softly; she squeezed his hand fondly, smiled. He smiled back. She stood up, reflecting on how giving speeches had become easier over the last few months.

"Since Grace, here, asked me to tell her what the *stand-your-ground* law means, I've been thinking." Grace beamed. "Truth is . . ." Andi paused. "I'm not a lawyer, so it's above my pay grade."

Everyone chuckled.

"But here's what I think. Take the word *ground*. What's that? Land, territory, your home, your castle, sure. But our ground here in Adams County is also our people. And our ground is the fields and mountains and rivers that we love. So, maybe standing our ground, for us, here in the valley, doesn't just mean shooting an intruder. Maybe it means that we take care of each other and our county the best we can, build each other up, not tear each other down." She looked down at Ed. "My boyfriend here, who's soon going to be my husband—" Everyone gasped, then started to clap. "We're already husband and wife in our hearts and our heads, but we'll be making it official in the spring."

Xav Contrerez said, "Give your bride a kiss, Ed," and everybody clapped more.

Andi lifted her hands. "Okay, thanks, but that's enough. As I was saying, you may know Ed took Latin in high school. He tells me the Latin word *patriam* means 'fatherland'—kind of what I mean by our 'ground.' I guess the idea is, you love your home ground like you love your father, and I for one loved my father a lot." She looked fondly at Ben. "Just like Sheriff Ben Stewart loved *his* father."

Another round of applause followed that, and Bernie had to dry Ben's cheek again.

A long, quiet moment followed.

Then Xavier said, grinning, "What happens when our new sheriff screws up?"

Grace jumped in. She held up seven fingers. "You say, 'It was just seven votes, Brad.'"

THE END

AUTHOR'S NOTES

Standing Our Ground is based on a true story from Montana. In 2014, twenty-nine-year-old Marcus Kaarma lured a nineteen-year-old German exchange student into his garage and shot him four times, claiming the "stand-your-ground" defense. Montana does not use the terms "first-degree murder," "second-degree murder," and the like. Instead, they charge five types of murder: *deliberate homicide, mitigated deliberate homicide* (murder committed under the pressure of mental illness), *negligent homicide, aiding or soliciting suicide,* and *vehicular homicide while under the influence.* Deliberate homicide (called first-degree murder in many other states) would be the charge made in the Daniel Essex case, as it was in the Kaarma case, except that mitigated deliberate homicide was appropriate and more easily won. In 2015, Kaarma was found guilty and sentenced to seventy years in prison, with no parole for at least twenty years. Like the conviction of Daniel Essex, Kaarma's depended on a careful and exhaustive investigation's uncovering of evidence that the shooting was long planned by the shooter.

Some readers have wondered whether conducting an exit poll during an election would be valid if done by high schoolers. No doubt, they've suggested, designing the proper questions, collecting the data, and doing the resulting statistical analysis would be beyond their capabilities. But along with the fact that Grace and her girls were helped by Ed Northrup, they had the guidance of a very helpful web page: https://www.wikihow.com/Conduct-a-Local-Election-Exit-Poll.

Remember too, Ed Northrup is a doctor of psychology, whose training included writing research questions and analyzing and interpreting stats.

You might wonder if my having Andi lose the election by a mere seven votes is stretching the imagination beyond the snapping point.

But that margin—50.1% for Brad Ordrew, 49.9% for Andi Pelton, a difference of 0.2%—is neither impossible nor unprecedented. Consider: In the Florida vote for president in 2000, George W. Bush won the state (after intervention by the Supreme Court) by a mere 537 votes out of 5,825,043 votes cast in the state, which is a margin of 0.00009219. Read that as a bit more than nine-hundred thousandths of one percent. In Florida's presidential vote in 2012, Barack Obama's margin of victory was slightly less than nine-tenths of one percent: 0.88%. Close elections happen, although I'll gladly admit that the votes cast in Monastery Valley hardly measure up to the volume of votes in Florida's elections. But even in small towns, such as my town of Hope, Idaho, ninety residents, every vote still counts.

NOTE FROM THE AUTHOR

Word-of-mouth is crucial for any author to succeed. If you enjoyed the book, please leave a review online—anywhere you are able. Even if it's just a sentence or two. It would make all the difference and would be very much appreciated.

Thanks!
Bill

Thank you so much for reading one of **Bill Percy's** novels.
If you enjoyed the experience, find out where the
Monastery Valley series begins.

Climbing the Coliseum by Bill Percy

"A light, breezy thriller, but its tale of a troubled man acting as
a father to an equally troubled girl has exceptional dramatic
impact." –KIRKUS REVIEWS

View other Black Rose Writing titles at
www.blackrosewriting.com/books and use promo code
PRINT to receive a **20% discount** when purchasing.

www.ingramcontent.com/pod-product-compliance
Lightning Source LLC
Chambersburg PA
CBHW011955120726
47898CB00009BA/2881